BIRDING
IN THE FACE OF
TERROR

BIRDING
IN THE FACE OF
TERROR

J. PIERRE REVILLE

PUNKIN HOUSE
Trumansburg, New York

Birding in the Face of Terror

First Edition Release 2014
Library of Congress Control Number: 2014952296

ISBN: (Print)
(10) 1938391098
(13) 978-1-938391-09-5

Punkin House
67 W. Main Street
PO Box 122
Trumansburg, NY 14886

Printed in the United States of America

Punkin House Books are available at special quantity discounts to use as premiums and sales promotions or for use in corporate training programs. To contact a representative, please email us at **BulkSales@punkinhouse.com**

punkin house
Innovative Book Publishing
www.punkinhouse.com

"All the world's a stage.
You'll get over it."

--Jeffrey Bonfield

Prologue

My name, you ask? I am called by a great multitude of names, as many as there are beings to call me. None of them are true.

This may seem ridiculous. In a universe of infinite possibilities, you might say, surely *someone* has uttered my true name, even if just by accident. But no, not once.

Indeed, you name-callers dwell in an infinite space, and that space dwells within you. There has been no time when this wasn't so, nor will there ever be. The possibilities of your universe are indeed limitless. But when you open your mouth to describe me or count my appearances, you confine yourself to a small box. I am present in this boxy world of names and numbers too, but I cannot be contained by them. Nothing you are capable of saying approaches the infinite.

Consider the number of beings that are alive right now in your world. This number may be staggeringly large on the human scale, but still it is a number. To know me, you must forget all numbers.

Picture the grains of sand on all of Gaia's beaches, or drops of water in her oceans. These numbers added together are not a single step in the direction of infinity. It is equally futile to give me a name.

Ever since human beings began measuring time, you have wondered about my true name, and asked me to reveal my face. I have told many times, you will see my face when you merely open your eyes. But all of your names, like grains of sand and drops of water before a numberless space, are towers built to reach the heavens; they all fall short of me.

I am beyond all measurements of time and space. I am before anything was, and beyond when anything will be. I am above up, and below down. I am farther than the farthest conceivable edge of the known universe. I am closer than your heartbeat.

All of creation is like a vast multitude of jars in a house of clay, spun from a potter's wheel that is itself made of the same substance. What you are, is what I am, and more, for I am also the empty space around you and within you. I take my own essence and spin myself into beings of incomprehensible diversity and complexity. I set this wheel in motion. I create these beings from myself, and return them into non-being in a cycle with neither beginning nor end. Beings come and beings vanish; they never leave my midst. They all remain One within me. I am that. You are that, too.

So, for this moment, lose all concepts of names as well. Stop searching for my true name, and feel my presence within your being, in the space around you, in everything your five senses are bringing to you right now, and all your thoughts about them. Feel the ecstatic nature of my being within you, within all of creation, because I love to be what I am, and I am to be what I love. For I so love you that I have given you the chance to lose me in your own mind, and feel the exhilarating joy of rediscovering what you never really lost.

Indeed, if this world is a stage, a place for you to act out your roles as assigned and apportioned, your jars of clay filled with the emptiness of me; this is no accident; I have made it so. And in this great drama, I too must become like a character, an image you will recognize. I must hide behind this image that fills your sight, like the sky disappears behind the fog, like the whole world behind your closed eyelids.

Your image of me will appear to you time and time again throughout the drama, in many different forms, always challenging you to make a basic decision: to put aside names and numbers, open your eyes, and feel my infinite presence. You will either shun me because you love your minute role to distraction, or follow me because of an inkling that you were once something much greater, and that I know the way back to you.

Therefore, for the sake of the drama, forget this moment of illumination, but do not lose it. Obscure it behind the translucent veil of your mind, but let it be a dim beacon in your heart, and carry this inner light always.

When you see me--that is, when you open your eyes--forget my true identity. But not completely. When you give me a name, call me as the Rastafarians do. Call me I and I. This will remind you of that faint inkling, and provide a clue as to why, when you look out at that vast multitude of beings and things with their own names, you cannot help but feel something of that greater self within every one of them. It is all I and I.

The wise among you know that the purpose of creation is to tell a story. A single story, told from a multitude of perspectives. To write it in words would be impossible. It has been said that even the world itself could not contain the books that would be written to tell my whole story. Theatre is the preferred mode of storytelling, for this is where the universe's flair for drama is let loose and given free rein to shine, unbound by the structure of words.

This is the nature of the play as a whole. Within the whole, there is a virtually endless web of interwoven mini-dramas, stages within the stage, where the stories of individual perspectives are played out through the eyes of all sentient beings.

Most of these dramas come and go unnoticed, other than by me. A rose blooms because it blooms; it needs no reason why, no audience to approve. This is the source of its perfection. But you, who are so given to search for Why, you are perfectly *imperfect*. Humans are storytellers by nature and brilliant actors by vocation. I cannot hide myself in a rose; it knows me all too well. But you humans, with your sacred names and numbers--so prone to forgetfulness! How easily you lose all sense of yourselves as actors on a stage, so absorbed as you are into every character. And how mightily you struggle to learn anything of your most basic truth! It is this very damnation that makes you the most favored of thespians on this stage, for while no being is further from the truth than the human, neither is any more motivated to seek it. Indeed, there is no reason why your continued survival as a species makes one iota of sense, other than that you have mastered the art of forgetting me and searching for what you think you lost.

Human dramas are also easy to recognize as analogies of the whole, filled as they are with the most vivid enactment of that elemental struggle. You get the honor of telling the untellable story of the whole by allegory; your tales mean something much bigger than they are, and that fills your stages with an electric urgency unknown to the rest of creation. Spring comes, the rose blooms, the grass grows by itself, effortless and free. But to watch you wriggle and writhe in your self-made shackles, and deploy your cunning means of removing them by wrapping them like a noose around others--who wouldn't grab a front row seat for that?! It is no wonder why yours are the stories that are preserved to share with others across time and space.

The most treasured of the stories preserved by the tradition of human storytelling, however, are not these tragicomic farces that fill your history books. They are tales of *remembrance*--stories that use their allegorical significance to chart a course by which a being may *come home* to me. For you to recognize yourself as "I and I" while still being "you:" this is the triumph to which all life secretly aspires. When this secret is unveiled, the shackles fall of their own accord and a storyteller comes home, there are reverberations throughout human awareness, and new generations of storytellers will reorient themselves around this course.

It is such a tale that I am here to tell now. This is a story of connection and remembrance, of a search for home.

This is not a particularly important story, at least not as importance is generally measured on the human stage. No persons of renown will make an appearance here, and there are stories of far greater magnitude that will play out this very day. But for those interactors who grace this stage, whose stories are involved in this one, it may be of particular interest. There are many, many such actors, and the stage is set for a grand homecoming.

For those among you who desire to feel the full breadth and significance of this homecoming, it is essential that you forget that I am the only storyteller--but again, not completely. No matter whose voice is narrating at any moment, hear that voice and that alone, but also know that I am with you always, never far from the fore of each scene. And if you begin to suspect that each voice in the story is my own (not to mention the silence of the stage set and all the props), you are onto something; follow it to its rightful conclusion. For truthfully, I say unto you, there are none who see anything but my roving "I" who sees all, one being at a time.

Right now, for instance, I am New York City. I am a living, breathing organism comprised of many elements. I am a stage made of land and water and air where a great, broad river flows into an ocean. I am a manmade infrastructure of massive scale, comprised of buildings and thoroughfares and hidden networks of conduits moving all the energy and fluids essential to my inhabitants. I am many millions of humans and countless other beings, all coming and going with every moment--the constant cycle of life and death, the patterns of migration as I swell by day and contract at night.

How can a city be an organism, you may ask, when it is defined by arbitrary political boundaries? But can anything more be said of *any* organism? Is there any living body that is not a temporary confluence of many millions of cells, interacting with each other via a natural infrastructure that requires constant migration and interchange with its surroundings to survive? With its essential structure coming and going with every moment, what can the organism call its own? Its fundamental "self" is a political arrangement with its surroundings regarding what it believes it can control and what it is willing to trust to "others"--can anything less be said of New York City, and the arbitrary line that separates it from New Jersey? So yes, you human beings are among my most imaginative co-creators. You can incorporate anybody you choose and give it political life. I am that as well. You are ever faithful to forget this too, for the good of the drama.

Some people call me The City That Never Sleeps. In truth, no city ever sleeps. There is always some level of conscious activity in the pulse of a city's lifeblood. But as the world's largest center of commerce, I do have a unique breed of bustle that never ceases, and it is already quite vibrant at 5:25 am. Trucks from all over the hinterlands pour in through my tunnels and across my bridges to beat the morning rush. Their cargo will feed both my hungry inhabitants and the wallets of a country starving for my money, an exchange no less vital to these communities than oxygen and carbon dioxide to other organisms.

The roving I zooms down to the level of one of my arteries--Avenue of the Americas as it heads north out of Chelsea past block after block of high-rises, like a Euclidian river in a canyon of glass and steel, concrete and brick. Another hour will pass before the sun rises, so the sliver of sky above is the same off-black shade it has been since nightfall. It never gets fully dark here for the steady presence of manmade electricity, from lights in offices above, the pale orange glow of the streetlamps, the 24-hour delis and waking storefronts, and the white headlights and red taillights of thickening traffic below. When sunlight disappears, the city illuminates itself from within, a reminder to the night that it is still awake and life persists under its arching canopy.

I follow the avenue a few more blocks, past the green arboreal oasis of Bryant Park, then turn left on 42nd St into the heart of the Theatre District. Here the glow intensifies, and as I look right and follow Broadway up to Times Square, I see one of the greatest footprints impressed upon Gaia by humankind. Hardly an inch of the canyon here is not plastered with some iridescent monument to the imagination--flashing signs, enormous billboards touting everything conceivable, words zooming by on giant wraparound marquees telling stories of the day, all clamoring for attention in the world's epicenter for being seen, an open-air shrine to humankind's worship of itself.

Now, in this moment, I am aware of an event that happened

here just over fifteen years ago. There was a woman standing on the sidewalk, scanning the scene around her with great interest. (I see this as though it were happening now, because from my perspective there is no difference. But on this finite stage, it happened in the past, and her appearance now is more like an apparition than a living character.) She was an eighteen-year old farm girl from Middle America, and this was her first time in New York City. She wandered over from the Port Authority bus station because she wanted to see the place that had emblemized the city in her childhood dreams, and there she was in the heart of it, seeing with her own eyes, loving everything she saw. It should be noted that she was one of the very rare human beings who was taught to perceive I and I from the moment she could form a concept of herself, so she was more inclined than most people to fall in love with a billboard or a neon sign, or a pigeon, or even a stranger on the sidewalk.

The living memory of her fades from my attention--she will be back later--and she disappears from this stage. Now, without any time passing, I pull back from Times Square and the political body called New York City. I cross the manmade line into the adjacent political body called New Jersey. Then I zoom in--through layers upon layers of being and boundaries, some collaboratively chosen, some subconsciously assumed, until I look back out at the universe through the eyes of an organism that is roughly concurrent to a single human body, lying in a bed inside a suburban single family home.

My eyes are covered by eyelids, so there is not much to see just yet. I am only half awake, and I am wishing that I could go back to sleep, but the wishing is counterproductive to my wish so it is to no avail. As usual, I woke up at 5:00 am with my wife's alarm. She is in the room next door, performing her morning yoga routine. In three hours, she will be in her office in the city, doing a job she loves. I will probably be inching forward in commuter traffic, wishing I were headed anywhere *other than* my office.

I open my eyes, briefly. A faint hint of light crawls under the bedroom door, along with my wife's bizarre Tibetan throat chanting. She would love for me to join her, or at least feel inspired to do *something* to greet the day. I am aware that there is an elliptical machine in the family room that I bought last winter and have used three times. It crosses my mind that I could get up and start a new morning routine for myself. But I roll over on my other side and close my eyes again. If I were thinking that today might be the last time I will ever see my wife, I might choose to spend every minute with her that I could before she leaves for the train. Instead, I am wondering how the hell I ever got hitched to a morning person.

I will introduce myself later when I am more fully self-aware... Now I pan back again as consciousness departs this individual for a few minutes. I cross the continent (2,913 miles--a considerable time-distance to cover on the human level, not even a fraction of an eye blink for me). I zoom back to a level just above the human perspective, entering a small house near the ocean in California. It is the same moment, but three hours earlier on the clock, or 2:25 in the morning.

A man and a woman sleep together in this room. I will call the man Pedro; this is how he is known in California, except by his wife, Nadia, who calls him by a secret name of their own making. Pedro is called something else by his family and friends back east, but he does not like that name so I will not evoke it here. I do accommodate the whims of the human ego, for it is instrumental in your perfect ability to forget me. The drama of a single human, played out on its own unique stage, is of such little consequence to the whole story that no isolated plot twist or character development is off limits. But as an allegory for what is happening on the stage of the human family, to follow the path of the individual ego is not unlike watching an entire species perform a tightrope act without a net, the fires of hell below on all sides--or so the audience and actors are led to believe. This is the beauty of the universal drama as perfected in the human experience: life, which is cyclical by nature, seems like a razor thin line across a pit of oblivion in which every choice, every action is of grave consequence. In reality, they have no greater impact on the actor than what she does on the stage before the curtain falls and she sheds her character like a robe.

A wise human wrote that "every one of us is followed by an illusory person: a false self. This is the man I want to be but who cannot exist, because God does not know anything about him." (God is one of your more popular concepts of who I am). This is true on the human level, for God, though infinite and eternal, is thought to have dropped you into his finite and temporal creation and set you loose, recusing himself of any responsibility for your actions as you run amok, chased by shadows that he does not acknowledge. Only the most adept God-seekers catch this contradiction and realize that this shadow, the human ego, is also one of my characters, and even the most vicious, loathsome characters torn in two by inner conflict are me in disguise.

So Pedro can have this false self, a minor indulgence of his ego. There are far greater issues on his agenda today.

Right now, Pedro is in deep sleep, experiencing rapid eye movement for only the fourth time in more than a month. He is dreaming about a garden, on a farm where he used to work but is no longer welcome. The garden is exceptionally lush with greens made of emeralds, huge ruby tomatoes and golden squash. As Pedro walks through this garden, he sees God making beautiful, intricate patterns in the soil with a rake (he knows this is God because it looks exactly like the cartoon images of God he had seen in *Playboy* magazines as a kid).

Pedro looks perturbed. He asks God what is the point of growing beautiful gemstone crops that no one can eat, but God does not answer him.

Pedro asks why this frivolous artistry that no one will ever see, when there is so much that needs to be done to improve the state of the world. Still no response.

Then Pedro throws up his hands in exasperation and says, "Do you even listen to our prayers anyway?" God just keeps plying his rake to the sand like a Zen monk, absorbed in his detachment from world affairs, his back turned to the inquisitive human. Pedro turns and walks away in disgust, more bitter and alone than before. He does not realize that this particular manifestation of God is a deaf mute, and he is so because Pedro, inspired by one of his favorite fictional characters, has secretly longed to be one for years. *Ask and ye shall receive.* How many times do I have to tell myself that before I understand?

But all is not lost for Pedro. At least he still dares to dream of God, something many of his fellow death-defying tightrope walkers stopped doing long ago. And he is about to wake up anyway.

I will soon disappear. I will zoom into Pedro and tell most of this story from his perspective, completely forgetful of myself until the time comes to remember. Meanwhile, it should be noted that today's date is September 11, 2001. This is not an ordinary day on most stages involving human beings. There is no such thing as an ordinary day of course, but it is extremely rare that so many characters are aware of this at once. Interesting times will soon be upon us.

Here comes the alarm. Places, everyone...

BIRDING
IN THE FACE OF
TERROR

ACT I

2:30 am (PDT) / 5:30 am (EDT)

Buzzer...Buzzer...BUZZER! I reach across my body and slap the snooze button with my right hand. The sudden motion simulates that too familiar feeling of waking up with alcohol in my blood stream, and I steady myself on my left elbow while the head-rush passes. My eyes focus on the fuzzy crimson digits of the clock until they form numerals and make sense. I collapse onto my back and stare at the ceiling.

Only four hours. Goddamnit.

How long can I keep this up?

Quick math...half-hour to the bus yard, another half-hour to Santa Maria...no time to snooze. I burned all the lag time last night. This is the deadline for me to start this gig on time. I do need a couple minutes, though, to gather some strength. Gravity is very strong in our room this morning.

Blah. I am so thoroughly un-rested.

My body doesn't know whether to consider this early today or still late from the day before. Driving a bus for a living has destroyed any functioning internal clock I had left after five years of long haul trucking and a lifetime of mild insomnia. Each schedule differs from the day before, and in the past seven months I have reported to work at every hour of the clock at least once. So a 2:30 am wake-up call is not unusual, in the sense that the unusual has become routine.

Nothing really prepares a body for *this*, however...I lie in bed for a while, trying to cut through the grogginess enough to move.

Nadia is next to me, lying on her stomach. She has not stirred at all. Apparently it is too late/early for her to be bothered by my alarm. That is a relief. She can use the rest. This was a rough night even by our low standards.

The last time we sought crisis intervention, a wacky Catholic woman at the counseling center gave us each a laminated card with *Ephesians 4:26* printed on it:

"Be angry, and sin not; let not the sun go
down upon your wrath."

We were supposed to promise each other we would remember this verse and never forget to apply its wisdom when we were having trouble. Well, since then I would guess we have sinned more nights than we've sinned not.

Last night was typical: I got home an hour later than expected from a South County wine tour--damn tourists just *had* to add that *one last stop* at Phantom Rivers on the way back to town. Nadia was too upset to eat the dinner she had cooked for us, and that made her blood sugar level drop so low that she had to take a glucose pill, which gives her uncontrollable shivers no matter what the temperature. While dealing with that, covered in blankets and hovering over a space heater, she told me in very loud and not the least bit uncertain terms that her endocrinologist was an asshole for calling her out on not recording her glucose-meter readings, and the ophthalmologist suggested she might need a second laser procedure on her right eye to clean up the scar tissue from the first one and prevent further vision loss, and the last set of oil pastels I picked up were cheap, crumbly garbage that she couldn't possibly use to do anything decent. (All of this, by the way, was my fault.)

It is best if I do not speak at all during these onslaughts, I have found, so I usually try to listen as dispassionately as possible and keep all judgments to myself. This time I told her the doctor was right.

So the night ended as they often do: me sweeping up the contents of dinner, plus a couple shattered ceramic bowls and coffee mugs, from the kitchen floor, and Nadia yelling something about how I never listen to her.

She finally passed out from screaming into her pillow around ten o'clock. This left a precious half-hour of solitude to type the day's handwritten changes to my manuscript into the word processor. This particular story exists only in the farthest reaches of my mind, and to lose even a day of contact, it seems, is to risk never getting back there, so I guard my daily writing time at all costs, no matter how brief or how basic the task I can accomplish. Nights like this, which means pure transcription. By 10:30 pm, with the window for sleep dwindling until it was just a long nap, I gave up and logged off, ruing the day five years prior when I saw the shy chalkboard artist from the natural food store smile at me from across the room of a Pennsylvania diner.

But all of that is behind us. I watch Nadia sleep in the soft crimson light emanating from the nightstand. Her face looks as peaceful and unscathed as a baby's. This is still the image of Nadia I carry, a vision of innocence and beatitude that emanated from the saint-like way she tried to carry the cross of her disease when I was getting to know her. Only later did I learn about the dual poles of her personality, the real Nadia who oscillates from moment to moment between this sublime acceptance of her fate and hysterical rage and fear.

I have also learned how well-founded those fears are. Diabetes rarely acts alone when it tortures. The co-conspirators include every system where proper blood circulation and hormonal regularity are crucial, from brain function to eyesight to cardiac function to thermal regulation--literally everything from head to toe. Aside from the long-term high risk of stroke, heart attack, and amputation due to gangrene--all of which are caused by chronically high sugar levels--there is the day-to-day danger of stealthy low sugar reactions that zap her mental capacity to respond, or worse, creep up on her while she sleeps. Living with a brittle diabetic has taught me to sleep night after night with one eye open, praying I won't close it inadvertently and wake up to find Nadia lying on the floor in a puddle of sweat, unable to speak or move any closer to the medicine cabinet, slipping toward a hypoglycemic coma (that was one of our honeymoon nights). I do this knowing that in exchange for my vigilance, I will be subject to bursts of irresolvable wrath on a regular basis.

And yet, she is still alive, and we are still together, because hidden inside all that human rubble is the most beautiful, resilient spirit I have ever known, a true artist in the supreme sense. It is Nadia who has taught me everything I know about what it is to love another person for exactly who she was and not for whom I wanted her to be.

The dread thought of not being around when that spirit lifts itself from its corporal prison and takes flight, be it for an hour, a day, or a lifetime, she has told me, is what motivates her to keep going. Maybe that is the case for both of us.

I gently kiss the back of her head, her soft auburn hair. Then I peal myself off the sheets, and stumble toward the closet to fish for a relatively unwrinkled shirt to bring into the shower.

I'm curious what's in store for today. This was a last minute change to my schedule, and all I know is that I must be in Santa Maria at 4:30 am, take some folks up to the mountains northwest of Los Angeles, and have them back in town by 5:00 pm--a solid 15 hour day by the time my work is done.

I ponder this as I prepare for my wake-up ritual. That ought to bring in some decent tip money. I'll take Nadia out for sushi tonight. That place down in San Luis Obispo with the Elvis museum. Best yellowtail in town.

Possibilities are starting to unfold. The road energy percolates within me, slowly pushing out the fatigue as cold water hits my chest. Maybe I can do this after all.

3:15 am (PDT) / 6:15 am (EDT)

I step outside into the mild chill of a late summer night. The protest of my senses against awake-ness and alertness is mostly quelled, though I'm still fighting an urge of my overworked eyes to stay closed. It is always a tougher sell with them before the sun comes up. They get paid in a currency other than money.

Pacific waves crash on the beach a couple hundred yards away in the darkness. I pause for a bit, absorbing their timeless rhythm while I lean against the hatchback of the Civic, a slight land breeze from the canyon stirring the moist ocean air. I know I'm running a bit late, but I need a moment with these waves. Nothing else in California gives me such a sense of grounding as when I stand by the shore and let my worries be drowned by the sounds of the sea.

I need the waves this morning because just now, as I shut the front door, I was disturbed by a flashback to a moment not two full weeks ago when Nadia had pushed me past the edge, and in my overwhelming rage I stormed out this door, believing I was closing it for the last time. I am accustomed to a kind of anxiety about *opening* our front door for fear of what I'll find inside. But this is new to me, this wondering if I have what it takes to stay.

A bit of personal history should help explain. Nadia and I are both east coast natives, though I hesitate to call us "transplants." We came to California as part of a cyclical migration pattern I established years ago in my first effort to get as far possible from the desperate, drug-addled, hyperactive mass of humanity piled upon itself in an unbroken pandemic sprawl from New England to Virginia. I once heard the tendency to bounce back and forth between the east and west described as "bicoastal disorder." Some hypochondriac side of me must have enjoyed having a malady to blame for my dysfunctional behavior, so it stuck.

Nadia may have recognized something of herself in this disorder, and she hits the ground running as eagerly as I do. We travel well together, perhaps because we tend to be chased by unique but similar kinds of shadows that stay attached to us at the heels rather than disappear across the miles. I do feel that my pace is exhausting her more with each move, though. California is our fourth home in five years, and none of the moves were fewer than two thousand miles. Now, having turned our backs to the homeland one more time, we live out here in a present without a past. We have no roots, no sense of place deeper than the eyes' pleasant sweep of the fabled "golden rolling hills." And so, like tumbleweeds across the desert, we were blown by an odd wind to the western edge, and now we have come to rest along this Pacific coast because there is no more land.

Well, Nadia has come to rest. I haven't. That is why I drive a bus.

There is some method to the madness though, a discernable pattern that has emerged in my bicoastal tendencies. I head west when I feel stifled, craving its open spaces and open minds. But I never feel like anything more than a sojourner here, for something in these spaces only fuels my restlessness. I want to see it all, be everywhere at once. I grow very dissatisfied with being confined to a single human body, and I turn to the closest approximation of escape I have ever known: incessant motion. Soon the futility of this begins to weigh on me and I decide it might be good to just be me again...but can I turn around and head "out east?" Over and over I've tried, but going east always feels like a retreat, a step *back* into the past rather than forward. Life becomes too cloistered, too settled and rigid, like old ruts on a country road. So the claustrophobia sets in again--living people become like zombies, memories become ghosts. The itch

for relief and release back into the wide open spaces returns...
and so on and so on, ad infinitum perhaps.

I have always wanted to meet someone with an equal but opposite bicoastal disorder, a west coast native who ran away to the
east, and find out if he or she ever says "back west." Somehow
I have always imagined this as impossible. Historically accurate
or not, America imagines itself to have been born in the east and
grown westward, that our past is "back east" while our future
unfolds "out west." We see it physically in the path our sun takes
across the sky, and perhaps we instinctively follow it. I feel like
I am tapping into a cultural truth here and not merely a personal
one. Maybe venturing east is contradictory to the American mythos, and an easterner like me is bound to turn toward the rising
sun when the urge to be home arises.

But this time, I came determined to break the pattern, stake my
claim and make my life here on the west coast. We have come to
a long prophesied place where the Santa Lucia Mountains meet
the sea in the most spectacular manner I have ever seen, the most
magical place I could imagine.

This vision was planted in me on a family vacation when I
was 13. We were all packed into a passenger van heading down
Highway 101 from San Francisco, sightseeing with my relatives
from Nevada. I was every bit the cliché bored teenager lost in his
own Walkman world, a soundtrack of early 1980s punk blaring
in the fore as the Salinas Valley and Monterey County flew by
mostly unnoticed.

Then we took a detour from the freeway, heading west out of
Paso Robles toward the Pacific Coast Highway. This piqued my
interest. After all, this would be my very first view of the Pacific,
and to a 13-year old boy from the east coast, California first and
foremost means airbrushed pin-up poster models in bikinis on
the beach.

But something else took hold of me as we climbed past the
hillside vineyards, bishop pines and live oak groves, traversing
those last crumpled masses of land that wear the sun baked air
and salt water aura of *Eureka!* so unique to California. There is
something about knowing that a whole continent is about to bow

before the ocean's majesty and the end of land is *just over there*....then we crested the ridge and there it was. The culmination of three thousand miles of unfurling earth, the great Pacific Ocean spread before us, about 10 miles out and 2,000 feet down below, shrouded in summer's mist. The land below us leading to the coast was a dazzling expanse of rounded velvet hills and arroyos, smoothed by millennia of sea breezes and the golden blanket of tall grass and wild wheat, punctuated here and there by juniper and cypress trees and the distant specks of grazing cattle.

The headphones came off, and I was pinned to the window. It seemed like a landscape from the pages of a fantasy book, like something Tolkien might have dreamed up on an Ecstasy high. I had the palpable sensation that we were flying as we coasted down the slope, my waking eyes scoping the voluptuous curves of the hills, feeling the road caress them, unfurling up and over and around and down. I was not bound up in a metal box anymore, but expansive and free as I became what I saw. I couldn't explain it then and I hardly can now. All I know is that a lust entered my body at that moment, one that I have spent the rest of my life bent on satisfying...this strange angelic sensation of relating to the solid ground of this earth as if it were the very firmament of Heaven.

The place where we landed on Highway 1 is just up the road from where Nadia and I live now, sixteen years later, in the town of Cayucos. It has been described as a beach town taken out of a time capsule that was sealed in southern California in the early 1950s, the living memory of a simpler time when a day's concerns centered on catching a fat wave, not a stray bullet. We were lured by the charm of Cayucos from the moment we arrived on the Central Coast, and it took a whole chapter's worth of toil and tears, but after nearly a year of subsistence living on the fringe, we finally found an affordable bungalow apartment on the edge of town. It was just half of a tiny ranch-style house, part of a cluster of similar dwellings tumbled like dice into the gully of Old Creek, just upstream from where it trickles into the great blue expanse of the Pacific. Humble as it was, I treasured our new home like none I'd ever had before. Never had a western home given me such a sense of having *arrived*.

Since then, I have become pretty certain that there is no such place as heaven--not anywhere near here anyway--and that angels don't dare fly so low to the ground. The California dream is a soul-sucking nightmare for the poor and un-landed, and the stress of maintaining it as a home, financially and emotionally, has zapped my desire to be here.

And now, this flashback. The cut on my right arm healed days ago; the wound within me still throbs. This is something I have not yet reconciled: why am I still here? Did I not follow my bicoastal pattern and head back east because all hope of finding home is gone? Or is hope still alive, and still living right here on Old Creek Road?

The answer must be waiting for me somewhere around the bend, and whatever I was living for from birth until the end of August doesn't matter much anymore--I'm now living to find it.

3:30 am (PDT) / 6:30 am (EDT)

Thousands, perhaps millions of alarms have sounded across my metropolitan area over the past hour. Most are met with a somnambulant resignation or even hostility--Tuesday, statistically speaking, is the least favorite day of the week among humans, and these are New Yorkers after all. Fortunately, there is a Starbucks location on every other city block, gearing up to fuel a fresh horde of morning commuters with their black magic energy potion. My parkways and expressways and surface streets thicken by the minute, loaded with more traffic than anyone ever imagined they would carry, building to that point where traffic stops its own flow and everyone goes nowhere, slowly...

The Pacific Coast Highway is empty and dark. I could lie down in the left lane and sleep undisturbed for at least an hour. A lone am/pm service station glows in the void as I pass the Morro Bay exit. Its luminous sign beckons me with the sweet allure of caffeine. But no, I am running too late to stop, even for something as efficient as gas station coffee.

It would almost be spooky, this absolute quietude in a place that is vibrant by day, but I am accustomed to it. My redeye departures always start like this. No other place I have lived goes to bed as early and uniformly as the north San Luis Obispo County coast, and it will be 7 am or later before my neighbors are roused in any significant numbers. Such is life in a place where the average home price tops $400,000, and maybe half of those are owned by people who don't live here.

This is the heart of California's Central Coast region. We are exactly halfway on 101 between San Francisco and Los Angeles. (Or, as my puritan friend back east likes to say, "between Sodom and Gommorah." It was part of a grand apocalyptic vision he had during a mushroom trip. Personally, I say New York and Washington are the places that should be smote first.)

It is an ideal location to reach both metro areas for my employer, Eldorado Stages. The bus yard is a half-hour drive down Route 1 to the far side of San Luis Obispo, past all seven of the Seven Sisters--ancient volcanoes, now plugs of igneous rock jutting up through the golden grass of the low coastal foothills--and several other landmarks I have come to know intimately through this job, now blanketed by the night. I can give a nifty tour of this area in daylight hours. Much of the work at Eldorado serves the local communities and caters to people's desire to be elsewhere--casinos, tourist traps, school field trips, all the typical diversions from the day-to-day--but there are also many gigs that involve showcasing the Central Coast region for visitors coming here from other elsewheres. These jobs require an element of hospitality more akin to a tour guide than just a driver. My trainers crammed my brain with more tidbits, trivia, and minutia about north SLO County coast than one could imagine possible, and it was up to me to smooth it into a spiel that would keep the travelers engrossed.

It hadn't occurred to me when I took a job delivering people how much more would be expected of me as a social being--the degree of interaction with my cargo compared to, say, paper, aluminum cans, breakfast cereal, or lawnmowers. Truck driving is a solitary profession, and the fact that I got into it a couple years after dropping out of college, as opposed to the plethora of service industry options available to non-matriculated former honor students, is indeed no coincidence. As a trucker, I was told where to go and when to be there, and as long as I did it safely, nothing else really mattered much to anyone. Bus driving is a completely different beast, a socially dynamic art of contrasts that I am only starting to understand. While the wheels are turning, my job is to go unnoticed, blend into the vehicle; ready to help the passengers at any moment but to speak when spoken to and little more. My needs for entertainment or distraction are nullified. I am two hands on the wheel, two feet on the floor, two ears in the cabin, and two eyes on the road. When the bus stops, I take on any number of roles that include not just a tour guide, but a travel agent, a concierge, a baggage handler, and sometimes just a smiling face who is happy that so-and-so chose Eldorado Stages. This part of my job does not come naturally to me. Perhaps that is actually the reason I am enjoying it more and more. Safe operation of a large motor vehicle is not much of a challenge anymore. But crawling out of the shell I grew as a truck driver, pretending to be outgoing and chatty for a few hours, then reattaching my protective carapace on the drive back to Cayucos for a typically not-so-quiet night at home? That takes some practice.

I got into bus driving by accident--literally, I am sad to say. This part of the story begins back east, almost two years ago, in our most recent place of residence, where I *almost* found my ideal home.

Cachés Notch is a small paper mill town-turned-reservation for artists, anarchists, and freaks in the mountains of northern New Hampshire, one of those überhip enclaves where lefties like Nadia and me huddle together to escape the reality that we are surrounded by gun-toting Republicans and hillbilly biker gangs. The *Utne Reader* once named Cachés Notch "the most enlightened town in New Hampshire" (which is sort of like being the sanest resident in the loony bin) and lauded it as "6,000 people and six coffee houses." And, as *Utne* failed to note, at least twice as many bars, pubs, and watering holes of various repute, so there were plenty of downers to go with the uppers.

This was officially my longest and most successful stint on the east coast since high school--almost a full year and a half--but it was in eminent peril as I had just lost my job as a writer for the local weekly newspaper. Actually, I didn't really *lose* my job, the way that one loses car keys or a wager. It is more accurate to say that I had a job--a very good one in fact--and then, slow-ly, over the course of weeks, it vanished, never to return, and I realized that there was no reason to come to work anymore. A strange realization: one day you are covering a high school hockey game, or interviewing the mayor or a man who makes sculptures out of trash (or in this case, both), writing stories that earn you praise and build your sense of vocation, feeling like you are back in the groove that you left upon dropping out of college, etc. etc...and the next day your boss tells you that she can't afford to keep paying you $6.50 an hour and she loves your writing but...

So I started searching for work that would keep me close to home. Nadia and I had been married in Cachés Notch three months before, and we felt a lot of camaraderie with the quirky locals, so we were not eager to leave. But the Border Patrol was the only growth industry in the region. Another tour of duty with a long-haul trucking company loomed over me if I didn't find something fast.

The most promising prospect was the local *Quebecois* bus line that ran from Manchester to Quebec City, jumping the border at the top of Vermont. I could take a northbound bus as it passed through town, then relieve the Canadian driver of the south-bound bus at the border and begin my daily round trip circuit. I didn't have the endorsement on my commercial license to drive a large passenger vehicle, so I gave one of my last $100 to a guy at the local community college to give me a road test on his bus. When the day of our appointment arrived and he didn't have a bus available, he asked me four or five "what would you do if such-and-such happens" kind of questions over the phone--even gave me extra guesses when I got one wrong--and just like that I became a legal people hauler.

The bus company did not hire me. I suspect I failed my in-terview with my extremely limited communication skills; I am functionally illiterate in French. But a whole dimension of com-mercial driving I had never before considered was opened up to me.

Meanwhile, Nadia did some research and found an organic

avocado farm in the mountains outside Cambria, California that invited folks to come work the land and acquire skills. I recognized Cambria from my map-scanning fantasy travels as being just north of the magic highway from Paso Robles to the coast. One photograph on the farm's rudimentary website really grabbed me, an aerial view of the spread tucked so neatly into the Santa Lucia foothills, with the rugged peaks of the crest towering above, that it looked like a Chinese landscape painting come to life. The farmer couldn't afford to pay us, we were told, but there was an old custom converted school bus on the property where we could live for free, and of course we could forage the groves and gardens for food.

How divine it felt for this opportunity to arise! Especially in contrast to northern New Hampshire in early December: the fall foliage was long gone, leaf peeper excitement a distant memory, and for four solid months we would see only snow and lead pipe grey skies, and unrelenting coldness would coat our nerve endings with hoarfrost until Easter...ah, but now the gray clouds are gone and bright blue sky abounds. The air on my bare skin is a warm, gentle caress as I walk barefoot through an avocado grove. I reach up and pluck a willing fruit from one of the trees, peel back the alligator skin and sink my teeth into the soft, creamy green flesh, a bite-full of concentrated sunshine. This seemed heavenly to us, and the thought of consummating those teenage dreams while making a home in the storybook land of the golden coast was too compelling to turn down.

Plus I have to admit that Cachés Notch had started giving me some subtle nudges that suggested it was time to move on. For one, I was spending too much time, and way too much of my liver's life span, in those watering holes. There are also some downsides to settling down in one's home state--for instance, the expectation of my parents that I would be available for all of the family events I had deftly avoided for ten years, even though I was still more than two hours away by automobile. It was an unexpected blessing to find myself wanting to lay down roots there in a familiar niche, nestled between granite crags in a valley guarded by giant white pines and sugar maples, and sharpened by nature's full bore plunge into every season. But leaving that safe haven to go anywhere nearby meant coming face-to-face with all the same eastern seaboard ghosts who inevitably catch me whenever I cease to be a moving target. So settling down was not an option, not even in a place that felt more like home than any I had tried.

So we sold our snowshoes and cleaned out the log cabin, packed up the jalopy, said goodbye to the North Country, and headed west.

Before we had even left New England, we met considerable resistance as we unwittingly took off into the teeth of a "nawtheastah"--basically a winter storm that picks up the Atlantic Ocean and drops it on land in the form of snow. *Somebody* up there seemed to be punishing us for uprooting ourselves again. There were times heading down through Vermont when the wind blew so hard from the east that I held the steering wheel cocked at a steady 45 degrees left to stay in a straight line, and if it is physically possible for snow to fall sideways, it did, in huge piles that turned the interstate into a thin track of white between snow banks. Fortunately no one else was foolish enough to be out there with us and we survived the first night at about 15 mph. It did not get much better from there as the snow turned to ice farther south. We skidded across a bridge in Virginia, smacking the concrete guard on the left side of the highway. I remember looking straight down into a gorge as I stepped out into the frozen hell to survey the damage, fully expecting to see a mangled side panel on the Honda Civic. But we had been saved by the fact that at least three fingers of ice on both car and bridge had absorbed the entire blow. With one whole bag of kitty litter and a little pushing, we were back on the road, thanking those lucky stars that were somewhere on the other side of the charcoal clouds dumping all manner of calamity on us. I managed to get stuck again, not once but *twice*, in our fruitless attempts to find a vacant hotel room that night. That was how we spent Christmas Eve of 1999.

But we caught a break in the weather the next day in Tennessee as the signs started pointing us west, and in two days we cruised from the Smokies past Nashville, across Ole Man River, through an Arkansas night and all 833 miles of the Lone Star State. Before I had fully recovered from a bad case of the shivers due to slopping through the ice-slush of western Virginia in my tattered Timberland boots, we were ordering *huevos rancheros* at a greasy spoon diner in the outskirts of El Paso. The Rio Grande Valley of New Mexico lay before us as I beamed out the window, exhausted yet invigorated. We were sitting on the doorstep of the West, like kids on the edge of a 1.2 million mile playground. Our snow-covered hovel in Cachés Notch could not have been farther behind us, and all was good in the world.

Our money ran out before the land did. We swung down to the border in Arizona and visited some friends in our most recent western outpost, the one we left to try laying down roots in New England. We stayed a day too long and played a little too much. Then we cleared out our old storage bin in Tucson (having simultaneous self-storage units on opposite sides of the country is a symptom of bicoastal disorder) and hit the road. I soon realized we did not have enough gas money to reach Cambria. We holed up at some Sonoran Desert fast food oasis with nothing but fumes in the gas tank, sleeping in a truck stop TV room, waiting for an emergency loan from Nadia's father to show up in the savings account.

Once it did, we rolled confidently into California, past the dizzying expanse of Los Angeles, up the 101 through a sunscape of surf and vineyards and our first mesmerizing views of the Coastal Range, and into San Luis Obispo by sundown on New Year's Eve. It struck me as an impossibly cute and vibrant college town, a palm-dotted mecca for hikers, bikers, and sun-lovers of all stripes, the quintessence of what a California hometown should be. Nadia, who had also grown weary of the bone-chilling weather in our boreal hideaway, was opening like a flower in spring and loved everything she saw. *This* was finally going to be the place for us, she insisted, and I couldn't disagree. We rang in the new millennium with showers and pancakes at the local hostel, and then set sail up the last stretch of Route 1, the once exotic pleasure cruise through a *ménage a trios* of road, land, and sea that is now my daily commute.

I often think back to that feeling of optimism as I cross the same ground less than two years later, a lifetime's worth of hard lessons absorbed by a mind forced to age too quickly. How did it fade away so far and so fast? Like another well-known "ye of little faith" tale, I suppose, this one involves a mustard seed.

3:45 am (PDT) / 6:45 am (EDT)

I have just walked into the tiny drivers' room at Eldorado Stages. Far from being a relaxing place to prepare for a journey or unwind after coming home, this is a densely packed clearinghouse of company information, CalDOT safety paraphernalia, bus-themed calendars, several years' worth of business files in cardboard boxes, lost-and-found items (and some that are just plain lost), tools and bus parts spilling over from the garage, defunct coffee makers, a cornucopia of maps, pamphlets and tourist brochures, and recently, a misplaced soda machine. If more than two drivers report for duty at once, there is not much elbow room.

The first thing I always do is raid the communal fridge. An ever-changing stockpile of goodies--deli sandwiches, juice boxes, sodas, cakes, pudding packs, etc.--always populates the drivers' fridge, and it is free for the taking. Most of it consists of leftovers from the great bacchanalian feasts our customers indulge in on their trips. One group that I took to a Dodgers game, for instance--mostly Latino families connected through employment at a fiber optics plant--brought at least two Costco sandwiches, three bags of chips, and a six-pack of liquid refreshment for every man, woman, and child on the bus, and they left at least a third of it behind. Only in America.

Today I select two danishes--a raspberry and a cheese--and a 20-ounce Coke. As I sit down with my paperwork and open the raspberry, I hear the whirring grumble of an automobile, badly in need of a tune-up and new timing belt. It pulls up and parks right outside the office door. With the engine still running, the door opens and Floyd walks in, looking frumpier than usual in his standard-issue NASA white short-sleeve collared shirt and navy chinos. With the right costume and a long white beard, Floyd would look just like a lawn ornament gnome. He was raised among the rock piles and ranchlands of central Oregon, and given another career choice, he might have turned out more like the Marlboro man. But Floyd has been driving motor coaches for over forty years, and it shows. He has permanent indigo bags under his eyes, and his face seems to have succumbed to gravity long ago- -in fact his whole body has assumed the shape of a pile of sand poured onto the driver's seat. Floyd spent most of his career with a company that ran month-long loops across the country. Who knows how many millions of miles Floyd has under that 44-inch belt, and when I can get him to wax nostalgic, he has a wealth of great road stories and practical advice, a valuable resource for a rookie driver. But most of the time Floyd just gripes about the passengers and how he is too old for this shit.

Floyd heads straight for his bin and grabs his paperwork, scanning it with his brow furrowed. He shoves it back in with an exaggerated sigh, clearly unhappy with his lot in life for the day. A minute or so passes while I wonder if he even knows I am sitting there, but then Floyd turns to me and bursts forth with an affected conviviality.

"Yo, Pedro! Whaddaya know?"

"Not much."

Floyd turns his attention to the refrigerator, leading his own expedition through the motley contents. It can be hard to tell the magnitude of Floyd's disapproval of anything--it all generates the same staccato breathing pattern and some variation on "*Uy-yuy-yuy!*" pronounced under his breath. It is a habit that has occasionally unnerved at least one of his trainees, because it is nearly impossible to know if one has forgotten to do a head count of the passengers after a meal stop, or if Floyd cannot find his favorite soft drink. This morning, it is the latter. He mumbles something incoherent to most human ears.

"Behind the meatball grinders and applesauce on the bottom," I say, without looking up. I hear the sound of a glass jar moved over a plastic shelf, followed by the fridge door closing and the fizzy pop of a once-shaken Dr. Pepper bottle opening.

"You *heard* that?" He sounds more concerned than curious, which makes me grin. I have been thinking that I ought to find some innocuous occasion to let him know.

"Yep."

He suddenly seems afraid to move.

"What are you, goddamn Superman or something?"

"I don't think so. Unless Superman also has two wonky knees and a lazy left eye. But yeah, my ears are hypersensitive. Annoyingly so."

I turn to look at Floyd and shrug my shoulders slightly, a mute acknowledgment of the cat now out of the bag. I can almost see him making a mental note to clean up the language of his not-so-private mutterings when he is working with me.

Floyd looks away, absently scanning the laminated posters on the wall with riveting information like Hours of Service regulations and diagrams showing how to properly inspect a Van Hool. He throws himself dramatically into the seat beside me, landing with a grunt. His face has all the pizzazz of leftovers from yesterday's dinner left out on the counter overnight. I can tell that, he too, was drawing on his deepest reserves just to get out of bed in time for this gig. He reaches for his mailbox and has a second look at his paperwork. It does not seem to hold his interest, for soon he has let the papers slide off to the side and, as he often does when we drive together, he starts scanning me, intensely, with a strange kind of eye. I have often thought that I must remind him of himself about forty years ago, when he was a young buck and life was simple and spread out before him like a boundless, uncreased roadmap. I feel him trying to tell me something, and I can almost hear the telepathic message: *Don't do it! Don't give your life to this! You'll lose everything else!*

Another half-minute passes, then he speaks in his trademark grumbly western drawl.

"Hey, did I ever tell you you're the whitest looking spic I ever seen?"

"About fifty-seven times since January. But not yet this week, so it's OK."

Floyd smiles and extends a pasty, droopy right arm to shoulder-chuck me, which I accept with a smile.

"So you're going out with them *bird people*, too, huh?" His emphasis makes them sound ghoulish, like B-movie science fiction villains.

"Looks like it. I've been reading the itinerary and it looks like a bird-watching group. We're going to Bonanza for some reason, then Azucar Mountain and a campsite in the foothills. Long day, but pretty easy. How about you?"

"Christ, I gotta take 'em to Santa Barbara so they can go to the Goddamn Channel Islands." Floyd shakes his head in astonishment at the stupidity of the entire world outside his cerebral cortex. "They're gonna spend two or three hours on a boat, go look at birds for an *hour, tops*, then two or three coming back. Ain'datta bitch!"

This is one topic on which Floyd and I will never relate. Just as nature abhors a vacuum, most drivers seem to despise the downtime that comes from waiting for passengers to do their thing at the places where we bring them. I love the free time. I get more done than I do at home, and it is all on the clock. But Floyd would rather drive laps around a parking lot than sit still and make use of his time.

"Well it should be a nice group anyway. Bird watchers can't be too rowdy."

"*Uy-yuy-yuy!*" Floyd's eyes roll to the top of his skull and back. "I never seen such *weirdoes* in my life! I've been taking this group out for the last three years, and lemme tell ya: *all* they talk about, *all day,* is birds. This bird does this, that bird looks like that. Christ almighty, there ain't a goddamn person in this group that knows *nuthin'* about anything else besides birds. Buncha loony tunes I tell ya...Christ I'm too old for this shit."

I am only half-listening now. My other half has moved on to the paperwork. Something caught my eye on the time sheet, where the customer's name is listed. I do not even know if I am interrupting at this point, but I blurt out, "American Birders Association?"

Floyd is uncharacteristically silent.

"*Birders?*" I say, in reply to myself.

"Yeah. That's what they call themselves. Why?"

"Well....in order to be a birder...one must be able to 'bird.'"

"Yeah, so?"

"'Bird' is a *verb?*"

Floyd looks off into space. "I guess so. Never thought about it much."

I have been leaning back in my chair to this point, but I suddenly bolt forward with my elbows on my knees to concentrate.

"'Cottleston, cottleston, cottleston pie...a fly can't bird, but a bird can fly. It always seemed to make so much *sense*. I never questioned it."

Floyd looks at me like I had spoken Swahili. "What the hell was *that?*"

"A.A. Milne. *The House at Pooh Corner.* Winnie the Pooh sang it. I've always assumed it was a true statement, but now I don't know. Maybe a fly *can* bird."

More silence. Now I know how to shut Floyd up when I need to.

"I gotta look this up." I reach down to the floor where I had parked my ancient army rucksack. It is ten years old to me--and much older to a WWII-era soldier named "Delvecchio"--and torn in a half-dozen places, but I still use it as a day pack. Despite many comments and admonishments from the unsentimental public-at-large, my wife included, I cannot seem to replace my rucksack. It is the only constant of my adult life.

Inside it I find my red hardcover *Webster's College Dictionary,* which has only slightly less seniority than the sack, and is held together by duct tape at the binding.

"You carry a *dictionary* with you?"

"Sure. Doesn't everybody?"

Floyd looks away and chuckles, shaking his head again no doubt. I flip through the "B" section until I find the entry for "bird."

"OK, let's see, there are twelve definitions altogether...noun: any warm-blooded, egg-laying vertebrate of the class Aves, having feathers, forelimbs modified into wings, scaly legs and a beak...slang: a person, especially one having some peculiarity... informal: an aircraft, spacecraft or guided missile...

(Floyd may have gone out to warm up the bus during this presentation. I can't be sure.)

...'the bird,' slang: a hissing, booing, etc., to show contempt made by raising the middle finger...ah-hah! Here it is. Verb: to bird-watch. Wow, *Winnie the Pooh* was wrong. A fly can bird."

I close the dictionary and look up at Floyd, who is back in his chair. At some point he must have decided to play along.

"C'mawn, how can a *fly go birding?*"

"Why not?"

"It's too Goddamn small! How's it gonna carry a pair of binoculars?"

"True. But I wouldn't be so sure. What about the one from that old Vincent Price movie? It probably could have birded if it so desired. And anyway, what species on earth has better *God-given* optical equipment to observe *any*thing than the common housefly?"

Floyd throws up his hands and laughs big. It is good to see such an unhappy man laughing when I play the clown.

"Jesus, it's true what they say about you, Pedro. You really are a loony tune. You should join up with the birders!"

"Maybe I will, Floyd." I smile back, to show I appreciate a genuine backhanded compliment. He gets up and makes that sweeping "come along" gesture with his arm.

"Awright, young man, let's go. We got people to pick up."

4:00 am (PDT) / 7:00 am (EDT)

The time of day which my people call "rush hour"--though it involves hardly any rushing and persists far longer than an hour--has arrived in earnest. Both Hudson River tunnels are backed up well into New Jersey, while the George Washington and Throgs Neck Bridges have turned from smooth-flowing conduits into hardened arteries. The platform of Grand Central Station looks like a human anthill, and at this moment, one hundred swarthy, sweaty men in identical yellow cabs on the island of Manhattan are laying on their horns and giving someone the bird. Gridlock has been achieved.

After a truncated once-over on the bus, I follow Floyd out of the Eldorado parking lot. We take the back way out of town, down Edna Valley Road to Price Canyon and shoot over to Pismo Beach. It may cost a minute or two, but we tend to start southbound trips this way because Price Canyon is a fun road to drive, a real snakeskin trail with enough curvature to invigorate the senses and let an artisan driver like Floyd practice his craft. As much as he tries to dull and downplay it with his words, Floyd's forty years on the road have made him a master at the wheel. I try to follow his exact path, easing into the curves, sailing through and accelerating as we pull out, all without shifting the center of gravity or nicking a line on the road.

You want your passengers to feel like they aren't even moving, Floyd explained to me once as we were laying over in Tahoe.

Every one of them is on vacation. This is their magic carpet ride-
-let them believe the bus is driving itself. Well, I think his exact
words were, "You ain't part of their party, so keep your mouth
shut and drive," but that's how I interpreted them anyway. Disappear into the vehicle, become the bus. That is the task of a
driver who aims to be superlative.

In the daylight, Price Canyon looks a bit like a broader, more
tamed version of its sister road to the north. Santa Rosa Creek
Road was the original land passage across the coastal ridge into
Cambria, before they built the highway to my storybook land.
Now it is a ghostly, seldom-used trail of cracked blacktop for
locals in ancient pickup trucks and daredevils seeking a wilder
ride than Highway 46. To travel it now is to realize experientially what a hardscrabble life even my grandparents' generation
and all who came before had to wrestle from this land. There
are places on the western slope where the switchback grades
would rival the best roller coasters at Magic Mountain. Down
below where it runs along the creek through the dense canopy
of overgrown moss-covered oaks, there are spots where the road
is simply not wide enough for two vehicles, and with the stark
combination of sun, shade, and sudden jutting hills, the visibil-
ity can be so bad that you can only *hope* there is no one coming
the other way. If a person wanted to hide from the world while
staying mere yards from the posh reality known to Hearst Castle
tourists or Route 1 Winnebago warriors, Santa Rosa Creek Road
would not be a bad place to vanish.

It was here that we made our first California home at the avocado farm, about five miles east of town, hidden deep within one
of the arroyos just beyond the main highway. It was such primal
farmland that even up close, one would hardly notice the formal
signs of agriculture. Avocado groves clung to the hillsides in a
manner that defied the typical linear layout of large-scale farms.
Tucked in between the trees were two terraced gardens in which
cash crops for the local grocery store and weekly farmers' market were raised. Water came from a year-round mountain spring
not far above the farm, so there were none of the fabled chronic
shortages that plague California growers. The hills rose sharply

to the north and east, cresting at the treeless ridge of the Santa Lucias. Far above, you could watch the meditative swoop of red-tailed hawks circling the skies like airborne sentries. I imagine this spot looked much like it did before any kind of conquistador arrived to claim it as his own. It was every bit the Eden we were seeking.

The farmer was one of those evil geniuses who lost his marbles somewhere long ago between acid trips and retreated to a hermetic life in the hills. He clearly wished he didn't need other people to run a profitable farm, and his general cantankerousness was a challenge to handle at times but mostly harmless. There was another young couple living in a tree house--New York hipsters with another acute case of bicoastal disorder--and a rotating cast of local characters and stray cats, earth children, and black hoodie punks. Together we made up a ragtag crew, but for a while we really gelled and turned out some great produce. Our lives became a nourishing routine of working with the earth, reaping the bounty we had sewn, and playing with like-minded souls on our little patch of paradise. For a while, I forgot all about the urges to be everywhere and elsewhere.

But like I said, the problems all began with one mustard seed. One of our tasks was to seed trays of lettuce starts that would become part of the farm's locally renowned mesclun mix. We were working with red mustard that morning, one of the smallest seeds in the agricultural plant kingdom. We would grab a small pile and hold them in our palms, carefully scrape two or three seeds into each portion of the plastic tray, then cover it all with topsoil.

There was no tangible buildup to Nadia's eruption at all. I only recall the sudden burst of motion out of the corner of my eye, a shriek of horror and frustration, and a black tray sailing through the air, crashing with a sodden explosion of soil and flimsy plastic against the translucent wall of the hoop house. Unbeknownst to me, Nadia's eyes had been doing strange things for a few weeks--inexplicable bouts of fuzziness that came and went. That morning, it took a turn for the much worse, and for the first time, she could not distinguish the seeds she held in her hand well enough to separate them. This was the onset of diabetic retinopathy, a degenerative condition of the vision for which there is no cure.

Nadia was inconsolable. Loss of vision cannot be an easy thing for any human being. To a person whose soul is devoted to a vocation such as painting, it is the beginning of the end of a worthwhile existence--or so I was told, very loudly, many times in the following weeks. She lost interest in farming, and found ways to back out of work and alienate our co-workers almost every day. One particularly troublesome habit she always had when falling into a long-term downer was to start binging on carbohydrates and comfort foods--things she knew would spike her blood sugar levels and throw off her very tenuous balance of health. When she started driving herself into town to different restaurants instead of eating on the farm, I knew this was going to be one of the vicious cycles, and sure enough her body became sicker with each indulgence, her outlook darker and more desperate. Meanwhile, tensions rose between us and the other workers. The farmer, normally aloof in his perpetual malcontent, started throwing venomous barbs at the freeloaders living off his labor. I tried to work twice as hard to carry the load for both of us, but no one saw that. They only noticed the absence of Nadia.

One day I was laying drip lines in a newly planted root crop patch of the garden, and I heard the telltale screams, the crash of something thrown against the metal mesclun wash tub, and a retaliatory barrage of profanity. I knew that our time on the farm was over. Apparently word had gotten back to the farmer that I picked some avocados from a tree that we had been told, for no good reason, to leave alone, and he decided it was all Nadia's fault. I did not bother to get in the middle of it. I just headed straight for the bus and started piling our stuff into the car. We stormed out of Eden in a cloud of plinking gravel, dust, and indignities, and didn't even bother to look back at the flaming sword that we knew would be there at the gate.

It was a major relief to be heading west on Santa Rosa Creek Road into town, leaving all that hostility behind and knowing we would never go back. But where to go next? Less than $200 was left of our emergency loan provisions, thanks to the restaurant tabs and extra gas money. This is how we learned first-hand the reality known to generations of California dreamers--the gold rushers, Dust Bowl refugees, runaways, and would-be starlets and leading men of Hollywood, endless summer lovers, dharma bums and nirvana seekers, and now the "undocumented aliens" whose ancestors called this land home before it was stolen from them--that believe it or not, you won't find it so hot if you ain't got the do-re-mi.

For all of the popular conceptions of California as the heartland of the hippie counterculture and a place full of people on the go (San Luis Obispo was the home of the world's first motor hotel, or "motel" as they came to be known), the equally true flip side of this is that nowhere in America is the static, conservative notion of private property so ingrained in the culture. There is a pervasive air of social Darwinism, a survival of the most affluent in which fitness is ultimately measured by the holding of property. People are as friendly as can be during the day, but after nightfall everyone on the north San Luis Obispo County coast retreats to some private castle or ranch, and it becomes the loneliest place on earth. It is very different than a place like Cachés Notch where *everyone* is poor, and there is an inherent bluesy camaraderie in being down on our collective luck. I felt the same culture in other bicoastal outposts in the Northwest, where an ethic of socialism validates the needs of the poor to a much greater degree. And even back home in the Northeast and the Rust Belt of the Midwest, there is a sense that everyone is rooted in their neighborhood, their town, or an ethnic enclave where notions of family are expansive and a "we're all in this together" mentality gives everyone a sense of place. In fact, anywhere that a harsh environment has forced people to band together for basic survival, one finds a degree of community across class levels and social strata, reflected in some element of common space, be it of mind or earth.

But paradise was parceled into private landholdings from the start, from the ranchos of New Spain to the subdivisions of today, and what is "mine" has never been "ours." Even along the dirt roads of Cambria's most inaccessible back country, properties are clearly marked by fences, driveways gated and often surveilled, NO TRESPASSING and NEIGHBORHOOD WATCH signs posted conspicuously. Whoever coined the aphorism "good fences make good neighbors" was probably a Californian.

That is all fine and good, I suppose, if you like your privacy and feel that you've earned it through hard work. But what happens when you combine this ethic with a highly mobile society, however, is that it becomes all too easy to shoo the poor away, without even considering how they contribute to the greater community. "Keep moving, stranger:" that is the California landowner's response to poverty in his midst. For individuals without the resources to play the predominant economic game of the local community, there is simply no place to be, especially at night. And failure to move on means coping with an existence that is ignored and unwelcome, and in some cases, even criminal.

The first indication of this came as we tried to find a campsite. It was the beginning of summer, and every campground from Big Sur down through Santa Barbara was booked solid. We found out that reservations were made through a system that requires a credit card, a great way to keep the rabble out. On top of that, there were ominous signs all over San Luis Obispo County posting a local ordinance that forbade sleeping in a vehicle. The fine was $250. For the crime of not having enough money to rent a room or stay in a hotel, the county threatened to take away our money. The justice in arrangements like that has always escaped me. But the true message had nothing to do with justice, and it was unmistakable: this is my piece of earth, sayeth the County, and you are welcome here to the extent that you serve my interests. If not, keep moving, stranger.

But Nadia and I were not interested in moving. There was way too much marrow to be sucked from the life of this place. So we went outlaw and lived out of the car. We moved up and down the coast to stay inconspicuous, showering in public facilities on the beaches, finding food wherever it availed itself. Some would call this freedom, and we tasted that joy from time to time, but it wasn't true freedom for us because we wanted something else. We *wanted* a place to be. We wanted to matter to shopkeepers and waiters and baristas, anyone who spoke the common language of currency in which we were temporarily illiterate. I checked the papers daily for driving jobs and applied for a few, but my New Hampshire license and lack of a local address really handicapped me. Nadia tried the entrepreneurial route and stole peanut butter, jelly, and bread from the Morro Bay Albertson's and sold sandwiches on the Embarcadero. It earned us some gas money and a couple meals, but nothing we did during those 40 days in the car ever overcame that language barrier. This was the hardest lesson to accept: that the crushing weight of being poor in a wealthy society is not just about a lack of security or opportunity--it is simply being on the wrong side of that most basic invisible wall between those who matter and those who don't, those who can speak and be heard and those who cannot. This is how one man's California dream becomes another's nightmare.

I had some acclimation to this from prior experience, but nothing prepared me for the intensity of it in California. Compounded by legal blindness in one eye, it was completely debilitating to Nadia, and eventually she did what she always does when she is desperate enough: she got sick to the point that she needed hospitalization. Pneumonia was the diagnosis. For Nadia, it meant a clean bed, three meals a day, constant care, and temporary deliverance from me, and I guess that was all worth it.

4:30 am (PDT) / 7:30 am (EDT)

We have driven thirty miles south from the yard, arriving in the urban/agriculture-clash city of Santa Maria. Though it still lies in the heart of a rich farming valley that grows all the iceberg lettuce for McDonald's and most of the world's broccoli, the city itself has mutated over the past twenty years into a genetically modified clone of San Fernando or Orange County. The contrast between the two largest communities in this portion of the Central Coast region could not be more stark. San Luis Obispo prides itself on "the SLO life," and has local ordinances banning box stores and drive-thrus at fast food restaurants to prove it. San Luis Obispans never tire of berating Santa Maria for its willingness to succumb to California sprawl. As best I can tell, Santa Marians just count their money and ignore us uppity types to the north, where it is debatable which is more impossible to find: a job or a rental unit. But that is Central Coast California as we round the corner into the 21st century. Like the rest of America, we sell our souls to the developers and the corporations, or we get left behind, like an old gold mining town.

We are now parked by the palm-dotted driveway of the Santa Maria Inn. I meet the conference manager, an affable man named Ken. He shakes my hand with a hydraulic crush and slaps me hard on the shoulder, which I don't take as well as Floyd's chuck.

"Good morning! I hope you're ready for an exciting day."

I never know what to say to things like that, and my answers are unfailingly awkward. "Of course. Just hope I don't fall asleep on the way." Ken laughs. He doesn't know I'm not kidding. I also meet the group leaders for my bus, a couple from Lompoc whose names escape me, as most names do. They both begin with a "B," so I will call them Bird #1 and Bird #2. They are dressed for a safari, somewhere between Congo green and Kalahari khaki. My first impression, after talking with them for a few minutes, is that she is a ventriloquist, and he is a dummy with laryngitis; she has been double-fisting black coffee since midnight, and he is ready to fall asleep standing in the driveway.

"Good morning, hi how are you? I'm Bird #1, this is my husband Bird #2, did you receive a copy of our itinerary? We want to make three stops. First one is off of Route 33 in Bonanza, we can show you the way we scouted the spot yesterday, then we're going to Azucar Mountain. Have you been there before? It's gorgeous. We'll spend a couple hours there and have lunch. Be very careful on the road going up there; very dangerous I'm told. Then one more stop on the way back at a campground. Pretty easy day. We'll be back at the hotel by five 'kay?"

"OK."

I'm glad we had this talk.

The Birds take their one-woman act elsewhere, leaving me to stand by the bus and watch the diffuse flock of birders slowly congeal into a transportable group. This is a lengthier, more difficult process with adults than with children--all the unleashed excitement of a school field trip without the fear of chaperones and official discipline. I also watch Floyd as he works the crowd by his bus, hobnobbing with the very people he dismissed as "loony tunes" an hour ago. Floyd has a vibrant personality he puts on when the paying customers are around, and he is already in midday form. He is especially good with the silver haired set. He becomes every man's best old chum from the neighborhood, and the ladies all think he is a grandpa Casanova, especially the ones with impaired vision. That is why Floyd usually gets the coveted "seniors" runs.

Before long, Ken whistles and booms over the din of the crowd that it is time to leave. I take my seat as the birders begin to board, filing one by one up the stairs to the aisle. I choose my greetings from a pool that includes "Hi," "Good Morning," and "Welcome Aboard," so they do not get stale. Most of the people, who only have one driver to greet, say "hi," but cordially. They all seem happy and exuberant despite the hour. This is the first trip of the week, much birding lies ahead. I scan the name tags as they pass by. They indicate that this conference has truly drawn a national representation, from Seattle to Maine to Key West and all points in between--a litany of familiar names, mostly places I have passed through on my way to Somewhere Else, but with enough regard that I carry a snapshot of each in a mental scrap-book, and that the people attached to these places are not total strangers.

I don't always take such an interest in who is riding on my bus. There are many groups for whom the bus is merely a cab big enough for four dozen people, a practical but cold model of efficiency, part of the annoying interval between Points A and B. For these passengers I find myself being only slightly more social than I was to my cargo as a truck driver. But it only makes it all the more intriguing when a truly dynamic group like this comes aboard, and it makes me pause to reconsider what it means to be a hauler of people. On a busy week, I can carry over two hundred and fifty passengers, each with a life story and a long winding road that leads them together on my vehicle for a spe-cific shared experience. Then, in most cases, their roads diverge and they disperse back into the far-flung world. But for that al-lotted time, I get to take a vicarious vacation with up to fifty six of my closest temporary relatives. In a very important way, a bus is the anti-California of mass transportation, where we *are* all in this together. There are no separate compartments, no first-class seats, and the difference between driver and passenger is only a matter of function. Even if that function is indeed to simply shut up and drive, I am still doing it *with* them. Not at all like the roll-ing isolation chamber of long-haul trucks that I gave up when I accepted this job. Maybe I knew instinctively that this was the only chance I would have to satisfy my craving for western expansiveness--to let myself be absorbed into that great wandering tribe of passengers, and let them carry something of me back to the four corners of the earth--while keeping my sanity enough to let me function at home.

In any case, it gives me comfort to know that all of America is with me today. It is a welcome break from the routine of high school football teams, wine tasting tourists from Fresno, and old folks getting fleeced for their Social Security dough at the local casino.

After a quick breakfast of juice and muffins is served, we are ready to roll. Floyd pulls out of the driveway first. His silhouette waves to me as he turns onto the boulevard, and I send back a right-handed salute. *Happy trails, my friend,* I think to myself, hoping he can hear.

I start up the bus--Number 477, an old warhorse with three-quarters-of-a-million miles of stories to tell. We head out into the empty Santa Maria streets. They are uncommonly broad and nondescript, like somewhere I might have rolled through in the Oklahoma panhandle. We go north a few miles through the slumbering town and turn onto the freeway for a short jog before exiting to a two-lane highway heading east.

Every bus, no matter how steady a course the base of its frame follows just above the ground, is tall enough to have an unmistakable sway. I have felt it many times as a passenger. If the driver is jerky or erratic in steering--too much of a hurry perhaps--the sway becomes an irritating wobble. The idea is to harness this natural momentum into something that feels more like the gentle rocking of a cradle. Maybe it is the wee hour of the morning, or I am actually in better form than I think I am today, but ten minutes into the run I am pretty certain that all forty four passengers on Bus 477 have been lulled back into sleep.

The valley in which Santa Maria sits is long and fairly narrow, running northwest to southeast. It does not take long before the road begins a steady climb away from the fertile lands by the ocean and into the dry, forbidding Coastal Range. Where the artificial luminescence of urban life enveloped us before, now a sea of twinkling orange dots float in the side view mirrors. Then the sea, too, disappears as we top the first ridge, and we have reached the Big Empty. In a matter of minutes we have left man's overburdened, overrun earth and landed on the moon. The highway follows a dry river bed, a long meandering gully carved by water from winter rains as it seeks its home, in no particular hurry. There are no human settlements along this route for the first fifty miles. For those whose image of California consists of smog-choked cities and parking lot freeways, places like this must seem other-worldly.

No one is stirring behind me now, all is quiet. The bus hums with meditative calm, bathing me in green dashboard glow. There comes a time like this on every long bus journey--all the more so when a portion of the night is carved off to cover the vast distance between places in the West--when the full measure of what I do hits me with epiphanic power and grace. To permit oneself to enter the mental space required to sleep while riding a land-based projectile, hurtling down a strip of asphalt at up to seventy miles an hour through all manner of weather--it seems to me that this requires a kind of trust that would be gradually earned, not blindly given. Yet here they are, those forty-four fellow travelers from communities all over America, each not merely a person herself but part of a family tree, branches inter-twined with others, all dependent upon her survival, all trusting me with safe passage through the night and day to come.

My mind revisits so many scenes where the skills to make good on that trust were honed...the first days of mangling a 10-speed transmission in the school's training trucks, when I *knew* that I would never be able to drive the damned thing and what did I get myself into...a couple winters later when the black ice of Nebraska taught me how to steer through a skid without jack-knifing or fishtailing into the car sliding next to me...the broiling summer day when I tackled the western slope of Donner Pass with a malfunctioning engine brake and I guessed wrong on the gear setting, and learned how to coast with forty five thousand pounds of laundry soap and eighteen smoking hotcakes all the way into the foothills. ...the endless uneventful minutes, staying alert and covering miles while catastrophe lay waiting just inches on either side of two thin white lines. Wyoming has shown me blinding snowstorms in late June and early September; Iowa, a tornado that crossed the highway maybe two miles behind me in the night; the New Jersey Turnpike, rain so hard it was like driving under a miles-wide waterfall, and a lightning strike that lit up the cab with a sizzling purple glow. The memories of it all are burned into my eyes, hands, and feet, and they could not forget if they tried.

And then these moments come when the mind remembers that the body knows all of this, and the heart fills with gratitude that a time-crafted gift has been given to me to give to others--tonight, in the form of peaceful sleep.

There is still a gap to cover between Nadia landing in the hospital and me in the driver's seat of this gilded steel Prevost. It is strange how these kinks in the smooth flow of one's life story, like a lost job or a case of pneumonia, so often lead to new chapters that feel nothing less than providential. Not long after I started visiting Nadia at the hospital in San Luis Obispo, I heard that one of the night shift nurses wanted to talk to me. She had caught wind that I was a truck driver. Her husband had an excavating company based in Cayucos, and needed a driver for one of his 13-speed dump trucks. It was unlike anything I had ever done as a driver, or really wanted to do for that matter. But I had crossed a certain vocational threshold where no vehicle seemed too intimidating to master. Plus, hunger speaks a language that does not include the word "No." A couple days later, I was gainfully employed by Oceanside Construction Company. I was a mover of earth.

The job was amazingly simple. Every morning I showed up at the truck corral just a ways up Old Creek Road and coaxed one of the old temperamental beasts into starting. Sometimes there would be equipment to move on a flatbed trailer to a new site, but most of the time I just drove to the same spot where we had worked the previous day--anywhere that someone was willing to pay a large amount of dollars to have the ground moved, smoothed, dug, leveled, or otherwise altered--and staged the rig where the crew wanted it. There, a small fleet of machines would be busy creating piles of dirt and debris for me to haul away to a prearranged site, then dump and repeat, for about eight hours each workday. The whole operation never took me more than fifteen miles from home, all within the grand coastline and canyon lands between Morro Bay and Cambria. I loved the ever-changing yet intimately familiar scenery, tinged with that sense of magic I had known since the first time I crested that peak. It was like Story-book-land had hired me to drive for its Public Works Department.

Every day, there were moments when my eyes would survey the landscape--perhaps the morning fog licking the hillsides as it retreats before the sun-baked crystalline California sky--and I would meditate on where I was and what it had taken to get there, and a delightful shiver would shoot down my spine, the unspeakable sensation of being in the midst of perfection. Once again for a time I was able to forget that there were roads leading away and beyond, uncharted lands to be discovered and redis-covered.

On top of that, Oceanside paid me the highest hourly wage I'd ever received for local work. Once again we were fluent in the local language of commerce. Within two paychecks we had enough to rent a room in a shared house in Morro Bay. It wasn't luxurious, but oh the joy of sleeping without pedals at my feet or a gearshift where my knees wanted to be! About two months af-ter that, with the loan from Nadia's father paid off, we found the bungalow apartment where we now dwell on Old Creek Road, just a five minute stroll from the truck corral. By Central Coast standards we were still among the peasantry, but we were peas-ants with a *home*, a place to be, and no castle dwellers were ever more grateful than we.

Nadia decorated the place with her newly discovered medium of oil pastels--broader than paint brush strokes with brighter colors more visible to her weakened eyes--and I fell into a pro-ductive routine of writing for a few hours each night after work while she drew. Three of the best weeks of our lives together, as I recall.

That idyllic world unraveled slowly this time, but the onset of its undoing was no less jarring or out-of-the-blue than a plane crash, on an otherwise ordinary December day.

The job we were doing was a house demolition right there in Cayucos. Someone hired us to knock down an adorable 1950s-era ranch house so it could be replaced by a tri-level condo, and probably triple the value of its quarter-acre lot. I remember walking through the house before we did any work, noticing its different layers of presence. Clearly, families had been raised there, with the telltale sign of faded height measurements penciled onto the door frame of the smaller bedroom. This was a place that at least two generations of someone's now-grown-up children must long for when they think of home. I wished like hell that I could buy it and preserve it for them, just on the off chance that I might meet them one day. But dreams like that stand in the way of Progress, so Progress knocks them down.

It had been a routine demo job until that day. We had worked most of the way down to the concrete slab. I was doing some light ground work in between dump runs, mostly clearing debris from a portico area between the house and a small free-standing garage. The crew was clearing the house of the last of its vital organs, while the boss was working with the backhoe side of his excavator chomping up the roof of the garage. I pulled up some plants at the base of the garage wall and walked them around to the organic matter pile around the side of the house.

All I remember next is a tense commotion of voices, and I turned around to see the boss leaping off his machine. As I got closer, I saw that the garage wall closest to the house--the one that had been above me no more than ten seconds earlier--was toppled and lying on the concrete. Also on the concrete, by the top of the wall now turned to rubble, was Santos "Splash" Rios.

Splash was a Mexican immigrant with almost no English, and surprisingly the only non-*gringo* on the crew, so he hardly ever spoke. He had earned his nickname, I was told, on a scorching hot day when they were leveling the ground for a new driveway on an oceanfront lot in Cambria. At the end of the day, he was having the usual beer and smoke session with the crew, when out of nowhere he said, "*Quiero nadar,*" and proceeded to sprint at full speed toward the bluff in the backyard. He hurled himself over the edge screaming "*Ayyyyyy!*"--I picture Acapulco cliff diver meets kamikaze pilot--and then all that the others could see from their perspective was the top of what had to be an enormous splash. They raced to the edge to find the newly christened Splash floating on his back like an otter, laughing hysterically. He had cleared about five feet of beach and dropped ten feet, and somehow managed to not die (they were pretty sure he belly-flopped, as it was way too shallow for other means of entry).

Splash's work ethic and skill set for his job were unparalleled. He could grade the slope of a yard, for instance, to the exact degree required using nothing more than his eyes, his hands, and a rake. He worked in the manner that I imagine a monk would tend to a garden, absorbed into his labor, completely free of distractions. All the gossip and bad jokes and sexual innuendo that were volleyed around him from morning until dusk were given no quarter in his brain. How I envied him for that. I later learned that Splash slept on a couch in someone's den and sent all his money back to a wife and children in Cuernavaca, just to complete this picture of a latter-day Latino saint.

On the day that all of this became past tense, Splash was walking across the portico with debris in his hands, right into the path of the falling wall. He was hit by the top of it, the part falling with the greatest speed and force, and slammed flat on his back onto the concrete slab. There was no blood or visible injuries, but he could not move aside from the involuntary spasms of breathless convulsion, like he was being choked by invisible hands he could not grab. Most of his skeleton had been crushed, and his airway was completely severed. Some feeble attempts at resuscitation were made, but there was no kind of CPR that could keep him alive. We all watched helplessly as Splash Rios surrendered the fight for his last breath, and left us on a sunny December day on the California shore.

It was the first time a human life had disappeared before my eyes. The other living witnesses on the scene ran the gamut from disbelief to hysteria to a shocked, sobbing terror. I somehow remained very still, observing. A few memories are etched from those moments...the surprise at how quickly the body changes when the breath is gone, his tan skin turning pale and face rigid like an off-white plaster mask within seconds.

And my first conscious thought: *Where did you go, Splash?*

I don't mean anything so banal as heaven or hell. I mean *where?* What looked out from those eyes while he drew breath, and where has it gone now?

I had never occasioned to ask those questions before, at least not since a series of terrifying waking dreams about death as an unending oblivion had scared them out of me (or pushed them deeper within?) over the course of my childhood. My existentialist fears drove me toward a life of meekly cantankerous shallowness that I find typical of people in this era. But then a building collapses, a life just like ours is lost, and suddenly the mind is forced to grapple with questions it would rather ignore.

No answers came that day or soon thereafter, but it was the day that I started asking better questions of myself. We can all probably look back at one point in our lives and remember one such person or event that woke us up from the nightmare of feigned immortality. Mine, if you will accept the paradox, was an anonymous Mexican laborer named Splash Rios.

I did not last very long with Oceanside after that. Asking unanswerable questions may be good exercise for the soul, but for the mind still operating from the confines of a human body, with a reborn awareness of the transience of such, it gets a little harder for a while. The accident happened on a Thursday morning, and we all took the rest of the day and Friday off to calm our frazzled nerves. But Monday we were back on the job. Unfortunately, we were also short our most productive laborer, and that meant that I needed to pitch in on the ground even more in between dump runs.

Some quick background on my physical health: it has been almost spotless in every way since birth. But as I alluded to Floyd, I have one humbling malady that has bugged me most of my life:

a pair of genetically defective knees. My kneecaps didn't fit correctly into the groove that nature designed--a minor detail it would seem, but it left me susceptible to knee sprains and accelerated cartilage wear. I went under the knife twice at age thirteen to fix them. While my left knee healed solidly and had never so much as whimpered again, my right had plotted against me ever since, and a slew of aggravating injuries ensued, all while doing things quite normal to most of the world. It has also been an internal barometer for measuring my stress level--generally speaking, when my right knee feels stiff and brittle like a plaster of Paris mold, something is not right with my head.

So there we were, my right knee and I, lifting enormous chunks of concrete and cinder blocks and tossing them into the front end loader's scoop. Barometric pressure was extremely high, and I dragged my right leg behind me, letting my back do all the work. I was the "how not to" model in the construction company safety videos. But in typical male fashion, I was also trying to prove myself to the *real* men who did that kind of work all the time, and the worse my knee felt, the more I tried to overcompensate with my upper body.

One Friday afternoon, eight days after the accident, I went to grab a particularly large chunk of the garage floor, and realized I couldn't get it with my back and arms alone. So I crouched down to lift with my legs like a good boy. As I lifted myself up, I felt something pop...in my left knee.

Did I mention I was also putting all of my weight on one leg? Yeah.

It did not seem that bad at first--nothing painful, just that queer, somethin'-ain't-right feeling. I noticed it getting worse throughout the day as I climbed in and out of the truck, and loaded some equipment on the flatbed at the end of the day. Not drastically, but enough swelling to make bending the knee feel like something that was not supposed to happen. I was limping on both legs, if that is even possible, but I did not tell anyone at Oceanside. It didn't feel like a big deal.

By the end of the weekend, as I lay on the couch with the knee iced and propped up, wishing the swelling away to no avail, it was clear that it was a very big deal. Nadia was always a little agitated whenever I got ill or injured. Anything that even temporarily threatened her status as The Sick One in the relationship drew more consternation than empathy from her. I had fixed my own right knee so many times through ice packs and rest that I was sure I'd be back on my feet by Monday, so every hour that I lay inert on the couch with no results only increased the hostility. I slowly resigned myself to the fact that this one was going to call for pills--one for my knee, and about four for my aching head.

When I came into the office Monday morning on Salvation Army crutches to file a workers' comp claim, I became Public Enemy No. 1 at Oceanside. The boss contested the claim, which wound up delaying payment for the full ninety days allotted to an appeal. It was true that I had not reported it as a work injury as I should have, but they had nothing on me as far as proving the claim was false, because it was not, and they bore the burden of proof. In the meantime, with me confined to "limited duties" (I was allowed to drive the truck, but no groundwork), my workload diminished drastically, and the boss did everything but verbalize that he wished the wall had fallen on me instead. And I certainly did not take the high road in response. I called him "pond scum" in an official document, and insinuated that none of it would have happened if he had not killed off twenty percent of his work force. It was the ugliest confrontation I have ever had with someone not married to me.

And it wasn't paying the bills either. What little bit we had squirreled away over the couple months of full-time income was quickly gone, and our bungalow haven was in jeopardy. The local classifieds were skimpy as always, so I turned to my most effective means of job hunting: skimming through the Yellow Pages listings for trucking companies, food distributors, anyone who had something with wheels and might need someone to propel it. No one was interested in me, and the anti-inflammatory meds had not taken full effect, so operating a clutch was still very difficult. I resigned myself to calling the dreaded temp agencies for desk work.

Then I remembered the special endorsement in my pocket--my license to haul people. I let my fingers walk to the Bus listings....

Two days later, in early January 2001, I limped into the office of Eldorado Stages and met Annie O'Fallon, the most blindly beneficent and trusting employer I've ever had. The doors she would open for me as a novice in the bus driving business were hard to fathom, but open wide they did. Paychecks started coming again, rent got paid, and I...well, for better or for worse, I caught the scent of the road, infused with adventure and liberation, an antidote to the stench of death that pervaded my life at Oceanside.

One might think that having gone through the travails of being penniless and homeless, to what was in most respects the simple home of our dreams, and then to the brink of losing that home, any employment situation that could pull us back from said brink would harken another period of gratitude for our prosperity, and warmth between each other who were manifesting our own dreams.

It did not. In fact, in many ways, the times ahead were the most desperate of all.

But a smooth empty road swallows despair like nothing I have ever known. All feels right when I am at the wheel, and the troubled nights I leave behind in Cayucos always give way to glorious mornings...and if I tell myself that often enough, I might start to believe it again.

Right now, it is oddly dark in the predawn sky--no moon, no stars, no lights, no traffic, just me and the bus and forty-four birders in peaceful slumber. I feel a yawn coming, but I choke it off and cup it with my hand. It is bad form to yawn in front of the passengers, I have been told several times. Makes them nervous. So I acquiesce, knowing that no one is awake to witness this display of fatigue. If a bus driver yawns, and no one is there to see it, is he still tired?

A sign: 25 miles to Cuyama. Good. We are almost halfway

there. The bus reaches a right-hand bend. It drops into fourth and chugs up an incline, headlight beams slicing the inky western darkness.

There is a city to my north, a mere fraction of my size and significance, yet somehow it has the gall to call itself "the Hub of the Universe." Such is the fantastic nature of names, after all. But I digress....The morning sky in this miniature metropolis is sunny and clear, as it is above me as well. It is one of those pristine September days in which our human residents delight, heralding the shift from muggy summer to the refreshing cool of autumn on the Atlantic seaboard.

Into this fair New England sky sails a jet airplane, bound for another city that dares consider itself a rival of mine--Los Angeles, irony apparently unintended--on the far western coast. Fourteen minutes later, another plane leaves Boston with the same destination. Routine daily departures, unusual only in that flightless creatures take to the air and cross the continent in five hours. This is the marvel of the human imagination, that after centuries of fruitless imitation and envy of birds, the proper concoction of engineering principles would lift a man off a North Carolina island and bring him down where he wanted to land; and more so, that so soon after the Wright Brothers' success, the day would come when thousands of these metallic birds would carry millions of people safely to places all over the earth, a kinetic web of motion that less than one hundred years ago would have been revered as a miracle.

These two birds will not be among those successful flights. For humans can also imagine their own annihilation, and on the other side of the world, someone realized that a Boeing 767, with a top speed of over 500 mph and a fuel capacity of 13,900 gallons, could be the greatest Molotov cocktail ever made. This person organized a crew of compatriots to make his dream a reality, some of whom hide among the passengers on these planes. For reasons known only to them, they are willing to die and take a small cross-section of humanity with them, and their scheme is about to culminate in my airspace, bringing total destruction to my largest buildings, terror to the hearts of my people.

Within a half-hour of takeoff, both birds have been hijacked and re-routed by trained pilots among the murderers. They are now guided missiles, and their new destination is lower Manhattan.

ACT II

5:45 am (PDT) / 8:45 am (EDT)

My name is Joseph Bijan D'Angelo, and I'm not going anywhere.

I'm supposed to be inside the Goddamn Holland Tunnel by now, maybe seeing daylight on Canal Street as I near the exit. But I ain't even reached the end of the Turnpike yet. Still inching across the elevated freeway here in Jersey City.

I am really starting to hate this drive. It's my own damn fault. The wife wanted to stay in the East Village, but I didn't want the kids to grow up in the city. So she said, "Well how about Brooklyn? We could get one of those lovely brownstones in Park Slope, become members at the co-op, blah blah blah...." But I was so sure that Jersey was the place to be. I mean, I'm used to losing a half-hour every morning at the tunnel, no big whup. But when I can't even get to Bayonne before the gridlock starts, that's bad news. That's an hour at best.

I know the PATH train would have me almost all the way to Penn Station by now, and then a short ride on the C train would bring me to the front door of my building at 9:01 am. Don't think that I ain't heard that a couple hundred times from the wife already. I just prefer the freedom of driving myself. Who knows, I might want to go uptown for a long lunch, dazzle a client or something....alright, that might have happened three times in the last two years,

I don't really like going out too much. But still, once you invest $300 a month in a parking space, spending extra money on train fare seems like such a waste. Carpooling? Fuhgeddaboutit. Two hours of forced conversation every day? No thanks, pal. So I handle the 8:00 am day care drop while my wife, the dedicated passenger of mass transit who actually likes her job, catches the 7:25 am.

On the other hand, this is really getting old...maybe I shoulda gone home after all.

Let's see, what else...I'm a middle management schlep at a public relations firm in Tribeca. We get paid buku bucks to make evil Wall Street bankers look like saints. Basically I'm an overpaid paper pusher. The last time I felt any professional satisfaction was about four months ago when I wrote a moderately defiant email to a senior partner on the matter of tax evasion. Bastard probably never read it. I guess I ain't really the whistle blower type. So the job pays the bills--barely, you'd be amazed how much it costs to live around here--but that's about all. Frankly, I think I'd rather be doing just about anything else today.

I'm 35, and I live in Union with my second wife and our two girls. We have a three-bedroom house, the whole suburban dream thing, yada yada yada. Not a bad spot, I don't have neighbors all on top of me or anything. It ain't as exciting as the East Village, but the wife's gotten used to it. Now she says riding the train into the city is like this fantastic event that brings her back to the first time she came here. Hey, whatever turns her on.

Damnit, this traffic. I don't know what I expect to happen. The guy in front of me rolls two feet, I roll two feet. He stops, I stop. My life in a nutshell.

It hasn't always been like this for me...I could get ahead of all this traffic. I can drop the girls off at Small Wonders anytime after the crack of dawn. It's just that, lately....I don't really wanna get out of bed in the morning. It ain't like I'm sick or anything, I mean physically I feel fine. I just...I wake up, and I know pretty much how the whole day's gonna go--there ain't much variation in it, know what I mean?--and more and more lately...I just don't want it. I'd rather go back to sleep and wake up later and be someone else.

Just this morning, I'm lying there half-awake, and the wife's in the other room listening to her crazy Himalayan shit, like someone's gargling mouthwash for twenty minutes...and I just start thinking: Really? Is this it? Am I going to drag through today, and every other day just like today until I retire, and then we go to Florida and buy a fortress by the sea so we can have a beautiful place to die? Is that really what this is all about?

Actually, I don't want this to get around too much so I'm hesitant to even mention it. But I think it has a lot to do with this...a little while ago, I did one of those internet personal ad deals. It ain't what you think so don't go getting crazy ideas about me, awright? So they have this part when you're filling out your profile where they ask about your interests, your hobbies and whatnot. And I totally froze. I had no idea what to write. I mean, there was a time when I might have called myself "outdoorsy," when i got out to the Poconos a couple times a year, the Catskills, go hiking, camping, all that stuff. I can't even think when was the last time we went camping. Before our oldest was born, so four years ago at least. I used to love car trips *anywhere* really, didn't matter where we went. Now it's all I can muster to get the will to go anywhere west of the Parkway.

So I was trying to think: nowadays, what do I do for fun that replaced it? Something that could involve other people, I mean...and I just couldn't think of anything. I love Thai food and microbrews for instance, but I don't really like bars or restaurants, so nine times outta ten, I'm enjoying them at a TV tray in the family room watching football. What kind of woman is going to find *that* attractive? Seriously though, I am a one-woman guy, I'm just...it's complicated.

Until the traffic killed any chance of arriving at work on time, my primary thoughts of the morning involved the Giants' pathetic rushing attack in Denver last night and the fact that the wife denied me sex for the third time in a month--right about when she started taking that yoga class with the pony-tailed hippie freak.

The car in front of me rolls forward about three feet, then stps. I do the same.

I glance at my hairline in the mirror again. Pretty sure it's getting farther north on my forehead... whoa...damn, this crazy broad in a silver hatchback almost rolled into me. She had to jerk to a stop..And of course it's because she's applying her makeup. In the left lane, I got a man in a plumbing contractor's pickup truck wolfing down an entire three-course breakfast. To my right, I'm looking out over the rooftops of Jersey City and the office towers down by the river, with Manhattan poking up behind. I'm just about even with the World Trade Center now, which at this rate means at least a half-hour before I leave the tunnel.

My God, when did life become so...uninspired?

I reach down and pickup my large cup of *Dunkin' Donuts* hazelnut coffee from the drink holder. I bring it to my lips and tilt my head back to suck up the last of my morning caffeine fix. It honestly takes about three of them to get through a day lately...Man, I'm so tired of these thoughts. I flip on the radio, only to hear fools laugh over an anecdote about groping a woman. I swear, it's enough to make ya crazy.

I begin to lower the empty Styrofoam cup toward the cup holder, when suddenly my head bolts forward. I crush the cup in my right hand as I grab the steering wheel and brace myself against the seat. Enormous plumes of smoke rise from the upper floors of the north tower of the *World Trade Center*. It's on the other side of the building so I can't tell…what floor is that? I can't--oh no. No, no...Oh God no, no please, please don't--oh God, please don't make me live through that again...VERA!

* * * *

My eyes are getting heavy again, and I have a sudden dire urge for coffee. The hypnotic procession of center stripe dividers is all I can see outside the windshield. I am slipping into microsleeps--my mind eases, gradually, heading toward that unconscious place of rest...eyelids start to slide...then a little jolt comes from somewhere, cocks my head back a couple inches, and I am alert again.

Damnit, why didn't I just stop at the gas station in Morro Bay? Large coffee and hot chocolate mix ("the poor man's mocha"). Poison myself just enough to get the nerve endings frantic and clamoring for relief. That would get me going better. But I'll be fine. I am accustomed to working through this condition. Daybreak will come soon enough. *It's always darkest before the dawn, I remind myself. A few of the passengers are awake and quietly* talking shop. Most still appear to be in deep sleep, visions of short-billed do-whichers, undoubtedly dancing in their heads.

Roads like this are what I crave about the west, and yet I have to say they fall under the "be careful what you wish for, you might get it" category. I am so devoid of external stimulus that my mind has no idea what to do with itself, and it lets go of its grip on the physical body.

Something similar happened to me once as a passenger, on a Greyhound in the desolation of Interstate 5 through the Central Valley. I am a notoriously poor sleeper inside any vehicle, as I would hope that most professional drivers are. But this time I fell asleep from absolute exhaustion at a similar hour for some timeless interval, and when my consciousness came back I was completely unaware of who or where I was. This lasted for maybe a minute as my mind groped in the darkness for something to grab and call Me...and the first things it got were my body, and the old rucksack at my feet...and motion--pure motion: no location, no origin, and no destination. A being moving freely through space, with no discernible relation to what was around me. I wasn't oblivious to my surroundings, I was just surrounded by oblivion.

I stayed in this state for a surprisingly long time, maybe another full minute. My eyes instinctively scanned outside the window, trying to get a sense of location. It looked like a giant dark sea, with rocks and sand and patches of grass zooming between shadows in the fore. I wondered if I were sailing along the edge of a beach, maybe on a train or some kind of hovercraft... but soon my waking imagination fell in line with an emerging memory--I was on a southbound bus in California. I had left my home in Seattle two days prior, and I was on my way to see a girl (of course) in San Diego. There were forty-some-odd people making this leg of the journey with me, including the young flannel-clad Latino gangbanger, sleeping peacefully next to me, heading home to Riverside. It was just a few days before Thanksgiving and I was warmed by the thought that everyone was going home. Everyone but me.

That happened almost eight years ago, but I remember the sensation as though it were last night. It has always seemed complementary to my teenage experience of cresting the mountain above the Central Coast. If the road had given me a taste of heaven then, this was more like a glimpse of nirvana, the void beyond all notion of self and being.

When I look at them together, assimilate their essence into one sort of non-linear experience without the dimension of time, I can feel what Kerouac was talking about during his Buddhist days when he told us that we are all "empty and awake." The mountain was my awakening; this, my introduction to emptiness.

I have made similar efforts to reproduce the experience, all without the desired results. The closest I have come was on a night that I smoked way too much ganja, and as I drove home I had to remind myself where I was going every ten seconds. But that was just chemically-induced stupidity, more annoying than enlightening. I have never been able to harness the emptiness anymore than I could bottle the sensation of being awake.

It is interesting to me, though, that both of the authentic experiences happened in California--less than 100 miles apart, actually--while I was traveling through...and now I've come back here to try to put them together.

I am writing about them in fact, indirectly. That is my current project, "The Valley and the Mountain," an allegorical tale about finding the middle road between the two extremes where our minds always seem to want to take us. It is coming along very slowly, partly because my life is one continuous distraction, but mostly because I never walk this road long enough to be able to describe it or draw a map to it. I keep working at it though, in the hope that writing about it will help me find it.

Usually a night like this is the perfect time to let my writing mind take flight, with the drama of home left behind, basic motor skills occupied, and the rare quietude of all social functions provided by a bus full of unconsciousness. But I am too mentally fatigued to reach the space where the characters dwell, where the allegory comes together in a way that I can translate into words. The irony of the fact that I am depending on such lofty trips into rarified air to write a book about the middle road is not lost on me; indeed, it is why in my weaker moments...most of the time...I fear that I don't have what it takes to finish it.

But that is still the aim--to find a way to live fully empty, fully awake, and to put it all into words.

Meanwhile, Bus 477 rolls on with its distinctive grumbling hum, like a yogi pronouncing OM through a sore throat. I appreciate the weathered pitch of our older bus engines. The new Prevosts--and by "new" I mean fewer than a quarter-million miles--are almost *too* sleek, kind of like driving a monorail. But a bus like 477, well into the autumn of its life, has picked up enough idiosyncrasies along the way to have a personality of its own. Now that I think of it, if there is a word for the opposite of "personification," then Bus 477 is the *THAT* of Floyd. If any driver's blood and sweat has been tapped and co-mingled with the inanimate life force of ol' 477 and its brethren at Eldorado, it sure isn't a young whipper-snapper like me. It is Floyd who runs through these fuel lines.

Floyd was the primary trainer placed in charge of orienting me to bus driving. We started with a road test. We cruised all around San Luis Obispo--city streets with the tightest turns he could find, parallel parking, etc.--then down to Santa Maria and back to see how I would handle the freeway. It was my very first time driving a bus, thanks to my *theoretical* road test back in New Hampshire, but Floyd wouldn't have guessed. He reported back to Annie that I drove like I was born in the driver's seat, which delighted her. It seemed that she had me pegged to be one of Eldorado's all stars--a square-jawed, broad-shouldered protégé of Floyd to lead the new hyper mobile generation of drivers through the first decades of the 21st century.

Annie was one of those women who projected the energy that she was everyone's mom. I was half-surprised to find out that she had no children of her own, though I suppose that was why she threw her life into adopting a quirky family of bus drivers. She must have recognized me as a bicoastal orphan, 3,000 miles from any source of maternal care.

"How Wonderful to Have You on Board, Pedro," she said when she hired me (Annie has a knack for speaking in capitalized words; she is the anti-ee cummings). "It's Rare to Find Someone with both a Truck Driver's Work Ethic and the Social Skills of a Bus Driver."

"Well, it is rare for me to be accused of having social skills," I retorted, "but I'll do my best to live up to your misconception."

Any way you look at it, Eldorado Stages opened its doors to me in ways that an employer never had before, and for the first time ever, the place that wrote my paychecks also felt like home.

I was a little dismayed about the starting wage on those paychecks--I earned almost fifty percent less per hour to haul people than dirt, a number that still baffles me--but I quickly learned that this figure was offset by the vast abundance of hours available to work. A short day in this line of work is eight to ten hours. Most are designed to fall within the range of what is legal for a single driver to handle in a day: fourteen hours, according to the arcane logic of the Department of Transportation. There are some itineraries however, like my current one, for which I know from the beginning that, adding up all the high mileage or slow road drive time, the waiting around time, and the less glamorous activities that punctuate the day (cleaning the vast array of trash, food, and other sundry left-behinds, inspecting and fueling the bus, emptying and refilling the port-o-john at the back of the bus, etc.), I will be expected to write short works of fiction in my log book. This is accepted and understood with a kind of wink-wink ignorance on the part of the charter bus companies because it makes customers happier and all of us wealthier. String a couple "normal" days together along with a blockbuster, and a driver can easily clear forty hours in three days. This is perfect for a would-be starving artist like myself, but with that puny hourly wage, for a driver trying to raise a family in this part of California (or one with an even more starving artist at home who claims she cannot work anymore), forty hours doesn't pay the rent, which keeps us hungry to be overworked. And with the robust economy of the first half of 2001, there were plenty of people wanting Eldorado's services, and more than enough work for those who wanted a fourth or even a fifth day to make ends meet.

The bottom line: after training, I was banking a good chunk more per week than I was at Oceanside--and taking twice as many hours away from home to do it. That is where the trouble began.

6:00 am (PDT) / 9:00 am (EDT)

Black smoke now billows from all sides of the north tower, and it thickens by the minute. It is almost as though I can feel it filling my own lungs now. Across the river and nearly a thousand feet below, my heart pounds inside my throat and I have to remind myself to breathe. What time is it? Oh man, she's up there. She's up there for sure.

The radio snaps me back to my immediate space. Wait a minute; did I just hear those men on the radio? They're still talking about that woman? "SHUT THE FUCK UP!" I scream at the radio and stab the power button with my shaky finger. After a couple painful misfires, I have silence. What a fucking waste of breath.

I guess I'd better explain. My wife, Vera, works for an agency called the Metropolitan Transportation Council, and her office is on the 82nd floor of the north tower...and whatever is happening up there is very close to her. I figure there must be some news on another station, so I turn the radio back on...OK here we go...oh my God. They're saying an explosion was caused when a large passenger plane crashed into the north tower..."Holy fuck," I say out loud to myself, "could that have been an accident?" Anywhere else, I would believe it was. But not the *World Trade Center*. This feels bad.

Only now does it dawn on me to try calling her. We just got the cell phones about a month ago, and both often forget...straight to voice mail. She probably left it at home on the charger...and of course her office line is dead. Oh God, please, don't take her now. To lose her now would be too much to bear....

It looks like we aren't even going to try to get into the city. People are walking around the turnpike and gazing at the tower. The plumber and makeup artist both pulled over to the shoulder and are out of their vehicles now, wandering toward the concrete wall on the right. Maybe I oughta do that also. All of a sudden I don't feel like dealing with this alone.

The plumber is a white-haired man in baggy green overalls and a grease-stained Mets hat. He speaks with a thick *Hell's Kitchen* accent, a throwback to the days before everyone was raised by the same television.

"Whatta ya hoid?"

"Just that it was probably a plane, flew right into the building."

The older man shakes his head and turns away.

"Goddamn towelhead bastids again..."

I bite my tongue, hard. I never know quite what to say in response to comments like that, and I really wish people knew better than to say them around me. To the average jamoke, I probably look like the typical Italian-New Yorker you see everywhere in the city, and half of me is...I just wonder how my Iranian mother would feel if she could hear that slur against her people. I decide to see if Makeup Lady is a little better company.

Her left hand has been covering her mouth since she got out of the silver hatchback. She looks a little off-kilter with her one eye bare and the other painted with dark blue eye shadow. A slender, wavy raven-haired thirty-something, not unlike the kind who would inspire a second glance, either from interest or envy, if encountered in the supermarket. She drifts past me without averting her eyes from the inferno, then starts stammering to no one in particular.

"Oh God, oh God, I would've...I would, I would have

been there right now, on the, on on the...if I didn't have to, to go to that...the doctor and...and all the traffic, and and and...Oh God...what is happening?"

"My wife is up there right now."

"Oh my God, REALLY? Where does she work? You must be going CRAZY right now."

"She's an urban planner for a New York State transportation agency, they have an office on the 82nd floor."

"Oh my God, no WAY! I'm temping at Cantor Fitzgerald upstairs. I just started two weeks ago. I would have been there now if I didn't have to....oh God, is your wife OK?"

"I don't know. Phone is off. Could mean any number of things I guess."

"Oh God, I have been so nervous about working in the Trade Center too. Was it about eight years ago, someone tried to blow it up with a car bomb in the parking garage? I can't get that out of my head while I'm working."

"I didn't want my wife to work there either, but to Vera it seemed like an acceptable level of risk--somewhere between the odds of getting struck by lightning while walking in Battery Park and getting run down by a rogue cabbie while crossing Broadway, she said."

"Oh goodness, I sure do hope she is OK. She'll be in my prayers."

"I think I'm going to listen for more news now. I'll let you know if I hear anything."

Makeup Lady waves for a moment, then her left hand resumes its post as protector of her mouth as I start to walk back toward my car. I always feel slightly annoyed when someone says "I'll pray for you" or "I'll pray for so-and-so," like they are arrogant enough to think that somehow those prayers will make a difference...I don't know, I just know that religion and I have a quarrel going way back. That kind of talk really gets under my skin somehow.

Maybe I'll wait this out inside the car after all. I grab the latch of my car door. People are so disappointing. If they ain't racist hatemongers, they're religious nut jobs.

I start to lower myself into the driver's seat...but something stops me in my tracks. A plane, descending from the southwest...way too rapidly. Planes flying low over this part of New Jersey are not unusual with Newark Airport nearby, but not like this one...not this sharp and fast. It gets larger and louder as it streaks over Staten Island... now the harbor...and now the plane, no more than 600 feet overhead, veers right and then banks hard left so I can see both wings, silhouetted somewhat against the bright morning sky. It roars past the gape jawed onlookers like a screaming angel of death and then... BOOM.

Cuyama comes and goes in the night. Two of them, actually-
-first New Cuyama (apparently the first one wasn't working
out so they started a new one), which has the town market, post
office, liquor store, and some semblance of a neighborhood to
the south of the highway. Then a couple miles down the road,
we pass the old town, an eye blink of a place with its "Tacos Y
Mariscos" restaurant and not much else. During the day, one
would see that *los dos Cuyamas* sit within a patchwork of fields,
a 10-mile long agricultural oasis amidst the moonscape of the
Coastal Range. Tonight, it is still too dark to see much beyond
the headlights' scope, though the eastern sky has turned from
black to a mix of purple and mauve, and surely out there in the
shadows the ranchers and farmhands are getting ready to earn
their daily bread. California is waking up.

We are still a half-hour from Bonanza. The emergence of
colors in the sky and landscape invigorates my senses, and I am
feeling much sturdier. The microsleeps have passed. The confidence that I am a steady hand at the wheel, an agent of the
Preserver of Life, is back. It will be needed. There is still much
driving ahead today.

I guess you could say there are always more colors in my sky
when I am on the road. This was the case long before I met
Nadia. She did nothing to cause it in any way. I can *pretend* to
be content staying close to home, and if ever there were a place
where this *should* have worked for me, it would be here on the

Central Coast, that fabled land of my dreams, the grandest homeland I have ever claimed. But something happened when I turned my fantasyland into a home: it became *real.* And real, to me, is stagnant, cold, and hard. Gridlocked. Even when surrounded by the most majestic natural beauty I can imagine, it isn't long before it starts to feel like living inside a plastic snow globe, just another trinket on a souvenir store shelf, and it is all for sale.

So you can imagine what happened when I was let loose on the world in the buses: I took off like lightning sprung from a bottle. I went *everywhere* they would send me. There was some financial incentive too, as we were still almost broke from the worker's compensation income that had yet to be approved. But the fact was, I needed it. I was ravenous for new land and I wanted to taste it all at once again. The list of places Eldorado sent me would read like a western 11-state version of that Johnny Cash song ("I've been to Portland, Porterville, Point Reyes, El Cajon, Monterey, San Jose, Santa Fe, Yellowstone..."). I devoured it all and kept asking for more, and Annie kept feeding it to me. I was her perpetual motion machine.

Along the way, I started to take more notice of the people I transported as well, and the appreciation they showed for being brought out into the great big world and back home safely. Going back to the idea I was developing earlier, the epiphany of trust--it is all the more amazing in a world that seems to value safety over everything, even over experience. It occurs to me as well how common this epiphany *could* be, but probably isn't. Millions of us step onto buses and trains and planes every day, and feel as blasé as if watching the morning news over breakfast. How easily we suspend our belief in the nearness of mortality as we enter these machines! It must be a necessary disconnect in the brain that allows us to take this completely unnatural action as though it is second nature. Or perhaps it is not this at all--perhaps our ease at traveling in superfast people-moving machines is owed to the service of so many people who came before me who, like Floyd, perfected their labor over the miles and essentially disappeared into the vehicle. What comes from this kind of mastering of craft, in this case, seems to be a collective peace that turns the extraordinary act of safe travel into the ordinary. I consider it a minor miracle, for instance, that any plane can propel itself upward and onward from one location and land somewhere else in what is described as a controlled plummet from the sky, and do it with such precision that not even a passenger's coffee will be spilled, let alone blood--yet this miracle happens many thousands of times a day all over the world.

You don't have to be fanciful or superstitious to see some kind of mysterious hand at work, through the personage of the trained professionals, but also beyond. In my clearest, sharpest driving mode, I am well aware that I am drawing on a power beyond my own to not only keep 'er 'tween the lines, but to keep all other objects from entering our space between the lines. To the Hindus, that sustaining force is personified and known as Vishnu. In the Muslim and Judeo-Christian worlds, it is the same God who also creates and destroys all forms. Others will call it fate, kismet, blind luck...maybe the last of these is the most scientifically apt depiction, but it is very unsatisfying. I am grateful that science has helped us learn to fly planes, build better buses and safer roads, for instance, but it will never explain *why* I drive them, or what keeps us wanting to travel them.

I bring this up mostly to segue back to Nadia. There are sides of her I inferred to but have not really shown. They didn't make a whole lot of sense in the previous context, but I think they will now.

There are two dominant themes that have spanned most of Nadia's life. One started to emerge when she was a public school fifth-grader in the Paulus Hook neighborhood of Jersey City. Her parents got a call from the school, and for once it wasn't the principal's office after censuring the rambunctious child. It was her art teacher, telling them that Nadia could go as far as her heart desires in the visual arts, she was that kind of prodigious natural talent, and perhaps they should consider getting her some formal training.

Twenty years later, that talent is still struggling to find its audience and come to full fruition, almost entirely due to the *other* dominant theme that has already been given some elaboration.

I do not often think of Nadia as a New Yorker since I never knew her in that context and neither of her parents live there anymore. But she is definitely one of the many millions who have transplanted roots that can be traced back to the city. Her father is a second generation Hungarian-American from Jersey City (which calls itself "America's Golden Door" due to its proximity to Ellis Island) and Nadia was raised there along the river in the shadow of the Twin Towers. When she was eleven, her dad made it big on Wall Street and moved the family to the north shore of Long Island. Not long after that--why is this almost a given in this kind of story?--her parents divorced, and for several years she and her sister were volleyed back and forth between Northport and her mother's new home in the upper Delaware Valley. This generally involved train trips through Penn Station, at which point the rebellious kids would often come up from underground and spend their LIRR fare money exploring the city. So Nadia got to know the manmade splendor and opulence of midtown Manhattan (not to mention the Great Gatsby airs of her dad's new neighborhood) as a wide-eyed child, imprinting them on her burgeoning life expectations (this manifested in many peculiar ways, such as her favorite pastime of driving around through ritzy neighborhoods in our bungee corded clunker to gawk at the houses, and her disappointment that I could never provide her with that kind of material comfort).

This was also when Nadia was diagnosed with type 1 diabetes--a fact that neither parent seemed to manage well, as sweet treats were always part of their arsenal for luring the kids back from each other. Her worsening illness led to some volatile teenage years, including a slew of expulsions from New York's best prep schools. At age seventeen, Nadia and her car thieving boyfriend ran away, and after a short stint in San Diego, returned to the anonymity of the Manhattan streets. This began a period of hard and fast living that did irreparable harm to Nadia's already flailing endocrine system. By twenty three, the boyfriend was facing five to ten on Riker's Island, and Nadia retreated to a quieter life near her mom in Pennsylvania. She turned to yoga and Vipassana meditation in an effort to quiet her racing mind, but the damage had been done. After a relapse with alcohol landed her in the hospital on the verge of death--about six months before I met her--Nadia was diagnosed as a bipolar depressive, and given a bottle of pills that to my knowledge she has never opened.

Though I would consider her one of the many who the city has chewed up and spit out, New York still holds a strong allure for Nadia. Even now she still talks about getting her diabetes under control and all her other sundry ducks in a row so she can go to the Cooper Union art school and become a renowned graphic designer as she dreamed of doing before it all went haywire. She knows how I feel about big cities, so it is a bit of a pipe dream on the logistical level, before any question of her physical and emotional fitness. But somewhere in the sad realm of the What Could Have Been files of my imagination, I can see Nadia, healthy and robust, sitting at a sidewalk cafe in Chelsea or the Village, unbothered by the noise and the air pollution, sketching her latest designs in a notebook over a light lunch and cappuccino. Free of her partner and her body, I think Nadia's soul would choose to live in New York City.

I don't doubt at all that she could do it, if her ducks were not completely scattered to the wind. At some point during those years of self-abuse, there emerged another voice inside Nadia's mind. "Alter-ego" is not quite right, but her ego was definitely altered. Although the voice spoke to her as "you," she knew it was just part of her "I," which is a very important distinction and the reason why she had a fighting chance to overcome it. But make no mistake: there was real dissonance in there. This voice hated Nadia, and endeavored to destroy both her and everything beautiful she created.

I have a theory about the relationship between bipolar disorder and psychosis. When I first arrived out west as a twenty-one-year old college dropout, I lived in a basement room in Seattle where I was flanked by schizophrenics on two sides of paper-thin walls. There were many times that I was privy to the candid, sometimes graphic conversations between the "occupants" of each single room (sometimes simultaneously, which was like having a stereo set on two bad talk radio stations at once, with access to neither volume nor tuner knob).

Nadia never does that. She is aware that any extra voices in her head are hers, no matter how at odds they are with her. That led me to the idea that bipolar disorder could be part of a defense mechanism of a mind prone to psychosis, designed to keep it from making the schizophrenic split. To volley back and forth, after all, between such distinct and disparate personalities creates an elasticity of the ego that someone like me, clinging to a single integral self, would find philosophically disorienting, or altogether unfeasible. But in a world in which what is normal is so thoroughly divorced from what is natural, the rigidity of the normal mind will not withstand even the most basic existential crisis. An ego fabricated as such, by nothing but the normal, rational mind and concurrent to the organism that imagines it, is like a grand, polished porcelain statue, standing in the path of the tornado of nature that one way or another will scatter its supposed existence to the wind.

If sanity is defined as successful adaptation to what is normal, perhaps insanity should be seen as more than a mere failure to be sane. It could also be the mind's noble effort to cleave to what is natural, and accept the self as part of an organic whole that includes both the organism and its surroundings--and the oncoming storm. For what people like Nadia do have in common with schizophrenics, if the theory holds true, as that something has ripped open their portal to the infinite. The barricade across this portal is a human fabrication, a part of the way the brain works to orient us to the viewpoint of the organism, which is a fantastic adaptive device for an intellectual being in an increasingly complex, manmade world. But that does not mean it is natural. To have the barricade removed prematurely, without the proper intellectual framework provided by some established pattern of understanding, exposes the human being to a completely new realm of stimuli--the natural world exactly as it is, interconnected to the core, with a tattered intellectual filter or none at all. With the proper framework, I am convinced, the world through this open portal resembles heaven. Without it, in the case of most

most schizophrenics, the same world will be a lot more like hell.

Then there are the curious ones like Nadia, for whom it is both, often in rapidly oscillating succession.

They who succeed at insanity do not really have a place in society--they are probably the ones who end up in monasteries and ashrams. Maybe they become the wandering pilgrims of the eastern traditions, or settle into a more hermetic existence surrounded by lush forests and gardens. Yet their influence is absolutely essential to the nuts and bolts functioning of the society they leave behind. So communication with the insane becomes a key measure of a society's vital signs, more so than gross national product or military might. A nation must listen to its lunatic fringe, lest its collective mind be fractured by its effort to stay rigidly sane, and it winds up shouting at itself in the existential equivalent of a dark basement room.

The violence so common to the bipolar condition is an indication that, in this particular mind, insanity is struggling to stay afloat but it is not going well, and I suspect that a persistent urge to be sane is the usual culprit. I see this all the time in Nadia--her daily struggle to let go of her parents' expectations of how her life was supposed to be, her clinging to material comforts while at the same time rejecting the means to obtain them, her constant vacillation between abject dependence on Western medicine and something akin to a fundamentalist faith healing. Her art--and this is the case with most tortured artists--is the clearest expression of her constructive insanity. Its surreal aspects speak to the part of us that is longing for a safe portal to the world beyond what we take in with our senses. This has been her primary function in society for as long as I have known her, and even more so once she lost the ability to rely on her external vision. But the expectations of modern American sanity are ingrained in her ego, rooted deeper than the artist has been able to reach to weed them out. Essentially, Nadia's sanity waved the white flag years ago, and ever since has been trying to negotiate the terms of a surrender in which it officially wins the war. Yet on some basic levels, her insanity has an extremely strong toehold and will not budge.

This is very important to remember, because Nadia is not just a sick person--that is merely the part of her that makes the most noise. First and foremost, Nadia is an artist, a Creator of supreme beauty to the highest degree.

In the Hindu cosmology, the creative force of the universe, that which makes ideas out of abstract potential and forms out of ideas is personified as Brahma. Nadia is as thoroughly tapped into the energy of Brahma as any person I have ever known. I wish I could do her artwork justice, but I am afraid I'm not artistic enough to put it into words. It isn't merely *what* she creates anymore either--it is largely *how* she has to do it, and the constant rebirth of herself as an artist that her physical body requires of her.

Before Nadia lost any vision, she was primarily a pen-and-ink artist, but really any implement with a fine point would do. Her portfolio--currently packed away in our woefully inadequate closet--contains some of the most stunning detail work I have ever seen in any motif. Mostly abstract images, and that's where my verbal skills seem most lacking, but images that come to life because they are so brilliantly conceived and finely rendered. I picture what one might see inside a spinning kaleidoscope, only the images are still and the spinning is happening in the mind. She had a fascination with fractals, and her mind seemed to produce them as commonly and intricately as mine might envision a map of California--only I cannot take credit for being a Creator of the map (nor California). Nadia drew what she saw, and what she saw was indescribably beautiful.

She is also a very skilled folk artist. When I met her, Nadia made a significant portion of her modest income by doing simple free-lance drawings for people upon request. One I remember was a portrait of someone's dog that had just died. She designed greeting cards with messages of love and kindness, with images of hobbit houses and angels and all manner of warmth she would fantasize about. To see this side of her art is to get a glimpse into the kind of life she wanted to live, and has always somewhat naively felt possible.

To say that losing much of her vision was an enormous challenge is a gross understatement. Diabetic retinopathy begins as spots in the visual plane that are like looking through fogged-up lenses. Nadia's foggy spots move around, and they vary in size and opaqueness, but the largest and most persistent spot is right in her central line of vision, as though she just walked from a cold room into warm air with glasses on. Except in her case, she *cannot take the glasses off.* Ever again. Even after two laser surgeries. They will be there for the rest of her life, they will gradually get worse, and the only way to make the spots go away is to close her eyes. I can understand why Nadia sometimes wants to close her eyes and never open them again.

But Nadia's great triumph as a Creator is that she adapts to this change rather than let it kill her inspiration. It started as soon as she picked up a set of oil pastel crayons in an art supply store in San Luis Obispo. The pastels burst with bright colors that she could see through the foggy spots. No more fractals or fine details in her drawings, but the images she started creating with pastels were even more whimsical and fantastic than before. It was as though she decided "what the fuck!" about depicting this world and let her imagination loose to explore all the other ones she could access. I have no doubt that losing external vision helped her sharpen her internal one.

Physically, she learned to work within her limitations--broad, bold strokes instead of fine ones; loud, garish angles instead of peaceful, genteel ones. Pug dogs and macaws and giant goldfish bowls strewn across verdant fruit orchards in front of her hobbit house, all under a starry sky-scape with a rainbow in the distance--that's what Nadia's great gift to the world is now. People respond to it like she has transported them back to their own childhood. It is mesmerizing to watch.

And to me, her creative gift extends far beyond art. It is in the meals she prepares for us--always from wholesome ingredients; she is a whiz at whipping fine meals together from whatever we have in the house. It is in the life lessons she imparts; I wouldn't know the first thing about the importance of organic food, for instance, if not for Nadia introducing it to me and patiently explaining why it is worth spending more for it. It is in the humor she brings to our lives; she is actually quite self-deprecating when she is in her creative mode, and clowns herself with a zest I have never seen in anyone else. Lastly, but far from least, it is all of this wrapped into a genuine walk of the spirit across this strange turning earth, and the quirky Zen master stick beatings she imparts on those closest to her, me first and foremost. Many of the saints of antiquity, across all traditions, were certainly more *successful* at communicating these lessons about living life with faith and zest and gratitude, but none tried more authentically than she does.

But that too is just one side of Nadia--and by "side," of course, I really mean something much more than just an aspect of a single personality. Let us not forget that a person who is bipolar almost literally has two minds, and they are at war with each other. If Nadia spends most of her waking hours in the mind of the Creator--and even at her worst, I believe she does--her life is still dominated by the more powerful force of Siva, the Destroyer.

The Destroyer, after all, has disease on its side. When Nadia's blood sugars swing, she is completely at their mercy. Too many years of destructive habits and self-abuse have left her brittle to the point that the normal preemptive measures a diabetic can take are ineffective, and even insulin shots and glucose tablets lose their ability to stabilize her extremes. Worse yet, the Destroyer within her continues to make bad choices against her better judgment--the carbohydrate binges, indulgences, with sugar and alcohol being among the worst; ignoring the advice of her doctors--because its objective is not her survival."Hell on earth" is how she describes this battle, and in times like these I can indeed see the devil in her eyes.

The heart-grinding truth of this is that I know the outcome of the war. The Destroyer is going to win. It overcomes us all in the end, but there is something more poignant about that in Nadia's case: her creative energy is so strong and so needed in this world, but at the rate she is going it will be snuffed out long before its fruition. And if she herself is powerless to stop the onslaught, imagine how I feel as her life-partner and would-be Preserver.

So here I am, with my wanderlust and Vishnu complex, finding fulfillment for both every day I go out on the road. Then I come back to a modest home I can barely afford, to watch a war unfold in front of me to which I cannot fight nor affect a truce. I think the only reason I don't ask to work seven days a week is that I know my absence gives the Destroyer free rein.

Abandonment issues go way back into Nadia's childhood, and the Destroyer preys upon them as readily as it does her disease. This is perhaps the saddest fact of all for me, because I know that a steady presence and companionship helps keep the Destroyer at bay. It does not stop the war, and there is plenty of collateral damage--I still bear some scars that go back to our time in Caches Notch, after I retired from long-haul trucking and took the newspaper job, and watched our money rapidly dwindle, not to mention our previously chronicled adventures here in California--but it does have the potential to pacify her much more, and buy some time for the Creator to strengthen herself and do more good work. Those few weeks in which we had our home, I did my eight hours on two healthy knees and came back to it at five o'clock every day, this was the closest I have ever seen to Nadia being at peace within herself, day in and day out. I still wonder how things would be now if we had been able to continue that way. But I know we couldn't. That isn't me. I have to face up to the fact that *I* continue to make bad choices against *my* better judgment where Nadia is concerned.

As I jumped into the driver's seat at Eldorado and drove off full-throttle into the Wild West, I snapped Nadia out of her peaceful phase, and into something very dark and hopeless. I knew this was likely to happen, and I could not stop myself from doing it. All the wrath I feel from her after her sun goes down, I have brought upon myself--let us permanently disabuse this narrative of any notions otherwise. On the other hand, who could turn down an opportunity like *this*?! Floyd said it himself--I was *born* in this seat! Or *re*born, at least. I had found a creative mission that was just as vital to me as Nadia's artwork is to her. I am an agent of the Preserver, the bridge upon which my fellow travelers may walk to journey safely into the yonder and back.

There is also the simple fact that I write better when I am on the road. *The Valley and the Mountain* has come further along and seen higher quality work in the past nine months than any other period of our marriage. So I have no reason to doubt that as I was escaping from the violently dichotomous world of my life at home, I was answering a calling as well.

Or is the Destroyer leading me to an early grave of my own?

There are two sides to my story, too.

Time will tell.

* * * *

The explosion in the South tower ripples through the sky like an atomic blast--first the searing orange flames and black smoke, then the ungodly roar of metal striking metal at over 500 miles per hour, like a portal to hell had been ripped open.

Like most people in my Hollywood demographic, I imagine, I have always been a big fan of "action" movies, cannot get enough of them. I have seen more of their artificial silver screen explosions than I could care to count, some of them pretty ferocious indeed. I have never seen anything like this. How many real human beings were just incinerated before my eyes? I can't even fathom. I just know that their images are burned onto my retinas, like shadows left behind as permanent scars on the walls of buildings in Hiroshima.

I absently drift back toward the wall when I am almost tackled by a wailing, hyperventilating woman. She throws her arms around me and buries her head in my chest, shrieking as if she had just watched the beheading of her firstborn child. It is Makeup Lady (who, incidentally, has neither children nor a uterus, though I don't know this yet). Her sobs punctuate an almost indecipherable chain of "OH MY GOD OH MY GOD OH MY GOD OH MY GOD!!!" It feels so sharp against my body that I start to recoil. I catch myself, braced against the grille of the BMW, and, awkwardly but with sincere intent, put my arms around her. I am unable to cry myself, so perhaps it is right to let her cry for both of us.

Her boiling, hysterical cries slow down to a simmering whimper as I hold her snuggly. We both seem to become aware of the strangeness of the scene, and the questionable decorum of a woman burying her head in a stranger, but she cannot move. Neither do I. I'm holding on for dear life in fact, as somehow letting her go now would feel like disconnecting from the only other person on earth.

"I'm so scared." Try as she does to make the words come out audibly, she can barely whisper them. I hear her though. She speaks for us both.

6:20 am (PDT) / 9:20 am (EDT)

We are cruising in a northeasterly direction on Highway 33, descending from the plateau where Cuyama Valley lies toward the semiarid heart of California's oil country. We are very close to the intersection of the giant V formed across a topographical view of California by the Coastal Range on the west and the Sierra Nevadas on the east, with the southern tip of the great Central Valley in between. Sunlight has slowly filtered into the scene, revealing a strange, unseasonal overcast of high gray clouds, not at all like the lower coastal fog that often visits our region on summer mornings.

The cloud mass must have come overnight, and now it is passing us by, leaving a mix of scattered cumulonimbus and sky to the east. A cool cobalt blue persists above us and across three horizons, with the eastern front opening like a majestic stage curtain. This is creating a phenomenal palette for the sun as it rises over the distant Sierras. Whereas a cloudless California morning yields a simple crystal and orange cream sunrise, this is one of those purple and hot pink explosions, like something Odysseus would have witnessed. Heavenly light pours down in beams through the windshield and the right side windows, as if half of the passengers on the bus were about to be raptured. The birders are waking and they are all watching in awe. I steal glances as I steer down the windy mountain slope, descending toward the valley.

I wish Nadia were here to see this. She would love it, might even inspire her next drawing. She rides with me occasionally, but not as often as I would like. Night-time jaunts into the wilderness are a little too grueling for her. But she loves small doses of the road. Nothing seems to sooth her nerves better than the little getaways we take in the car. Sometimes we go out right on the heels of my own trips. If I come home right after a ten--or twelve--hour day and Nadia looks frazzled and agitated, we will just head back out the door and cruise. Our favorite trip is north on Route 1, up through San Simeon over the coastal plain to the part where the mountains drop straight into the ocean and the road looks like a bowl of elbow macaroni. We will stroll around the cliffs at Ragged Point, 400 feet straight above the water. She gets back into Brahma mode here--vital, vibrant, at ease. We can joke and laugh together, walking hand-in-hand while hawks circle and soar above the golden peaks, and I once again recognize the adventurous woman who dropped everything to go west with me four years ago. We can usually count on a few hours of freedom from her demons when I get her out of the house, provided she is not physically ill or dealing with volatile sugar levels. But a 2:30 am wake up isn't happening any time for her, nor can fifteen hours elapse between chances to prepare her own fresh food in our kitchen, so the majority of Eldorado trips are out of bounds.

Moments like these--the sacred minutes our eyes can perceive the dazzling array of colors before the sun bleaches the sky and the landscape, and the mind turns to more mundane tasks like watching the odometer click--these are what drew me into the driving profession. We all find our secular religion somewhere. Some people climb mountains, some pilot sailboats, others stroll through forests or hand glide or snorkel or golf or watch birds. I climb into commercial vehicles and chase the *Ahhhh!* Moments of life. I need them like I need water and oxygen. But I am finding them harder to enjoy alone now. I think of Nadia, and I realize that half of me is missing. More so, half of me is left home to dwell on a disease. I want to tell her about what I see and let her experience it through my eyes, but how can I? How do you reproduce *this* with words? Whenever I try it becomes all the more clear that we are having separate experiences and we feel more apart. So I don't say much about my trips. But then, what does *that* leave us?

What I am saying is that I see and appreciate the sunrise now, but something strips me of joy. Most of the passengers, according to the roster, are married and sitting next to their spouses right now. Assuming they both find this more interesting than the complimentary copy of *USA Today* from the hotel, they have a clear path to joy. They have the sun, the sky, the earth, their eyes, and they have each other.

I would give anything to feel what they are feeling right now.

Because here is the paradox of *my* life with Nadia: I would love to provide the home that she so desperately wants, and to actually live there with her. I just feel completely ill-equipped to do it. I cannot sit still...but I never seem to get anywhere either.

Like I suggested before, in many ways my whole adult life has been an effort to recreate the experience of reaching that peak of the last westernmost ridge, looking down from the top of a world I wanted to leave behind (or, at times, the valley of dissolution into oblivion, though this is a less conscious drive). It is not part and parcel with that idea that I have to *come down* from it, though, or so I imagined.

The California Dream has always been an elusive but cherished American goal, some manner of castle--a mansion, a ranch, a three-bedroom house in suburbia--planted in a land not far from paradise. For me, that dream is to be perched atop a mountain overlooking the ocean. Not like Hearst in that monstrosity up the coast, God no. I could live happily in the cabana for one of his swimming pools. Nothing fancy at all, the more modest the better, in fact. An anti-castle would be perfect. Just a simple quiet place to *be,* away from this world full of people who just blindly *do* all of their lives. We have talked about this dream many times together since coming to California. I have often thought that I could walk away from any manner of vehicle if I had that place on the mountain by the ocean.

Nadia and I would go up there and never come back, disappear completely. I would write, she would draw, the world would crumble all around us and we would shout great Zen belly laughs down into the canyons.

But something has to get us there. Without a rental car paid for by my parents, there was no peak experience sixteen years ago. And with Nadia out of work, it is up to me to drive us to whatever dream we will get to share here. The reality of it, therefore, is that I am a rat racer just like everyone else. Everything I do on the road is in some manner trying to please the paying customers so my stock will keep rising with Annie. Nadia may be losing her visual acuity for perceiving the details of the world, but as an artist, at least when we travel she still *sees* the world exactly as it is, and bends it into what it could be. I am starting to see the world from the road as a series of measurements by which I assure myself of achieving my passengers' goals for their trip. The rising sun now is not unlike an alarm that tells me things such as "I have two hours before the Bayshore Freeway turns into a parking lot; better not make that optional rest stop in Soledad" or "this is when the elk are most active along this highway; stay extra vigilant from here to Kemmerer." I understood from the beginning that there were to be some costs involved in disappearing into the vehicle--which I would lose all control over where my travels took me and how I got there. That I was more than willing to let go...but did I have to lose the soul that would be stirred by what I saw along the way?

So I spend most of my time taking people to visit someone else's Castle, running back and forth to the City of Angels, or idly reading newspapers and dozing in Anaheim hotels while children frolic through the *Magic Kingdom*--but the magic is fading fast for me. I can see a small swatch of ocean if I stand at the end of our driveway--my version of the postage stamp green grass homestead of the suburbs--but I don't have much time for that. My chosen profession does not pay enough to support the California Dream, and I have to put in ridiculous amounts of overtime to keep it going. No time for timeless things like mountains and oceans when drunken bowling leagues and frat boys need to barrel through the desert to get their Vegas fix.

Besides, the mountain I am searching for does not exist. There is no place left in this society for a person to be--not without playing the real estate game. This is the point where I lose my grip on the reins and have to admit that I will never be a home-owner. I am not going to stick my neck before a predatory institution and beg for a mortgage. I am not going to build a grand plastic hotel. I am not going to charge rent to anyone who wants to share space with me. I am not going to collect $200 every time I pass Go. And I am definitely *not* going to cash in on my landholding when the game is over. If this is what it takes to get ahead in our world, I will gladly stay behind, thank you.

It seems to me that there are two primary categories of evil that human beings do unto each other. One is the direct expression of violence and the taking of life, limb, and property or the assertion of a political agenda by the means thereof. This is the loud, painful kind involving gunshots and explosions that makes the news everyday and needs no further explanation. The other kind--far more prevalent and subtle--is the evil of participation in a system by which *all* access to basic human needs is commodified and callously allowed to be priced beyond the means of large numbers of people by the "invisible hand" of market forces. This is a dull, throbbing pain in our souls that *never* makes the news until someone stands up to oppose it or circumvent it, often by violent means.

The real estate market is the purest form of the latter evil in our world. The very land we dwell upon is a commodity by which great fortunes are amassed, while other vital community members cannot even enter the game. All notion of stewardship is lost in this culture. Land is capital, and capital that is not being used to generate more liquid forms of wealth is going to waste--or so say the capitalists. Our houses are no longer homes. They are stocks that we hold in private corporations that will gain or lose value, depending on how desirable they are to others.

I concede that it is virtually impossible to conceive of a functional system in our culture that does not assign a certain value to a piece of property that is in sync with the medium of exchange we use for everything else. The problem comes from attaching that value to blind market forces, and attaching to *that*, our popular idea that we all must maximize the return of our "investment" in our real estate. Everything is about the building of equity into a property, and if we dwell on it and actually make it a home--a place to raise a family and, hell, maybe even pass it on to the next generation--we are "wasting" the equity--we need to turn it around at a higher price and buy something bigger. It has gotten to the point that there is a whole class of people who have made a profession of "flipping" properties--buying them without any real stake other than financial, then turning them around a short time later for a profit. And the problem is that we have an ingrained idea that this is simply how it goes--real estate should *always* continue to gain value, and it is virtually the property owner's legal right to make a profit every time she sells.

When this happens frequently enough, the average price of a home in a community becomes greater than the average citizen's ability to pay, because wages sure don't inflate so rapidly. This would damage the economy, as disposable income drops on account of all the money earmarked to living expenses, so we all need credit to maintain the standard of living we have come to expect--and conveniently, the same people pushing the mortgages are only so happy to extend it. A second artificial boost to property values!

In areas like the Central Coast, this is compounded by the fact that so many properties are owned by people who have made their money elsewhere and are buying vacation homes or retiring or simply investing in a hot location. This creates a totally warped property market that bears no resemblance at all to the local economy, so all the people who mow their lawns, clean their pools, collect their trash, stock their groceries, police their communities, and yes, even drive their charter buses--we are playing against a stacked deck. But oh, we *must* keep playing, must keep that American dream alive! Or so say the savage predators we euphemistically call "bankers." Here, Mr. Laborer, you don't have adequate income to buy that house for your family?

Well I have this special mortgage deal for you that will take care of all of your problems. You'll pay a higher interest rate, but no need to worry, just call us in a couple years for an equity loan to pay off your credit cards that you maxed out while devoting sixty five percent of your income to your mortgage...this is the third prong of the Devil's pitchfork.

It is all such a fucking house of cards. I can see the day when this system finally spirals out of control, not just in exclusive communities like San Luis Obispo County, but *everywhere*. *All* the real estate markets will collapse; no one will be able to afford the mortgages they obligated themselves to while the bubble was expanding. The banks will cry poor but hey, guess who owns all the properties being foreclosed! We will all blame the banks when that happens, and we'll be partly right, but we are the ones who buy into the get-rich-quick schemes of their crooked system. The banks sell us the illusion that the American Dream is healthier and more sustainable than it really is--first through credit cards and now through high-risk "subprime" mortgages--and we are eager buyers. No one to blame but ourselves really.

The depressing thing is that renting is hardly any better. I'm just paying someone else's mortgage. When property values rise, so does my rent. When they rise to the point that the owner decides to sell, we will probably find ourselves looking for a new home. This happened to us at our first house in Arizona. It was a horrible experience for Nadia. She had really been making the space her own and was an avid caretaker of the property while I was gone trucking, and losing it brought a stigma that she still carries. I think she has been looking for me to take the leap and buy us a home ever since. I go through the motions of being interested, I push myself to work like a speed addict and save up the money for a down payment. But it isn't in my heart; I cannot buy into the evil. The mountain I am looking for was sold to the highest bidder long ago.

So I drive on, with the ever-present hope that somehow I will reach that horizon, and the knowledge that I never can. Meanwhile, the foxes have holes, the birds of the air have their nests, the sharks and jackals have their high-rise condos by the beach

beach that block everyone else's view, but Pedro hath not where to lay his head.

6:30 am (PDT) / 9:30 am (EDT)

Bus 477 has not needed any fuel for about 10 miles. Like a plane coming in for a smooth landing, we have coasted down the eastern slope of the foothills--one of those classic California scenes where unbroken planes of wild wheat and golden-brown grass cover the smooth sculpted hills and arroyos, treeless seismic up thrusts mellowed by centuries of sun and wind--and just as the ground begins to level out, we arrive at the edge of Bonanza.

As the name suggests, this was once a prosperous town, fueled by the black gold of the southern Central Valley, at a time when being rich in mineral resources was a sure means for a community to secure local jobs and money that stayed in the community. Now that the infrastructure is built, however, and the minerals are owned by corporations that transcend national boundaries--never mind state or municipal ones--there is no telling where the oil wealth of California goes. But one thing is certain: it does not stay in places like Bonanza. The town is now little more than a haphazard smattering of cinder block ranch houses and vacant lots, laid out like a gap-tooth mouth on a grid pattern of crumbling paved streets. What once would have been called "downtown" is now a single block with a cafe, a social club, and a couple shuttered thrift stores disguised as markets. Everything else is boarded up or otherwise empty, no sign of anyone even trying to rent them out or sell them. The only businesses that show any sign of vitality are the gas station/ice cream shop with a Subway restaurant at the intersection of the two state highways, and a boxy stucco church with a tall white cross that overlooks all from the center of town. Everywhere else, I see evidence of a town forgotten by progress and time. If Bonanza were a person, it would be a doddering old man with a walker and oxygen tank cart, whose wife died long ago and children moved away and never bother to call.

Yet the oil pumps, sprinkled around the town and concentrated in greater numbers to the north and east, perpetually bob with their slow, methodical gait, too busy to notice that they are the only ones left in town with employment. I remember reading a short story as a kid, about a society full of machines that were performing all kinds of automated functions for people like cooking breakfast and getting them ready for work, only there were no people present in the story. Later we learn that some kind of apocalypse had wiped out the human race, yet the machines kept running. Bonanza reminds me of a low-tech version of that.

A few miles outside of town we turn due east on a quiet county road and head out into the geometrically flat land that marks the Central Valley. Bird #1 instructs me to pull off to the side of the road by a chaparral field. All my untrained eyes see from here are a flock of those bobbing pumps and the occasional pickup truck. I pull the parking brake plunger and it engages with that satisfying hiss--bus speak for "job well done."

The birders begin to mobilize and prepare for action. Everyone is abuzz. From my roost at the front of the bus, I can hear maybe a dozen conversations distinctly, and every one of them centers on the subject at hand. It seems as if all the cares and concerns of life--the bills, the news, the world at large--were left behind at the lobby of the Santa Maria Inn, and nothing remains but an extreme singularity of purpose, and a passionate love of birds. This is why they have come from far and near. This is their shining moment. Let the birding begin.

With few exceptions, the people on Bus 477 fall neatly into one of two camps. The majority as I mentioned are married couples, age forty something to seventy(ish). No matter how old, they all give the impression of being retired, or at least having a good deal of money and leisure time. They are well-versed in species and habitat, and handy with the Petersons field guides to find birds they do not know. As best I can tell, these people find in birding anything from an engaging hobby to a nearly consuming passion.

In the other group, of which #1 and #2 are typical, are the professional naturalists, the hardcore birders. These are slightly younger, hyper-intelligent, pocket-protector-meets-crunchy-granola creatures. They use words like "riparian" and "avifauna" in casual conversation. They write articles in scientific journals about the migration patterns of the sooty shearwater. They spend weeks camping in rice paddies in Laos to chase the elusive semi-palmated plover. They can identify a marbled godwit at one hundred yards without a field guide merely by the curvature of its wings in flight. In short, these folks are the real deal, and their leadership is crucial to the success of the mission.

Every participant is given a checklist--a birding scorecard--upon which is printed the categories and species names of each bird they might expect or hope to find. Here they will record which birds they bird and where they bird them. This serves as an historical record for individual birders, a far more humane version of trophy heads on the wall. Some groups have a competitive side to the scorekeeping, according to the Birds, but not the ABA. When one person spots a new bird, the protocol is to announce it to the crowd so everyone can see. The goal is group success, not just personal.

With four field trips in dramatically different bioregions of California, the ABA Regional Conference offers an exciting variety of bird prospects. The scorecard includes fifty two categories and two hundred seven species, everything from the acorn woodpecker to the yellow-rumped warbler. The red-necked phalarope may be mingling with the black-headed grosbeak. A European starling might be sharing airspace with an American coot. By week's end, with any luck, this group may get to see a tree swallow, a loggerhead shrike, a Lazuli bunting, a white-breasted nuthatch, and of course, everyone's favorite sight, the bushtit.

Here at our first stop, though, the range is limited due to private property. The ABA has to make very specific arrangements with the oil companies to bird in these parts, so birders must keep to the shoulder of the road and rely on high-powered binoculars and scopes, some of which I am told run upwards of $1,000. I marvel at the fact that some people have birding equipment that is worth more than I am.

Bird #1 approaches me as I stand by the door to offer a hand to those disembarking. She seems mellowed out by the long drive and nap, and she is speaking with proper punctuation now.

"OK, we'd like to be here for about an hour, so 7:30 departure? And please, you are very welcome to join us if you are at all interested. We're a pretty fun bunch once the feathers start flying." (I would give her props for that line, if I weren't pretty certain it is her catchphrase.)

"Thanks, I will probably do that later. Right now I think I need some rest and recovery time."

"Fair enough," she says, flashing an exaggerated smile, then turns around to begin giving instructions to her flock.

When the bus is empty, I grab my rucksack and bring it back to the three-person bench seats at the very back. I feel overdue for some new material for "The Valley and the Mountain," so I figure I'll try to cut through the haze and churn something up. I reach inside behind the dictionary and...wait a minute...aw *hell*, it's not here. I left the composition notebook on my desk in my haste to get to sleep last night. Well that's just ducky. I can't even remember where I left off, it has been so long since I added to the narrative. With a disgruntled sigh and more indignation than I wanted to express to myself, I toss the rucksack onto the bench against the water closet, the buckles clanging on the wall in protest. I fluff it up as best I can, and lay my head on it, lying on my right side, legs not fully outstretched. I guess the transportation gods want me to get some shuteye, cursed masters of my traveling fate that they are. Goodnight...morning. Whatever.

6:50 am (PDT) / 9:50 am (EDT)

Both of the inbound lanes of the Turnpike are now parking lots. They will stay that way for a long time, as every bridge and tunnel into Manhattan is now closed. People have left their cars right where they sit and wander around in an agitated daze, eyes locked on the twin infernos across the river. Shrieks and lamentations from the gathering crowd punctuate the steady faraway din of emergency vehicle sirens from lower Manhattan. Otherwise, the world within earshot has become chillingly silent and still.

Makeup Lady has disengaged from my chest and watches with left hand over mouth again. She seems just a little steadier now, though I can't ignore a notion that her steadiness was a bit compromised before everything started this morning. Even if I know well that I am looking at her incomplete makeup job, I can't help but think that I see the remnant of a black eye.

A disheveled old man walks up the shoulder toward us. He has long gray hair under a tattered bandana that was once red, and looks like he just woke up from a night's sleep on a bench down at Liberty Park. He shakes his head repeatedly as he walks and mumbles. I'm not the type to lend an ear to lunatics, and I look away when the man meets my glance.

"You can't ignore the facts, young man!" His arms flail

out as he speaks. "The end is coming! It's underway!"

He stares at me and waits for a reaction. I realize he ain't going away without one.

"I'm sorry. End of what?"

"The *world, man!* Don't you know what Nostradamus said about this?" Now he holds his arms out with Shakespearian flair as he proclaims his Truth. "The end will come when two metal birds crash into tall statues in the new city, two brothers torn apart by chaos."

"Yeah," I say, barely concealing a laugh. "I'm sure he did."

"Well *don't look so frightened,* young man! I'm sure you have *all your* affairs in order, doncha?" The man then continues on with his tortoise-like gait, shaking his head and muttering about the ignorance of youth. I let out a disgusted sigh.

"You don't believe there's even a chance that he's right?" asks Makeup Lady. I look at her with a smirky glare. Another blip on the flake radar screen.

"Who, *that guy?*"

"Well, not him per se. Just the words he spoke. You know what they say: the world's biggest fool can say the sun is out, but that doesn't make it dark."

I snicker. "True. But A: I'm sure no one said anything of the sort until this morning, and B: I think Nostradamus is as real as the Easter Bunny. The idea that someone could see events hundreds of years before they happen is ludicrous."

"Well, I'm not saying I believe *everything* the man supposedly wrote, but I wouldn't say what he claimed to do is impossible either. Time only appears linear because of our perspective within it, but in reality it moves in cycles, so I don't see why someone who is attuned to that couldn't glimpse something from the future and maybe even make sense of it. I mean hell, I've had dreams of planes exploding in the sky that I didn't understand until now."

I look away and shrug. I ain't about to admit that I have,

too. "Ehh, to me that sounds like new age mumbo jumbo. We're desperate to feel like we have a grasp on *all this*, and we invent these semi-plausible scenarios that always bend reality *just enough* so the ordinary person can't perceive them. Then we speak of them as though they're scientific facts for long enough and *voila*, we have beliefs...but did you ever notice that everyone who is considered a prophet is conveniently dead? Forget about hundreds of years-- show me someone alive who can see *ten minutes* into the future consistently and I'll say there's something to it."

She grins, not the response I was expecting. I will learn that she is extraordinarily difficult to offend.

"Well I guess that means we agree to disagree."

"Agreed," I'm relieved that my burst of candor was well-received. It is never my conscious intention to tear down what others have built, but my defenses are so strong that I rarely know when to quit. It has long been a problem.

Just then a fire hydrant-shaped man in a *Gold's Gym* tank top wanders by from the other direction.

"Holy fawk," he says in a Jersey shore accent, without any particular segue. "I just heard there's like dozens of people jumpin' off the top floors of the towers." He is one of those people who forget to breathe while talking when excited. "My friend says they're splattin' like eggs all over the streets. Shit, that's fawked up."

Makeup Lady freezes. All signs of the relaxation that came from our repartee disappears as she considers the implications of this news, and she starts sobbing loudly. I rush over to hug and comfort her, then turn to fire hydrant man.

"She works upstairs in the north tower."

"You mean those bond traders up there?"

"Yeah, I believe so."

Fire hydrant man shakes his meaty head. "Aw fawk. Yeah, bro, they're all goners."

His voice dropped a few measures as an indication of sympathy, which only made the content all the more baffling. Makeup Lady's crying becomes more hysterical. I turn her away from him and cast a "get the hell out of here" glare back over my shoulder.

"Maybe we should just sit in my car until we're able to move."

She nods her agreement. I start walking her toward the passenger door when she suddenly turns to face me again, and grabs the lapels of my suit coat. She holds one tightly in each fist, as if they are all that is protecting her from falling into a dark abyss, and pulls herself closer to me.

"Please, please don't leave me today," she stammers under her jagged breath. "I can't handle this alone. Please."

"OK." I'm not sure where my words are coming from now. "I promise."

She loosens her grip on my now somewhat crumpled lapels, then slowly steps back and releases them. It seems like a bad idea to make eye contact with her right now, but I do anyway. That one black eye still speaks distress to me from some place I don't understand. Her other eye seems childlike, both in its unadorned simplicity and vulnerability. They are among the prettiest shades of blue I have ever seen--almost turquoise in the direct sunlight. There is a place inside them that seems strangely unafraid, and for a moment, I want to go there.

The moment disappears as her gaze shifts past my shoulder and her eyes bulge to enormous proportions. Her left hand reports back to its station above her mouth as she gasps, "OHMIGOD!" I turn around to witness the massive plume of ash and smoke rising up from where the south tower had just been.

7:00 am (PDT) / 10:00 am (EDT)

My eyes open, for at least the tenth time since I lay down. I check the clock on my cell phone. Only twenty minutes have passed. Birders are constantly hopping on and off the bus, and at little more than sea level with the windshield facing due east, it is already too hot to be at the back of the bus with the sun baking the stagnant air through the windows. If I am going to get any sleep at all, I will have to use the luggage bays.

It is a rather brilliant idea that one of the veteran drivers taught me, perfect for days like today with no suitcases taking up valuable space. Open the doors on both sides for cross ventilation, crawl inside and voila, instant king-sized bed. It often works wonderfully--say, a group is taking five or six hours at an amusement park or a racetrack, too short for a hotel room, too long for that uncomfortable doze across the seats.

But this isn't going to work here either. The group is confined to a close proximity to the bus, and I am too much of a spectacle with forty-four people standing nearby. Rather than let me rest, they all have to offer their two cents about my strange nesting habits. That's OK, I think, the next stop will offer a couple hours of solitude, and it is shaping up to be an easy day anyway.

Eventually someone calls out, "LeConte's thrasher!" across the street and the whole flock makes a hasty retreat, leaving a lone figure standing by the edge of the chaparral field. I poke my head out for a closer look at the straggler. A slender, silver-haired woman smiles at me, genuinely, with no indication that she considers the encounter unusual. In her white windbreaker and matching slacks, she gives the impression of a small but sturdy birch tree, which is somehow enhanced by hoot-owl bifocals.

"Good morning," she says, more as a declaration than a greeting.

I crawl from my nest to make a proper introduction. Sometimes, for none of the typical reasons, a person will interest me more than others before saying a word. Generally it is something invisible, a spiritual trait that I lack but desire. In this case, I think I sense an elaborate root structure. Some people do not end at their feet.

"Hey, I'm Pedro. Good to meet you."

"Betty Pickett," she replies.

"Hello Betty. Seen one LeConte's thrasher, seen 'em all, I presume?"

"Not exactly. I am what they call a 'non-birding spouse.'"

"Oh...interesting. So you're just coming along for the twelve-hour bus trip then?"

"I've endured much worse. Picture this, only on a Bengali airboat." We share a laugh at that image. "I've been tagging along with my husband for many years now. He has brought me to the four corners of the earth chasing birds. I've been to places I'd never imagine seeing otherwise."

"I see. Right on. So why aren't you a birder yourself?"

She smiles just as before, neither smirk nor grin. Surely she has answered this question a zillion times, but the answer seems unrehearsed.

"I prefer a good walk," she says. Not a hint of derision, but there is an undeniable silent emphasis on "good." I dig that.

"Hope you don't mind if I linger by the bus at times while they do their thing," she continues.

"Of course not," I say, "we'll just bird the birders together." She is delighted by the suggestion.

"Wonderful. Well for now I am going to stretch my legs a bit more. Very nice to meet you, Pedro." And with that, Betty turns and begins strolling back toward the hills to the west.

"You as well." I feel like I just got a visitation from my own grandmother, only better. Betty is not going to make me eat all the gross overcooked butternut squash on my plate. Actually, everything about Betty seems so grandmotherly and gentle, but *solid*. I keep coming back to the tree image, because it is the most important aspect I can relate. Trees are the silent unsung heroes of all animal life on earth; by the end of the day, I will feel the same way about Betty Pickett.

7:15 am (PDT) / 10:15 am (EDT)

The birders are milling about, looking a little underwhelmed. By general consensus this is a tough spot to bird, and they are looking forward to more intimate settings later today. I have abandoned my nap plan and now wander among the birders, looking for a glimpse into their world, to see what they see.

So far my perception of people who actively seek communion with our feathered friends is that they are a peaceful fellowship--mellow, carefree, much like how we perceive the birds themselves. Frankly, I could use a bit of that vibe. In spite of my best effort to feel and appear otherwise, I cannot deny that my insides are pretty tightly wound. I cannot blame that on Nadia. She may have ratcheted my spring a few turns, but it was there long before her dramas became an integral part of mine. Driving used to be such a reliable tension release for me, but one small setback over a notebook is all it takes to show that this does not always work anymore. I don't think I have fully answered the question of *why* yet either...some last factor of the equation eludes me.

Another thing I have observed about birders: these people are dead-on focused. There is an extreme singularity of purpose that I have never seen in any other group I have transported. For instance, we do a lot of work for the Paso Robles High School athletic department. When I take one of their sports teams to an intersectional road game, they talk about everything *but* sports on the bus, players and coaches alike. I have never heard a theological discussion amongst the peanut gallery while taking a church group to a conference or a mountain retreat. But for all of Floyd's wacky observations about the world, he seems to have the ABA birders pretty well pegged. I am sure that every one of these folks has rich life-stories and cubist complexities to their personalities like everyone does once you see them in an array of settings. But to observe them now, if I am truly birding the birders in their most natural habitat, gives the impression that I am surrounded by one-dimensional giants. It is staggering how much avian knowledge has been dropped all around me since they woke up this morning. The sheer volume of technical details that distinguish one species from another, the shape of one habitat relative to another, and the techniques necessary to identify the nest of the northern shoveler, or reach the mating grounds of the gadwall, etc...it just feels like so much *stuff* to carry. I have never wanted to be a packrat, be it the physical or mental kind. Too much of a drag on mobility.

An unclaimed tripod scope stands by the bus facing south. No one seems in a huge hurry to pack it up, so I walk over to have a look. It is amazingly powerful, reaching hundreds of yards across the semiarid scrub with perfect three-dimensional clarity. Quite a gizmo.

A round woman in khakis approaches me. She is out of the hobbyist-retiree camp, and she has a great-to-be-alive smile this morning.

"So're we gonna make a birder outta ya?" she chuckles, one of several such questions I'll field today.

"Perhaps."

"Got anything in yer scope?"

I look again, and then pantomime as if I got a bite on my fishing line. "Yes! I have a metal-crested petroleum woodpecker. It's foraging for food!" She does not laugh. I don't know if she didn't hear me or understand me, or if birds just ain't no joke in these parts. Instead she commandeers the scope and scans the field for a specimen. Immediately she spots something about one hundred yards away.

"Ooh here ya go. Sage sparrow. Adult male. Beautiful."

I peer through the scope and yep, there he is, a little brown bird, perched atop a fencepost. He sits still for a moment, tilts his sage sparrow head a couple times, then takes flight, probably in search of some grub.

"Pretty cool, huh?" she says, even more aglow than before.

As I thank the woman kindly for her guidance and expertise, part of me is thinking, so this is what brought you out from Oshkosh, Wisconsin? But I have traveled farther on flimsier pretenses. Actually it is pretty exciting in a way. I have *seen* birds all my life, birds of all kinds. My first spoken word, I am told, was "apple," which was an attempt at saying "airplane." And members of the class Aves were plentiful as I explored the backwoods of my New Hampshire home as a child. Yes, like many folks, I have always admired and envied the beauty of birds in flight.

But this is the first time I have ever *birded*.

My biggest question: do the birds feel like they are being watched? Wouldn't that be a little spooky--forty-four people zooming in on your every move with high-tech surveillance equipment?

And what of the people, their bird brains chock full of genera and species, descriptions, characteristics, endless classifications? Do they better appreciate what they see for all that knowledge? Maybe it's just me, but I don't see how. It is a feeling that surfaced earlier in the morning when I started reading someone's scorecard. All the technical data was laid out so...*methodically*, like a medical chart with better handwriting. Some classification is inevitable I'm sure, but I can only take it so far. I mean, if I am walking along the beach in Cayucos on a classic summer afternoon, and I see a little cream-colored bird with orange toothpick legs flitting playfully in the sea foam, I may recognize it as a sandpiper, but what do I care if it is a willet, a whimbrel, or a wandering tattler?

I don't know, but the day has just begun and I am already starting to feel that, for me anyway, birding, to paraphrase Mark Twain and Betty Pickett, is a good walk spoiled.

7:25 am (PDT) / 10:25 am (EDT)

Mesmerized. That is the only word that comes close to describing my state of mind at the moment. Everyone around me seems to be in the same state, or a neighboring one. Some are weeping, some pacing with their hands on their head, some still cursing or expressing their outrage, but not quite as loudly as when the second plane hit the south tower. That was a moment where we all found out for sure that something sinister was happening, and someone did it very intentionally. Difficult to swallow, easy to understand. But watching the total vertical collapse of one of the towers of the *World Trade Center*-that is surreal. It is something that *no one* could expect. I guess nothing shuts up the noisy part of the brain like something so surreal it can't be believed.

The quiet dissolves moments later as words resurface, and not in a good way. For me, a particular flash point occurs as I hear someone loudly proclaim that it is "time to nuke all them sand niggers."

Now, I grew up as a working class Brooklyn kid, so I was pretty well-versed in the art of street fighting. One of the first lessons I learned was how to quickly size up an adversary. So I know immediately that I can make the fat goomba who said this swallow his teeth. It takes everything I have not to do it, too. Fortunately, I have learned to fall back on something Vera taught me the one and only time it happened in her presence, when some drunk grabbed her ass as we left a Broadway show. She said fighting is never worth the pain I cause myself by inflicting it on others. She also said turning the other cheek wasn't about protecting the other guy, it's about listening to conscience over my own anger. I didn't get it at first, or didn't want to anyway; too much like something my mother would have said. But Vera has a way of getting through to me slowly, and I remember it now whenever something makes me boil. So, I turn my cheek on this asshole as well and help Makeup Lady to the passenger's door.

The radio is still playing, and as I settle into my seat, I hear the details of an enormous fire at the Pentagon. My companion looks more frayed than ever, holding her head up with her right hand on her forehead, elbow propped on the arm rest of the door.

"A third plane, from Dulles," she says in a beaten-down monotone. "They turned it right around and crashed it into the Pentagon. Someone's declared war on us."

I breathe deeply. "This is too much. I need to turn the news off for a while." She does not protest. The silence inside the car is the most refreshing lack of sound my ears have ever reported. I watch without emotion as the cloud of ash and dust across the river spreads horizontally, swallowing whole piers and city blocks at once, while my prized airtight model of German engineering protects me from the growing insanity all around us.

"So tell me about your wife."

The sound of her words slicing the silence almost startles me, while their odd content falls onto my verbal receptors with a thud.

"My wife?"

"Yeah...what is she like? How did you meet her?" A short silence ensues while I process these questions. "You know you're going to see her again, right?"

My eyebrows raise sharply as I spin around with a scrutinous glare. There was a certainty in her question that harkened back to the Nostradamus conversation, and not in a bad way. I am not going to admit to this either, so I choose to address the first questions instead.

"Well..." I struggle to find a place to start. The candor required of me here is not something that comes natural or easy, but there is something about her that makes me need to try. "That story probably requires me to start with my first wife, Isabella. The love of my life...so I thought, anyway. We were high school sweethearts, went to college together at St. Francis, and were married right after graduation, ready to start popping out babies. We were the all-Italian-American love story, except the babies didn't pop out."

"Oh no, what was wrong?" I wonder if she could already feel the synchronicity.

"Endometriosis in her fallopian tubes. It was just starting to become evident as we began trying to conceive. The laparoscopy did nothing, and we were feeling desperate –if you weren't raised Catholic, you might not understand the pressure we felt from our families to reproduce, but it was *enormous*. So we started looking into progesterone therapy."

(Now all along I'm thinking *Wait a minute! Who the hell you sharing this with? Retreat!* but she keeps looking at me from that fearless place....)

"Then about eight years ago, Isabella left the fertility clinic one evening and was driving to visit with her sister and newborn niece in Pittsburgh..." I stumble slightly trying to get through this part. "But a…a Greyhound driver fell asleep at the wheel…and veered into her lane on the Turnpike. The bus slammed her into the barrier and crushed the car like an aluminum can. She had no chance."

My companion's left hand assumes its vigil by her mouth. "Oh my God! Oh God I'm, I'm so sorry..."

I nod softly. The shock never goes away entirely.

"I would have been with her if not for a stupid project at work that swallowed up my weekend. And the only reason she was on the road so late was the doctor's appointment. Otherwise, she'd have been sleeping peacefully at her sister's...they said the driver had gone over 40 years accident free, and he was on his last run before retiring...."

I stop, needing to turn in a different direction. I've slopped through this pile of ironies before and it never leads to anything good.

"I would have just killed myself if it weren't so engrained in me as taboo for a Catholic, but I figured no one could keep me from drinking myself to death. So I proceeded to become a raging alcoholic. It was Vera who saved me."

"Wow, how fortunate! What happened?"

"Actually it was one of the strangest first encounter stories I've ever heard." I chuckle, feeling the guard slip a little more. "Vera was in a master's program at Columbia and she was taking the A train home from midtown. I was trying to get back to my apartment in Red Hook, but I stumbled onto the wrong train. I wound up puking and passing out at her feet just before her stop."

I swivel my head and flash a toothy, embarrassed grin at my companion, who suddenly bursts into laughter. Comic relief probably was not expected in this setting, and she seems to appreciate me not passing up the chance to provide it.

"The next thing I remember, this tiny woman is dragging me off the train and onto a bench at the station. She managed to coax me into walking home with her, and she let me sleep on her couch. I woke up around noon the next day with a killer hangover, and she's sitting there typing a Goddamn thesis paper, smiling at me."

"Wow!" says Makeup Lady. "That is...I don't know if it's incredibly admirable or stone crazy!"

"She's definitely both, in great abundance. So yeah, here we are, seven years later, married with two kids, living the suburban dream in Union."

"Aww, you got your family after all," she beams. "What a beautiful story! I wonder what magic she worked on you."

"Ya know," I say as I look away, "I still don't really know myself. She said that she saw this *brilliant light* inside of me, and it was starting to flicker but it was still strong. It was *begging* to be rescued from drowning in my sadness, that's how she put it. I've never seen a Goddamn light in anyone before, to be honest...but I've been thinking about that since Captain Bizzaro gave us a piece of his mind earlier. Your response was exactly like something Vera would have said. She will lend an ear to anyone, no matter how bat shit crazy they are. I'm sure I sounded like that when she met me. So she's been trying to teach me her way of seeing things all these years, and I have so *much* resistance to it because it makes no Goddamn sense to me...but I see how it made her capable of saving a pathetic drunk like me, and it sorta makes me stop and think...maybe it doesn't matter so much if it's *true*...maybe all that matters is that it *works*."

"Well, truth is relative anyway, so all you're really saying is that what works for her is her truth."

I turn back to my companion and smirk. "See, that's where you both lose me. How can there not be an objective reality that we're all experiencing? That's completely illogical. There's no basis for *anything* to exist without one."

"Oh, there's an objective reality for sure, it's just that none of us experience it directly. Except for enlightened humans, microorganisms, and plants. And inanimate objects, but that's a given."

I raise my hands toward the sky in mock praise.

"Well *hallelujah!* It all makes sense now! I just have to be reincarnated as a fern." Makeup Lady laughs heartily, but I'm not satisfied yet. "Seriously though, so there's a special class of people who know what's what, and they're gonna tell the rest of us that we're cursed by something we didn't even do. But the same God who cursed us--who only they can see, mind you--also has the solution for us. *But it's gonna cost ya!*" I say the last line with a hammed-up

New York wise guy accent. "Where I come from, that's called a shakedown. That's not religion, that's organized crime."

My companion shrugs. "Don't blame me. I voted for Zeus."

I slap my thighs and shake my head.

"Nope. You and Vera and your enlightened vegetables can have your alternate universes, I'll stick with this one, for better or worse."

"Well, me still thinks the gentleman doth protest too much, but I can let it go. I bet your wife and I would get along wonderfully. We seem to have a lot in common."

"Yeah, you're both absolutely *bonkers*."

"Maybe so. How about your kids--what are their names? I just *adore* children."

"Our oldest is Mirabai, Mira for short, she's four. And Rabia is two.

She gasps. "Oh my goodness, those are the most divine names. What lucky girls!"

"Vera's choice, of course. My votes were Lisa and Danielle."

"I'm with Vera. Ha, you know we've been talking for an hour, and I know your wife and kids' names but I don't know yours. I'm--*OH MY GOD!*"

Her face becomes the same freeze frame image of horror I saw before, and she spastically reaches for the door handle and jumps out as it opens. I follow suit, and see the north tower now plummeting toward the ground in the same uncanny manner as the other, each floor seeming to give way one at a time starting below the impact zone, until all 1,368 feet have collapsed into a hellacious heap of debris and dust clouds further engulfing lower Manhattan. Vera's office no longer exists.

Neither does the Cantor Fitzgerald complex near the top floors, nor anyone who was in it at the time. The woman standing by the front corner of my car would have been one of them if not for the appointment to follow up on her emergency hysterectomy. But I am in no mind to care or console her. A dread panic is spreading through my body, wiping out all memory of her certainty that Vera is alive.

Just as I feel on the verge of breaking down, I hear a dreadful thump behind me. I look to my right, and see Makeup Lady lying in a heap on the ground, blood gushing from a deep gash above her left temple.

7:30 am (PDT) / 10:30 am (EDT)

The Birds commence the roundup process. It is time to take leave of the flatlands and make our way to the peak of Azucar Mountain. We will drive forty eight miles and climb 8,000 feet to reach the highest point in the Coastal Range this side of Los Angeles. You would be hard-pressed to find two more different birding environments within such a short drive of each other.

I close the left side luggage bay door and stroll back around the right to close that as well, grabbing my rucksack in the process. As I do, I catch a glimpse of the cover of my multi-creased, dog-eared copy of Mark Twain's *Life on the Mississippi*. I have been reading it lately to draw inspiration for "The Valley and the Mountain," for it occurred to me that someone with my extreme case of bicoastal disorder might not be the best spokesperson for the middle road. If anyone ever spoke for the sensibilities of middle America and lived them out through his stories, it was Mark Twain.

It's funny that Betty Pickett evoked Twain earlier with her "good walk" comment. He has been floating in and out of my mind all morning anyway, as I have been trying to pinpoint what feels off to me about the birders' singularity of attention, and their amassing huge mental archives of technical knowledge about birds. Something I read a couple weeks ago seemed to speak to it perfectly. I just haven't had a chance to go back and look it up. But it is clawing at me now. I am sensing one of those breakthrough moments that writers will later wax nostalgic about when being interviewed on NPR. Better devote some time to this at the next stop.

I start walking toward the entrance to assume my post...but something diverts me. I drift east, past the open door, angling past the flat vertical plane of the front of the bus, across the gravel of the shoulder until I come to a stop on the road itself. It is empty in both directions, both the road and the land as level as the most monotonous stretches of the Great Plains. Even though we are not too far from the dust-bowl smog-tropolis of Bakersfield, this suddenly feels like the most desolate place in the world. My eyes are drawn past the valley to the humps of the Tehachapi Mountains hugging the eastern horizon, and beyond them to all that I have explored and learned and loved across the vast stretch of land back to the place I once called home--and then *zoom*, right back to the blacktop beneath my feet.

This happens to me often, and when it does I realize in the keenest sense that what I am standing on is an unbroken stretch of pavement that leads to anywhere I could dream of going on this continent. Just because we give the road different names as it changes forms and crosses political boundaries, this does not mean it is broken into separate entities--it is one indivisible whole. To realize this, and to identify oneself with the road and not merely the one organism standing on it like a dot on a roadmap: this is to achieve something like that dream of being everywhere at once. And I believe it is akin to leaving behind the mortality of the individual and experiencing the eternal life of the whole.

This is not always a comforting experience. The road leads down many dark passages, and the pain of the whole where it *feels* broken and isolated is just as real as its ecstatic pleasure in being whole. As I feel this now, I am suddenly overwhelmed with foreboding. Something on that road ahead does not feel quite right...and somehow, I immediately know what it is I need to find in Twain. I take out my copy of *Life on the Mississippi* and flip to a spot just a few pages in front of my bookmark. It is a section where he shares his insights about what he lost when he fulfilled a boyhood dream and became a river boat pilot:

The face of the water, in time, became a wonderful book--a book that was a dead language to the uneducated passenger, but which told its mind to me without reserve, delivering its most cherished secrets as clearly as if it uttered them with a voice. And it was not a book to be read once and thrown aside, for it had a new story to tell every day. Throughout the long twelve hundred miles there was never a page that was void of interest, never one that you could leave unread without loss, never one that you would want to skip, thinking you could find higher enjoyment in some other thing. There never was so wonderful a book written by man; never one whose interest was so absorbing, so unflagging, so sparklingly renewed with every reperusal. The passenger who could not read it was charmed with a peculiar sort of faint dimple on its surface (on the rare occasions when he did not overlook it altogether); but to the pilot that was an italicized passage; indeed, it was more than that, it was a legend of the largest capitals, with a string of shouting exclamation points at the end of it, for it meant that a wreck or a rock was buried there that could tear the life out of the strongest vessel that ever floated. It is the faintest and simplest expression the water ever makes, and the most hideous to a pilot's eye. In truth, the passenger who could not read this book saw nothing but all manner of pretty pictures in it, painted by the sun and shaded by the clouds, whereas to the trained eye these were not pictures at all, but the grimmest and most dread-earnest of reading matter.

It is clear to me that I am looking at these birds today as a collection of pretty pictures, wondering why anyone would invest all the time and head space to learn to see them as an italicized passage with a string of shouting exclamation points...but what is that peculiar sort of faint dimple on the surface of the road ahead? Why can I not take my eye off of it?

He goes on:

> *Now when I had mastered the language of this water, and had come to know every trifling feature that bordered the great river as familiarly as I knew the letters of the alphabet, I had made a valuable acquisition. But I had lost something, too. I had lost something which could never be restored to me while I lived. All the grace, the beauty, the poetry, had gone out of the majestic river! I still kept in mind a certain wonderful sunset which I witnessed when steamboating was new to me. A broad expanse of the river was turned to blood; in the middle distance the red hue brightened into gold, through which a solitary log came floating, black and conspicuous; one place along, slanting mark lay sparkling upon the water; in another the surface was broken by boiling, tumbling rings, that were as many-tinted as an opal; where the ruddy flush was faintest, was a smooth spot that was covered with graceful circles and radiating lines, ever so delicately traced; the shore on our left was densely wooded, and the somber shadow that fell from this forest was broken in one place by a long, ruffled trail that shone like silver; and high above the forest wall a clean-stemmed dead tree waved a single leafy bough that glowed like a flame in the unobstructed splendor that was flowing from the sun. There were graceful curves, reflected images, woody heights, soft distances; and over the whole scene, far and near, the dissolving lights drifted steadily, enriching it every passing moment with new marvels of coloring.*

I stood like one bewitched. I drank it in, in a speechless rapture. The world was new to me, and I had never seen anything like this at home. But as I have said, a day came when I began to cease from noting the glories and the charms which the moon and the sun and the twilight wrought upon the river's face; another day came when I ceased altogether to note them. Then, if that sunset scene had been repeated, I should have looked upon it without rapture, and should have commented upon it, inwardly, after this fashion: 'This sun means that we are going to have wind tomorrow; that floating log means that the river is rising, small thanks to it; that slanting mark on the water refers to a bluff reef which is going to kill somebody's steamboat one of these nights, if it keeps on stretching out like that; those tumbling 'boils' show a dissolving bar and a changing channel there, the lines and circles in the slick water over yonder are a warning that troublesome place is shoaling up dangerously....'

No, the romance and the beauty were all gone from the river. All the value any feature of it had for me now was the amount of usefulness it could furnish toward compassing the safe piloting of a steamboat. Since those days, I have pitied doctors from my heart. What does the lovely flush in a beauty's cheek mean to a doctor but a 'break' that ripples above some deadly disease? Are not all her visible charms sown thick with what are to him the signs and symbols of hidden decay? Does he ever see her beauty at all, or doesn't he simply view her professionally, and comment upon her unwholesome condition all to himself? And doesn't he sometimes wonder whether he has gained most or lost most by learning his trade?

I shudder. A chill comes over me, as if a sudden cold wind hit the back of my neck alone and no one else. I glance over my right shoulder and realize that I am the only one left outside the bus. *How long was I standing there?* I wonder. I turn around again and face the eastbound stretch of road. Something out there is shoaling up dangerously, but *what*?

I had been pretty certain when I started in reflection on that passage of Twain what it meant to me. Now, going back over all the thoughts of the morning--my life on the road, my reaction to the sunrise this morning...my wife...I am left to ponder: am I thinking about the birders...or myself?

I return to the bus and fire it up. All the birders have alighted on their seats as scheduled. I use all the width of the pavement and shoulders to execute a textbook three-point turn, and we are back on the road, returning from whence we came.

* * * *

I spring to action immediately, ripping a piece of my shirt to fold into a compress. I hold it tightly against the wound, propping her body up against the tire of the car. With my free hand I yank my tie off and start wrapping it around her head to hold the compress in place. Some people notice the ruckus and a small crowd is gathering around us. It must be quite a spectacle. I have never seen so much human blood escape a body at once.

"Yo what happened, man?" one of them calls out.

"She fainted and bashed her head on my car. Quick! Someone call 911!"

I keep the pressure steady on the wound with my left hand, but blood is still trickling down into a fearsome puddle on the concrete roadway. No one is able to get a call through on a cell phone. All the major service providers had transmitters on the Twin Towers, so the already overburdened communication systems of New York City just lost a huge amount of capacity. Besides, there is no way an ambulance could get to us fast enough. She does not have time to lose. I make a quick assessment that the fastest way to the surface streets is to backtrack to the Columbus Drive exit, then I scoop her up, careful to keep the pressure on the wound and her head up, and lumber toward the off ramp. Only later will it surprise me how completely unconcerned I am for the welfare of my car or anything in it.

Meanwhile, across the river, the eruption of chaos and grief continues, though the mountain stands no longer. A great number of my people left their bodies this morning, many of my bravest and finest among them. There is a deep wound near my heart, but I am not dead. No, I am not dying; I am coming to life. For from the scattered presence of millions of I's who witnessed these events, there is emerging a spirit of We. These people, who dwell in the most diverse city on earth, with so little in common beyond all being a part of me, awoke this morning as separate creatures in their minds, but now they are learning that survival--in life and death--means never forgetting that we are one. I have lived almost four hundred years because I am one with all who live within me. We are resilient; we are New York strong; we are One.

Many of us are suffering. Many of us are scared. We care for those of us who are afflicted, we honor the fallen. Those of us who have the strength begin to dig.

One of these persons has overcome incredible odds just to be alive and walking on September 11, 2001. She has no business being among the ones who are sturdy enough to lend a hand to her brothers and sisters. Given her medical condition, she cannot possibly be among the New Yorkers with a shovel in her hands and a fire in her heart.

But she is.

ACT III

I have never seen a person die.
Not even my mother. I refused to stay in the room with her when she took her last breath.

Damnit, that seems so cowardly now to think back on it. But at the time, as a thirteen year old boy losing his mother, I was so angry at her, so filled with bitterness. How does someone just *decide* it is time to die? What kind of God lets a woman raise a family and then "calls her home" when they need her the most?

But I'm not thinking of this right now. All I am thinking is there is no way in hell I am letting this woman die in my arms today.

I descend the off ramp in a clumsy gallop. She ain't particularly heavy, but the awkwardness of supporting her weight while keeping pressure on her wound is slowing my gait. Blood streams down my left forearm and leaves a trail of drops behind us. It's showing no sign of letting up. She needs to be stitched up fast.

The surface streets are nearly deserted. Everyone is either by a television or somewhere with a birds-eye view across the river. Fortunately, I spot a payphone a block ahead on the right. *Thank goodness there are still public phones, we're not all completely dependent on these damn cell phones yet.*

A young Latina woman approaches from the opposite direction, drifting stuporously as many eyewitnesses have been doing all day, but the sight of a man carrying a woman drenched in blood seems to shock her back to where she is. I implore her to call 911 so I don't have to put her down, and the woman dutifully responds.

"*¡Dígale que ella tiene una lesión en la cabeza con hemorragia grave y necesita atención inmediata!*"

The woman relays the relevant information in Spanglish. She hangs up and turns to face the bleeding woman with sincere concern, then mutters some words under her breath and makes the sign of the cross. Normally, I would be annoyed by that superstitious ritual that I too was trained to perform and gave up shortly after Communion. But not now.

"*Muchos gracias. Ella va a salir bien.*"

"*De nada,*" she responds, still aghast but appearing more calm.

Within two minutes, I hear a wailing siren approaching, to my tremendous relief. It arrives on the scene and the EMTs immediately pop out with a rolling stretcher. I hand her over with great care, my arms and back glad to be relieved of the strain. I wait off to the side, wishing for the first time in who-knows-how-long that I were not so out of practice with prayer.

G ridlock....
The word looped into my thought stream about a month ago, and I keep coming back to it like the tip of a tongue to a canker sore. It is the arch nemesis of anyone who earns a living operating motor vehicles. Makes me wonder if Superman ever fixates on the word "kryptonite."

My trusty companion in the rucksack describes gridlock as "a major traffic jam in which all vehicular movement comes to a stop because key intersections are blocked by traffic." *Webster* does not like to repeat himself. It is unusual to see a word used twice in the same entry as "traffic" is found there. But it seems part and parcel of the definition: it is traffic stopping traffic by getting in its own way. No external force needs to come along and put up roadblocks, walls, traps. All it takes is a critical mass of vehicles funneled into the narrow, rigid channels of our roadways, and stagnation manifests out of motion. Traffic brings itself to a halt. Gridlock is the universe's natural reaction when too much is trying to happen in one place at one time.

I hardly ever encounter gridlock driving in California, even in Los Angeles. Contrary to popular imagination, LA traffic flows pretty smoothly because there are so many freeways in every direction. The volume can be intense at times, but four or five lanes in both directions are usually enough to carry it all with only moderate slowdowns. The exceptions to this rule are notorious and chronic, and everyone knows to avoid them if at all possible (which brings to mind a quote attributed to the great koan master Yogi Berra, who said of a popular restaurant, "No one goes there anymore, it's too crowded.")

One of these is the San Diego Freeway, "the 405" as it is popularly known--especially between US 101 and Long Beach. The only time you can be sure to avoid gridlock on the 405 is the middle of the night. Back in July I was assigned to take a group to the J. Paul Getty Center in Brentwood, yet another palatial estate built by a silver spoon megalomaniac, so stuffed to the gills with art and antiquities that millions of tourists feel compelled to swoon over the Great Man who assembled all this cultural wealth in one place for us (I never took the tour there, but I would bet my next paycheck the guides don't talk about the time Mr. Getty allowed kidnappers to mutilate his grandson while he stared them down over a ransom payment). With a strong throwing arm, one could almost lob a brick from the long driveway of the Getty Center onto the 405 as it slices through the southern slope of the Topanga Hills, so there is really no feasible way to avoid using it as the access and egress--and someone had the brilliant idea to schedule this group's tour to conclude at 4:45 in the afternoon. Suffice it to say, we were gridlocked from the get-go, the three-and-a-half- hour drive to San Luis Obispo turned into four-and-a-half, and yes, I ate a cold dinner alone that night too.

Predicaments like that are exceptions in southern California, though. I find gridlock a much greater problem in San Francisco--a city surrounded by water on three sides--and places like Phoenix and Seattle, which simply outgrew their infrastructure. In between these clusters of concrete jungle, in the vast open spaces for which the West became known--places like Route 33 as we head back south out of Bonanza over the ripples of the Coastal Range foothills--the idea of gridlock could not be more foreign. This is the kind of place where you will see postcard photos of a cattle drive clogging up a dirt road in an empty pasture, and the caption will say "Rush Hour Traffic." The allusion to a land-based vehicle as a ship sailing the open ocean does not stretch the imagination out here. The road energy flows unimpeded in all directions, constantly, like an untamed river or the shifting tides. These are the roads that keep drawing me back to the West, even after I think I am ready to embrace my eastern roots.

I know I have yet to give a really satisfactory explanation for why I developed this acute case of bicoastal disorder, what keeps chasing me off the east coast into the Big Empty of the west. But I think I am on to something here. Gridlock is the key.

The first eighteen years of my life were spent at the northern end of the great megalopolis of the eastern seaboard, in the hinterland rural-burban reaches of the city they call "the Hub"--and like any wheel, it turns slower the closer you get to the Hub, which is an apt way to describe the gridlock patterns of the small patch of reclaimed tidewater swamp known as Boston. After that I went to college at the southern end--and trust me, the notorious stagnation that everyone complains about *inside* the Capital Beltway has nothing on the chronic gridlock on the Beltway, both the freeway and all the feeder roads around it. In between Boston and Washington, there are most of the key intersections of my adult life--travels back and forth; the junctions of my life with the byways of my closest friends, who mostly grew up in their own gridlock patterns of Baltimore and Philadelphia; the roadside attractions of all of our shared experiences; homes where I have tried to plant myself up and down the Mid-Atlantic. Hardly anywhere in this region is there a place I can go where I will not see multiple images of myself from the past, doing something I no longer want to do, in a life I do not want to live. Why do I haunt myself this way? Who is this person that should only be was, and why does he persist? I don't know...I didn't know him very well then either. Perhaps that is a clue.

I know I am not alone in this phenomenon. I see it in my friends too, when we are back east. The images pile up, all the unforgotten feelings associated with them spewing behind like exhaust fumes, until all the key intersections are jammed, and then...emotional gridlock. The old feelings choke off the flow of anything new.

I have always known my own personal escape route: any highway sign that points "West" will do the trick, as long as I have the means to follow it. But I already know the loop that puts me on, so it is more of a reprieve than an escape, a band-aid instead of a cure.

So I find myself back in gridlock time after time. I could probably deal with the lack of motion, let it become a kind of meditative stillness. I even wrote an essay on this once while I was stuck for an hour on the Key Bridge outside Baltimore, which was the basis for that idea of identifying with the whole unbroken road, not just a dot on the map.

But it's the noise that kills me. Every damn driver who thinks that laying on his horn will part the gridlock like the Red Sea and let his people go--or at least himself. When you get down to it, that is what I really cannot stand about the east coast: the noise. There is no appreciation of quiet in the northeastern subculture. Silence is like dead airtime on the radio, a void where no money is being made. We have an incessant need to fill this space with noise. The quiet of the New Mexico desert, or the Montana mountains, or the red rock canyon-lands of southern Utah, or hell, even here in the big empty of central California--that all started to disappear the moment some Dutch dude plunked down twenty seven dollars in shells for Mannahatta Island.

Of course this is especially problematic for me with my stupid rabbit ears. And it isn't just the acuity--I do not have much ability to filter background noise either. So I hear every one of those Goddamn horns, sometimes better than a conversation I am trying to have within my own car. Interesting, how a single physiological feature can have such an enormous impact on a person's life: Nadia's pancreas stops working and turns her world into cauldron of inner conflict. Others may have a single facial feature considered unattractive or grotesque, and they grow into a reclusive shell. One might not think that hypersensitive hearing could have that kind of effect. But here's what I tell people when they ask what it is like: imagine if everything in your visual field stimulated your brain and commanded attention, even the smallest objects in your periphery? Would you desperately need to shut your eyes most of the time? No wonder I crave these open roads of the west. People are such downers when the words that they think are private are not. I hear every single discouraging word spoken in my presence--of course I am drawn to find my "home on the range" where they are seldom heard. Something to help preserve the illusion that people are kind and actually like each other.

So it's not just the ability to keep moving. It's the quiet, just being able to hear myself think. Gridlock deprives me of that.

For those who still live and work in the heart of the northeast corridor, gridlock has a reality that is far more than metaphorical. And the undisputed heavyweight champion of gridlock is the Big Apple. I am glad to say that, unlike Nadia, I have almost no personal connections to New York City. My father's family escaped Manhattan and moved upstate in the 1950s--that is as close as I get, unless you count a gazillion trips on the Cross Bronx and a couple Yankees games. If I set neither foot nor tire in the city again, I shall be a happy man for all my days. Whose idea was it to put eight million people on three islands and a peninsula, surround them with about ten million more--many of whom need to reach the islands for work--and give most of them a car? An urban planning student would flunk out of college for suggesting it, yet here it persists in the 21st century, in the most mobile society in human history. It made a lot more sense when the primary modes of transportation were boat, horse, and feet, and water provided a barrier of protection against various kinds of beasties. But in the age of the automobile, the anthrax bomb and the nuclear missile, New York City is an illogical conundrum. It is already a crumbling shadow of its former self, and the internet will make it obsolete within a generation if something else does not do it first.

But the reason why it will exist long beyond its usefulness is the same reason why I keep coming back to dwell among ghosts. It is home for eighteen million people, and the roots of countless millions more. As monstrous as it can seem to people like me as an outsider passing through, for all those people it is the two-bedroom ranch house in Cayucos that they will never forget, long after it is torn down. This has an even stronger pull on most people than it does for me. The reality is that most would rather deal with gridlock everyday of their lives and know just who they are, than risk the liberating experience of emptiness.

Hmmm. New York...I wonder what got my mind going down *that* track.

But now I need it back here. Bus 477 has been retracing its tire prints for a while. We climbed back nearly all the way to the ridge of the foothills on Route 33, and we are now turning east onto Azucar Mountain Road. The climb will continue for about twenty miles on a narrow switchback trail. We are just a stone's throw from the San Andreas fault now, and the gentle undulations of the land have morphed into a seemingly endless series of mogul-like hills and gullies--too steep to climb head-on, so we will spend many miles in second gear, traversing back and forth in ascending corkscrew turns.

Before it gets too bad, and while we are fairly close to civilization, I decide to call Nadia, for I imagine we will soon be out of cell phone range. Bird #1 also calls one of the conference higher-ups for the same reason. Nadia does not answer and I get our machine. The signal is already very choppy and she probably gets every other word of my message, but at least she will know I thought of her before disappearing for the day. There have been too many times that I have not thought to check in with her, and that is a fault of mine I need to fix. It suddenly feels much more important to me that I never forget to see her beauty.

Bird #1 is still on the phone when I hang up. She is evidently straining to hear as well, but her overall reaction to whatever she is hearing is unusual. I can't afford many backward glances, so it is hard to read. She says very few words, but they have a tone of incredulity that is not quite right. When she hangs up she immediately begins whispering with her husband, adding to the intrigue. I imagine, though, that it is a private, family affair, and judging by their reaction it could be anything from a child taken ill to something dreadfully wrong with their prized cockatoo.

Upon closing their mini-conference, however, Bird #1 gets up and approaches me. She leans down and whispers into my ear with calm, calculated precision.

when we get stopped up here, you might want to turn on the radio. there's a national crisis.

Something inside me sinks when I hear those words. I don't know what it is but it goes straight down and stays there. *There's a national crisis?!?* What a perfect non-sequitor! We are also headed for another Ice Age, someday. Words without meaning. This will not stand. I ask her to please, pray tell.

someone's been hijacking airplanes and crashing them. they've hit the world trade center and the pentagon.

OK, now *that* has meaning. Yes, national crisis, yes.
Oh God...

i'm driving

                                       this bus

    people, back there

                we're moving

space and time, space and time...

                we're safe....right?
                     right, yes

         for now...I have to keep us that way.

For now.

    Focus on the road.

        Focus.
                On.

                        The.

             Road...

THE ROAD! veers left, hard, like a dog chasing a rabbit. I fling the steering wheel in the general direction, and the bus makes an awkward lunge but stays on the pavement. Beyond it lies a black diamond ski slope of rocks, tall grass and sagebrush. Before we are fully straightened out, a yellow sign foretells of a right U-shaped turn and advises fifteen miles per hour, or about half of our current speed. I stab the brake on the edge of panic. The centrifugal force drops, keeping us on the good side of the center stripe, but my overcompensated steering takes us over the white line and onto the dirt.

Ugh. This is not good. The passengers must think I am falling asleep. I'll have a mutiny on my hands if I don't pull it together. Mercifully the road straightens out as it climbs the bank. Now we are almost directly above the first turn. We crest the incline and ease back left. Steady now, steady...

A sickening feeling has overcome me physically. Everything from my throat to my loins is one giant knot. I am shaking. I want to cry. I don't want to cry. My hands and feet and eyes are completely autonomous now. They have to be--everything else has stopped functioning, and it is a long way down these ravines. This is a tough road to drive with *no* national crisis.

Bird #1 has returned to her seat. There is still a deliberation going on, but it is clear that they intend to keep this information from the rest of the bus. Do they expect some kind of ugly panic? One big nervous breakdown at 5,000 feet and climbing?

Forty-three other human beings on the bus and the one person they tell is *THE DRIVER?!*

Composure. Keep it. Somehow.

My head is a giant switchboard ringing with questions. What happened to the Twin Towers? Is the Pentagon *destroyed*? Are we being invaded? Where is the President? Are we mobilizing troops? Is this World War III?

How much information do the Birds have?

I cannot ask direct questions without undermining their decision, so I simply inquire if there are more details. She leans over again.

all we know is they closed every airport in the country.

Good. I am glad someone is on top of things. No more crashes.
Contain the damage.

Then I hear Bird #1, in a hushed tone, say to Bird #2 what will
be the crux of my discontent for the next several hours.

"God, how do we do our jobs today?"

How? I believe the proper question is "WHY?" Jesus Henry
Christ we need to get *home*! We need to be plugged in with the
rest of the nation! Are they really considering birding through an
unprecedented and unquantified national catastrophe?

I mean, regardless of my earlier pontifications on the merits of
birding, there is *nothing* I can imagine doing at this moment that
is more important than contacting family and loved ones and
finding out *what in God's name* is happening in the world!

But I jussa drivah, suh.

I feel like telling the Birds what I think of their policy and
shouting something to the crowd, but professionalism overcomes common sense. I keep hearing Floyd's voice in my head,
and Annie's as well, for she would certainly agree (and say it
much nicer). It would be very uncouth to argue with a paying
customer about their agenda, to dictate to them what will happen
with *their* bus. Actually, by this point I am pretty well self-contained. This road demands my full attention and somehow I have
to pay it. My eyes are watering and I feel five ulcers starting, but
I keep the news to myself.

My first cogent thoughts about the situation are a dispassion-
ate and well-trained journalistic attempt to answer the missing
"5W" questions. We have a good idea of "What," "Where," and
"When," but are totally in the dark as to "Who" or "Why."

The last time something like this happened, we all learned that
we need to be careful when looking for these answers. I still
remember that morning--April 19, 1995--when the news came
over that a bomb had ripped open the Murrah Federal Building in
Oklahoma City and at least one hundred innocent victims were
dead. I was working at the front desk of an international hostel in
Flagstaff, Arizona. It was one of a half-dozen such places in that

that Grand Canyon gateway town, and the one that had culti-
vated the greatest eat-drink-and-be-merry reputation among the
backpacker set, so rare were the days that I did not wake up trying to shake some kind of wine- or whiskey-induced fog. The
reports from the local NPR station that day, therefore, almost
seemed like a hallucination...a *truck* explodes on the street and
takes out half a building full of people...in *Oklahoma?*...For the
next two days the papers were chockfull of chest-thumping war
cries, editorials about how we should nuke every Islamic country in the Mideast on general principles. But something did not
feel right to me, and I told everybody who was sober enough
to listen, "No, it wasn't the Muslims, this was an inside job."
Generally, my companion would then offer me the bourbon and
say, in a thick Aussie accent, "'ere mate, 'ave anutha swig." And
generally, I would oblige.

Then, of course, I was proven right, when we all learned the
main culprit was a blonde-haired, blue-eyed kid from Buffalo. A
Marine even. That was the peak--and subsequent downfall-- of
the mid-90s "militia movement" in America, a loose confedera-
tion of self-propelled paramilitary groups that vowed to fight the
supposed excesses of the federal government and the alleged
transfer of American sovereignty to the United Nations. The
Oklahoma City bombing flew in the face of the adage that "there
is no such thing as bad publicity." It became much harder to
sympathize with the cause of grown men playing Rambo in their
backyards when the media was flooded with stories of children
turned into charcoal in the Murrah Building's day care center.

There is also nothing new or un-American about the idea of
raining death and destruction upon highly populated areas from
the skies. We are still the only nation that has made good on that
threat in the atomic age. Hollywood has indulged our Armageddon fantasies for decades with meteor showers, alien spacecraft
attacks, and the like. And just before those two Colorado punks
shot up their high school a couple years ago, they filled their
diaries with wistful images of hijacking a jumbo jet and crashing it into the heart of Manhattan. Nobody owns a copyright on
senseless mass murder.

But the *World Trade Center*...this is not the work of American psychopaths. This has *jihad* written all over it. Islamic militants have wanted to bring down the Twin Towers for years. A car bomb in the underground parking garage shook one of the towers visibly and injured hundreds in 1993. With its grandiose vertical scale and cold glass-and-steel sheen, the World Trade Center carries a symbolic presence that is far greater than its mere physical existence. It means something that the tallest building in New York City is not a church or a temple or a mosque, or any other place of worship aside from the invisible hand of the gods of the free market. Whether we call this good or bad, or both, or neither, it means something, and it is something that many people in our world fear. And the Pentagon...good lord, is *that* dripping with symbolism...our largest building on a *horizontal scale,* a five-sided fortress of military might, shaped like a symbol known for satanic connotations. Nope, not much mystery there either. This, for all the inherent contradiction in the phrase and its massively flawed concept, is an act of holy war. And it has finally crash landed on our shores. America can no longer imagine itself safe from the swarms of enemies it creates by stirring up the hornets' nests of the world.

I soon realize that this train of thought is taking me further from the truth. This is the inevitable result of an over-reliance on media and news commentary: an inability to feel. I am dealing in mental abstractions, and they have no truth, no reality. There is nothing I can think that can even hold a candle to the reality of a jet plane crashing into a building, hundreds of human lives extinguished in a fiery moment of hate. There must be something deep within me on the soul level, something that witnessed these events--I have had dreams about exploding planes throughout my life, and it only makes sense that my mind could not fathom a building getting in the way. There is something in me that felt the horror, the sorrow of lost life, something that wept out loud and beat its breast for God's mercy, while this crazy bus driver body struggled to stay awake almost three thousand miles away. It is there, but I don't know where it is. I do not know how to find it. I cannot make it be *here*. I am not an eyewitness on the eastern stage. There is a wall between these two stages, and somehow I have the notion that I helped build it because I decided that *this* is happening *here* while *that* is happening over *there*. I am a single speck of dust on tumbleweed in an empty desert. I am a blind man groping in the dark for the controls of a radio, so I can know and not feel. I will never feel what happened this morning in New York and Washington.

That is where the hopelessness sets in.

Bird #1 leans over again from across the aisle. "How are you doing?" she asks, in a less focused whisper. Her words bring me back to the bus, back from the torture chamber between my ears. I have been better of course, but I assure her I am fine.

"Would you like a cold drink?"

Why? Am I visibly shaken? Probably.

"Anything with caffeine. Please." Then I remember the 20-ounce bottle of Coke down by my feet, so I tell her I am covered.

I reach down with my left hand--the right one planted firmly on the wheel and eyes upon the more gently winding road--and fish around for the Coke, which evidently took a tumble on those spastic U-turns. It is now lying on its side in the spot where the clutch pedal would be with a standard transmission. I retrieve it with a good stretch--egad! so much tension in the shoulders. I feel like a marble bust of myself. The plastic cap unscrews with little ceremony, no satisfying thrust-and-pop action like the cans or the old glass bottles. But the liquid itself feels good on the throat. Somewhere between refrigerator cold and lukewarm, mellow...ahhh. Great. In fact Coke has probably never tasted better.

It is funny, the things one thinks of at times like these, the ways the mind will sling out a lasso to pull us back and draw a connection with the greater world. It occurs to me that the soft drink I am holding--one of many millions in circulation across the world at this very moment--is in a sense a microcosm of the World Trade Center. It does not take a major stretch of the imagination to see that this long, cylindrical bottle was conceived and designed from the same realm of inspiration that brought forth the Twin Towers. In fact, even better than the Twin Towers, Co-ca-Cola, both as a product and a marketing entity, represents everything that is capitalist America on the world stage. Omnipresent. In-your-face. Bombastic. Magical.

And some people hate all that enough to kill themselves, and take as many Coke drinkers with them as possible.

I take another swig. Yuck. This time all I taste is acid and high fructose corn syrup. So much for the magic. I screw the cap back on and stash the bottle between my seat and the console where it won't roll around, thinking it is a good time to heed Nadia's advice and quit the stuff.

Before too long the roller coaster ride smoothes out completely and we reach another crest. We are quite a bit higher than the junction now. Unobstructed views extend for many miles on both sides, with a sweeping panorama of the valley to the left. So beautiful. Over there is Bakersfield and the agricultural heart of Kern County, then the Tehachapi Range, southern terminus of the mighty Sierra Nevadas. Beyond that, all the raw land, huge and unfurled, rolling in the invisible distance toward the eastern seaboard, which burns, burns, burns...

"Oh!" shouts Bird #1. "Look everyone! A red-tailed hawk at ten o'clock!" Forty-three heads turn in unison.

What is going on out there?

After a long while, a senior EMT approaches me. He hands me a clear plastic bag containing a tie that was once solid blue, and is now mostly purple.

"Good job on the bandage." I can tell from his voice and demeanor that he is a grizzled veteran of homeland carnage. He sounds like he has been working for about thirty-six straight hours. "I don't suppose you need the piece of your shirt back."

"Thank you, no. How is she?"

"Definitely a concussion, a little whiplash. Vitals are stable. Hopefully for her sake she'll stay asleep through most of it. We finally got her plugged so I think they'll get her stitched up alright, but that blood loss is still a concern. Do you know her? Any kind of identification at all?"

"None. This happened up on the freeway. We were stuck in traffic up there together. She fainted when the second tower collapsed and hit her head on my car on the way down. Hadn't even gotten her first name yet. I suppose I could go back and check her car for ID."

"Anything to go on would be helpful. I'd bet my house she's on some kind of blood thinner. That stuff's runnin' like red Kool Aid."

"Gotcha. I'll head up there and see what I can find, and I'll drive her car over to the hospital when traffic clears. Where are you taking her?"

"JC Medical Center. It ain't but a half-mile west on Montgomery up there," he says, pointing to the next intersection.

"Wow, she picked a great spot to take a header on my car."

"Only because you done what you done. Seriously son, we been watchin' people panic and do the strangest shit all morning, but you made two quick decisions that probably saved this woman's life, keepin' as much of that stuff in her body as you did and runnin' her down off that gridlock up there. You should be proud of that."

"Thanks." I feel a little surprised at being praised for something I hope anyone would do in my shoes. "I'll probably appreciate it when I find out she's OK."

The older man offers a closed fist, and it takes me a quick second to remember that in some Afro-American subcultures this is equivalent to a handshake. I give the man a meek bump, and receive one back.

"Aw'ite," says the older man. "We'll be waitin' on you." He returns to the ambulance, and they whisk her off to the hospital.

Just like that, I am alone now, for the first time since I saw the fire in the north tower. I know it is probably a moot point, but I check my cell phone just to see if I missed any calls during the fracas. No service. Wow. Just a few weeks ago I had finally convinced Vera we should buy a pair of cell phones so this exact scenario would not happen. Now here I am, surrounded by millions of people and holding in my hand a device designed to communicate with any of them at any time, yet I feel more isolated than I did without it.

I had imagined that at this point I would wait out the traffic, then pick up the kids and bring them home where Vera would hopefully have called with her whereabouts. This is still my intention at the moment, yet I cannot seem to get up from the curb and make tracks in that direction. I can't help but think back to the certainty in this woman's voice when she said I would see Vera again. What *was* that? And why do I feel compelled to trust it? Somehow this fact starts to feel settled in my mind, while what is completely unsettled is who this mystery woman is, and what is causing the pain in her that is rooted far deeper than the horrors we just witnessed.

I can't believe I'm saying this to myself, but something just told me that Vera is either gone, or is managing just fine on her own, and I can live with not knowing which just yet...because there is someone alive who I promised not to leave alone.

While I pause and consider that, another voice that I don't yet know that I have speaks up. It moves my lips, forms words I don't understand. Then for an unknown reason, it moves my right hand across my chest, faintly but distinctly, making the shape of the cross.

I rise, and head back up the off ramp to find out who this person is.

10:00 am (PDT) / 1:00 pm (EDT)

I have never needed Tom Brokaw as much as I do now. The president of my country is vowing to "hunt down those responsible for these cowardly acts," but I do not know this yet. I am still trying to make first contact with the outside world.

We have stopped in a large parking lot near the summit of Azucar Mountain, 8,200 feet above sea level. This is one of the highest points in the vast mountainous terrain between Los Angeles, San Francisco and the San Joaquin Valley, and the only peak that wears a consistent snowcap through the winter, hence the Spanish word for "sugar" in its name. Only the top few hundred feet are above the tree line, though, and here we are still in the thick of a coniferous forest that we entered several miles before reaching the access road--an eight mile, twenty minute climb up a narrow one and a half-lane path shaped like a spiral staircase.

The last of the innocents has long since deboarded and headed for the woods, in search of Steller's jays, Clark's nutcrackers, western wood-pewees, and violet-green swallows, to name a few. So I am free to search for whatever news I can find through the rudimentary technology available to me. Cellular service seems to be null and void up here. Both the bus phone and my wireless have a big X where the little bars should be. I tried repositioning the bus all over the lot and it made no difference. Radio should be better than it is up here, but we are hemmed in by the dense evergreens of the Los Padres National Forest, and

Bus 477 happens to have the weakest radio reception in the fleet. In the age of instant information, this is extremely unsettling.

My first news is mostly unintelligible--it's in Spanish. There is a general rule in California that no matter how bad the radio reception is where you are, you can always get a Spanish station clearly. My four years of high school study, enhanced by a period of hands-on practice during that short stint near the border in Arizona, are enough to help me pick up many individual words, but the clunky pace of my translation is too slow to build intelligible sentences at the speed of a native speaker. I keep hearing *aviones*--plural of "airplane," from the same Latin root as *ave,* "bird"--and *Estados Unidos*, but I cannot put much together beyond that.

The next station is out of Los Angeles. It is English, but they keep talking about the "tragic events of the morning" without explaining what those events are. The discussion is also limited to the effect they are having on Los Angeles, mainly the closing of LAX. Typical southern California solipsism. The DJ reads an enormous list of closed facilities and canceled events in the region. For all I know, Los Angeles could be in the throes of a freak blizzard.

It does put things into a strange perspective though. Everything, from kindergarten classes to Major League Baseball games, is coming to a sudden halt. 2,600 miles from the nearest terrorist attack, everyone has stopped to watch, to weep, to try and wrap their minds around the magnitude of this tragedy.

But the American Birders Association Regional Conference marches on. Birds do not recognize a national crisis, I suppose, so neither shall the birders.

No, there's no way to spin this and make it come out right. Someone is fucking with me. This is not happening. I am not sitting here in a bus waiting for a bunch of people to bird while the rest of America huddles together with one eye on the TV and the other anxiously scanning the skies. I mean, what's next? Are my family and friends in Boston and Philadelphia sitting in someone's crosshairs? What about military bases? Refineries? *Nuclear power plants?*

Christ, there is one on the coast not ten miles outside Cayucos. Someone could attack Diablo Canyon from the air without even crossing American soil, and Nadia is within the instant melt-down zone right now. How safe should I feel today?

Groan... My dander is not all the way up yet, but it is rising rapidly. I want to blame the Birds straight-up, but I realize this could be unfair. The decision may have been handed down from above, from that executive they had on the phone. A nameless, faceless force with no mercy in its soul, bidding us to bird in the face of terror. The Birds could merely be good foot soldiers, like I, handling edicts from above with aplomb.

Plus, who knows what would happen if the masses were told immediately. I think they deserve the choice, but the freak-out potential is large. Could they have reached a consensus? Would a majority have wished to return to the hotel? I guess we will not know until they are told. But when, if ever, will that be?

On my third try the radio bears some informational fruit. It picks up a Bakersfield station that is running the CBS national news. I soon realize it is audio from the TV broadcast--they keep referring to video footage, maps, and diagrams that I am supposed to be able to see--but at least my questions are starting to be answered. This is how I learn each of the Twin Towers was hit by a different plane. It also reports that all four of the hi-jacked planes were bound for California: three for Los Angeles, one for San Francisco. Some of my passengers could have been on those same flights just yesterday. What seemed before to be an east coast event now has bicoastal ties, and I think about how many people on this side of the country were preparing to pick up business associates or friends or loved ones at LAX and SFO today–people who will never arrive.

They mention the Pentagon and a fourth plane that crashed in Pennsylvania, but barely, which seems like relatively good news. No reports of other planes hijacked before everything was grounded. Sounds like the worst is over back east--it is a living, waking nightmare, but the attacks are over.

Wait...what are left of the vital organs in my torso sud-denly hit the floor, and the air escapes from my lungs...did I just hear that right? The *World Trade Center* is *GONE?*

Suddenly, before I can mute the radio, Betty Pickett appears in the open doorway of the bus. She was strolling through the woods last I saw her, but now she is standing in the doorway with a look of pure shock.

"*What is going on?*" Every syllable is stressed. Her affect is pale and faint.

I tell her. She climbs the steps and stands by the radio, listening with palpable intensity. Her eyes close and she shakes her head, almost imperceptibly, like a mother who has warned her children a million times about their reckless behavior, and now it is too late. She does not speak. Here we are, I think, two people, two islands, sharing the same grim news. What is she thinking? How does this add up with the sum of her life experiences until now? I don't know, I cannot be her. I will never know.

A timeless interval is spent in this manner. I mostly stare at the radio and feel blank. When I glance at Betty now and then, her eyes are still closed; she seems to be in some contemplative state. Then, just like that, she says something cordial and returns to her seat near the back of the bus. She never struck me as the chatterbox type, but this seems unusually curt.

The radio continues its inverted mime routine, using words to fill in the pieces of a puzzle that we cannot see.

Once again, you are looking live at the World Trade Center in Manhattan, where about 90 minutes ago the second of the two main towers collapsed after being struck by a hijacked Boeing 767 earlier this morning. As you can see from this aerial footage looking east over the Hudson River, there is an enormous cloud of smoke and dust where New York's two tallest buildings once stood, and eyewitnesses on the ground tell us all that remains at the site are twisted metal and shattered glass, all manner of debris scattered everywhere and--"

I quickly twist the power knob off. I cannot hear anymore. How many people were in those buildings when they came down???

My stomach convulses and I dash out the door. There is hardly anything in my stomach so all I do is cough up some bile. No dinner last night, and no breakfast this morning except for that horrid prepackaged danish. I am now strangely aware, by its absence in me, of the emotional release experienced by bulimics when they binge and purge.

This suddenly makes me feel desperate to talk to Nadia. In my mind I am seeing the family photographs of some of the birthday parties she had as a young girl in the fancy restaurant on the top floor of one of the towers. It was not yesterday, but it wasn't that long ago either, as little as 15 years I am guessing. Some of the people who cooked and served her food might have died there this morning. Does she even know yet? Nadia is more of a media recluse than I am, but sometimes when she is especially uncomfortable in her body, she will use TV as a way to vacate. I could picture her needing that today after last night's disaster.

If she does know, there will undoubtedly be a half-dozen voice mails on my phone by now. I really need to find a signal. There are spots along the sides of the access road where the slope is too steep for trees and a clear path to the sky opens up. Hoping I will find something down there, I take off in that direction, checking the clock on the phone to see how much time before lunch is served.

I hike down the road about a quarter-mile before the first opening in the trees. As best I can tell, I am facing southeast, looking down and out at a whole flotilla of mountains stretching beyond the horizon. We are not more than fifty air miles from the San Fernando Valley and the western edge of metro Los Angeles, but there are probably no cell towers in that whole fifty miles either, nor a single square mile of flat land. Interstate 5 snakes through the hills to the east about twenty miles from here near the crest of Grapevine Pass. But I have seen the cell phone coverage maps of California and they are a bunch of blobs where the cities are, with very thin lines radiating out along the major roadways. So I already know that the place where I stand is well within a blank zone. I am just wondering if I can try the same thing again and expect different results.

Sure enough, no service. That was the last hope. I am officially incognito until at least three o'clock.

I stare out at the small blue-gray humps on the horizon. Just beyond those hills, ten million people are huddled together and mourning, and here I stand alone, wanting nothing more than to be among them.

Suddenly, they are all gone.

Everyone out there, all over the world--gone, laid to waste. I am the only survivor.

The silence I perceived as refreshing a few moments ago as I walked down the access road is now eerie and foreboding, and I am feeling claustrophobic, as though invisible walls are closing in. My heart races and I feel slightly short of breath; anxiety is swallowing me whole. I do not panic, though. This will pass. I know it will because I have experienced this before. But the perception seems to eclipse my knowledge. In this moment, on some level of meta-cognition I cannot explain, I am aware that I killed everyone on earth, and I am standing here utterly alone.

"Well _____," I whisper to myself, using my real name. "You finally got your mountaintop." Ask and ye shall receive, I suppose.

The perception fades as I start to think about birds, a loophole that mercifully leads me back to the present. I trudge toward the bus, feeling heavy of foot and heavier of heart. Here and there through the trees I hear gaggles of birders, the rustle of footsteps on the pine forest floor and the sharing of scorecard details. I consider asking if anyone needs an albatross, since I have such a fine specimen hanging from my neck.

When I get back to the bus I flop into the driver's seat and rub my eyes; the tired is starting to come back. I absently turn the radio back on--same broadcast of the TV news audio--but quickly decide that this one-way forum is a very poor form of companionship. I desperately need to talk to someone. Betty is still in her seat with her head slightly bowed. I notice that her lips are moving, and I wonder if she is praying.

It is not like me to approach strangers like this in search of connection, and the natural flow of communication is often choked with anxiety. *What should I say?*

I rest my right knee on the seat in front of her, facing back as she continues to speak silently to herself.

"Excuse me, um...I was just wondering if you...do you have anyone you want to call?" *Now that's brilliant.* "You could try to use the bus phone."

She looks up and smiles again. "No, I'm OK. My family is in the Midwest. I imagine we'll contact them from the hotel. I do have a niece who lives in New Jersey and works in the city." Betty tails off briefly, as if reconsidering my offer for a moment. "But I surely would not be able to reach her now anyway. I know she is OK though. She's a real survivor. Besides, I'm sure there isn't much of a signal up here."

"Yeah, it's pretty bad." *Oh I can be such an idiot!* I lean forward a bit more, and notice that she has not been praying.
She is doing cross-stitch, counting to herself. A round frame sits on her lap, with a stitching of a small bird with a bright yellow chest and a black and white speckled back, with a prairie scene as a backdrop. Pretty and simple.

"That's beautiful," I tell her.

"Why thank you. It's almost done."

"What kind of bird is it? I don't have my field guide handy."

She laughs. "Western meadowlark. The black V over the yellow breast is the distinctive marking, I am told."

"Ah, your state bird. Cool."

Betty looks up now, intently, and amusingly puzzled. "How did you know *that*?"

"Your nametag." I point to the plastic badge pinned to the left side of her white windbreaker. It says "Betty Pickett--Smith Center, Kansas." She holds it up and reads it upside-down, then chuckles.

"Oh for heaven's sake, I forgot we were wearing these silly things! Well, I am very impressed that you know our state bird. I don't imagine that is common knowledge in California."

"It isn't. Probably not anywhere," I reply with an inward smirk. There is no way she knows what she is getting herself into here. "I just have kind of a freakish memory for details when it comes to geography. No other field of knowledge, mind you. Just geography."

"Oh? What else can you tell me about Kansas?"

"Ha, I'll do you one better than that. I can tell you that Smith Center sits at the junction of US Highways 36 and 281, right about where the Great Plains in the west transition into the eastern prairie. Population of, oh, about 2,000? And it's maybe twenty minutes west of the geographical center of the 48 states in Lebanon."

Betty looks at me as though I had just recited the atomic weight of each element in Group 18 of the periodic table. She lets out a laugh that slices through any tension remaining from "the tragic events of the morning." I wish everyone had to wear a nametag telling the world where they are from. It makes for the perfect icebreaker.

"Nineteen hundred, actually...I have never, ever, met *anyone* on my travels who has even heard of Smith Center! I usually have to tell people I'm from fifteen miles west of the middle of *nowhere!* Or as the locals like to call it, "the Middle of Everywhere." Are you from Kansas, too? Or did you really learn that from studying geography?"

"Well, before my wife and I moved to California, I spent most of the past ten years cris-crossing the country, both as a professional and amateur vagabond. There are only so many roads you can take from east to west across America, and I'm pretty sure I've tried them all. So there aren't many towns that I don't know with some intimacy. Although I have a particularly good story for how I met Smith Center. I found Highway 36 when I was getting around by delivering cars. The agencies that match drivers with cars to be delivered always put a strict limit on the mileage, enough cushion to give you some room to roam, but not an unlimited amount. Well one time, I discovered that Route 36 saves about fifty miles on the trip from Denver to Indianapolis as opposed to staying on I-70. That saved my bacon more than once."

"Oh my goodness, we have a son in Denver, and we always drive down to Russell to get on the interstate. My husband insists it's faster."

"I'm sure it is. Ol' 36 slows down for every town it crosses; I don't think there's a single bypass west of St. Joseph. But if time is ever the lesser part of making 'good time' for you, I highly recommend it. I just love the sky in your part of the world. So unbelievably vast. I could stare into it and get lost for hours when I'm there...so I'm curious: how does one make a living in a place like Smith Center? I find myself drawn to towns like that, but I always get sucked back into long haul driving when I try to settle down in one."

"My husband had a position in the Smith County government that kept us comfortable. He retired four years ago with full pension. Now he works for himself leading local birding expeditions--I bet you didn't know that we are the upland bird capital of America?"

"Huh, no, that fact had somehow escaped me."

"Well you've never been on one of Melvin Pickett's birding adventures! He also writes free-lance articles, mostly for birding journals. And I operate a bed-and-breakfast out of our home on Main Street."

"Really? I wouldn't have guessed that Smith Center could support a B & B."

"Our connections in the birding world definitely help. And you'd be surprised how many people still pass through, probably a lot of folks like yourself drawn to the big sky country."

"No kidding, that's fantastic. How many rooms?"

"Just five. I should say that the front half of the house is a B & B. The back half is run more like a hostel. We overcharge the B & B folks so we can afford to run the other half on donations. Many guests end up staying for free."

"What a brilliant idea! All businesses should be run on that model."

"I've found that people with money find more value in something if they are asked to pay more, and people without money appreciate the chance to experience something they wouldn't otherwise. This way, everyone is happy."

"That's *amazing*, Betty. I wish I'd known you were there; I would have stayed with you that one time. Oh, so how I got to know Smith Center--you'll like this story. So the next time I took 36 I was heading west, and I decided this time I could spare the eight mile round trip to head up to the monument marking the center of the forty eight states. It was close to midnight by the time I got there, and I swear I didn't pass a single car all the way from Belleville. Just as empty as you can imagine a road ever being. So when I got there I felt like I was on my own planet. I thought it would be a real hoot to spend the night at the center of the forty eight states. It was close to midnight by the time I got there, and I swear I didn't pass a single car all the way from Belleville. Just as empty as you can imagine a road ever being. So when I got there I felt like I was on my own planet. I thought it would be a real hoot to spend the night at the center of America, and I got settled into my little nest I had set up in the hatchback. Maybe a half-hour later, it was getting a little warm inside the car so I went to open the window a crack...and I looked over at some kind of caretaker's shed, and there was a light on inside that I could see through the window. I hadn't even noticed if it were on before, but I looked around and there were still no other cars...and then I saw someone pass in front of the light through the window. I don't know what I thought was going to happen to me, but I got so spooked by it, I jumped back in the driver's seat and tore out of there as fast as I could! I drove straight to Smith Center and got a twenty dollar room at the Prairie Winds Motel."

"Goodness gracious! I think I would have been spooked, too. You know, I grew up on a farm about four miles due east of that spot. I even remember when they built that monument: 1940, I was eight years old. The whole town was there. Everyone thought it would turn Lebanon into a tourist attraction."

"Ah. I guess the boarded-up hotel nearby suggests how well that went over."

Betty laughs. "Yes, it wasn't exactly Mount Rushmore. But it's our little claim to fame, I suppose. Do you know how they determined the exact center? They took a cardboard cutout of the United States--this was before Alaska and Hawaii, remember-- and they found the place at which it would balance on a point! Isn't that something?"

"Interesting... I guess that might make you one of the most balanced Americans in history."

"I never thought of it that way, but maybe so," says Betty with a smile. "And it's a chapel, by the way, not a shed."

"Really? But it's so *tiny*."

"Room for four in there, I've heard."

"Huh...well then that makes total sense. Someone was just having a midnight mass at the geographical center of America." We share a laugh about that. Interesting that at the balance point of the continental United States, there is a place of worship, be it ever so humble.

"So how about other family? Do you have brothers or sisters that stayed local, too?"

"I have an older brother named Alasdair who stayed in Kansas. He passed away in 1980. And I have a younger sister named Ione; she owns a bookstore and coffee shop in Kansas City. They each have two daughters, one of whom is in New Jersey, and the other three are in Missouri, Nebraska, and Iowa. And I have five boys who are scattered. We're a far-flung family, but mainly based in the heartland"

I nod, not sure where to take the conversation from there. I am very curious about what it was like to grow up--and, perhaps, spend all of one's life--so close to the center and not ping ponging from one side to the other. But I am having trouble formulating a question for some reason. Then Betty beats me to it.

"Where do you call home?"

Her question catches me strangely off guard. I had been wandering in the ethers of my road trip mind, and I seem to have forgotten it is possible to have a place called "home."

"Huh?"

"Well, you mentioned that you and your wife moved to California recently, so I was curious where you are from."

"Oh right, of course." I chuckle a bit at my inability to understand her straight-forward question. But it is a genuine stumper. I honestly do not know what to say. "Jeez, I guess I have many homes. Too many perhaps. So many that none really stand out."

"OK, so where were you raised?" I can tell by Betty's expression and tone that she is not just making small talk, that she is genuinely interested and wants to help me put together this puzzle.

Yes, that would be a fine answer. Concentrate.

"Well, I grew up in a small French-Canadian farming village in New Hampshire. Not all that different than Smith Center, with more trees."

"Oh, that sounds quite nice. Did you like it there?"

"No. I hated it. It felt like everyone was in everyone else's business, and there was so much pettiness and backstabbing. Kids were mercilessly cruel to each other because everyone knew every kid's weaknesses. And as I learned more and more about the world through my geography books and map-reading fantasy trips, everything in my hometown felt so...insignificant. I couldn't wait to get out and go someplace where things happened that mattered. So I went to Washington DC for college to study political journalism."

"Oh, how interesting. How did you like that?"

"Well, I learned pretty quickly what it means when 'things happen' in the political realm--I don't know how *anyone* could want to devote a life to documenting that much foolishness. City life was the equal and opposite kind of undesirable. People were so disconnected from each other and afraid of crime. And everything they did had this layer of, I don't know...self-im*port*ance... and it all seemed so fake, because in reality it is no less small and insignificant than what happens in a small town, maybe even less so because people are less likely to help each other now and then...so no, I didn't like the big city any better. I got out of there as soon as I could, kind of forgot to get my diploma first."

"I see. And I'm guessing that was when your nonstop travel began?"

I start to wonder if we should move to the bench seat at the back, so I could halfway lie down and treat it like a therapist's couch. But it feels refreshing and nice to be asked these kinds of questions by someone who seems to care about the answers.

"Yeah, more or less. I guess I had the idea that the extremes would be more tolerable if I kept moving. And that works in some ways. But it gets lonely...I think that's why I have always traveled with an eye out for someplace that would be different...something more like a community. I learned that it really isn't the size or scale of a place that makes it a community--the suburbs, for instance; somehow they feel like the worst of both worlds, despite what developers and real estate agents want us to believe. I think what makes a community is a special state of mind; people can find it in the country or the city, or anywhere in between...but it's rare. The more elusive I find it to be, the harder it feels to keep it myself. What I have been dreaming of lately feels more like a hermitage than a community...that scares me a little. I'm not always my own best company."

"I hope you'll pardon me for saying so, but it sounds like you've been pretty unhappy wherever you go."

Her polite bluntness strikes a good chord with me. It produces a gentle forcefulness that I find exceptional. Most people will give you one or the other, but rarely both at one time. My contrarian nature is no match for it.

"You're right. I hate to admit it, but that's one thing I have learned from trying so many different places. I always think each one is going to have the special ingredient that makes it feel like home, but they never do because it's not something missing in the places I live. It's me."

A few moments pass in which Betty looks pensive, like she isn't sure how to ask her next question, or maybe whether she should ask at all.

"...May I ask you a question about your name?"

Uh-oh. I'm busted.

"Sure."

"I've been curious ever since you introduced yourself this morning...you don't look much like a Pedro."

I have to laugh a little at the difference in decorum between Betty and Floyd. I do not know if my face conveys how thick and thorough the mask about to be pulled off is, but I am feeling it.

"I'm not...a Pedro, I mean. I'm someone else."

"Oh?"

I didn't think she'd accept that answer.

"It started as an inside joke between my wife and me. I guess I just turned it more outside than it was intended to be. Now it's to the point where everyone I know in California knows me as Pedro--even my boss, who has seen my driver's license."

"May I ask what your real name is?"

I tell her. Even as I say it, it doesn't sound like me. Everyone is born and given a name, and most people are content to call themselves by that name. Some realize that is not who they really are, and choose to call themselves something that feels more appropriate to who they have become. My chosen name is Anonymous.

"Well, I think that is a beautiful name," says Betty, just a touch defiantly, "much more becoming of you."

"Thanks. I don't disagree really, I just...it reminds me of things I don't want to remember."

Betty's expression shifts from sympathy to deep concern.

"Like *what*?"

Her emphasis softens the question rather than sharpens it. She probably expects to hear something much more shocking than she will. I always feel stymied at this point in the What's-Wrong-With-Me conversation. I was never abused or neglected, in fact if anything my parents cared too much about me and not nearly enough about each other. To be an empathic heterosexual son of white middle class America is to suffer greatly, but entirely from confusion and guilt. So much of what I feel and identify as painful does not happen to *me;* to talk about what *does* feels whiny and ridiculous. But to propose that one could feel the suffering of others as *though* it were one's own--this seems to be taken as an invitation to question my sanity. I have learned that there is no good course of action except to pretend there is nothing wrong from the start. But I have already let the proverbial cat out of the bag, and Betty's concern is genuine, so it deserves to be addressed thoughtfully.

I am not feeling very creative right now, though, so I rely on one of my stock answers.

"A few years ago I was reading an interview with one of my favorite punk rock musicians, and he was asked about his reputation for being particularly misanthropic, even by punk standards. His reply was, 'Unfortunately, yes, but only because I care so much about people that I can't stand how they treat each other. The world seems to provide endless justification for defending the honor of the weak by hating the strong. And the problem is everyone wants to be the strong one all the time. Where is the honorable person who is content to be moved by the world on its own terms? Why wait to inherit the earth when it's all for sale, and you can steal the money from your neighbor to buy it?' That really resonated with me. I think I started feeling that at a very young age, too young for it to make any sense. It's something that I'm still working out in my mind."

Betty's eyes still express the same concern, but her overall expression is shaped more like a question mark, and she has no words for it. Maybe I lost her at "punk rock." Or maybe the only appropriate remedy for someone who claims to hate people for hating people is to slap him across the face and say "Stop it!" and Betty is too kind to do that. In any case, we seem to have hit a wall. It is a familiar wall, the same one I cannot get past on my own.

Maybe someday when someone asks me the same questions, I will have the temerity to talk about Celine Lafleur, the beautiful strawberry blonde from just up the road, the girl of my 6th grade dreams who openly stared at me one day while I walked down the school bus aisle--mouthful of metal and face prematurely peppered with zits--then turned to her friend and whispered *"he's so ugly."* Maybe I will talk about all the times my parents said the most horrible things to each other, supposedly in the seclusion of their bedroom, apparently unaware of the audible conductivity of heating vents. Or just the endless barrage of backbiting comments meant to go undetected by the world at large, but rendered all too real by my supersonic ears and unrelenting memory. I might go on to explain how I have blamed myself for being there, how the cruelty would not exist if I were not there to hear it. Someone might respond with a great platitude such as how I need to let go of all that, to accept that there is cruelty and ugliness in the world because without it we would not recognize the kindness and beauty that comes with it. And maybe I will feel desperate enough to buy into it. Until that happens, I guess I will have to remain an enigma to the Betty Picketts of the world, and they to me as well.

Having exhausted our momentum with this topic, I search my mind for anything else, but we inevitably return to the news of the day.

"So you are from the east coast then," Betty says, down-shifting her expression back to friendly conversational. "Do you have any family in New York?"

"No, I don't. Everywhere else, but not there. My wife does, though. She's really the one I'm concerned about reaching. Haven't been able to yet..." My voice trails off as I picture Nadia curled up in the fetal position on our couch, sobbing while televised dust clouds rise to the heavens from a hole where the greatest landmark in the cityscape of her childhood memories used to be. The bile comes back to my voice as I think about why I am not home to comfort her.

"Yeah, I can't believe we're still *out here* so a bunch of people can watch *birds.* The LA station says everything there has been *cancelled*, and we're...it just makes no sense."

"Well, I'm sure the group leaders just don't know yet. When they get--"

"They do. She talked to someone right after we turned on Azucar Mountain Road, and she told *me.* That's why I had the radio on."

Now Betty looks a little perplexed, too. "I see...I guess I agree with you then. This doesn't seem like a day for business to go on as usual."

We continue along that line of thought, agreeing that this news should not and cannot be sat upon indefinitely--somewhere between here and Santa Maria, the birders need to be told. Great, I'm thinking, I have an ally. Maybe we can lead an insurrection against the Birds and I will steer this bus back to civilization, putting an end to this veil of blissful ignorance.

But even as I fantasize about this, I know Betty would not relate to this mode of thought, no more than she does to the ruminations of a punk rocker. It is not in her nature. There is a Midwestern mildness in the way she expresses herself. She may not agree with the Birds' decision, but it is clear that she yields to it unquestioningly, as though her own opinion is a dubious guide that must not be trusted. It is not a matter of "my leaders, right or wrong." The decision happens before thought. She seems to make a subconscious choice that, in any given situation, imposing her will cannot make things better, only worse.

It is an interesting worldview. I associate it mostly with the rural areas of the heartland, what we pretentious bicoastals call the "flyover states" as if they are wasted space with nothing of value. You do not encounter it much on either coast or in big cities. Not anymore. We urbanites accept things when we are happy, and when we're not, we try to change them. If we do not, we feel passive, weak. We are victims.

Today is a perfect example. Our country is under attack. The group leaders are protecting the passengers from this information; I want to tell them. They say the show must go on; I say we should go home. Therefore, I want to challenge their authority. I am resisting out of a sense of professional duty, but I am hardly at ease. I feel subjugated.

Their will has nullified mine.

But wait. That is just an assumption, on many levels. Like I mentioned before, it is not clear who made the call on the news embargo. Whose will would I be challenging? The Birds? Or someone above them on the ABA hierarchy?

Or (gulp) someone even higher than that?

I do not know if Betty Pickett is a religious person. I tend to assume that all people from the Smith Centers of this country are at least semi-devout Christians, just like they all have pink houses and white fences and moms who bake apple pies. She could be a militant atheist or a voodoo priestess for all I know. But there is no mistaking a person with true peace in her heart. And the more I study her, the deeper her source of steadiness seems to be. She is not immune to pain; her initial reaction to the news showed that. It is what she does with her emotions-- or does not do, perhaps--that makes all the difference. I think I demonstrated earlier where suppression of my feelings is getting me. But Betty does not suppress her feelings; she subordinates them. There is a higher power involved.

Here, this is what I am trying to say. I'll rephrase an earlier statement. It will explain everything:

She may not agree with God's will, but she yields to it unquestioningly.

This is a huge assumption of course, but I would bet my life on it. God's will. That is what Betty perceives and I don't. That is why I fight and she doesn't. I have a hundred questions for her now, but the birders are coming back from their hike and I am pressed into action. I help Bird #2 unload the boxed lunches from the luggage bay and distribute them to the hungry crowd. We will do lunch up here for a half-hour or so, then move on to a campsite farther back into the forest. Bird #1 is chirping about what a great spot this is for mountain chickadees. I resist the temptation to give her a bird of my own. Sorry, but over 5,000 people are dead or missing in New York City alone, so I am not in the mood to hear what a treat it is that the green-tailed towhees are lingering after the breeding season.

When all the lunches are served, Bird #1 confides to me that she is worried sick and she intends to tell everyone before the next stop, a little while after they have eaten. Good plan, I say. Proper digestion is crucial. The birders have scattered about the lot, many sitting on the porch of a wooden lodge. How odd it is to walk among these elders, all munching on turkey sandwiches, apples, and chips, sipping juice boxes like school kids. I feel like the sole possessor of some horrible knowledge that will rip them from their second childhood. I know so little about today's atrocity, but they know nothing. It does not even exist in their worlds yet.

But it will. There is no escape.

ACT IV

12:20 pm (PDT) / 3:20 pm (EDT)

*M*ark this date on your calendar, babe...wherever you are. I say these words to myself very deliberately, almost moving my lips with them. There have been times when Vera seems to hear me telepathically, and I would not put it past her to have mastered the trick if it is humanly possible. So why not give it a try?

What I want Vera to know right now is that, while sitting in the waiting room at the Jersey City Medical Center, I tossed aside the *Sports Illustrated 2001 NFL Preview* issue. It completely disinterested me.

Initially, I was curious what the pundits thought of my Giants' chances this season after the butt-kicking they received in the Super Bowl back in January. But as soon as I found out, I realized how utterly irrelevant that information was, adding nothing of value to my life. Even worse, it stole valuable attention from what does matter.

I also realized that for all the time I had logged in doctor's office waiting rooms with Vera over the past several months, I had actually spent very little time *with* her. Vera is not one to ask for attention, and damn me, I have exploited this fact to vacate myself into magazine world and avoid the situation at hand. Like my mother all over again.

Knowing Vera, I'm sure she is just waiting patiently for me to learn that this is my loss, not hers. She could have repeated that fact to me hundreds of times over many years and it would never sink in. I had to hear it from myself.

Then something even more amazing happened. I started in with what I usually do when I realize the error of my ways, which is to feel dreadfully sorry and sort of pummel myself with guilt (Vera often teases me for holding onto the worst aspects of Catholicism while keeping none of the best). But then I stopped. I felt a new directive. I'm still not sure where it came from...it sure *sounded like* something Vera would say, and I don't have the foggiest clue where else it could have come from...but it distinctly felt like my own voice, only like nothing I've ever heard before. At that moment, I knew with absolute certainty that I was already forgiven. *"Don't belittle yourself,"* the voice said. *"You are growing into a greater being. This is a time for self-expansion."*

Now I don't pretend to know exactly what that meant, and I'll be damned if I understand why I'm suddenly hearing a voice in my head that refers to itself as "you." But I do know how grateful I am for the one person in the world who has taken the time to assure that I wouldn't think I was going bat shit crazy if I ever did.

Thank you, my dearest. I have a lot of time to make up...please be safe, my love....

Right now, though, I know Vera would insist, this time belongs to a woman named Estelle Platt, who lies in the Critical Care unit, still unconscious. At least, that is the last I heard about her, more than 45 minutes ago. It has been very difficult to squeeze any information out of the hospital staff. Alas, showing up with her purse in order to establish her identity was a dead giveaway that I'm not a family member.

The purse did not have the loosest of lips either. It did reveal her driver's license with a Kansas City address, which matched the Missouri plates on the hatchback. There was nothing to immediately tie her to any family members. Her cell phone was locked, and she carried no address book. I did find a half-completed form to file for divorce in Missouri, which indicated that once official, Estelle will go back to her maiden name, Boncoeur. I considered looking up the Edward Platt character who is still officially her husband, until I saw "physical abuse" listed as one of the reasons for the divorce...*that black eye premonition...spooky...* so there could be a damn good reason she is living in New Jersey and doesn't want him to know where she is.

I also found a receipt for lab work that was done this morning, showing a local address. She too happens to be living in Union. Looked like a lot of blood was drawn, but no indication why. Maybe that was why she fainted under distress?

The most valuable clue in her purse was a matter of pure coincidence. I was scanning the photographs in an accordion-style sleeve inside her wallet, and recognized a woman who was in several of the pictures--long, curly blonde hair, fairly stocky build, kind of a tomboyish type. She wore a cowgirl hat and boots with blue jeans in most of the pictures, but not in any of my memories, so that threw me off for a moment. But then a couple photos included a small boy about Mira's age with coffee-colored skin...ah, right: I had seen them at Small Wonders. We've crossed paths a few times in the morning when I need to be at the office early, not often but enough to leave an impression.

(I'm ashamed of this and would never speak of it to anyone, but that impression was a mild uneasiness at seeing a "mulatto" child among Mira's playmates. My Nonna Lioni--the D'Angelo family matriarch and a very old school Sicilian--blamed every social ill since the 1960s on "race mixing" and never missed an opportunity to ingrain this in her impressionable descendants. Even now, ten years after she died, I must remind myself that children of interracial parents are not "neither black nor white," but *both*, and culturally richer for it.)

The last picture in the sleeve came from one of those formal portrait studios where families go to look as stiff and respectable as possible for posterity. This photograph included the boy's father, a tall, dark-skinned man who I did not recognize. It did appear, despite the rigid poses orchestrated by the photographer, that this was a happily united couple.

With this as my only real lead, I called the day care center to ask about the woman.

"She has long blonde hair, looks like a country western singer."

"Oh," said the receptionist at Small Wonders, "you don't know how appropriate that is. Her name is Melody Weaver. And her son Malcolm is Mira's best buddy."

"No kidding." Ah, life.

"Oh yes, they are *inseparable*. I'm surprised you haven't met Melody yet. Vera says they've been having weekend play dates at your house."

I cringe as I contemplate whether this will get back to Vera, and the "beautiful world outside your man cave" lecture I will get if it does.

"So have you heard from Vera?" She continues, her voice now weighed down with gravity.

"No, not yet. But my cell phone is useless and I haven't been home yet, so that doesn't mean she hasn't tried."

"Well we are all praying for her, of course. If I know Vera, she's probably rescuing people from the towers right now."

"Thanks Lynette, you're probably right. I've been thinking that myself, but it's good to hear someone else staying positive. You know how pissed she'd get if she found out we were worrying."

"That's the spirit, Joseph, keep it up. I'll try to reach you at the hospital if I hear anything. The girls are just fine here of course so don't worry about them. We're keeping everyone safe within their playful world today. No use worrying the kids with things they're not ready to understand."

Excellent. I feel much more connected now, having touched base with Small Wonders. If Vera lost her phone,

I figure, she won't know my number but she surely knows theirs. All the security I sought in a machine, I now have through connecting with another human being. The life lessons are coming fast and furious today.

I sure hope I can connect with Estelle Boncouer Platt very soon....

12:30 pm (PDT) / 3:30 pm (EDT)

We are backtracking again. Azucar Mountain was our turning point as well as our pinnacle, and the steep, winding access road is now a playground slide leading back to the main drag. Then we will head west a few miles along the ridgeline before turning south through the pines to our last stop of the day, the Meseta Centrada campground.

It has been almost seven hours since the first metal bird plunged into the behemoth facade of the World Trade Center; seven hours since the loudest wake-up call America has ever received; seven hours since the American Birders Association hit the snooze button on Bus 477.

Of the forty-five people taking this chartered trek through birding Shangri-la, only five have any knowledge of the devastation in the northeast part of our country: Bird #1 and Bird #2, Betty and Melvin Pickett (assuming she told her husband), and me. The rest of our flock, for reasons that defy rational explanation, has been kept in the dark. An entire nation is in shock, activity everywhere has ceased, yet Bus 477 keeps on rolling like nothing has happened.

And I am at the helm, captain of a captain-less ship.

I am starting to regret how I handled that conversation with Betty. As the only other non-birder on the bus, I suspect she shares my opinion that there are some wacked-out priorities in keeping this show on the road, that someone decided the pursuit of brown creepers and common snipes should go on in the face of a massive terrorist assault on American soil. I could almost understand if the only consideration were whether to give us a chance to contact our families and whatnot, but who is to say the assault is over, or that the east coast is the only target? This could be a planned lull in the action before a whole different phase of operations begins. We are all vulnerable, and being incommunicado actually endangers our lives today. Aside from my earlier thoughts about subordination of her own will, Betty seems level-headed enough to be able to explain to the Birds that the will of forty passengers has not even been considered because they have not been informed. That seems like the only hope for common sense to prevail here.

That is just a small portion of the regret, though. In a culture that is obsessed with expressing itself at all times, it can be painfully hard to find a good listener when one is really needed. Betty strikes me as just that kind of person. She demonstrated a willingness to help me, and I think I pushed her away with a tinge of my punk attitude. How nice it would be to have that moment back and simply come clean...but what's done is done, of course, and I cannot change that decision. I can only hope to get another chance before the day is over.

We arrive back at Azucar Mountain Road, and turn onto its straighter, flatter track. We are about twenty minutes from the campground now. Bird #1 stands up and takes the bus microphone in her left hand, chewing the fingernails on her right. I guess she has decided it is time to spill the beans. She queues the microphone but stalls, still very uncertain of how to proceed. I wonder what is going through her mind. Never in a kajillion years would she have imagined her role would entail such statesmanship. I guess I have to give her credit for dealing with such a difficult situation that lies far beyond her ken. The Birds were christened as leaders because of their knowledge of gadwalls, lesser yellowlegs, and American wigeons, not how to handle a national crisis.

She struggles, but the words get out.

"Ladies and gentlemen, I'm afraid I have to report some very unfortunate...um, some tragic news. This morning, four planes that took off on the east coast were hijacked, and crashed."

A collective gasp, then a soft din of "oh my God" and similar offerings. No hysterics, just a handful of questions, mostly "where?"

She tells them: two in New York City, one at the Pentagon, one in Pennsylvania.

There follows a period of what you could call "subdued unrest." Many of the statements that will be overheard in public for several weeks are said: laments about airport security and why we are so hated, how life "will never be the same again" (an odd phrase--when was life ever "the same?"), and so on. Not much emotion really. Maybe they do not feel personally affected yet. Not many conference participants hail from that sprawling east coast city known as "BosNyWash." Too much destruction of natural habitats for that to be a birding mecca, I imagine. Right now, for this group, it is probably on the level of a devastating earthquake that flattens a foreign city--it is horrible and tragic, but it doesn't affect *my* family.

All I want to hear, though, is someone get up and say we should consider quitting early, that we know too little about the state of our world, and that this is far more important than a birding expedition.

No one does.

Not a single person.

The Birds are not a rogue element controlling the flow of information, disallowing grown men and women from making a crucial life decision. They are just on the same wavelength. They knew how the people would react. They knew it would make no difference to their birding day. Betty probably knew that too, seeing as how she has globetrotted extensively among this subculture. My insurrection idea would not even get a talonhold with this flock.

Holy freakin' hell. Floyd was absolutely right. These people are total loony tunes. So much for my scheme to liberate them. Welcome to the Hotel California. The birders are prisoners of their own device.

Wow, Floyd.....I wonder how he is doing now. Our groups are

scheduled to swap trips tomorrow, and Annie's typical strategy is to keep driver and group paired together as much as possible, so I am almost certain that he will be doing this run tomorrow while I take my flock to Santa Barbara harbor to get their shot at chasing pelagic species. Perhaps it was nothing more than luck of the draw that our assignments were not reversed.

That is an intriguing thought, because as far as "where were you" stories go, Floyd and I could hardly be writing more contrasting ones about today, considering we started the morning in the same place. His birders left him alone for six or seven hours today to search for black skimmers and elegant terns. Meanwhile, Floyd is stationed in an active neighborhood in a bustling small city, the kind of place where I imagine normal life skidded to a halt this morning and everyone is gathered in front of a television or by a radio, in restaurants, stores, offices, gyms, barber shops--anywhere that they will not be alone in their grief. There are probably a half-dozen payphones within a two block radius of where Floyd is parked, too, so communication with anyone he might want to reach by phone is possible.

There is a heartbreaking irony in that. Here I am with a wife, plenty of family, and some good friends back east who I cannot reach, while Floyd has the world at his fingertips...but outside of his co-workers, I don't know if he has *anyone* to call. I really don't.

See, I know a little more about Floyd than I let on earlier... quite a bit more, in fact. And he knows *a lot* more about me.

Back in late July, Floyd and I were working together out in the arid northeast corner of SLO County, not far from where James Dean went splat in his Porsche at age 24. We were part of a three-bus gig that was supposed to involve running a continuous shuttle from a hotel to a wedding site and back. The father of the bride was a big time rancher with a spread of several thousand acres in the hill country northeast of Paso Robles. He had rented all the rooms in one of Paso's finest hotels, so our task was to meet his guests there at 5 pm and take them to the site somewhere on his ranch for the ceremony. After dinner, we were to start running shuttles back to the hotel, with the departures staggered to happen every half hour, until the winding down of the party, which we were told would be about 1 am.

It all looked good on paper, and the site itself was an absolute study in gorgeousness, the picture-perfect essence of the golden rolling hills of California. What rancher's daughter wouldn't dream of having her wedding on this hallowed land and dancing the night away under the diamond sky?

The first indication that this was not a fully baked idea, though, came when we arrived at the ranch and the end of the paved road and turned onto a primitive trail carved through the grass by pickup trucks. Two tire tracks of dirt were all that delineated our path, and the trail was just barely the width of a bus. It was hilly terrain so the trail was not the least bit straight, meaning there were many places where the rear tires of our forty foot buses off-tracked onto the rough stuff. We even had to ford a couple creek beds, one of which was almost impassible and even gave Floyd fits trying to clear it without bottoming out. It was only a four mile stretch but it took a good twenty five minutes to traverse, and was definitely the most hair-raising stunt I was ever asked to pull off with a bus--tops on a long, bizarre list.

The drive back to the hotel on the highway was about twenty minutes, making it roughly an hour and a half round trip. So the simple math of having three buses departing from both locations every half-hour made sense. But add some complexity to the math--I picture one of those word problems from grade school: if a bus leaves The Oaks at 7:30 going 55 mph, and another leaves the wedding site at the same time going 10 mph (and don't forget, there's a third one somewhere in between), where will the two buses meet? The answer, inevitably, many times over the course of the night, is on the Goddamn trail. And when a bus meets a bus coming through the ranch...there would be nowhere for one of them to go but *back*. As much as two miles. In the dark. So yeah, that was not happening.

But that was not even the most egregious error in planning made by the father of the bride: he stiffed us on dinner.

We found that out as we finally got to the front of the enormous line and were ready to sink our teeth into the tri-tip steak that had been tantalizing us for a half-hour. There were no meals apportioned for the drivers, we were told. Sorry.

Floyd was absolutely livid. "You don't bring people out into the fuckin' sticks," we all learned at great length and volume, "tell 'em they gotta work all night, and don't feed 'em. There's a way things are done in this business and that ain't it." I have never seen him so visibly put off by the carelessness of a customer--and Floyd is not one to shrug off an opportunity to be insulted. After going toe to toe with the head chef, Floyd took some time to cool down, and then took a more diplomatic approach with one of his lackeys. We were told to keep it on the down low, and we literally had our plates handed to us through the back of the tent, Jim Crow-style, but we were hooked up with healthy portions of dinner rolls, soup, side dishes, and salad. Floyd puffed out his chest and looked heroic, and we thanked him profusely (I did not have the heart to tell him that I didn't know we were supposed to be fed, so I had brought some leftover goulash).

If not for the Dinnergate scandal, I am sure Floyd would have worked out a deal where a bus would leave roughly every ninety minutes, waiting for the previous one to arrive back at the site before launching. But he was not going to lift a finger for "that dumb cowpoke fuck," even if he did own half of northeastern SLO County. We offered to stagger our departures an hour apart starting at 11 , but that did not work because only a few people wanted to leave at 11, which would have left too many passengers for the two remaining buses to carry. It was an utter fiasco. We all left en masse between 12:30 and 1:00. I did not hear a single guest complain, but the dumb cowpoke fuck sitting catty corner from me spent the whole ride to Paso talking about how he would "damn sure get that old troll farred," and by that I'm pretty sure he meant "fired." (Annie backed Floyd completely after she heard our version of the story.)

All this was a roundabout way of explaining that Floyd and I unexpectedly had over three hours to kill that night. Generally, drivers come prepared for layover time with one form of distraction or another--usually movies to watch on the bus VHS player--but no one had anything on hand that night. I didn't even bring my rucksack. So we did what men of the road have done for centuries, long before the VHS player was invented: we made a campfire, we sat around it and we shared stories. With the rear tires of Floyd's bus as a wind block behind a natural clearing, we dug a three-foot radius pit, gathered up just enough live oak and manzanita wood for a substantial fire, and used my logbook pages to get it started. It was the best layover of my career.

The third driver that night was a guy named Paul. He was a little younger than I, a former school bus driver who was Annie's most recent hire. He was a trim, athletic fellow, typical blonde-and-bronzed California outdoorsman who dabbles in every physical fitness activity under the sun. There was an infectious youthful energy he brought to the job; he was too green for the road to have taken its toll on him in that regard. I think Annie liked to pair us together with Floyd, mostly so we could learn from his experience, but also in the hope that our enthusiasm would rub off on him.

Despite working with Paul often over the previous three months, I did not know a whole lot about him. But I learned a lot that night. Like me, he had been pegged as an academic stud at an early age and carried great expectations into college, but drifted off that path due to restlessness--only for Paul it was exercise that motivated him, not wanderlust. When his would-be Cal Poly graduation class was matriculating, he was in the middle of hiking the entire length of the Pacific Crest Trail (I believe I was manning the fry station at a Jack In The Box in Seattle during mine). He grew up in Arroyo Grande and had barely been outside of California. His dream was to move to Hollywood and become a personal trainer to the stars. And he insisted that at age 27 he had never had a serious girlfriend--many casual ones, of course, but none whom he had considered marrying.

"That's the ticket, Paul," said Floyd while finishing up his bowl of Alaska king crab bisque and sourdough croutons. The din of revelry and up-tempo country dance hall music resounded from just a couple hundred yards away, a reminder that two lives had just merged in our presence. "Don't let *no one* tie you down. This is a single man's job. Don't be like this knucklehead here and try to keep someone happy at home while you're living your life out here."

That led me to talk about Nadia, which I do not usually do in too much detail--and definitely not much of the *true* story. No one who has never spent time with Nadia and me can really grasp our complexities or understand why we are still together, and these two were not likely exceptions. But there is something about a campfire in the hills under a starry night sky that acts like a truth serum...or maybe a funeral pyre to how you wanted everything to be.

"Damn, Pedro," said Paul when I was done with my eulogy. "No wonder you work so much."

I shrugged. "I just love to drive."

Floyd let out a snorting laugh. Few people have as good a knack for inappropriate laughter as Floyd.

"C'mawn, Pedro. No one loves to drive *that* much!"

I knew he was right, but I was feeling oppositional. "Alright, Mr. 30 Day Tours of America, what's kept *you* rolling all this time? I have a hard time believing you've been single your whole life."

Floyd stared at his empty bowl for a few seconds. Across a patch of sagebrush, on the other side of a gently sloping hill, the bride tossed her bouquet.

"Yeah. I was married once.... Twenty-one years."

Whoa. Paul and I looked at each other, both raising our eyebrows. I had no idea how right I was about that. Floyd seemed to be hoping that was enough information for us, but the silence betrayed our curiosity. He took a deep breath.

"Our youngest daughter had turned 18 about a month before. She ran off to live in some hippie commune in Mendocino. You know, *whatever*...so I was doing five-day runs down the coast out of Eugene: Crater Lake, Redwood Park, San Fran, Monterey, all that shit. I'd come home in the middle of the fifth night, then have two days off before going back out. I did those for several months. Easy gig, made great money, piece o'cake."

"So one day I wake up, and my wife's sitting at the table reading the paper. She'd made breakfast for us just like she always did. I sit down next to her and I ask her what's new. She says, "Floyd, I'm leaving." So I says, "Oh, where ya going?" and she says, "I don't know yet. I'm just leaving." She doesn't even look up from the paper! So I'm thinking, Yeah right, she's leaving, and I just went on eating breakfast. She didn't mention it again the whole two days.

"But when I came back from the next trip, she was gone. Moved in with her sister up in Beaverton. Even took all the goddamn furniture. Ain't datta bitch!"

Floyd guffawed at the memory. Paul and I were speechless. I didn't know whether to laugh with him or hug him and try to get him to cry. After a few awkward moments, Floyd seemed to get his gravity back, and continued in a more subdued tone.

"So that's when I started doing the thirty-day loops. I figured there wasn't nuthin' to stay home for. The kids were all scattered all over the place, and they acted like they had no idea who I was anyway. So I went to my boss and I told him to work me...and he sure as hell did...."

Floyd's voice tapered off at the end. I was transfixed on a cluster of stars near the eastern horizon, then suddenly noticed there was no sound aside from the crackle of the fire. It stayed that way for close to a minute, before an eruption of hootin' and hollerin' from over the hill broke the spell. I have been to enough textbook weddings to guess that this somehow involved a garter belt.

"So that was it?" said Paul, speaking for both of us. "You never tried to reconcile after that?"

"It was like she disappeared completely. Never even saw her in court, she let her lawyer handle everything."

"And your kids?"

"Haven't seen 'em since. I think she trained them to hate me like some people train their dog to roll over. Never laid a hand on any of them, neither. I guess I just wasn't there. In-laws wrote me off completely too. Her parents called me "son" for twenty-one years, and then they didn't call me nuthin' ever again!"

This was the closest Floyd seemed to being genuinely angry during the whole conversation. Maybe this was a particular sore spot. I just couldn't take it anymore.

"Jeez, man, I just...I don't know what to say...I'm so sorry. This must have been killing you all these years."

Floyd rubbed his chin for moment, as though trying to decide whether to accept my sympathy. Then he let out a throaty "Naaah!" and dismissed it with a backhanded wave.

"Don't feel sorry for me. They just forced me to do what I shoulda been doing all along. I know you guys think I complain too much on this job, and yeah, there's lotsa things I'd change about this business if I could. But at the end of the day, I love what I do, too, and that's why I'm still out here. I've seen some amazing, beautiful shit out here. Shit that'd make your eyes pop outta your head. Never woulda seen *none* of it if I stayed in Oregon, know what I mean?

"There was this one time I had a group way out on the coast up in Maine, right up next to FDR's place up in Canada. We pull in late, like maybe 10 o'clock, and it's the end of a 16-hour day so I'm just beat to shit. So I'm getting everyone checked in at the hotel, and the desk clerk says, 'You oughta get up and see the sunrise. It's gonna be at 4:30 tomorrow.' So I laugh at him and I says, 'Ha, I'm gonna be sleeping til 4:30 in the *afternoon* tomorrow.' But damn if I didn't think of what he said before I went to sleep, and I set my alarm for 4:15. And when I woke up and went outside--oh my fucking Lord, the *whole Goddamn* sky was pink and orange and purple, and it was all reflecting on the ocean, and all the bunch of dark islands there in the harbor standing out like shadows...most beautiful Goddamn thing I ever seen in my life. Took my breath away. Now how you think an Oregon country boy like me is gonna see the *sunrise* over the ocean in *Maine* unless someone sent me there in a bus? That musta been thirty years ago, and I can still see it like it happened yesterday."

I had heard Floyd monologue about a great variety of things in my time working with him, but that was the first time I ever heard him wax poetic about something he saw while driving. What a wonderful feeling to see that dimension emerge from him, as if he had been a cardboard cutout of himself all that time and suddenly became a real person with life and breath and a beating heart.

"Christ," he continued, "I'm 67, I could retire tomorrow if I wanted to! But there's nuthin' I can imagine doing that gives me more satisfaction than getting out on the road and doing what I do best, and showing jokers like you how to do it right, too."

Paul and I both seem to recognize that, coming from Floyd, "joker" is something of a term of endearment. Floyd had been leaning back on the milk crate he was using for a seat with his back against the bus, but then sprung up and leaned forward with his elbows on his knees, talking with his hands like he had suddenly turned Italian.

"Now I want you two to listen to this real good, OK? There's some men that are meant to stay home and raise a family, and there's some that ain't. The way I figure it, there's gotta be some folks that are born to do this kind of work, or else nobody'd be able to go anywhere! If you're one of these people, that's great, don't be ashamed of it...but be *honest* with yourself and the people in your life. Don't find out the hard way like I did. Cuz this ain't just a job. You gotta be dedicated to this like you would be to a family. If you're doing this just for a paycheck, it's gonna break your back. You ain't gonna be good for the people and you ain't gonna be safe. Every company's got a handfulla these guys and they're the most miserable sons a'bitches to work with cuz they're only half there."

Paul and I both nodded and chuckled under our breath. We knew he was talking about Annie's husband. He had the most seniority at Eldorado, got the choicest assignments and probably the most hours as well, but in half a year of working with him I don't think I have ever seen him smile.

"OK, so here's how I see you two. Paul, you're a first class guy, always cheerful, the passengers *love* you. You work like a mule, and you're safe as hell while you do it. School bus training did you great. And you love your independence. That's something a person just *has*, you can't train that. The only question I got about you is, do you really love life on the road enough to do this week after week, year after year? Cuz it seems to me that you'd rather be bangin' movie stars after they take your aerobics class.

And that's great, I get it. You just gotta decide if that's your thing in life, and if it is, *go do it!* Don't try to do this while you're heart is somewhere else, it'll never work."

Paul nodded softly. Seemed from his expression like Floyd had him pretty well pegged.

"Now *you*, Pedro," and he turned square to me as he said that, "don't you dare let this go to your head...but you got everything it takes to be the best driver I ever worked with."

Really? He had never said anything like that directly to me before. I must have had a puzzled look on my face as he continued.

"See, you have no Goddamn clue about it either, and I like that, so I have no idea why I'm telling you this. But in forty years I ain't never seen a rookie driver like you. *Forty years.*"

I looked at Paul, and he smirked and nodded in agreement. "He just tells me to watch whatever you do, and do that," he chuckled.

"I mean," continued Floyd, "you keep your mouth shut and you listen, you take directions perfect, you have a fuckin' photographic memory of every Goddamn *map* you ever *looked* at, which is ri*dic*ulous. And you drive the bus like it's part of your body. I noticed that on your Goddamn drive test--*nobody* is that smooth on a drive test! You react to shit before it even *happens*, and you got Goddamn ice water in your veins. There ain't a place I been in this whole Goddamn country where I wouldn't let you ride my tail to get to--hell, I'd even follow *you* to most.

"But the biggest thing of all I've noticed about you, Pedro, is that you care about the passengers more than anyone I've ever known. *Anyone.* That's another thing you can't teach no one, they just gotta have it."

I was starting to wonder if Floyd had brought a whiskey flask and snuck a few swigs. He turned and started speaking directly to Paul.

"So back in February Annie tells me she's gonna send Pedro with me to Mammoth on an overnight run. So I says 'Annie, what the hella you doin' sending a Goddamn truck driver to the mountains in the winter? If we gotta chain up, he's gonna think he can sit on the side of the road and wait til spring!' And you know how Annie gets, so she says to me, "Oh *Floyd*, he'll be *Fine*. He's Handled Stuff like that Before."

(I laughed inwardly upon hearing that. At that point I had not chained a tire since driver training school, and that was indoors on a dry carpeted floor, not outside in a snowstorm. And Floyd was right about truck drivers--every trucking company I have worked for tells its drivers, "If it's bad enough to chain 'er up, it's bad enough to shut 'er down".)

"Sure enough, come afternoon of the second day, we're getting walloped up there, it's a Goddamn whiteout. Plows can't keep up with the snow coming down on the access road. Hell, it's even been a few years since *I* dealt with shit like this. So we're loading up all the skis and stuff, and the group leader on Pedro's bus starts panicking about how we'll never make it down the hill, oh my God, she has to get home for such and such that night, blah blah blah...she's getting everyone worked up, the parking lot's turning into a total mob scene. So Pedro goes over and starts calmly explaining how he's done this for *years*, used to go back and forth over Donner all *winter*, he's seen a helluva lot worse than this. Then the sum'bitch starts throwing his chains on, and it looks like he's done it every Goddamn day of his life! And they're all watching him, and everyone just kinda settles right down. It's all bullshit of course, but he's *selling* it and they *believe* it, and it's *working*. I woulda ignored the bitch and just done my thing, but he didn't want them to be afraid.

"Before we leave I take him aside just to make sure he's really OK, and he says, 'Hell, it's just powder, we'll push right through it.' And I says, 'Yeah, powder coming down a couple inches an hour!' And you know what this kid says to me? He smiles and says, 'We got it.' Ain't been bus driving for *two whole months,* and he's telling *me* 'we got it!'

"So we start rolling, and damn if I can see any more than a bus length ahead of me, it's Goddamn brutal. I'll admit, I get a little white knuckled at times. But I look back and there's Pedro right behind me, keeping just the right distance. They said he drove it like it was a sunny summer day, not a drop of sweat."

(One of Floyd's favorite training catch phrases, which I think he borrowed from a deodorant commercial, is "never let them see you sweat.")

"Takes a good long while, but a few miles down the road, we drive out from under the storm, chains come off, and we're home free. I swear, they wrote him up like he saved every one of their lives."

Floyd looked back at me, probably noting in my face that it all seemed a little incredulous. "Hey, don't take my word for it, Pedro. Just ask Annie. She'll show you all the brown nose cards"--referring to the Customer Satisfaction Surveys handed out by Eldorado after each trip--"you already got about a dozen A-plus marks. Took me *four years* to get that many. That's why you're getting all the veteran jobs, *dude.*" Floyd adds in the mock surfer accent he likes to use with Paul and me. "It ain't just cuz Annie's got the hots for you."

That was the first statement that actually made me blush...and come to think of it, I thought to myself, she does like to mention how fortunate we are as a company to have a couple good-looking young drivers in the stable.

"Now the problem with you, Pedro," Floyd went on, halfway interrupting at that point, "and no offense to your lovely wife--your problem is, you married a sicko."

I don't think that was intended to make me laugh, but it did. "Ah Floyd, I'm so glad you prefaced that with 'no offense,' or I might have thought you were about to say something inoffensive. I knew I shouldn't have tried to explain Nadia and me in one sitting."

"No no no, I ain't talking 'bout what you told us tonight...look, I hear the stories, I see you come in day after day on no sleep, I see what she looks like when she picks you up...your wife is not a healthy person, Pedro. You know it, I know it, Annie knows it...we're all concerned for you."

"I appreciate your concern, I really do. But Nadia and I are fine. We're going through some rough times lately, but we always--"

This time Floyd interrupted without any words. I looked up, and his eyes were riveted to mine. Times like these you can see the ancient remnants of Floyd's cowboy roots in his eyes, and they are fierce. He did not actually get up and get within an inch of my face, or grab me by the arms and shake me. It just felt like he did.

"Son, you have responsibilities on your shoulders that I never *dreamed* of taking on. *My own kids* didn't need me as much as your wife needs you. You deal with that at home, then you come out on the road and somehow keep it all under control, and it's a fuckin' miracle that you can. But meanwhile, *your wife is going blind*. So what the hell are you doing out here?"

I felt a lump come to my throat. No words came with it.

"*Or*, what the hell are you doing *back there*? That's only for you to decide. I got a good idea what you were born to do, but I can't tell you what it is. I *can* tell you that you'll have to decide before long, for your own safety and Eldorado's passengers. I can see this all crashing down on you one day, Pedro. I hope like hell it don't, but I think it will."

The camp fell silent after that. The fire had dimmed to a few red embers, and the chill of a cloudless night in the hills was coming upon us. In the distance, the music kept twanging on, the guests invariably trying some form of drunken line dancing. Floyd checked his watch.

"Alright, gentlemen," he said as he strained to stand up. "Guess we'd better go see if fuckhead lined up any passengers for the first trip."

"Hey, Floyd," I called out as he started off in the direction of the music. I did not want it to be forgotten that whatever was said there that night, there were some very kind words among them, from one craftsman to another. "Thanks."

"Sure, kid...but like I said, don't let it go to your head. You're still the bottom of the food chain in this business, no matter how good you are. The best ones always remember that. So don't forget, it all just comes back to the first rule of driving."

"*eeeeYeep*," added Paul, in an exaggerated grumbly drawl not unlike Floyd's. "*Shut up 'n drive.*"

The conversation haunted me for several days, especially the image of Floyd coming home to an empty house. It correlated a little too closely to a waking nightmare I have had ever since moving us from the safety net of life near Nadia's family in Pennsylvania to the isolated wilds of the desert southwest.

A few weeks after the move to Arizona, which had been relatively free of tribulations, several incidents unveiled Nadia's emotional instability that she had heretofore kept well hidden from me while I bopped around the northeast in a truck for a living. It is much harder to hide a whole aspect of one's personality while spending a week sharing motel rooms and a small moving truck. So the cracks in her foundation had just started to show--not the major fissures that were revealed later, but cracks all the same.

This was around the time I also started to realize how tenuous Nadia's grasp on life really is, and that her trademark stalwart independence was a complicated mix of genuine grit with bravado and wishful thinking. Despite what her words were telling me, I knew she did not want me back on the road. Yet there we were, settling into a beautiful new hometown where artistic poverty and minimum wage service jobs were the two choices for employment. After a fruitless week of exhausting the few local options that might have earned our combined living, I called one of my former long-haul employers, and they were only so happy to bring me back. Turned out that this was because someone decided I owed them four hundred dollars because I abandoned their truck last time I left their employment, even though I "abandoned" it exactly where a supervisor told me I could. This is a great example of what Floyd meant about "the food chain."

It also meant going back to a "3-and-3" operation--home for three days, on the road for three weeks--so it was not ideal for either of us, but in a border town with a primitive economy and a stagnant housing market, being paid on a national wage scale meant that we would live like royalty, which seemed like it might be fun for a change.

Nadia drove me to the truck terminal on the outskirts of Phoenix--a strange city made up entirely of outskirts--and stayed with me while I was reoriented to the company. It was a quiet couple of days. I did not realize while it was happening for the first time in my presence, but a quiet Nadia means something is simmering and heading for a boil. She reached 212 degrees the night before I was set to ship out. It was the first fight that had the qualities of viciousness that I would later attribute to her fears of abandonment and bipolar condition working in tandem. With the ultrathin skin I had at the time, I was completely unprepared, and when she threw her engagement ring at me, I told her to get the fuck out of my room and out of my life. I even repeated those horrible words when she came back a couple hours later to apologize--after I had cast our rings onto Interstate 10 and started telling my sorrows to Jim Beam. Nadia drove the three hours back to Bisbee in the middle of the night, and I fell asleep not knowing if I still had a fiancée.

By the time we got to reconcile, I was doing it from a truck stop payphone on my way to Indiana. We cried together about the rings and promised we would never take the next ones off. She reaffirmed her gratitude for my willingness to work for both of us, how excited she was to be in a thriving artistic environment surrounded by unspoiled land and clean air. She talked about the person she became that night as though it were a stranger she did not recognize, and at that time, she was probably right--it did feel as though an intruder had entered her and spoken through her mouth. Less than a year later, when the intruder seemed to have taken up permanent residence, we were spooked enough to head back to the northeast to be closer to our support network again. That was when we chose Caches Notch, just a couple hours from my family and even closer to Nadia's father, who had retired to northern Vermont.

But for a good while after I hit the road, there was a genuine detente, a calm after the storm that felt like the life we had promised each other when we donned those rings. That was when the visions started. I could have been anywhere--say, Kansas City, picking up a trailer full of Cheez-Its bound for Piggly Wiggly in Alabama--and maybe I would still be a week or two out from home. But like any truck driver from time to time, my mind would wander away from where I was and start following that unbroken ribbon of road, back across the miles we know like a childhood memory or favorite song, leading us back to our hometown. The vision would take me to my front door, a smile in my eyes as I imagined coming to rest, ten thousand miles in the rearview mirror, and the loving reception I would get as I come through the door.

But then the door would open, and she would be gone. Everything else in the house would be just as I left it, but no trace of Nadia. Somehow I knew that she wasn't gone like Floyd's wife was gone. He could have found her if he wanted her back; Nadia had gone to a place where I could not go. This was a few years before Santos Rios, when death was still a shapeless dark void that did not engage my imagination. I had to distract myself, pretend it was only a daydream and not some kind of prophecy sent by the Destroyer to remind me that he could come for her at any time.

Fast forward to San Luis Obispo, early August 2001. The empty home image was fresh in my mind when, about ten days after the wedding gig, Annie called me into her office before a routine casino run for what she had promised over the phone would be a "Very Exciting Opportunity."

I had an inkling what it was. Back in the spring, Eldorado had landed a major contract with a company based in the Bay Area. Starting in June, we had been running four buses a week from a satellite terminal in San Jose, doing a whole smorgasbord of multi-day trips for busloads of Chinese tourists. The crème de la crème of these trips was a massive seven-day sensory overload extravaganza that somehow involved two days at Yellowstone, the north rim of the Grand Canyon, and just about every park, lake, and hole in the ground in between. I had been hearing the stories from the veteran drivers as they cycled through for two or three weeks and came back to home base. Their tales were lyrical and epic, brutal at turns, but always rich with the majesty of ordinary people being stretched beyond themselves by situations larger than life. One could sense that true poetry was being written at the wheel. Floyd said Yellowstone was "the ultimate ball-buster," and after one tour of duty he swore he would never eat Chinese food again (most of the meal stops were at greasy spoon Chinese buffets). Still, I was mesmerized. And for all my cross-country travels and western adventures, Yellowstone was a place I had never occasioned to visit. The rest of the agenda was just as mouth-watering. But even Annie would never trust a rookie driver to such an important and lucrative gig...would she?

"Now Pedro," she said in her trademark bubbly soprano, "I want you to know that I would Never Ever Assign an Ordinary Rookie Driver to the Landmark tours. But You and Paul have been getting Such Good Marks, and I Know you can Handle Yourself out there. So I would like to give you a Shot at Yellowstone."

My heart raced. I felt like a baseball player finding out he had been voted to the All-Star team while still playing in the minors. The Nadia vision flickered in my mind. I pushed it away.

"Alright! I'm in!"

"Wonderful!" she cheered. "Now it's Only Fair to Warn You that the Reason this is Opening Up for you is that some of the Veteran Drivers are Complaining that Yellowstone is Too Grueling and they Don't want to Go Back. You will be Worked Harder than you ever have in your Whole Life I'm sure...but you'll Come Home with Thousands of Dollars in your Pocket to show for it."

Ah, that was another thing I had heard. The tour guides encourage the passengers to tip the drivers for just about everything we do. There is a base price of five dollars per person per day for the full week, and an optional tour of the Las Vegas Strip on the night that we layover there coming home, with a suggested donation of ten dollars each. Add it all up and, with a full bus, before hourly wages are even considered, it is realistic to come home with over two thousand dollars in cash for each trip. This had me salivating almost as much as the driving. It had been so long since Nadia and I had a nest egg of any kind, let alone multiple thousands of dollars.

"Now the Only Part of this that Concerns Me," Annie continued, "is Nadia. Generally the guys are doing either Two or Three Week Rotations. Paul says he would Like to try Three, but David is Coming Back the weekend Before your Third Week for our

Anniversary, so I can Get You Home after Two if you Prefer. That would make this Shorter than your Trucking Trips. Do you think Nadia would be Alright with That?"

Again, from somewhere in my mind I saw my front door open and Nadia was gone. I scrambled that signal with a quick shake of my head.

"I'll sell her on that point. And the thousands of dollars of course."

"Excellent! Oh Pedro, you are going to Love Yellowstone. I think You were Tailor Made for This Trip. The Chinese are just So Sweet, they Appreciate Everything we Do for them. Of course the Schedule is Impossibly Hectic, and you'll Wonder How in the World they can be Enjoying Themselves, but that's just the Way they Like to Travel I guess. I don't think they Know how to Relax!"

"Great, I'll be in excellent company then."

Annie went on to explain how it would work. That coming Saturday, Paul and I would depart for San Jose in a bus that would also be new to the rotation. The other four buses would converge from their various directions sometime that day--all the trips were scheduled to arrive back in the Bay Area on Saturdays. Two drivers would stay and do another circuit, and the other two would drive back to home base in the bus that had been running for Landmark the longest. Sunday morning would begin with pickups at five locations across the Bay Area, and then each bus would go its own way. Paul would be doing a pair of three-day trips up the Oregon coast. Another would do a similar set of treks heading south on Route 1 toward San Diego. There was another week-long trip that headed straight for the Grand Canyon and took in all the Arizona and New Mexico sites before jetting back.

But my Yellowstone trip was indeed the undisputed heavyweight champion of the Landmark tours. Over three thousand miles in seven days--the equivalent of a coast to coast trip across America at one of its wider latitudes. Along the way we would take in five national parks: a full day at Yellowstone, and whistle stops at Grand Teton, Bryce, Grand Canyon, and Zion. Other st-

ops and photo-ops along the way included one of the many gorg-
es along the Snake River in Idaho; Jackson Lake and the town of
Jackson, Wyoming; the Mormon Temple in Salt Lake City; the
world's largest copper mine in the hill country of Utah; a night
on the town in Las Vegas; and a whole slew of trinket shops
and outlet malls where tour guides had arranged for bounties for
themselves and their drivers--anywhere from $10 to $40 in food
and/or merchandise credit--for bringing in busloads of souvenir-
hungry tourists. The hardest day of all, I was told, was the last,
with an early wake up after doing the Vegas Strip past midnight,
followed by a 620 mile assram of a drive across the Mohave
and up the Central Valley back to the Bay Area, then dropping
passengers at the five pickup locations in reverse order and performing the standard ablution rituals on the bus before finally
crashing at the hotel in San Jose (because this was a sightseeing
tour with a hefty price tag, in addition to the daily bus cleaning
and fueling duties, Landmark expected all the windows to be
washed and squeegeed every night, a task normally performed
by a contractor back at home base). On my second Sunday, I
would be up at 5 am to start the whole loop again with a new
batch of passengers, "not even a Full Night to Sleep or Lick your
Wounds," warned Annie (which reminded me of the oft-quoted
line of future governor Jesse Ventura's character in the movie
Predator: "I don't have time to bleed.")

Just to be sure I had a tangible sense of what I was facing, Annie showed me a typical time sheet. I admit, I was a little daunt-
ed when I looked at the Total Hours box and saw a three-digit
number: 105, to be exact. That was in seven days. To put this
in perspective: legally we are allowed to work 70 hours in any
eight day period. So we can do the 14-hour days as long as there
are shorter ones and time off mixed into every week. But by the
time I finish my eighth straight day on that turnaround Sunday
(insert joke about "even God rested on the seventh day" here), I
will have put in right around 120 hours. That means the amount
of time I would work *beyond* my legal limit in eight days was
greater than the standard work week that my boss would be doing. I suddenly did not feel bad at all for taking a tourist's money

that he would otherwise blow at Caesar's Palace or the Barstow Levi's Outlet store--I was going to earn every fucking penny. Render unto Caesar what is Caesar's, and unto Pedro what is Pedro's.

The next morning was my first chance to discuss the Yellowstone trip with Nadia. I caught her in a very good mood, one of those times when she seems to float just above her body and loves any new idea. But I wanted to take no chances so I led by telling her that I had a chance to make about six thousand dollars in take-home pay in two weeks, more than half of it cash. I saw her eyes light up, and it was not hard to deduce why. In her mind, six thousand bucks was starting to sound like a down payment on a house. Normally I might have burst her bubble while it was relatively small by asserting that it would take about *ten* weeks to earn enough for the typical down payment on even a modest house in our area, and by then she would also have to pay for my cremation so that would cut into the profit margin. But I *really* wanted Yellowstone, and I needed all possible positive angles to help me get there, so why not let her believe this would get us one step closer to owning a house. The truth would come out as soon as we contacted one of the pimps they call realtors.

When I filled in the details of what the Yellowstone trip would entail, Nadia immediately decided that what I really wanted was a Chinese girlfriend. The thought had never crossed my mind as a possibility. I imagined Chinese tourists to be more like birders--older folks carrying a great deal of optical equipment, except these ones would be shooting non-stop barrages of photographs of each other standing stoically in front of every natural and manmade landmark in the western United States (this stereotype was 95% accurate). The idea of meeting someone in my age range and connecting romantically seemed very far-fetched. But I had never spent a whole week at a time with one group before. *And what if there was someone who...no, not going to happen.* I jettisoned the idea as specious and dangerous mind junk, and Nadia seemed more inclined to joke about it than worry so it did not derail the Yellowstone train.

And that was that. Three days later, Nadia dropped me off at Eldorado, a duffle bag stuffed with two weeks' worth of clothes as my only cargo. No time for laundry, I was warned, and forget about entertainment or other pastimes. It would be work, eat, and sleep, in that order of priority and volume. I did not even bring the rucksack, figuring that it would taunt me while it sat untouched in the luggage bay and hotel rooms. But the atmosphere in the car as Nadia saw me off was optimistic, as though I were a young invincible solider headed off to battle, and she fully expected me to come back a decorated war hero.

Three weeks later, on Saturday September 1, 2001, Nadia dropped me off for another Landmark tour, and I felt like I wanted to be zipped up in a body bag. We had been fighting for about five straight days and I still did not even know why. Finally I called Annie and begged her to get me back out there before I snapped. She said she would hold her husband back another week and let me relieve Paul on the Grand Canyon run. She was deeply concerned for me, and I said there was good reason to be, but getting away for a week was the only thing that was going to help. What I did not tell her was that I was pretty sure this was going to be my last trip for Eldorado, that when I got back to San Luis Obispo, I was going to use my cash income to buy a train ticket and start a new life somewhere back east.

1:00 pm (PDT) /4:00 pm (EDT)

I am thinking about taking a break from my experiment with meditation and giving in to the allure of *Car and Driver*...but then I hear a woman barrel into the lobby and rush to the front desk, frantically inquiring about her sister. I look up and see that this is Melody Weaver, dressed much more conservatively, as I remember seeing her, in a white blouse and long, pleated tweed skirt. Even on a day of uproar and heaving emotions everywhere, Melody gives me the strong impression of a bull in a china shop.

I approach her timidly and introduce myself. Melody spins on her heels and looks right at me with blazing intensity, then leaps toward me with a boisterous hug that almost knocks me over. It persists much longer than I expect.

"Thank you thank you thank you," she intones in my ear. "I got here as fast as I could after hearing your message." Then she steps back. "Wait–Joseph...you're Mira's daddy! We've met before. My son is her best friend. I've been to your house for play dates a few times! Your wife is the most adorable person I've ever met. What a small world!"

"Yes, it sure is." I was too embarrassed when I called her to mention the connection that I had learned through Small Wonders, and I'm hoping to figure out a graceful way to dance around it now. The truth is, I feel a peculiar apprehension when any person comes to my house. I mean, that's why we moved to the burbs, so I could engage with people as little as possible.

"I'm sorry, I'm really bad at remembering names and faces at first. Vera keeps my head spinning with new people to get to know."

"I totally understand," says Melody, which puts me at ease. "That was the hardest part of becoming a teacher for me: how to learn the names of a hundred new kids every year. Well I am so glad you recognized me from Estelle's photographs anyway."

"So am I. I was starting to think she was all alone on the east coast. Everything in her purse seemed to tie her to Missouri."

"Yes, those are our roots alright, they run pretty deep."

A nurse arrives to escort us to the ICU. Melody vouches for me as a "family friend," a contradiction that is not caught due to a shift change. She keeps a reassuring hand on my back as we walk together, which I don't seem to mind despite my typical need for personal space.

We arrive in Estelle's room to find her lying still, neck immobilized, and head wrapped in a thick turban of bandages.

"Her CT scan was negative for intracranial bleeding and hematomas," the nurse reads from her chart, "so that was very welcome news. The excessive bleeding seems to be solely due to the anticoagulants, and there should be no issues with continuing them now that she's closed up. We will need to monitor her concussion symptoms when she regains consciousness, but we don't expect them to be severe. Scary and a little gory, in other words, but your sister has a very hard head. She should come through alright. Rest is the best thing for her at this point."

"Thank you for everything," Melody says. "You can imagine what a relief it was to get a call from a hospital in New Jersey instead of the coroner in New York."

"I have been absolutely sick with worry all day," she

continues as the nurse leaves the room, "for her and for Vera. To be honest, though, it has been hard to stay focused. I teach sociology at a prep school in Summit, and at least half of the kids have parents who work in Manhattan, many at the Trade Center itself. I can't tell you how exhausting it has been to keep them reassured while I had so much doubt myself."

"Well at least we know Estelle wasn't up there. That doctor's appointment saved her life."

"Amen to that," she whispers, holding her hands together in prayer below her chin. "I can only hope we were so fortunate with Vera."

"I know it's likely that she was in her office, and that the plane hit somewhere above it. Just not sure how far above yet."

"Oh, well darling, if you want to get home now, please don't let me keep you. I would be glued to the phone if I were you."

I ponder this for a moment, staring at Estelle's IV unit. "You know...that was all I wanted to do all morning, until I had the chance to do it. But for some reason, I don't feel like being home now. All my life I've been retreating to my home whenever there's any discomfort with the world...but I'm not going to do that today. I know Vera is safe. I know she's somewhere on the island doing something important for someone. I think it's essential for me to trust that...."

I look over and see Melody gazing intently at me, eyebrows arched. Such an interesting appearance she has: a strong, sturdy jawline and high cheekbones, like she has some American Indian blood in her family. Even in her prep school teacher's uniform she gives the impression that she could rope a calf or wrestle a steer to the ground. But then all that curly blonde hair, and the softest, kindest-looking sky blue eyes I have ever seen... I never took note of her this way before, yet at the moment she is indescribably beautiful to me. I don't even mean it like that. I just mean...beautiful.

"Besides," I continue, "I promised Estelle I would stay with her today. I'd like to keep that promise."

Now Melody's expression turns incredulous, but gratefully so. "You have no idea how much that will mean to her… in that case, why don't we have my husband pick up your girls when he gets Malcolm and bring them to our house? Tyrell will be there in about a half-hour. Just call Lynette and she'll make sure he knows."

I hate that my first thought upon hearing this is not simple, pure gratitude. If only I hadn't heard the word "moolie" a thousand times before I ever had a positive impression of an African-American man while growing up...but if I learned racism as a child, I could certainly unlearn it now as an adult, one moment of acceptance at a time.

"That would be wonderful, thank you. I'll go call her now."

Melody smiles as I leave, a hearty robust smile that fills the room. Later she will tell me it was because of how relieved she was that her first impression of me could not have been more wrong.

1:10 pm (PDT) / 4:10 pm (EDT)

As we pull into Meseta Centrada campground, I hear nothing but idle chatter, mostly about birds again. I want to crash into a big tree. Instead I follow the roadway to a parking area surrounded by modern camping amenities: indoor restrooms and showers, a clubhouse, and a caretaker's residence. I momentarily forget my frustrations as new hope of contact arises, but the caretaker is away and there are no outdoor phones. The campground is deserted. I beseech the cell phone gods to reach down and touch me Michelangelo-style, to let me connect with the world again. I maneuver all over the site, but it is useless. I might as well be on Mars.

My heart turns to lead as I watch the birders traipse through the campground. To my bilious discontent, the group will be staying within sight and earshot at this stop. They are drawn to several hummingbird feeders like moths to a porch light. They will also be looking for band-tailed pigeons, white-headed woodpeckers, and pygmy nuthatches in the fringes of the open space.

What a bunch of ostriches! I swear this is an episode of The Twilight Zone. I am working with aliens. Soon I will hear that irritating music and they will all slip out of their humanoid disguises, revealing slimy green beasts with tentacles and long fangs. Maybe their race is responsible for the hijackings, and they have been scouting locations to launch a west coast attack. They will eat me and drive the bus back to the rendezvous point, and await further instructions from the mother ship.

This would explain a lot, actually, but not everything. I wish it were an inhuman act to fly loaded planes into office towers, but history does not bear that out. No other species has our penchant for gratuitous self-destruction. Our alien invasion fantasies are just tricks to disassociate ourselves from our genocidal tendencies, and mine are no different. I am trying to hide from the fact that there is a cold-blooded killer inside me, waiting for a moment of rage and desperation to strike.

Exaggeration? Not if I'm honest with myself. Like most people, I have an exoskeleton of social restraints and fear of repercussions before I even reach the flesh of conscience keeping the killer contained. But what if those layers are pierced by an event as horrific as what happened today--would the tender flesh be strong enough? What if I found myself face to face with the devil who orchestrated this mass murder of innocent human beings? Would I still be able to turn the other cheek? Or would I take an eye for many thousands of eyes? At this moment, I would tear his body to shreds and spit on the heap of organs and bones that remains, and my sole regret would be that I could kill him only once. But then conscience speaks--would not his brother have the same imperative to retaliate against me? When would it ever end? The mind cannot process both at once. It has to disassociate from one or the other, but both the rage and the conscience are true, so they pull from equal and opposite directions. When this happens long and hard enough, a split occurs. Huge trouble. I am starting to spin.

Extremely heavy of foot, I lumber back to the bus, where the radio speaks to no audience. Betty is gone, off on another trek. I sit and listen some more, almost against my will. I cannot stand the radio now, it is getting repetitive and the news is too full of holes to make any sense. But no radio is worse, so I keep it on. The news has become my crack pipe.

It all seemed so simple back in August. I would do my 200-plus hours and come back two weeks later a relatively wealthy man. We could rest easy and not be on the brink of eviction for a while. Maybe I could even cut back on my hours, ask for a four-day workweek instead of five. That extra day off could do wonders for my writing, not to mention Nadia's outlook.

It sure felt like we were on our way to that, too. The Yellowstone trip was just as grueling as everyone warned me it would be, but it reached the level of craziness that I embraced it instead of complaining about it. A 70-hour work week is a dull pain in the ass sometimes, light enough to tease with some small doses of recuperative time at home in between 14-hour sessions on the rack. But 100-plus hours in seven days--that is a fucking threat to life and limb--so energy reserves never needed before start to kick in. The result of this adrenaline-fueled perpetual motion combined with sleep deprivation was that I felt, looked, and behaved a little bit like a speed addict. But that was just enough to keep me on pace with the Chinese. Good *gawd*, their motors never slow down. Whether they were eating, talking to each other at incredibly close proximity and high volume, or dashing from one photo opportunity to the next, even the most senior of the citizens on my bus vibrated on a frequency to which my senses could only acclimate after about the third cup of coffee. I learned really quickly that Annie was dead-on right about them. The Landmark itineraries were not overly ambitious for their customers' tastes. That is just how the Chinese roll. I suspect it was this culture shock just as much as the volume of work that was creating the battle of attrition in keeping the buses staffed with Eldorado drivers, accustomed as we are to life back home.

What more than made up for this, in my opinion, was Annie's other observation about the passengers. They were by far the most gracious and friendly people I have ever had the privilege to haul. They had an effervescent curiosity and they loved to talk and exchange ideas across that cultural gap. I did not get to learn much of their language as they were all so eager to use their English with me. The one phrase I heard day and night from every one of them, for literally everything I did, from handling their suitcases to holding a hand out as they disembarked to simply pulling in safely to each stop, was "Thank you" (although it sounded more like "Sang Q"). It never got old; in fact I doubt I have ever appreciated the sound of those two words more than the endless mantra of Sang Q. Many times it felt like the extra boost of nitro I needed to keep going when the tank was getting empty.

There was also about three thousand miles worth of virtual solitude on each trip (I drove a rental bus with an elevated passenger section, so everyone behind me was also about three feet above, giving the driver's compartment much more of a cockpit feeling). For that I had the constantly invigorating, ever-changing gorgeousness of the wild intermountain West. As soon as we leveled out from the long steady slope on the dry side of the Sierras in northern Nevada, I could feel that we were in a new milieu of land that I had not experienced for a long time, and I felt unleashed.

(People have asked me what was my favorite part of the drive, but one could just as well send a fine food connoisseur to sample every menu item at a five-star restaurant and tell you his favorite. He would surely insist that the entire dining experience must be evaluated as a whole. On the short list of what I remember most vividly: the back roads through the rugged high country from Idaho Falls to West Yellowstone, Montana; sharing the road with bison and antelopes as we spent the day touring Yellowstone Park; coming down out of Wyoming through the jagged peaks of the Wasatch Range into Utah; the otherworldly feeling and stark emptiness of the Kaibab Plateau heading to the north rim of the Grand Canyon before dawn; Interstate 15 as it clips the northwest corner of Arizona and drops 800 feet through the Virgin River Gorge, a canyon hardly less grand than any I have ever seen from within. One could spend a month exploring the territory we covered in a week and still not do it justice. The endless stream of photographs started to make sense to me when I realized later that my mind could only retain it all as a blur, and I was grateful when a couple families made good on their offer to mail me some snapshots. Ah yes, proof that I really did see Yellowstone Falls, Jackson Lake, etc.)

Despite the obscene workload, I managed to keep in touch with Nadia at least once a day. I made good use of the small nibbles of free time that were built into the schedule, mainly meals and the fifteen minute photo ops. I was elated to find that Nadia had found her way back to the mindset that worked so well in some of my long-haul heydays. With my absence assured, Nadia seemed to treat each day as a whole, self-contained parcel of time for her to own unto herself, and do with whatever pleased her most. She went for walks almost every day. She finally visited the Morro Bay library and brought home some large print selections and books on tape. Not coincidentally, I am sure, she started a new self-portrait. It was an image of herself as she wanted to be, a portrait of the artist as a self-realized freak with short pink hair and the matching knee-high boots for which she was ever on the lookout, and multi-colored leggings, sprawled out in a big comfy chair with a steaming mug of tea by her side. As customary with Nadia's drawings this would include companion animals, in this case a pug dog and a tropical bird that may have been either a toucan or macaw. This was all to be drawn on a very large canvas she had been saving for a particular inspiration, so it was definitely the most ambitious project she had undertaken since she started using pastels.

We also got some tremendous and unexpected news in the mail near the end of the first week: Nadia had been approved for Social Security disability benefits. This was going to make us a two-income family going forward, which we had never been aside from the sporadic (and in my eyes, always undervalued) sale of Nadia's artwork. But the news was even better: it was determined that her disability had begun when she first sought medical attention for her vision loss, more than a year prior. So her first monthly benefit check included back payments for that whole time, to the tune of over six thousand dollars.

Now, even I had to admit, we were starting to talk about a chunk of change that could become part of a down payment on a house. Nadia brought up the likelihood that her father, who was very supportive of us in general but understandably weary of watching us pinball all over the map, would loan or even give us a matching contribution for the down payment to encourage us to lay down some roots. Her enthusiasm finally got through to me, and it led me to many introspective hours at the wheel while the great wide open west zoomed by. Could I really do this?

Would my opinion of the game change just because I could suddenly afford to play it? Is California even the right place to think about planting ourselves, or should we look to go back east, somewhere that our roots were more likely to find nourishment? Am I ready to become mono-coastal? I came to no conclusions and made no promises to Nadia, just one to myself: that I would not lose the ethical compass that led me to reject the purchase of property. If life were to lead me down that path, I would embrace being appointed as steward of this portion of land under the sun, and pay no mind to abstractions such as equity and resale value.

Nadia inquired about my Chinese girlfriend a couple times. I assured her that I was far too busy to date, even if I did meet my Chinese soul-mate, and she seemed to take that at face value and with all due lightness of heart. I suspect Nadia would have been much less inclined to joke about it if she knew how close it came to happening.

I honestly do not remember the Americanized name she called herself because I tried very hard to forget it. Instead she will forever be known to me as Stargazer Girl. She was a Taiwanese college student traveling with her grandparents. She was petite even by Chinese standards, with shoulder-length black hair, bright almond eyes and a heart rending, angelic smile. I found the younger adult passengers to be more reserved than their close-talking chatterbox elders in general, but even considering that generality, Stargazer Girl stood out in soft-spoken contrast to her peers. She was on the first of the two Yellowstone trips, so I was still getting used to the passenger-driver dynamics of this peculiar group when by Wednesday I had noticed her quietly lingering a little longer by the front of the bus whenever we de- and re-boarded, looking for me at meal stops, etc. By Thursday, the Salt Lake-to-southern border of Utah day, we were looking for each other, and the Hellos and Sang Q-s were getting warmer, but a mutual shyness kept it from growing beyond that.

Friday morning was when I fell hard for her. That was the day with a 4 am wakeup call and 5am departure from the hotel in Kanab so we could cram in breakfast and a quick gawk at the north rim of the Grand Canyon. It was the only day on the schedule that involved an actual pre-dawn departure, and true to form. the passengers were all running at midday speed by the time I dragged my sleepy ass to the parking lot. The same people were milling about in the same groups squawking away, a couple dozen of the older folks gracefully awakening their bodies with tai chi (and I don't mean to minimize how beautiful that was because it was a truly amazing sight to see). But my Chinese soul-mate was not among them. She was out on the edge of the lot by herself, away from the bus and the motel lights, looking up at the sky. I ventured over to join her against most of my better judgments. It was a crystal clear night and the heavens were overflowing with twinkling lights that seemed about twenty feet above our heads. She was awestruck. We tried to share some words that conveyed our feelings about what we saw. I gathered by this point that her English was actually quite limited, and "beautiful" was about all we could agree upon word-wise. But the look on her face as she gazed at the stars, then at me, then back at the stars, was something I will never forget, damn me.

By then I was giving myself over to thoughts of what could happen if I invited her to spend that night with me in Sin City. I decided I needed to cool off a bit, and I avoided direct contact with her the rest of the day. Beyond shyness, there was probably a gender-based cultural imperative that would have held her back from pursuing me, so it seemed very likely that the parking lot in Utah was going to be Our Moment. And it was...until the very end of the trip. As it turned out, Stargazer Girl was among the many passengers staying with me until the last stop Saturday night in San Jose. I had been rehearsing for hours what I would say to her to convey how she had made me feel, yet keep everything on the up and up. After I pulled the last of the suitcases from the luggage bay, I walked around to the right side of the bus and noticed that she was standing alone with her back to me, facing the door and craning her head side to side. It seemed like she was scanning the lot looking for me. I came up behind and tapped her on the shoulder, and the look on her face when she turned around answered any questions I had about her feelings toward me. I immediately forgot everything I intended to say.

I did manage to thank her for coming along for the ride, and told her that I would have sought her out and talked to her a lot more if I were not married. I showed her my ring as I said that, and she seemed to understand. Then she said--and this is a God-honest direct quote straight from her lips--" The best thing of traveling was having you." I melted. By then, there were a half-dozen smiling old ladies standing around us, drawn to us like heat-seeking missiles, intent on finding out exactly what was going on. As a race, the Chinese are not big fans of things like privacy or personal space.

So that was more or less the end of that. I tried to tell her that I hoped she would always gaze at the stars, which did not seem to translate well. I wonder if she thought I were suggesting that she should literally never cease looking at the stars, which would be impractical, especially during the day. We did manage to hug--she was impossibly tiny in my arms--and she gave me a business card with her email address at school. I kept it for a short while, even cued up her address on an email the week after I got home when Nadia was not in the room and started to think of what to write, but I deleted it and threw the card away. It was not worth the risk.

So that was my Chinese girlfriend story. Stargazer Girl was like a ghost who visited me in a dream, never to appear in my waking hours, and she was not even a blip on Nadia's radar screen. She had nothing to do with our falling out after I got home. As I said, I did not know what could have caused it until much later.

In retrospect, it all started on the Thursday of my second week, when Nadia did not answer any of my four phone calls. We did talk early Friday morning while everyone was chowing down at the Grand Canyon, but it was brief and she was rather abrupt and evasive about the day before. I could not reach her that night from Las Vegas either, and we had brief, uninspired conversations on Saturday while I was barreling back to the Bay. Annie's husband was gung ho about getting home so we eschewed the layover at Eldorado North and made a midnight run back to headquarters that night. I pretended I was waiting for Nadia to pick me up, then when David was gone I made my customary bed in the back of the local shuttle van (Nadia's night vision was already poor enough for her to curtail driving after dark) and got some spotty sleep for a few hours. According to the time sheets I filled out in the morning, I had worked 214 hours over the previous fourteen days, and I could not fucking sleep because I was wondering what the hell had gotten into Nadia this time.

One thing we had decided we would splurge on with my Yellowstone haul was a bed-and-breakfast getaway to celebrate Nadia's birthday. She had turned thirty while I was gone. I got the first three days of the week off, and told Nadia to pick her choice of anywhere within a half-day's drive and we would live it up for two nights. She chose Sequoia National Park, and found a cute spot in a place called Lemon Cove in the Sierra foothills. Everything seemed on track Sunday morning as Nadia picked me up and we headed northeast toward the sequoias. Both the trip and Sunday afternoon and evening at the inn were pleasant enough, though--and again, this may be a case of 20/20 hindsight, it is hard to tell--there certainly were signs that Nadia was stewing over *something*. Nobody I have ever known carries a quiet tension like she does.

Some of this tension was probably evident on Sunday....and *a lot* of it was on Monday as we explored the park. The sequoias are staggeringly beautiful, a little overlooked I reckon compared to their smaller and younger cousins, the coastal redwoods, and with the spectacle of Yosemite so close. But virtually anywhere else in the country, Sequoia and Kings Canyon National Parks would be *the* place to see.

Nadia seemed like she desperately wanted to let go and enjoy herself, take in all the grandeur, but she was getting worn down by hiking even moderate terrain. There was one trail up a rocky bluff that afforded a marvelous view of a mountain range just to the east that includes Mount Whitney, California's high point at over 14,000 feet. Nadia could only make it halfway. She looked very discouraged, but told me I should keep going and she would meet me back at the base. When I got down, she seemed even more upset at my willingness to accept her offer and go on without her.

The tension grew from a dozen similar if less poignant moments. Finally, later in the afternoon, the dam burst, over the most innocuous miscommunication about our dinner plans, and a flood of hate-driven angst drowned out any semblance of normal getaway vacation from thereon. Something I said apparently cast a pall over the whole commemoration of her birthday, which showed that I obviously did not care about it at all, because why else would I go away for two weeks and miss her birthday in the first place...and it spiraled downward from there.

I learned many skills in the three years following the fight at the hotel in Phoenix that made even Nadia's worst episodes much more manageable. At our best, we honed in each other what one might call a rapier wit, and we used those soft-pointed weapons frequently in the verbal equivalent of fencing duels. Nadia has admitted that she enjoys this exercise and actually needs it in her life to keep her good humor up, and I have learned to enjoy it as well. At darker times, simple humility, self-effacement, or occasionally, the kind of departure from ego usually only required of those applying for sainthood are needed, and I have developed some aptitude for all of them as a way of maintaining peace. Maybe I was still too exhausted from the 214 hours, but when this particular flood came, I had none of these skills. I fired when fired upon. There could not have been a worse scene for this. It is particularly embarrassing to fight openly at a busy bed-and-breakfast. Who the hell goes to sleep at a person's house and *fights* all night, I pictured the guests and proprietors wondering to themselves. We were planning to stay and relax for the better part of Tuesday, but I felt so ashamed for our behavior that I could not stomach having breakfast with everyone. Nadia, who does not recognize nor have a working definition of the word "shame," insisted on having the breakfast we had paid for while I tried to rest outside in a hammock, hoping like hell the time apart would do us some good. When it proved not to, I got downright mean. I told her I was going home right away, and she could come with me or not. I think the ultimatum--an unusual tactic for me--put just a shade of fear into her, as it was intended to do. I was fucking sick of her, and not about to go on living like that, forever prostrating myself before a two-headed monster. The three hour drive home was almost completely silent. This was when I started devising my escape plan.

Not too seriously at first. I wanted to give it time, give everything a chance to simmer down. I worked the next two days. First was a North SLO County wine tour, which I normally love to do since I am so intimately familiar with the terroir (as wine people like to call "land") and love showing it off. But I slogged through this one. My tank was on empty. It was not a good day to run on empty either. Some of those roads up in the western Paso Robles hill country make Santa Rosa Creek look like an LA freeway. I wondered if this were what Floyd had prophesied by the campfire.

I received my answer to that question the next day. Wednesday night was just as hellacious as the previous ones, except this time I did not stick around for it. I had an early morning departure, so I drove to Eldorado and slept in the van again--well, I flopped around in the van for several hours. The plan started to feel more real, and urgent.

In the morning, I ran over to one of the local Hard Rock Churches that plays to the alternative crowd. I picked up a busful of young Christian hipsters and surfers for some four-day end of summer "Jesus is my brah" fest in the foothills past Fresno. With the destination being only three hours from SLO, Eldorado preferred to drop Christ's homies off and come back for them on Sunday rather than tie up a bus and pay a driver to layover for four whole days, so this trip was as simple as they come.

The group leader was a salt of the earth fellow who might have been the person on whom the Ned Flanders caricature on The Simpsons was based, except he was aiming for--and not quite hitting--an age about fifteen years hipper. (I did like his "And they will know that we are Christians because of our T-shirts" T-shirt.)

"Okaley Dokely!" (I'm not even kidding.) "Let's blow this popsicle stand and get the show on the road!" Yeah. Right on, dude.

When we reached the south end of Fresno, we pulled into a

spot well-known among drivers as a fast food mecca. Just about anyone can find something there among the dozen choices segregated onto a cul-de-sac spur off of a frontage road running parallel to the main drag. (If you are an omnivore in California, or simply a fan of the world's freshest and yummiest fries, there is only one choice that matters: In-n-Out Burger.)

As we left the meal stop, we had to turn left on the frontage road and then barely a full bus length after that, we would curve and then turn right onto the main drag and make what would amount to a U-turn to continue heading east. Meanwhile, a dump truck--ironically, one very similar to what I drove for Oceanside--had turned onto the frontage road and was coming up to the spur with its right turn signal on, which still signaled the turn he had just made, *not*, I must emphasize, an intent to turn right onto the spur. *Everyone* knows that you do not assume that a signal means an intent to turn until the signaling vehicle begins to make the turn. I have been in that situation thousands and thousands of times in my life, and I have never jumped out in front of a vehicle signaling but going straight ahead. Until then.

I heard the sickening sound of the dump truck screeching to a halt as I watched it helplessly over my left shoulder. Once I had started, there was nothing to do but keep going, so I did, and we missed being T-boned by probably less than ten feet. Only the fact that the dump truck had just turned and was not up to full road speed saved us. Had the spur been any further down the frontage road, it would have been a collision.

My heart leapt into my throat. For the first time at the wheel of a commercial motor vehicle, I felt paralyzed with fear. I realized at that moment that I was fully capable of being one of those people who, with a split second of poor judgment or lack of concentration, creates a front page disaster and rips a gaping hole in who knows how many lives. I could have been the Destroyer for a handful of kids and their families in the impact zone, not to mention a $100,000 bus entrusted to me.

As far as I could tell, the kids were completely unaware of the incident. Perhaps it was the In-n-Out high, perhaps the typical teenage inattention to anything happening outside of five feet from the center of their hormonal activity--or maybe I was shell-shocked and my rabbit ears were not functioning--but I did not hear any reaction as it happened nor anytime thereafter. They did *not* miss the reaction of the dump truck driver. After I made the right turn from the frontage road to the avenue, we came to a red light, and for about half a minute we sat maybe thirty yards from him facing the same direction. He wanted to kill me. His whole upper body was leaning out the window, as though he wanted to leap out but his feet were bolted to the floor. Both fists flailed around violently and he screamed an absolutely epic stream of obscenities. The Christian kids seemed to think it was pretty rad. Flanders turned kind of a chartreuse color as he fruitlessly tried to spin the situation. ("Heh heh, looks like our brother is having a little case of roa-diddly rage, heh heh.")

I just sat there meekly, thinking the earth was going to inherit *me* if this damn light did not change *real* soon. Then it did. I rolled through the intersection, the incident was over, and the day proceeded as normal. Flanders was as gracious as ever in parting and showed no signs of being dissatisfied with my service to him and his charges.

But I carried it with me all day. I felt hollow and fragile. I thought I could let it rest and put it behind me, but I was almost visibly dragging it around with me when I got back, so much that Annie asked me if anything was wrong (a topic she diligently avoids, surely afraid of what she might hear). I confessed, told the whole story. There was a small, insignificant voice of protest that feared losing my status as Eldorado's golden boy, but I knew I would continue to be a wreck if I did not get it off my chest. Annie was perfect. She told me she would Rather have a Driver who Recognizes his Mistakes and Learns From Them than someone who Thinks his Driving is Flawless, and I was That Much Safer now because I was Knocked Down a Peg and that was a Mistake I Wouldn't Make Twice. My esteem for Annie as a manager had always been high, but that day I really came to understand how lucky I was to work for her at that point in my life. She should have been cloned so that every small business in the world could have an Annie running the show. She asked if Anything were Happening Outside of Work that was Weighing on me. This time, I lied. It was so clear that she wanted me back in the saddle, and I did not want to her worry. I started to feel a little guilty about that while also having thoughts of bailing on her, so I put my escape plan on the shelf and decided to try another night of diplomacy with Nadia. I was hoping the humility of the day's lessons would carry over into our conversation and give her anger a place to rest where my defensiveness had been.

The plan hopped right back off the shelf and into full effect that night. When engaged in a power struggle with someone who feels completely powerless, I learned, too much humility can be a dangerous tactic--it can be seen as a weakness to be exploited. I started the conversation by trying to tell her about my day. She followed with a half-dozen barbed assaults on my competence as a driver, a husband, a writer, and an all-around human being, all of which went unanswered. When a seventh one came, I shot back hard. I questioned how anyone could ever love someone so heartless, and no wonder everyone else who cared about her before me had given up. I knew as I said it that it was not true and likely to hit a raw nerve, but I said it anyway. That was when I felt the knife graze my left arm.

There have been very few times that I felt threatened by Nadia. The sad fact is that her frailty makes her a toothless tiger when her anger spills out into physical violence. I can walk right through her punches and kicks without so much as a bruise, and her flailing limbs are easily subdued with minimal force. I also knew that even at her most ferocious, completely abandoned of her senses and lashing out with everything she had, Nadia's intent was always to hurt me, never to injure me or worse. She never went after my knees, and somehow I also never worried about being attacked in my sleep. This goes back to the important distinction I made earlier between a bipolar and a psychotic--she never lost touch with the self-preservation instinct that knew she needed me healthy and alive. She also knew that she could hurt me much more with verbal abuse than I could or would in return, so that was her form of asymmetrical warfare. Direct physical confrontation, when used tactically, was an act of desperation, but still a controlled one, and usually elicited an "oh not this again" kind of ho-hum response from me while I squelched it.

Having a kitchen knife thrown at me drew an entirely different response. Thank goodness she hooked her left-handed throw slightly, and the blade brushed my arm on its way past me instead of sticking into it, or a body part much more vital and vulnerable. It left me with something that looked like a big paper cut just above my elbow, with a bit of blood escaping where the sharp point of the knife hit. I erupted. I lunged at her, screaming at about twice the volume she could reach. She threw both fists in the direction of my head. I caught them both just below the wrist and pushed until they were both pinned against cabinet doors. I continued bellowing fire right into her face while she was immobilized. I gave her everything the dump truck driver gave me that morning and probably more, a full karmic exchange. By the look on her face, I think she expected me to start pounding on her, but my intentions were more sinister than inflicting pain. I wanted her to be afraid to speak or even move for at least an hour, or until I got my bag packed and got out of the house. I let her arms go and dared her to throw anything else at me, still leaning over her and posing as though my trigger finger were itchy. Her arms dropped to her side, she closed her eyes and sank her head, looking thoroughly defeated, regret already flooding her face.

This was the low point of my life. I was too jacked up on fury and buried in full emotional body armor to notice how much it was hurting though. All I knew was that I was out--out of patience, out of reasons to justify living that way anymore, out the door. There were many times that I left our home in order to let things cool down, always knowing I would come back, but this was not one of those times. This was full-scale retreat. I assumed I was never again going to see anything I left behind. This was the "what would you grab if you woke up and your house were burning down" game that people play, only this fire was real. The priority was notebooks--a half-dozen composition books I had filled over the years, and a couple three-ring binders with contemporary projects. I took all the books I was reading out of the rucksack. They took up valuable space, and they were replaceable. I added the hard case of 3-1/2 inch disks I use in the word processor, making sure that the one labeled "Valley & Mtn" was among them. The machine itself: replaceable. So were most of my clothes. I grabbed about three days worth, including two combos that would be acceptable for the Landmark tours. That and a toothbrush was about all the rucksack could handle, and that was all I wanted to carry into the afterlife, to hell with everything else. Phone, wallet--got 'em. No keys, she can keep the Goddamn car. Checkbook?...no, I'm not going to tempt myself, I thought, I am walking away from that money. I don't want to be so easily tracked, so no ATM card either. It is all hers.

(This was, admittedly, the most premeditated part of my plan. I still had about $150 cash in my wallet; the rest was deposited in the bank before we left for Sequoia. I was well within my rights to take the half of the $12,000 nest egg that I had earned, but I truly wanted to minimize the struggle she would have in living without me. I felt no vindictiveness toward Nadia, just a desperate need to be away from her, and leaving her all the money was essentially buying security for her and space for myself. The cash on hand was plenty to get me through the next week, and if Annie cooperated I could have another two grand in my pocket by then--more than enough to get me back east and situated somewhere to lick my wounds and heal.

All this packing was done amidst an eerie silence in the apartment. I could not rule out the possibility that while I worked, mostly with my back to the kitchen, the knife could have been plunged into my neck at any moment. I figured all bets were off, since I had barreled across at least two lines that I had never really approached. So I was jittery and moved in rushed but purposeful spasms of action, trying to make sure in between that I was not overlooking something important, counting on my ears to pick up any deliberate soft footsteps. It was with much relief that I emerged from the bedroom to find she had only moved to the indentation in the wall that, in more jovial times, we referred to as the "formal dining room." She was slumped forward in her chair, her head and left arm lying flat on top of our sorry excuse for a dinette table. I did not want to tip off my intentions yet, so I told her I was going out, didn't know where, not sure when I would be ready to come back. I saw her lips form an OK, but even my ears could not pick up the sound. She was already in a faraway place.

It was a many-headed beast that confronted me as I stepped through the front door and slammed it shut, each head screaming a different emotion at me through the armor of numbness. Joy was not among them, not one bit. Liberation, yes, but the snarling kind felt by a caged animal let loose. *Someone's gonna pay for all that time in captivity,* they seem to say as they flash their eyes and teeth teeth at anything that crosses their path. There was relief at the narrow escape, but it was neutralized by a sudden wave of fear about what really would happen to Nadia if I followed through on this, and would my resolve be able to hold up through whatever it was? Floyd's words about her needing me more than his kids needed him echoed through my mind. If that were true, I would be orphaning her. She would be abandoned by the man to whom she trusted her life..*I can't carry that right now...it is crushing me.* I tried to push it aside, but the vision of that very door opening to an empty house was now lodged near the fore of my mind.

Above all: excruciating fatigue. The yellow haze of the pre-dusk sunscape was coating the land with drowsiness. It was going to be another long night if I did not find somewhere safe to sleep, and I didn't feel safe anywhere in Cayucos. I dragged myself over to Route 1 and scanned the horizons for my options. I had always thought I would know exactly what to do and where to go in this moment, but it was quite the opposite. I felt the stench of death and failure in every direction, and the expansiveness I expected to feel was replaced by a sunken chest and labored breath. The mountains of the north coast seemed like the best place to get lost, so I stayed on the east side of the highway and stuck out my thumb.

About fifteen minutes later, I had a ride to Cambria in the bed of a rattly Toyota pickup, shared with two Latino laborers and an unfriendly dog. One of the men looked so much like Splash Rios that it spooked the fuck out of me. What would he say if he had come back to tell me something? "'All is well'.... 'Resentment is like drinking poison and expecting your enemy to die'.... 'Get them before they get you'"? We nodded at each other, but there was no inclination to speak. Good, I thought. I could not have handled that. Instead I just mused quietly as I leaned against the tailgate, once again just me and my rucksack...but emptiness was not working for me this time, and I was barely awake.

Actually--and this is something I had rarely done before--I started daydreaming about Home. The home I had as a little boy, the first one of which I have clear memories. Just a simple cookie-cutter house in an ordinary neighborhood in that quiet New Hampshire village. But my parents used a lot of imagination and made it unique with some renovations. The run of the mill basement became a cozy family room with a coal stove, pool table. and a splash bar. A patch of grass on the sunny side of the house became a garden. And the backyard, which always had the perfect dimensions for whiffle ball except for a couple pesky trees, was opened up to give it the kind of *feng shui* that has earned other ballparks comparisons to cathedrals. This all happened within a year when I was twelve, and it seemed to portend that this would be the home I would kiss goodbye when I went off to college, come home to on breaks and holidays, bring my future wife to meet the parents, etc.--all the American Dream stuff we see in the movies.

This daydream has since become kind of a recurring theme for me at odd times. I see myself at what seems to be my current age, walking through the house and upstairs to my room. It looks just like it did when I was thirteen. The roadmaps of childhood had been replaced by posters of sports heroes, heavy metal bands, and of course, those bikini-clad cover models. But there was also a new addition, scored from a poster shop at the mall a few weeks after the California trip: a photograph of Route 1, snaking along the coastal plains north of Piedras Blancas, then disappearing into the rumpled mountains at the edge of Big Sur under a cool blue sky. I didn't consciously set it up as an altar to my first and still most powerful deity, but looking back, that is certainly what it became.

So in this daydream, I walk into my room, I slip under the covers of my bed, and I fall asleep. That's it. Nothing else happens. I never wake up feeling refreshed or suddenly young again. I just sleep, timelessly. I wonder if I long for the waking world to turn into one of the dreams I might have had while sleeping there, when everything still seemed possible...or simply that it could be possible to *go* home.

My home was not demolished in favor of a tri-level condo, but it might as well have been. It belongs to someone else now. My parents sold it when I was 14. *It's a booming market,* their friends told them, *get the most of the equity while you can.* So they did, and they bought a fancy new house in a neighboring town, with nice fancy things like a two-car garage, vaulted ceilings, polished oak floors, swimming pool, and forced air heating ducts.

That house was the beginning of the end of their marriage. My father took a second job once they realized they had overextended themselves on the mortgage, and the typical litany of downward spirals followed. By the end of my second (and final) year of college, that house was gone too, and neither parent lived in a place I could call home.

I have never forgiven them for that, I thought to myself as twilight fell on the coast, Cayucos disappeared behind the hills, and I drifted off to sleep. Not my parents, not anyone's parents. No one.

Just as genuine emotions are starting to break through, I am jarred back to the bus as I feel it lean with a creak to my right, and I hear first one and then a second plodding footstep on the platform by the door. I do not need to look; I have already had the pleasure. It is Bob from San Pablo (which, he has reminded me more than once, is pronounced, in defiance of its Spanish origin, like "tablet," and I would rather have a cheese grater scraped across my ears than hear him say it again, so I will not forget). Bob is an oafish character in hiked-up jeans who loves to talk about the 30 years he spent working at the Golden Gate Bridge. He must have the world record for the largest set of hand-held binoculars, and as he wears them hanging from a heavy duty strap around his neck, they look like some kind of public humiliation device that a puritan tribunal would force him to wear as punishment for lewd behavior or perhaps a Sabbath violation. Bob has been following the bus in his own vehicle, presumably because he cannot fit comfortably in a bus seat. Maybe that has negative effects on his feeling of birder camaraderie, because even this morning he spent a disproportionate amount of time seeking conversation with me. Now he looks forlorn, like he really needs an ear to bend. A pleasant enough fellow I am sure, but right now he is a 300-pound mosquito that I feel like swatting.

"Pretty disturbing news, huh?"

I agree.

"Yeah," he replies, in a deeply knowing tone, and then trails off. He is searching for the right correlative story from his memory banks. It takes some time. I brace myself.

"'Course when I worked on the Golden Gate we got bomb threats all the time, and I yoosta hafta go out 'n'spect the bridge 'n look for the bomb."

"Really?" *Oh God, this is what I feared.*

"Yeah. I never found one though." He sounds disappointed. "Always just a hoax I guess."

Mmm, yes I can see the significance of your story. It had the word "bomb" in it. Very interesting. Now go away and let me fester in peace.

That is what I want to say, but I try to play nice first instead. I ask if he has ever been to New York. Maybe there is some common experience to bond over.

"Naw. I been to Worshington once when I was a kid. Mostly I just been in California. Not too many bomb threats here. We just watch out for earthquakes mostly. I was on the Golden Gate when that quake hit in '89. It shook a piece of the Bay Bridge right off, landed on some poor bastards in their cars. But the

Golden Gate was OK. It's a sturdy bridge, lemme tell ya. In the 30 years...."

I can't handle this. The spin is getting worse. I need to go for a walk. I excuse myself from the conversation as brusquely as possible--made all the more awkward by the fact that he took up the entire doorway--leaving Bob and his bridge to reminisce alone.

The birders are scattered about the site in small flocks, each pursuing its own agenda. Birds are abound and the action is intense, far better than they expected. The scorecards are rapidly filling with montane species and western migrants. The mood is absolutely unaffected by the outside world. A random bird-er walking onto the scene would have thought he had died and gone to some heaven where no one kills anyone and birds are all that matter.

All around me I hear people talking and checking their score-cards. The voices grow and accelerate like a TV nightmare scene. A woman near the hummingbird feeders shouts, "Hey Harold, c'mere! Are these Anna's or Rufous?"

"Rufous! Did you get the cedar waxwing nesting in the ponde-rosas by the driveway?"

"DOES ANYONE NEED A BROWN-HEADED COW-BIRD?"

My sentiments exactly! Does anyone need *any* of this?!

"All I need is a chipping sparrow and a dark-eyed junco and I'll have all the emberizids!"

"Dorothy and I saw a junco last week, maybe you'll get one in Morro Bay! I still need a spotted towhee!"

"How do you tell a MacGillivray's warbler from a Townsend's?"

"Check the nametag! (laugh, laugh)"

"Bushtit! I've got a bushtit!"

AWGH! That's it. I am coming unglued. This is the descent into madness. I have been teetering on the edge for years, now I am going down. *FUCK EACH AND EVERY ONE OF YOU.*

I run, as fast as my wing tips will take me. Soon I am in the woods and the birders are gone, but I do not stop. I want to get lost. I don't think I can go back to the bus. I can hide out here for a few hours, then find the road and hitch back to Santa Maria before dark. That would teach 'em: leave them forty miles from nowhere with a bus, no driver, and no phone reception. See if one of *them* can handle Death Wish Road in a 40-foot bus under extreme stress.

Tree branches force me to slow to hiking speed, but I lose none of the ferociousness. I smack things out of the way and trample anything I can. My path gets a little crooked, then a lot crooked. Now I do not know if I am going away or coming back. The sun cannot help, I have no idea what direction I started in.

Whoa. Now I really am lost. Once again, ask and ye shall receive.

I am too fried to figure this out now. We are still at least a mile above sea level, and the sudden burst of activity has me seriously winded. I am sucking air in fact. Goddamn poisonous bus driver food. I have gained at least twenty pounds since I started this job, about half of them at Chinese buffets.

Well this is a fine kettle of fish. I guess the only thing to do is pick a direction and trudge onward, and hope that I eventually run into someone looking for a hermit warbler.

ACT V

1:45 pm (PDT) / 4:45 pm (EDT)

Ugh. Nothing looks familiar.

I must have made the wrong choice back there. I have not heard a birder's voice for at least twenty minutes, so I must have wandered farther away from the campground. I cannot see the sky at all now, as the evergreen canopy has thickened.

Not all who wander are lost. Tolkien said it and I believe it. But some definitely are. I think I will backtrack to where I was and pick a different direction.

This is *not* how I want my Eldorado career to end. I was supposed to be on an eastbound train today. Might have been scheduled to pull into Penn Station tonight in fact. I would have been heading right into the heart of the carnage instead of speculating about it in a forest 3,000 miles away. Imagine that, the divergence of possible realities created by a decision as simple as whether or not to board a train.

But a funny thing happened on the way to the station. I decided to take one more shot at redemption.

I am not the type to search for meaning in dreams that come to me at night. There is a running joke between my subconscious and me in which God mocks me or otherwise messes with my head, and those usually come without much subtlety. But on a typical night, my dreams would make a David Lynch film look decipherable.

The dream I had that night after leaving Nadia was not hard to read at all. I was in a hospital visiting her just as I have many times before, only this time somehow I knew I had been keeping a long-term vigil--about five years. Whether this were the outcome of me leaving her was not certain, but it felt like it was. She had been lying in the hospital bed for the whole time, motionless and expressionless, but not comatose. This was more like a catatonic state. When I looked closely, I saw a lot of movement beneath her closed eyelids, like she was experiencing REM sleep. But nothing else happened. Five years had passed and the doctors still could not explain it.

So this one day, I had been there a while and was getting tired, thinking about getting a bite to eat or maybe just wanted to stretch my legs. As I always did, I leaned toward her to tell her in a gentle conversational voice that I was going to step out and I'd be back shortly. Before I got any words out, she opened her eyes, bolted straight up in bed, looked directly at me, and *screamed.*

I woke up with a jolt and a full-body shiver. It was sometime before daybreak, and I had a ghastly chill and a coating of moisture all over my skin and clothes. I vaguely remembered the night before, being poked awake by the Latinos in the bed of the pickup. They dropped me at the intersection of Route 1 and Moonstone Beach Drive in Cambria. In the haze of my half-awake state and my desire to avoid all people, I decided it would be a good idea to sleep on the beach.

I knew the contour of Moonstone well enough that I was confident I could find a spot back by the low cliffs where I would stay secluded and dry. One advantage to being in an exclusive and rural area like SLO County, I learned while living in the car last year, was that law enforcement was pretty lax. I am sure the police figure that few people here would be both desperate enough to sleep in a car and crazy enough to ignore the posted risk of prosecution, so vehicles parked on the streets overnight did not draw much scrutiny. I figured the same logic would apply to sleeping on the beach, as long as no one saw me walk down from Route 1. Evidently, no one did.

So I did sleep remarkably well and stayed clear of the high tide. It was not ocean water dampening me when I awoke, it was the thick marine layer of fog that envelopes the immediate coast on most summer mornings. I hadn't considered that factor when I made my overnight accommodations.

Things were off to a strange start already: first with Nadia screaming at me from fifteen miles away through the intercom of my subconscious, then waking up with the feeling that an animal with a very wet tongue had licked me from head to toe while I slept. I rose from my bed of sea-tumbled stones and mollusk shells in the shadowy light, feeling creaky and badly in need of coffee. The gas station back at the north end of town would be my only option at that hour, which my phone confirmed was 5:30. Amazing. My first solid eight hour night of sleep in at least three weeks.

I checked my call log to confirm I had actually called Annie before making my bed on the beach and did not dream that, too. As always, she was very sympathetic and ready to pull any strings for me. At one point it sounded like she covered the phone with her hand and had a short discussion with her husband. She came back and said that he "Grumbled a Little, but he Agreed to Swap Schedules" with me. Wonderful. By the way that he treats me when we work together, I am certain that David already thinks I am sleeping with his wife, and at least half the veteran drivers--maybe even Floyd--seem to agree. *Oh well*, I figured, *I won't be sticking around when I get back, so what does it matter anyway.*

Meanwhile, I had almost two full days to kill. I was the only driver heading north for the next round of Landmark tours, so I had all of Saturday to make the three hour drive to San Jose. I contemplated this as I sat in a booth at the Chevron station and sipped my Foglifter--best gas station coffee ever, from a local roaster, one of the perks of being back in Cambria--absently scanning the front page of the Los Angeles Times. It seemed like the thing to do was to continue on up toward Big Sur, spend the night wherever I wound up, and start heading south in the morning.

Once the sun was all the way up, I went back out to Route 1 and stuck out my thumb. Within a few minutes, I had a ride in what must have been a 1960s Volvo wagon, driven by an ageless man with flowing silver hair. The car gave the impression of a bicycle within a cage that seated four, so it would hardly have shocked me to look down at the floorboards and see him pedaling. The dashboard looked and smelled like my grandfather's old fishing boat. I am not even sure it had a speedometer. But the thing puttered along in its steady tortoise-like way, and the old man said nothing. He just looked at me with a Cheshire cat smile and nodded his approval. This is what he did for the whole ride to everything he saw. I imagined that he was on his way to spend the rest of his life at the *Esalen Institute*, or maybe to sit on a cliff in the lotus position for forty days to bring about world peace--or maybe he just drives his putt-putt wagon up and down the coast, looking for forlorn hitchhikers at which to smile and nod. I just wanted to put more distance between myself and Cayucos, so I was up for a ride with anyone.

We passed the flats of San Simeon and Piedras Blancas, covered by the gray marine layer that I imagined made the Pacific look like the Irish Sea. About an hour into the trip (normally more like 40 minutes), we reached the mountains from my teenage bedroom altar that slope straight into the ocean, their rounded peaks lost in the fog. The ancient wagon slowed to a near stop on the first incline switchback, but it had pulled these hills a thousand times and would pull them many thousands more, or so I was pleased to think. Soon we were into the thick of the clouds ourselves, and the little twigs that held the windshield wipers sprung to life, to the old man's smiling and nodding delight. Then we briefly poked above the cloud layer and saw the great expanse of their sparkly white sunny side like a marshmallow sea, clear blue sky above us to the heavens. Then we dipped back down into the clouds and up above them again. We did this a few times, like a dolphin swimming through the water and popping up for air. The old man just smiled and nodded and took all the curves and dips and hairpin turns like we were riding on rails.

I rode with him up past Gorda, but there were some trails in that vicinity I was itching to hike so I jumped out shortly after. I could have stayed with him forever. I wonder if I was supposed to, and together we would drive off into that good night. But I guess it was not time to go yet. Too much unfinished business here. The driver smiled and nodded even more vigorously as I stepped out, and then he surprised me with a graceful two-fingered wave, like something you would expect from a messiah. Then I closed the door, and the little Flintstone car puttered off to God knows where. I watched it disappear around the next looping bend, wondering if I was about to wake up on the beach in Cambria. Or did the dream sequence go back even further?

If it had been a dream, it somehow transitioned seamlessly back into a cold reality, its whimsy dashed on the rocks of my hard analytical mind. Nothing too noteworthy happened for most of that day, which was disappointing in itself, as this was something I had wanted to do since we arrived in California. Nadia never has enough energy to handle the heavy verticals of the Big Sur backcountry trails, so we generally limit ourselves to flat observatory areas like Ragged Point. I always envisioned having a day like this for myself to explore, maybe dream about where I would perch that mountaintop home overlooking the ocean after I become a bestselling author...but my mind was too full of things neither immediate nor grandiose. I was dwelling on the new life I was facing back east--where I would try to settle, seeing my friends and family again, what they would say when I show up alone. These things obviously did not come to pass, so there is no sense in rehashing them now and letting them obscure this story as they did my solo hiking day.

The one watershed moment that started to change everything came late in the day. After punishing my MSG-poisoned body for hours, I decided to make one last dash up the Vicente Flat trail. In contrast to its name, the trail starts with one of the least flat stretches in Big Sur, straight up and then out about two miles along rocky ridgeline parallel to the coast that all the trail guides lauded as being among the most stunning ocean views in the area. I knew I had been unusually absent all day, and I imagined this could be that one snapshot moment I could capture to commemorate this incredible place and this phase of my life here, something to hold onto until I could return on better terms.

So I pushed my exhausted legs up one more climb. And I reached the top. And there it was, again, the *Eureka!* moment I was seeking.

Only it was not the kind I was expecting at all.

I did not have a concept for what I felt at the time, and I had not truly developed one until I experienced it again, in the present tense, on September 11, at the top of Azucar Mountain.

All I knew at the time was a ripped-open feeling in my gut, and a pang of fear in my heart. I needed to get off the mountain and back to town. The thought of spending another night sleeping alone in the wild suddenly felt unbearable. I needed to be around people--anybody. Strangers would be just fine, just not *nobody*.

Time was short to get back to the highway and catch a ride going south. I guessed that I had come a mile and a half from the trailhead, almost all uphill or level, so the descent would be much quicker, although with my knee condition applying the brakes is more painful than climbing so I had to resist the panicky urge to go bounding down the hill. I reached the highway by 6:30 am, a little under an hour before sunset. Not desperation time yet, but considering the high percentage of tourists who would be passing me by without a glance, it was no guarantee I would get a ride before dark. About a half-hour passed, and all the time I wondered if my dreamboat was on its way back through to take me, smiling and nodding, back from whence I came.

The ride I did end up getting was the complete opposite in every way. It was a college kid in a shiny red Camaro that looked like it had just rolled off the showroom floor. He seemed happy, too, in his own vacuous way, and he talked my ear off while driving like hellfire all the way down the coast. He was from Pebble Beach, among the affluent communities at the northern gateway to Big Sur, and he was heading to Santa Barbara to start preseason workouts with the UCSB water polo team. The car, he felt the need to explain, was a present from his dad for his 21st birthday--it wasn't like he just bought it for him for no reason, of course. While he elaborated on the finer points of water polo strategy, I marveled to myself at the fact that I, an above average student who was excelling in my journalism classes, had been working my way through school and still amassing $10,000 a year in debt, while this dimwit whose father could afford to buy him a Camaro was getting a free ride for throwing a ball around a pool. When I told him he could drop me off in Cambria, he informed me that he "banged a chick from Cambria once...or maybe it was Morro Bay." I zoned out after that--*OK*, I whispered to the universe, *not just* anybody, please. But I did appreciate the timely and expeditious ride (even after he had the cajones to ask for gas money), because thanks to him, I actually got to Main Street Grill before closing time.

As much traveling as I have done, I have seen woefully little of the planet, in fact nothing has coaxed me off of North America yet. But in the wee little portion that I have explored with insane thoroughness, there are few sources of cheap eats that I would place above Main Street Grill. It is everything wonderful about the ambience of the north SLO County coast--I picture a sea otter, floating on its back in the lightly bobbing waters of Estero Bay, munching on abalone out of a shell sitting on its belly, not a care in the world-- without all the excess money. The ridiculously early closing time (8 pm) is in sync with the local culture as well, so it was kind of miraculous that I made it there in time to strap on the feed bag. It occurred to me as I was trying to decide what to order that I had eaten nothing all day but two protein bars I picked up at the gas station, so I went hog wild and got the ABC burger (avocado, bacon, and cheddar) *and* the tri-tip salad, along with the requisite oversized "small" bowl of seasoned fries. I even indulged in a glass of local pinot noir, just because I could.

I grabbed a corner table so I could soak it all in. Main Street was slammin' busy as always. Hearst Castle tourists, local families, vacationers in town on summer home getaways from the inferno of the Central Valley, teenagers on the prowl, even a pack of BMW motorcyclists fresh from an exhilarating Route 1 ride--they all blended into a mass of humanity that felt strangely cohesive. It may not have been community in the strictest sense, but there was a commonness I rarely allow myself to feel. A half-dozen wide screen TVs added to the attention deficit element. One showed highlights from east coast baseball games, flanked by live broadcasts of the Dodgers on one side and the Giants on the other. The Food Network and Animal Planet were also represented. Ahh...it was exactly what I needed: to be part of the human family, engaged in frivolous, perhaps even extravagant consumption, not taking themselves too seriously nor beating themselves up for everything they have done wrong, or for taking more than their share of the world's resources. It is the curse of the First World, this ability to consume at will, and the only cures for this disease of the conscience, aside from physically removing oneself, are to quit speaking the language (as Nadia and I attempted unwittingly), give away all one earns and follow one's God/guru of choice, or give up the fight and gorge oneself on the teat of the beast until one forgets that any among us lack. That night, I had to surrender. Something on the mountaintop scared the fight out of me.

I also found myself thinking of Nadia again, and not in the way I wanted to be thinking of her, as someone who would soon be in my rearview mirror. If my conscience was clamoring for me to contact her and offer to make amends, I stuffed the message back with food and wine and said *Give it one more night*. It was not unusual for me to disappear overnight after a major fight, but a second night would raise an eyebrow, maybe even make her think and realize there are lines she has to prevent herself from crossing. The cut on my arm still stung, and I wanted her to feel the pain a little longer.

When Main Street actually closed its doors at nine o'clock (they are good about refraining from chasing people away while they close), I rolled my fat belly toward the village center and found the hostel I had heard about. It looked so much like someone's home that it felt more like a low budget bed-and-breakfast than a hostel, and I thought nothing of shelling out $22 for a bunk. I spent the rest of the enchanted evening in the common space, pretending to read a Lonely Planet guidebook to Costa Rica, while completely enthralled by a coven of diabolically beautiful Belgian sirens. They poured over maps and spoke vigorously to each other in their guttural Dutch tongue, oblivious to the ugly American and his unclean thoughts in their midst. I fell asleep feeling stuffed and basted in comfort.

The next morning, I took stock of my situation over bagels and ollalieberry jam. My day of hiding in the mountains had morphed into a rather expensive turn of the page .With the money for the dorm space and the lavish dinner spent, plus $10 for Bitchin' Camaro Boy (it was the smallest bill I had, damnit), I was down to under $90. That would have gotten me through either of the two weeks on the Yellowstone trips, but I had decided that my body could not handle another solid week of Chinese buffets, so I was planning to ad lib some of my meals. My decision to leave the bank card with Nadia had now painted me into a corner. I would need to go back to the house one way or another. If I were doing that, I figured, I might as well pack up a duffle bug with provisions for a Level 2 escape: a few of the most important books, and maybe a week's worth of clothes instead of three days.

It was time to call Nadia. My heart raced as I cued up our home number and it rang. After five or six rings, Nadia grabbed it and spoke quickly as if she had pounced on it. I told her where I was. She sounded a lot more relieved than angry, which lessened my tension a bit. She had noticed my notebooks were gone, and was worried that I was serious this time. I told her a half-truth: that I was afraid she might become wantonly destructive and target my few cherished and irreplaceable things. She promised she would never do that, and then after a short pause, she asked if I had planned to come back. *Say No, say No!* I told myself...but I could not pronounce the word. The resolve had seeped away, again. That fucking mountaintop.

"Yeah. I was."

She said she was glad.

Then I told her about the Landmark trip, that Annie switched things around so I could do the Grand Canyon for one week, and I wanted to follow through with it. There was a lengthy pause, and when Nadia spoke again she sounded deflated. But she offered to pick me up and bring me home to pack, and then run me down to SLO to get the bus.

I met Nadia at the gas station. I did not want her to know I had spent a posh night at the hostel. She looked like she had not slept since I left. We hugged, but it was mechanical, devoid of the overflowing warmth that usually follows a severe fight. I gathered that whatever reconciliation would have come from causing her to reflect on the situation was spent on my decision to go away for another week.

And so that was what brought us to the Eldorado parking lot on Saturday, September 1, 2001. We sat there for the longest time with the motor off, both looking straight ahead, silent. Nadia had not said a word since we left the house. No jokes about Chinese girlfriends. Not even a protest against the trip. Silence never bodes well with Nadia, so I scanned my mind for some positive angle for her to take home with her. All I could come up with was a feeble "Hey, when I get back, we'll be about $3,000 closer to a down payment." She looked down, and her jaw tightened like she was gritting her teeth. Ouch. Time to cut my losses. I leaned over and kissed her softly just above the temple, and as I opened my door I told her I would see her in a week, and that I loved her. She mumbled something as I started to get up, and I started to say I didn't hear her when--

"YOU'LL APPRECIATE ME WHEN I'M DEAD!"

1:50 pm (PDT) / 4:50 pm (EDT)

I am keeping watch by Estelle's bed, falling into tiny naps. Melody has been gone for a little while, and the soft repetitive sounds of the medical equipment are lulling me to sleep. I am at least one large coffee behind in my daily routine, and I know I could get one from the cafeteria, but I've gotten to the point where I feel too lethargic to get up and help my situation.

The boost that I got from those realizations in the lobby seems to have left me. No voice is speaking to me now. It makes me wonder if that wasn't some kind of adrenal reaction, like an emotional version of the sudden power surge that makes an ordinary person lift up a car to save his child pinned underneath. I sure hope it wasn't.

Melody returns to the room, looking forlorn. She has been watching the TV news in the lobby, something I've diligently refused to do. Seeing it with my own eyes was enough evidence for me.

"Oh Joseph, I just heard that there were *hundreds* of people in Estelle's office when the first plane hit. They don't think anyone got out before the tower collapsed."

I close my eyes. I feel like the news *should be* stirring something in me, but everything stirrable has settled into a still numbness. I started feeling it the moment I was pressed into action while besieged by fear for Vera. It kept me from being paralyzed or shattering into pieces, so it served me well while it was needed. But now I cannot seem to turn it off. I wish I could, but I don't know how. Not because the feeling is foreign to me--it is *too* familiar.

It is nothing more than an extreme manifestation of what I've learned to get through *every* day.

"I can't wrap my mind around that...not at all. Maybe it will come to me later. Right now," I say, gesturing toward Estelle, "this feels like all I can handle."

"I understand," Melody says with true empathy. "I felt like I was wearing a suit of armor all day at school, and didn't get to take it off until I got home and heard your message. I cried hysterically into my pillow for about twenty minutes before I could do *anything*. Then I called her parents to reassure them that she wasn't in the tower, and I hustled over here."

I pick my head up from the slouch it had assumed. "*Her* parents?...I had a feeling you weren't sisters."

Melody smirks, and blushes a bit. "We don't look anything alike, do we?"

"Not in the slightest."

Melody raises her right hand. "I cannot tell a lie. We're not related. We've been best girlfriends since second grade back in Buchanan County, Mizzourah. But we're accustomed to having to pretend we are sisters. You saw how much better reception I got from the hospital staff than you did."

"Hmmm, yes. I'm guessing you have some experience with that?"

"More than I care to," Melody sighs. She pauses before proceeding, not sure what level of security clearance to give me. "Two months ago, Estelle was diagnosed with uterine cancer, one of the worst forms of it, too. She had an emergency hysterectomy that seems to have caught it before it spread. Thank God I wasn't teaching summer school, and I was able to go home to be with her for it. Her slime ball husband just got drunk the whole time, couldn't handle the pressure. Two weeks after the surgery, he split, ran off with his secretary. Can you *imagine* how low a person can be to do that?"

Unfortunately, I can. The picture is becoming much clearer.

"Did he ever hit her?"

"A couple times, when he was drunk. Not that it should ever happen for any reason. But that was the one form of abuse where he showed a bit of restraint. I think he was afraid to make her bleed."

"Oh right, the blood thinner. What's the story behind that?"

Melody exhales sharply. "*That* is the really scary story, long-term...a few years ago, she had a very mild stroke. It hardly even set her back really, but her doctor took it very seriously, said it was a huge wake-up call. She has a clotting disorder in her blood. It's a genetic condition, and it has affected many of the men in her family over the years, but she never showed any signs of it until the stroke. The doctor said if it had happened much closer to her heart, it could have led to cardiac arrest. He considered her fairly high risk, so he put her on Coumadin. Of course now she bleeds like a hemophiliac, so there's that kind of danger. She gets her blood tested monthly to make sure the clotting factor is in a manageable range. That's where she was this morning. I *knew* she was going to be too woozy from that. I should have driven her to the train station, but she said she needed her car later and insisted on driving."

"I see. That explains a lot."

"And the poor girl's still at above average risk for a heart attack because there has been so much plaque buildup, also genetic. She may be looking at stints before long." Melody turns to face her friend. "Basically, her body is a ticking time bomb. I've had to come to accept that the price of loving her will probably be losing her too soon." She exhales again, tension easing as she does. "But whattaya gonna do? You don't close your heart to a person just because she's not long for this world. Maybe *none* of us are...you just gotta love as deep as you can while you're here and never count the cost. You know?"

All I can do is nod. I have been a professional cost-counter for way too long. Twenty-two years, to be precise. For a few moments, there is no sound in the room besides the steady, soft beep of Estelle's pulse monitor.

"So Vera told me your mother was Sufi."

The abrupt change of gears catches me off guard. I shake my head, inwardly. *Damn you, Vera*...yet another absentee provocation of one of my greatest vulnerabilities. She knows how much I dislike talking about my mother.

"That's actually something you and Estelle have in common," she continues. "Her mother, her aunt, her grandmother, and even great-grandmother Estelle have all been Universal Sufis."

"Really?" I wish I could gracefully change the subject. "Wow. That's not something you'd expect to find out about a person."

"Of course this was the Midwest, so they had to pretend to be Methodist or Lutheran to avoid being ostracized."

I pause for a moment. It has been a long time since I unlocked the vault where this information is kept...but the voice is coming back now...it whispers, saying I have kept my mother locked in this crypt for far too long. I owe it to her to let her out. With lingering apprehension. I proceed.

"My mother...was raised in the old Mevlevi tradition that dates back to Rumi himself. She lived in Tabriz as a young girl in fact, home of Rumi's beloved mentor."

"Oh wow, Joseph, that's fascinating!" Melody leans forward in her chair, both elbows on her knees, hands propping up her chin, looking completely enmeshed. No going back now, I realize.

"Her family emigrated to America to escape a more menacing kind of ostracism from the growing fundamentalism in Iran. They settled in Brooklyn and were very active in the Sufi community here. Then she grew up and married a wop from Bensonhurst."

"Oh my. That sounds like a very interesting mix."

"The funny thing is neither family approved of the pairing. You can imagine how an airtight traditional Italian clan would respond to a Muslim woman from Iran. But her family was just as prejudiced toward him. Her father said if she married a Catholic she'd become a slave to her husband and the pope, and he came here to give her better than that, blah blah blah. So yeah, they were a match made in Babel. It was like Romeo and Juliet with less backstabbing. She kept her faith, though, kept it to the end."

"How did she die?"

I grimace as the irony slices my throat.

"Uterine cancer."

"Oh...I'm so sorry."

I stare off, getting lost in the methodical drip of the IV unit.

"She refused any treatment. Said Allah was calling her home and she wasn't afraid. She was ready to go. Yeah, she was ready. Try explaining that to your thirteen year old son, though...."

A tear starts to well up in my eye, but it does not fall. Melody takes my hand. I give her a faint grin as a thank you, then shrug.

"Papa was a long-shores-man, a simple guy. Times were tough for dockworkers then, and he'd just taken a second job to make ends meet. My mother was the rock of the family, she held us all together. And then she was gone...I know I've always blamed her for that, but I think I also heaped on all the blame for the whole conflict between my families, and the fact that Papa was left behind to deal with the alienation from both sides. She was the freak who chose death over life after all."

I stagger for a moment as I think of that. It sounds so wrong now that I've put it into words and shared it with someone else. The voice is speaking clearly and firmly now. *Set her free...let her go.*

For twenty-two years, you've made a dead Sufi woman carry

your own cross...it is time to take it from her.

"But that's not true really. All these years I've assumed that anyone who welcomes death has rejected life...I think I've been very wrong about that. My mother didn't reject *anything* during her life. She was the gentlest, most peaceful soul you could imagine. If anything, she had too much peace to stay in this crazy world. But it wasn't a rejection of the world....I think it might have been the greatest *affirmation* she could give. She knew the world would go on without her just fine. She knew that her family would be OK. She tried to share that peace with us when she left... but I didn't listen. And you know what? I still turned out OK."

Meoldy looks awestruck. I can hardly believe what I hear myself saying now. The words are not coming from me anymore.

"Papa was OK, too. He let her go in his own way that I never understood. He grew softer and kinder; I thought it was a weakness in him that accepted her going away. But I think he was growing into assuming her role. He knew he'd have to be a mother and a father to us kids...I can't believe I missed it all these years, but they really did bring out the best in each other. And they both encouraged each other to stay true to their faiths. Their families never saw it, but they were *both* the innocent ones. They loved each other beyond these archaic differences. I admire them both equally...I've never vocalized that until now."

Melody beams again with that room-engulfing smile. "That's so amazing, Joseph. I really commend you for realizing that."

Now *this* might be a sign that I've gone crazy, or it might not, but I'll be damned if I don't feel something (or someone?) release itself from this secret hiding place in my chest and fly away.

"It's such a strange world we live in sometimes, ain't it? Seems like there is always a reason for one group to hate another: these ones don't worship the right God, those do but they don't do it the right way, this one isn't pure enough, that one isn't strict enough, those ones aren't enlightened enough. Where are the people who are just content to be themselves, and let everyone else be who everyone else is? I want to be part of that group."

"I'd say that's where the Universal Sufis have it right," says Melody. "I don't know a ton about them, but I know they view all spiritual paths as valid, and they find inspiration from all sources, not just the Qur'an. They seem to be real freethinkers. I know Estelle's family has some very eccentric ideas. But they're also the sweetest people on earth, so they're doing something very right."

"But Estelle isn't Sufi herself?"

"I know she would like to believe and practice and continue that family lineage. She's just had an awful lot of hard reality thrown at her. But she keeps overcoming it beautifully, too, so she is doing something right herself. How about you? I'm guessing you didn't follow in your mother's footsteps."

I laugh, though inwardly I am already regretting the truth I have to speak. "Are you kidding? If I so much as see that guy's poems on a greeting card, I get tense... but I'm starting to wonder what good that has done me. I think if nothing else, I just want to be able to understand Vera better."

"How so?"

I formulate my thoughts carefully. Words do not come easy here. This is completely uncharted territory for me now.

"Vera is *so much* like my mother in so many ways. Well, a loony boisterous American version of my mother. But she can relate to *anbody*. I can see her being one of these people who exemplifies the best of everyone's spiritual path just like my mother did. I think that's a big part of what drew me to her, and also why I keep a distance between us. It scares the daylights out of me to be that open. And I tell ya, sometimes, I listen to the things she tells me, and I think, 'Holy hell, my wife is a total wingnut.' I'm afraid I treat her like that much more often than I realize. But then I look at how she goes about life, what she does for people, the values she teaches our daughters, and how much patience and love she has for a schlub like me, and I just *KNOW* that what she sees must be real. There's just too much personal evidence to keep ignoring it. I'd bet my life on it."

Tears are streaming down both cheeks now. I let them fall.

"I don't think she really knows how much I appreciate her...I pray that I will be able to tell her."

Melody embraces me and squeezes hard. I hold on, as if for dear life. Here comes the flood. Finally.

"You will, darling," she whispers into my ear under my wailing sobs. "I know you will."

2:00 pm (PDT) / 5:00 pm (EDT)

Not out of the woods yet, literally or figuratively. But at least I am back to a familiar spot, and I know which way I walked to get to it the first time I was there. I decide to try the opposite of what I just did, figure it has a 50/50 shot of working out. If I can make it before collapsing that, is. I do not know if I have ever been quite this tired.

So...you'll appreciate me when I'm dead.

On the Richter scale of vulgarity and volatility in Nadia's outbursts, this was barely a tremor. But truth moves at light speed and with laser precision, and this one snuck right through a crack in my armor and stunned me in my tracks like no inflammatory haymaker would. I could not walk away from the car, but I couldn't get back in, either. I did not want to go *or* stay. Damn her, she got me good.

Nadia actually made up my mind for me. With a surprising burst of strength, she leaned over, yanked the door out of my hands and slammed it shut while I scrambled out of the way. Then the car bolted forward, the right rear tire coming close enough to my toes to make me wince when I thought about it, and made a dash toward the driveway before she realized my bags were still in the back. She jerked it to a halt, jumped out and lifted up the hatchback door, grabbed both of my bags and tossed them to the ground--again, wow, this must have been pure adrenaline--then hopped back in and sped off in a thick cloud of dust. I stood and watched the dust settle for a good minute before moving toward my gear, not sure what to make of what I just saw. I wanted to be furious and consider it validation for my plans to escape. But there was something too admirable in the way that she turned the tables on me so quickly and so thoroughly, like only a born truth-bearer can.

One thing it proved to me that I already strongly suspected--and proof is far better than suspicion in such matters--is that Nadia's statement was *not* a suicide threat. In one of her more lucid moments, Nadia once explained to me that the reason she had not taken her own life yet was that she was too greedy for human experience, so there was no way she could voluntarily bring hers to an end. It struck me as such a beautiful self-assessment of the defiance that makes her tick. (Another gem from the same conversation that I have to remind her from time to time: she did not hitch her wagon to mine expecting me to provide safety and comfort, but the widest possible range of experience.) If she had slinked away silently with the same kind of demeanor she had when I left the house Thursday night, I might have been concerned enough to think about undoing all the plans. But explosive anger means business as usual for Nadia. This may or may not have pushed her to the point where she was also considering life without me, but either way, life was the only option. There was a better chance that I would drive off the rim of the Grand Canyon with a bus full of screaming Chinese than Nadia would kill herself over this.

As for me, there was nothing to do but trudge forward, and hope I would find some kind of sign in the desert.

From the moment I pulled onto Highway 101 North, I knew it was exactly what I needed, and where I needed to be doing it. To go three hours in either direction on 101 from San Luis Obispo is to experience one of the greatest freeway drives in California, in my humble connoisseur's opinion. But heading north jazzes me the most. The ground I covered that day on *El Camino Real* parallels Route 1 (if it is possible to parallel such a squiggly line) on the east side of the Santa Lucias. Here the mountains rise like a wall of earth, more sharply than on the coastal slope, from the arid rift zone on the edge of the valley. This is Steinbeck country, a rugged land where agriculture and the untamed wild meet in a dynamic compromise that brings out the beauty of both. It is also the last stretch of road I missed as a somnambulating thirteen-year-old, right before that fateful detour over the mountain to the coast. I was mindful of that as I retraced those footsteps, hoping to rediscover what was lost before the first awakening.

For an introverted driver like myself, three hours alone on a rolling bus is nothing short of paradise. I should qualify that: assuming I did not just nearly cause a catastrophic accident in that bus. The drive home from Fresno was fairly hellacious. I am curious about this dichotomy I experience in my own company, how it can vary to such extremes depending on my frame of mind. Makes me wonder if Nadia and I are really all that different.

I let that thought marinade in my mind while I cruised past sleepy towns like King City and Soledad. One of the tragic consequences of a condition like Nadia's is that its negative aspects are what people tend to remember because they are the loudest, and even I as her closest companion and life partner am not immune to that prejudice. The reality is that she spends about ninety percent of her waking hours going through the normal range of moods and emotions that everyone else experiences--OK, maybe what a highly right-brained, redheaded Leo semi-lunatic artist experiences. It is just the remaining ten percent that ranges from the highest highs to the lowest lows.

It gives me pause to wonder if the way I talk about her on the rare occasions when I do open up leads people like Floyd and Paul to assume the ratio is reversed. This would be a major disservice to her truth, for in my opinion, the true Nadia is to be found in the ninety percent. This is where she is when she creates her artwork, when she graciously and conscientiously pours herself into preparing nutritious food, when she extends herself into the community and inspires people with her wisdom and humor*--and yes, even the majority of her time with me is spent within this spectrum of wacky artistic normalcy, for better or for worse. Before we invented high-fallutin' terms and pharmaceutical treatments for every variety of mental illness, people like Nadia were believed to have a demon living within them. I used the word "intruder" to describe the personage I encountered on that horrible night in Arizona. Both terms suggest something that is not Nadia has entered her being and is now the source of her extreme reactions to inner turmoil. I can follow this reasoning most of the way to its conclusion, and frankly my biggest hang-up is not the tendency to imagine it as a phantasmic boogey-man with its own existential integrity, but rather that this logic presupposes a firm line between self and non-self. But that is another story for another time. For now, I believe it is fair to conclude that the demon-intruder is an entity that is *in* Nadia but not *of* her, and therefore, Not Her.

If I am going down that road, I think I will get much closer to the truth by going back to an analogy that I used at the very beginning--the shadows that follow us both as we migrate from coast to coast. The one that "stays attached at the heels," created by the physical body, is a perfect metaphor for what I mean here. The interloper is not something that afflicts only an unfortunate few, and it does *not*, I hasten to add, have an independent, objective existence, just as a shadow depends on a solid body and a light source to exist.

This idea started to percolate a couple months ago when I decided I might want to be a Quaker. I had heard that the focal point of their weekly prayer meetings was not a sermon, but a shared period of *silent* worship--O, sacred silence! My ears loved the sound of that! Then I learned that the purpose of silent worship is to provide the space for each person to get in touch with the "Inner Light" that is within everyone, not just an in-group of holy rollers or saved souls. The Quakers say that if we

---

*In general, Nadia has no difficulty at all drawing people to her and making genuine friends, even if most of them eventually recoil from the extremes of her behavior. The Central Coast was a glaring exception to this. Her initial adjustment to living with blind spots in her vision, and the turn inward that this necessitated, was partly to blame. I also believe the "keep moving, stranger" culture clash affected her powerfully and imbued her view of California with a stronger alienation than what I experienced. I have always felt a subtle alienation everywhere, and never truly expected to stop moving.

listen intently, we will hear the voice of the Inner Light and it will give us the counsel we need. So they gather to give each other silent space and wait to be moved by the voice of Inner Light before they speak.

If this is so, I pondered while the lush fields of Salinas and Prunedale flew by, why are most people unaware of their own Inner Light? Part of the answer might lie in my earlier ruminations on noise--we have no appreciation for silence and immerse ourselves in all manner of noise. But my experience told me it must be something more fundamental than that, for even when I escape the manmade noise of our world for a while, something within me keeps me just as blind to any Inner Light, and deaf to its subtle voice.

A little farther up the road, as I approached the savory aroma of Gilroy, the garlic capital of the world, a theory arose as to why we are unaware of the Inner Light: we aren't. We have known of the Inner Light since time began. Ordinary people from all over the world have sensed it time and time and time again. In fact, it is as familiar to us as our heartbeat.

But we perceive Inner Light in the form that our culture has taught us, like a filter over a lens, creating an iconic image that resonates most with the individual's mind and heart.

A Christian, for example, will see Inner Light and feel the presence of Christ or hear the voice of the Holy Spirit, or, for Catholics, an even more personified image like the Virgin Mary or one of the saints. I am sure other faith traditions have their own filters, creating their own images from the same source (I made use of a few from Hindu culture before). Each filter carries a whole host of cultural assumptions about the nature of the light, who it shines from or is intended to shine upon, the purpose of its voice, etc.--none of which are intrinsic to the light itself.

Nadia and I were both raised in what she calls a "dogmatically secular" culture, the new dominant paradigm in the modern western world, which denies the Inner Light altogether. Its perception is couched into vague, innocuous concepts like "intuition" and "conscience," without any exploration of the origins of these faculties. Some of the storyboards for these filters are left in the hands of New Age philosophers and their marketing teams; others, in the homilies of the moviemakers at Disney Studios. By and large, however, as I suggested earlier, to take with any solemnity or seriousness the perceptions of any form of Inner Light, in this day and age, is an invitation to have one's sanity questioned. Given what I've concluded about sanity and its viable alternatives, this seems to me a dangerous path for an entire culture to tread at once.

But if I was right in my theory about the Quakers, there is hope. For at that moment it seemed clear to me that there is a significant subculture that travels a middle road, swimming against the streams of both traditional religion and modern secularism, seeking the direct, immediate experience of Inner Light with as little filter as possible, finding inspiration and guidance in all of the world's scriptures but idolizing none of them. I see this as a loose affiliation of dissidents from all faith traditions or none at all--people who learned from the great exemplars that reforming an authoritarian institution only creates a new, more rigorous authority, so the only rational choice is to *de-form* it: boil it down until nothing rigid is left and only Inner Light shines through.

I would count the Quakers, who find all the evidence for Christ that they need in their own experience and do not deify the words of the Christian Bible, among them.

I would also count Nadia. Without a doubt.

Which is to say that following this middle road is no piece of cake. Being out there on what appears to be one's own, ontologically, alienated from the "normal" people all around--this has the potential to create its own kind of pathologies that feed on our vulnerability as individuals. When a light shines on any hard object, it also casts a shadow. Inner Light seems to be no different.

It was the shadowy aspects of the Inner Light that drew my attention as I reached the southern edge of San Jose sprawl, the slanty daylight of late afternoon cast upon the landscape. There seems to be a whole iconography in our cultural filters for the shadow as well, the most common and obvious being the devil and his crew of meanies and malignant forces. With someone like Nadia, the demon-intruder is more visible, more personal, and more bent on premature destruction.

But even this very real and grave perception, it must not be forgotten, is shaped by images that are lodged in our collective imagination. If the devil did not exist, it would be necessary to invent him, and that is the point: it was, and we did. God, too. It was necessary because of a twin experience that is universal, to some degree, in all human beings: one day we wake up and we are dazzled to see that all of life is a brilliant light that shines within us, all of us, without explanation; at the same time, we are spooked because of an equally unexplained, unrelenting dark space that follows us everywhere. Our brain and our five senses tell us that as life leaves our body, the darkness overcomes us and persists as a death without end...but the voice within us whispers the most inexplicable part of all: the Light prevails. In every life. Each and every time.

As the bus hissed to a stop behind the hotel just off the Southbay Freeway, I felt like I had just learned to formulate the question that *homo sapiens* have been asking themselves for thousands of years, without any definitive answer. We keep going because it swallows every other question whole. We have to ask. If we stop, we may survive, but we will cease to fully live.

2:15 pm (PDT) / 5:15 pm (EDT)

I am guessing on the time, since I have no timepiece. Seems about right. A trio of mockingbirds (another assumption on my part, but it also fits) follows me, calling back and forth to each other about the strange bird traipsing through their woods. Somewhere the sand in an hourglass that measures my opportunity to get the birders back to Santa Maria for the Day One wrap-up gathering is running awfully low. And I can only hope that my current path is leading me back to the bus. Still no birder voices in my extensive earshot. But something tells me this is the right way, so I keep going....

Motor coach drivers, whose job description involves some of the least adherence to routine in the history of labor, tend to be creatures of habit when off the clock. Typically on Saturday evenings at the Landmark outpost in San Jose, the incoming soldiers of the road and the fresh meat all convene across the street at Location #875 of some corporate restaurant chain to swap war stories and gossip and whatnot. I had joined them on my first two turnaround days. On September 1, I got my room and sequestered myself there like a monk in his cell. I had too much momentum to risk losing it in the vapid chatter of bus driver world. No one would expect me to be there anyway; I had a hard-earned reputation among Eldorado drivers as the Stargazer Boy of the pack.

I did not bring this portion of the story into the present tense in order to search for an answer to the questions it raised--though I now consider that a worthy endeavor, perhaps the most worthy. Instead, my intent is to show with as much detail as possible why I believe that Nadia's demons are essentially no different than my own nor anyone else's. The difference is in the magnitude: the immediacy of the question--I have every reason to think death is an event 46.7 years into my future; Nadia has every reason to think differently--and the fact that her body seems to punish her for being alive on a daily basis. But just as religion now seems to be a reaction to the experience of Inner Light and Inner Darkness, I am guessing that what we call bipolar disorder is a symptom of a reaction to a pesky shadow, not the cause.

Our varying reactions to the shadow explain a lot about human behavior. I suspect that most people never notice their shadow, so fixed is their vision upon only what is around them. If they catch a glimpse of it, they hide from it or numb their sensitivity to it with one drug or another. These are the ones who cast their darkness about carelessly and wonder why they find so much conflict in their lives. Others become aware of their shadow, but incorporate it seamlessly into their being, perhaps calling it their "dark side." Yet others, like me, become acquainted at such a tender age that they are liable to be frightened, and may spend the rest of their lives being chased by their shadow until they come to some kind of terms with it. These are the ones who compulsively wash their windows, or try to master parlor tricks like levitation and transfiguration.

Then there are the poor souls who at some point in their lives are assaulted by their shadow with such brute force that they are shattered then and there. They often wind up shadow boxing on the sidewalks and lost highways, or locked up in institutions. Those who survive the first blow and are feisty and resilient enough to keep fighting may wage an epic battle, and may even go the distance standing toe to toe with the enemy. This is how we get our mad poets and artists, our Vincent van Goghs and Allen Ginsbergs, our King Davids and Han Shans.

I hope it is clear by now that *both* Nadia and I exhibit varying degrees of maladaptive reactions to our shadows. The primary difference between us is our fight-or-flight response tendencies.

I almost exclusively choose the more socially acceptable flight option, whereas Nadia is engaged in a bare knuckle brawl to the death with hers. That is why I am constantly being chased back and forth across the country, while Nadia gets knocked up and down a precipitous scale of emotions that dwarfs what a "normal" human experiences. Both of us, however, are haunted by the same phantom.

When I came home and packed a second bag for the Grand Canyon trip, I decided to grab a few books, knowing the itinerary for the week ahead would be more merciful than Yellowstone. One book that made the cut was Nadia's collection of essays by the modern Catholic monk-visionary Thomas Merton. It had been sitting on the back of the toilet for some time (oddly typical of the bathroom reading in our house) but I had never been inclined to pick it up. The reason I was raised in a dogmatically secular household is that both of my parents are recovering Irish Catholics, so I have a nearly inborn disinclination to consult the Mother Church for any guidance. In fact, for a variety of reasons, the Roman Catholic Church might have been the very last place I would expect to find spiritual kinship. But I had recently learned that, like the Quakers, Merton himself had a lot of street cred among people I esteemed, both for his interfaith dialogue and his efforts toward social justice and human rights movements. And the book was pocket-sized, so I figured the wisdom-to-mass ratio might be very high.

It did not disappoint. Reading Merton was like meeting a new best friend. I gobbled it up well into the night in the sanctuary of my hotel room, mining nugget after nugget of pure mystic gold from those tiny pages. One of the first passages was a rather well-known excerpt from Merton's book *Conjectures of a Guilty Bystander* describing an epiphany he had while traveling "in the world" after seventeen years in a monastery:

> *In Louisville, at the corner of Fourth and Walnut, in the center of the shopping district, I was suddenly*

overwhelmed with the realization that I loved all those people, that they were mine and I theirs, that we could not be alien to one another even though we were to-tal strangers. It was like waking from a dream of sepa-rateness, of spurious self-isolation in a special world, the world of renunciation and supposed holiness. The whole illusion of a separate holy existence is a dream... Though "out of the world," we are in the same world as everybody else, the world of the bomb, the world of race hatred, the world of technology, the world of mass media, big business, revolution, and all the rest. We take a different attitude to all these things, for we belong to God. Yet so does everybody else belong to God. We just happen to be conscious of it, and to make a profession out of this consciousness. But does that entitle us to consider ourselves different, or even better, than others? The whole idea is preposterous.

In the past I would have stumbled over or consciously balked at phrases like "belong to God" and dismissed it all as anachro-nistic gibberish. But Merton's simple sincerity compelled me to assimilate his experience, not merely grasp at understanding his words. I could relate to the person at Fourth and Walnut, because in a very real, non-metaphorical sense, I *was* him, and he was me. That's what his writing told me. Onward:

I have the immense joy of being man, a member of a race in which God Himself became incarnate. As if the sorrows and stupidities of the human condition could overwhelm me, now that I realize what we all are. And if only every-body could realize this! But it cannot be explained. There is no way of telling people that they are all walking around shining like the sun.

A jolt went down my spine as I read the last line. Inner Light... Merton saw it, too. In its pure state, without the filter taught by his culture. There is no way the Catholic Church would endorse a testimony that people are all shining like the sun. Approve of that, and next thing you'll have people running around claiming everyone is saved...so Merton was a bit of a heretic to his faith. The Quakers were originally chased out of England because the Anglican church considered *them* heretics. Catholics and Anglicans still cannot get along well enough to share a united Ireland. But the heretics corroborate each other without contradiction. Interesting.

One could begin to question the value of Merton's religious training in this light. But then there was this:

> *This changes nothing in the sense and value of my solitude, for it is in fact the function of solitude to make one realize such things with a clarity that would be impossible to anyone completely immersed in the other cares, the other illusions, and all the automatisms of a tightly collective existence.*

The last phrase made me think of gridlock, in fact that must be what brought it to my consciousness to be submerged in other thoughts and resurface this morning. I wondered if there is any hope for those of us wound up in a "tightly collective existence," or if solitude is the only means of cultivating perception of Inner Light. The next paragraph contained a clue, probably a bigger one than I realized at the time:

> *My solitude, however, is not my own, for I see now how much it belongs to them--and that I have a responsibility for it in their regard, not just in my own. It is because I am one with them that I owe it to them to be alone, and when I am alone, they are not "they" but my own self. There are no strangers! Then it was as if I suddenly saw the secret beauty of their hearts, the*

depths of their hearts where neither sin nor desire nor self-knowledge can reach, the core of their reality, the person that each one is in Gods eyes. If only they could all see themselves as they really are. If only we could see each other that way all the time.

If only, indeed...By then I was starting to feel that I could open to any page of Merton's writing with a question and find an answer to it.

One last piece that struck me that night came from an essay on the Desert Fathers. These were a loose affiliation of monks and holyfolk (there were Mothers among them of course) who retreated to hermetic lives in Egypt in the 3rd century. They were among the rock stars of early Christianity, at a time when the faith was still free and untamed. They were to the modern Christian church what a pack of wild mustangs is to a pony show, and the testimony of their direct, experiential practice has influenced the progressive element of Christian spirituality both east and west throughout the centuries.

In studying what motivated these desert hermits, Merton observed that *"one goes into the desert to vomit up the interior phantom, the doubter, the double."*

As I drifted off to sleep, I supposed that was what I set out to do as well. I needed to puke up the false self that casts my shadow, the idol, the "Pedro." If I was not going to run away and start a new life in the safety of "back east," I would need to come home better to Nadia than I ever had before.

I saw Paul in the morning as he prepared to head out for his *fourth* Landmark tour. He had called Annie the same night I did and begged her to let him stay out longer, and she was happy to oblige, giving him his first shot at Yellowstone. Apparently, Paul had fallen in love with motor coach driving--and, he was so giddy to tell me, his Chinese soul-mate. She was also a college student, traveling America with friends before going away to study for a year in Thailand. He was already making plans to visit her in Bangkok once he earned some vacation time from Eldorado in three months.

"I think she might be The One, Pedro," he beamed. "Can you believe it?"

"Wonderful," I said, then had to suppress a momentary urge to go Tyler Durden on that beautiful face of his. *No, think: WWT-MD?* I highly doubted Thomas Merton would beat him to a pulp.

I kept to myself on the Grand Canyon run, at least as much as I could with fifty five tourists following my every move. Sunday began with a frantic inversion of the Yellowstone Saturday, ending with an unceremonious plop at an obscure casino-hotel on the outskirts of Las Vegas. Once again, I avoided distractions and bunkered up in a booth at the In-and-Out across the street. I was hoping that Merton would give me insight about the shadow. Instead, I got a formal introduction. From the section called "Real and False Selves:"

> *To say I was born in sin is to say I came into the world with a false self. I was born in a mask... All sin starts from the assumption that my false self, the self that exists only in my egocentric desires, is the fundamental reality of life to which everything else in the universe is ordered. Thus I use up my life in the desire for pleasures and the thirst for experiences, for power, honor, knowledge, and love to clothe this false self and construct its nothingness into something objectively real. And I wind experiences around myself and cover myself with pleasures and glory like bandages in order to make myself perceptible to myself and to the world, as if I were an invisible body that could only become visible when something covered its surface.*

And then, the clincher:

> *Every one of us is shadowed by an illusory person: a false self. This is the man that I want to be but who cannot exist, because God does not know anything about him. And to be unknown to God is altogether too much privacy.*

Now Merton was *really* speaking my language. The Buddhist influence in the first part is undeniable. This is the cause of our loneliness in a world of abundance; indeed, as the Buddha said, the cause of all suffering--the idolatry of self. We create our inner shadow by constructing an idol of ourselves and standing in defiance of the Light; that, and our unwillingness to be transparent, or empty in the Buddhist sense.

So we had a Catholic monk espousing Quaker truths using Buddhist concepts. I wondered who else was in on this great conspiracy to subvert the paradigm that says we all need to stand in our own way and cast shadows on each other.

Monday was relatively easy, just a 400 mile jaunt to Grand Canyon Village by way of Hoover Dam, Route 66 schlock shops and Sedona. It was good to be back in the wild lands across the mountains from home, this time with a southwestern flavor. I felt free as we zoomed across the high desert, watching dust devils swoop across the Mother Road, racing 18-wheelers along the interstate.

My questions that day focused on the idolatry. How do we turn away from this worship of a false self? How do we peel off the dressings and bandages and let ourselves be transparent? Merton gave no clear answers, but plenty of hope for finding them in my evening reading as I nestled into a spot by the fireplace in the hotel lobby:

> *If we want to understand alienation, we have to find where its deepest taproot goes--and we have to realize that this root will always be there. Alienation is inseparable from culture, from civilization, and from life in society. It is not just a feature of "bad" cultures, "corrupt" civilizations, or urban society...alienation begins when culture divides me against myself, puts a mask on me, gives me a role I may or may not want to play. Alienation is complete when I become completely identified with my mask, totally satisfied with my role, and*

convince myself that any other identity or role is inconceivable. The man who sweats under his mask, whose role makes him itch with discomfort, who hates the division in himself *is already beginning to be free....*

This passage seemed to have a Christian essence. I am far from qualified as a Biblical scholar, but I'm pretty sure it says something like "all have sinned and fallen short of the glory of God," and I'm guessing we are expected to take that at face value without question. Here, Merton provides an answer to the unasked question: everyone *does* have the glory of God, the Inner Light, within them. He saw it in everyone at Fourth and Walnut. It is hidden from us because we all commit the "sin" of following our culture's lead and choosing to be this brittle trinket of an idol instead, wrapped in the bandages of our words and symbols and concepts and everything that makes life in a civilization feel more substantial. Those who are satisfied with this idol worship while alive, Merton suggested (and I believe Jesus agreed somewhere in the gospels), had better enjoy it while it lasts, before the coming storm of death shatters what they hold to be the sum of their existence...but those who are dissatisfied with a divided life may find out there is way more to the story....

The only true joy on earth is to escape from the prison of our own false self, and enter by love into union with the Life Who dwells and sings within the essence of every creature and in the core of our own souls.

Merton took me somewhere completely new with that one. The Life Who dwells within every creature...my first thought, oddly, went back to Splash Rios, and how I pondered what was happening as I watched life vanish from his body. "Who looked out from those eyes, and where has it gone?"

With those questions echoing in my mind, I contemplated the Life of which Merton wrote. Capital letters, written by a Christian, are a sure sign of a reference to Jesus Christ--who, by all accounts, was a human being who lived in Palestine around 2,000 years ago. A carpenter, not even a rabbi or prophet, let alone someone who dwells and sings in the core of our souls. Those who believe he was more than that attribute to him many statements like, "I am the Way, the Truth and the Life." An audacious statement indeed, if he were talking about the frail idol the Romans executed by nailing to a cross. His people called him a blasphemer; history has made him look a lunatic or worse. I had hardly given him a moment's thought in my twenty-nine years on earth.

At *that* moment, however, I did. A new seed of thought, planted by Merton, began to sprout.

Maybe when Jesus said, "I am the Way, the Truth and the Life," he wasn't talking about himself at all.

Maybe he was indeed an ordinary guy, not unlike Thomas Merton, not even much unlike Nadia, who either gradually through deliberate effort, or suddenly by cataclysmic happenstance, saw through his idol and became well acquainted with Inner Light. His culture offered him no help in understanding it: their perception was squelched by an overabundance of religious law and other thick filters. So he turned inward for answers, and wound up doing the work that deconstructed the idol so thoroughly that he was able to look straight into the Inner Light, empty and awake, and say, "I am that."

Maybe Jesus and the Buddha are one and the same.

A chill came over me. I closed the book and moved closer to the fire. Nights at the Grand Canyon never fail to be colder than I expect, even in the summer. Looking back, I think that revelation was more disorienting than comforting. It meant that many people I was happy to consider enemies were just friends I hadn't met yet. And if I were to be a friend-in-training, I had *a lot* to learn about cultivating that kind of awareness.

The next day involved no driving at all. We gave the passengers a quick orientation to the park and let them go feral for the day. While they were gone, I hiked to a quiet spot on Yavapai Point and sat on the rim of the canyon. I stared across the great chasm to the north rim, the place where I had been not even two full weeks before. So much insight gained since then; so much further to go.

I immersed myself in Merton, focusing on the chapter about Solitude:

> *The world is the unquiet city of those who live for themselves and are therefore divided against one another in a struggle that cannot end...It is the city of those who are fighting for possession of limited things and for the monopoly of goods and pleasures that cannot be shared by all.*
>
> *But if you try to escape from this world merely by leaving the city and hiding yourself in solitude, you will only take the city with you into solitude. For the flight from the world is nothing else but the flight from self-concern. And the man who locks himself up in private with his own selfishness has put himself into a position where the evil within him will either possess him like a devil or drive him out of his head. That is why it is dangerous to go into solitude merely because you like to be alone.*

Oh. Yes, that makes sense...very much so.

The recognition was too strong, and the accusation too damning. I accepted the slap in the face, then flipped the pages, looking for a quick antidote:

> *The true solitary does not have to run away from others: they cease to notice him, because he does not share their love for an illusion. The soul that is truly solitary becomes perfectly colorless and ceases to excite the love or hatred of others by reason of its solitude.*

Ahh, now that felt like something I could embrace. I let the words melt over me and seep into my soul, my eyes scanning the unfathomable expanse that lay before me. Every work of art made by human hands, assembled together in one ridiculously rich man's Castle, could not hold a candle to what flowing water has done, just within the scope of what my eyes could see.

In that moment, the Grand Canyon felt like the perfect place to die.

Fortunately, I did not mean *that* kind of death--that was mere inches away from me if I desired that. I meant the kind of death the prophet Muhammad spoke of when he said, "Die before you die;" what the Buddhists mean when they say, "While living, be a dead man. Be completely dead. Then do as you will." I meant the death Jesus of Nazareth referred to when he said, "Greater love has no man than this, that he lay down his life for his friends." I meant perfect colorlessness. Transparency. If the idol must exist while we live, let the sun shine through it.

I read on:

> *I ought to know, by now, that God uses everything that happens as a means to lead me into solitude. Every creature that enters my life, every instant of my days, will be designed to wound me with the realization of the world's insufficiency, until I become so detached that I will be able to find God alone in everything. Only then will all things bring me joy.*

Yes. It was starting to come together. Disappear while still apparent...while apparent, disappear. Disappear completely. Then go where you will.

I sat there for hours. When I was done, I closed my eyes, and spoke a silent Thank You to the hole in the ground. Again, not out of the woods completely. But that was the day that the mountain started to lose its grip on me.

The next leg of the trip, I was pleased to find out, mirrored a road trip that Nadia and I took with my friend Woody Goodman. Woody was waiting tables at a restaurant in Albuquerque at the time. His shift ended at 10 pm one night, and the next one resumed at 5 pm the next day. In between, the three of us decided, we would drive to the Grand Canyon, and come home a rather roundabout way so that we could play Twister at the Four Corners monument where Arizona, New Mexico, Utah, and Colorado meet, the only such place in the United States. It was Woody's brainchild to play quad-state Twister, but Nadia had the brilliant idea to add the state abbreviations to the spinner to make it even more challenging. One must then not only place one's right foot on blue, for instance, but blue in *Colorado*.

We played for about a half-hour before my internal clock told me we had to leave to get Woody back for his shift. (It was on this part of the drive, somewhere south of Farmington, that I dozed for about ten minutes, and woke up having dreamed that I met God, and He told me "Unless thou can place thy left hand on red in Rhode Island, thou art not worthy of Me.") We made it with seven minutes to spare--900 miles in just under 19 hours. That Nadia could not only survive such a journey but thrive on it, says volumes about where she was then, physiologically and emotionally, compared to where she is now.

Our Wednesday followed the route of that trip precisely. We spent a lot of time showing them Monument Valley--that magic place with the giant red sandstone buttes that tower up to 1,000 feet above the desert plain, spoiled perhaps by one too many scenes in Hollywood westerns or jeep commercials, but to see them for real in person is to reclaim all their majesty. After a fun photo stop at the aptly named Mexican Hat rock in Utah, we proceeded to that monument to pointless abstract geometry (I wonder what the Navajo, who operate the Four Corners Monument, really think of our fascination with this spot--after all, before the white man drew arbitrary lines and carved their land into separate states, this, as everywhere, was just another sacred place within the four directions). No Twister games that day, although I did demonstrate for some of the passengers how the game would have been played if we had a board, to their amused delight.

We reached the hotel in Farmington that evening, so I turned back to Merton, looking to bolster the faith that I figured I would need in droves once I got home. As ever I found him to be right on target:

> *The man who does not permit his spirit to be beaten down and upset by dryness and helplessness, but who lets God lead him peacefully through the wilderness, and desires no other support or guidance than that of pure faith and trust in God alone, will be brought to the Promised Land.*

Sounded easy enough. But then he continued:

This is where so many holy people break down and go to pieces. As soon as they reach the point where they can no longer see the way and guide themselves by their own light, they refuse to go any further. They have no confidence in anyone except themselves. Their faith is largely an emotional illusion. It is rooted in their feelings, in their physique, in their temperament...but when the time comes to enter the darkness in which we are naked and helpless and alone; in which we see the insufficiency of our greatest strength and the hollowness of our strongest virtues; in which we have nothing of our own to rely on, and nothing in our nature to support us, and nothing in the world to guide us and give us light--then we find out whether or not we live by faith. It is in this darkness, when there is nothing left in us that can please or comfort our own minds, when we seem to be useless and worthy of all contempt, when we seem to have failed, when we seem to be destroyed and devoured, it is then that the deep and secret selfishness that is too close for us to identify is stripped away from our souls. It is in this darkness that we find true liberty. It is in this abandonment that we are made strong. This is the night which empties us and makes us pure.

What a fascinating perspective to add to the concept of the shadow. If complete darkness descends upon us and Inner Light seems to flicker and fade to nothing, the shadow disappears as well. Perhaps it is then, in the calm and surrender of this darkness that the work is done to elucidate the idol so there is no shadow when the light is restored. When light shines all around us, we are complacent and content. There is still that pesky shadow that follows us around, but we can turn away from it and forget it is there. Darkness strips away our ability to rely on ourselves to cling to pleasure and flee from pain. Eventually, then, when the darkness passes and Inner Light is restored, we know it is not merely our own--it is divine light within us. It was all starting to come together.

Thursday was a bit of a burner. We made a long horseshoe shape across northern New Mexico, weaving through the Sangre de Christo Mountains to the artist colony towns of Taos and Santa Fe. Then it was Los Alamos in the afternoon and an evening dip in Jemez Hot Springs before a late run to Gallup for the night to rest and stock up on Navajo tchachkes. I had been shortening my nights with all this reading, and it caught up to me. I was asleep before my head hit the pillow.

Friday had a few quick diversions at the Petrified Forest and some enormous meteor crater I had never bothered to notice, a hyper-quick stroll through my old stomping grounds of Flagstaff, and ended inexplicably at London Bridge. Yes, *the* London Bridge. Some genius had the vision to buy the actual bridge from the Brits, disassemble it and put it back together in the otherwise forgettable community of Lake Havasu City--therefore, we must go look at it.

In honor of the jolly old bridge, I opted for a quiet dinner of fish-and-chips instead of a last shot at the Chinese buffet, and dug into the final chapter of Merton, on Sainthood:

> *One of the first signs of a saint may well be the fact that other people do not know what to make of him. In fact, they are not sure whether he is crazy or only proud; but it must at least be pride to be haunted by some individual ideal which nobody but God really comprehends.*

Amen to that. An interesting word, "pride." It is one of the highest ideals of "the world," yet C.S. Lewis called it the deadliest of the deadly sins, the one from which all others spring-- which I take as corroboration of the idolatry of self as original sin. But "pride" is used in other connotations as well. I think of the last line in the final verse of that U2 song that is ostensibly about Martin Luther King Jr. but, like all of Bono's songs, is Christian rock in disguise: "Free at last, they took your life, they could not take your pride." What is this thing, then, that is left after one lays down one's life, and how does it relate to saint hood--which I understand to be the cultivation of the antithesis of pride?

A partial answer seemed to come next. This was the final entry in the volume. It seemed that the editor also saw this as Merton's triumphant culminating statement on where the path may lead us if well-traveled:

> *Be content that you are not a saint, even though you realize that the only thing worth living for is sanctity. Then you will be satisfied to let God lead you to sanctity by paths that you cannot understand. You will travel in darkness in which you will no longer be concerned with yourself and no longer compare yourself to other men. Those who have gone by that way have finally found out that sanctity is in everything and that God is all around them. Having given up all desire to compete with other men, they suddenly wake up and find that the joy of God is everywhere, and they are able to exalt in the virtues and goodness of others more than they ever could have done in their own. They are so dazzled by the reflection of God that they see in other men they live with that they no longer have any power to condemn anything they see in another...as for themselves, if they still consider themselves, they no longer dare compare themselves with others. The idea becomes unthinkable. But it is no longer a source of suffering and lamentation: they have finally reached the point where they take their own insignificance for granted. They are no longer interested in their external selves.*

Maybe pride, as used by Merton and Bono, is used almost ironically as a reclaimed word. Maybe pride is the imprint left upon the world after our work is done and we are taken out of the equation--the joy in others' joy, having been enriched by the life we surrendered to the Life. I started to feel like I finally had what I needed to bring home to Nadia.

The Saturday homecoming trip from Havasu was about fifty miles farther than Yellowstone's, but it seemed easier because

I was not driving the Chinese around town Friday night. There are only so many ways you can look at a bridge that had to have a canal built underneath it in order to appear purposeful. It was still a sixteen hour haul that whooped me pretty thoroughly, so I was glad that the other driver heading back to the mother-ship wanted to crash in San Jose too.

Even so, I hardly slept that night. My mind kept racing through variations of the conversation I was going to have with Nadia. We talked twice over the week that I was gone, both rudimentary but not horrible, enough to establish that we still carried some lingering tension, but neither of us were at DEFCON 1 anymore. I think we both felt remorse for our own bouts of irrationality and were ready to meet somewhere in the middle.

Ultimately, I figured, the question was simple: What was my pride? If I could die after tomorrow, either kind of death, what would I want to leave behind? It might not seem like much to accomplish in twenty-nine years, but at that time, a Nadia who felt loved and understood was all I asked from life.

The moment of truth came early Sunday afternoon. Nadia picked me up, looking unexpectedly mellow and collected. We decided to go to Pismo Beach and sit by the bluffs. We parked ourselves on our favorite cliff-side bench in front of the main cluster of rocks jutting up from the bay, where a flock of pelicans had nothing better to do than hang out and people-watch.

We both started to talk at once, and I felt relieved that she was not feeling silenced. Nadia yielded.

"Before we get into anything," I said, "I have to confess: I had every intention of leaving when I got back from this trip. I wasn't even going to come home, just go straight to the train station and head east."

"I knew that. You're a horrible liar."

"Well, I practice at being horrible. It felt wrong on several levels, bailing on Eldorado and everything, but that's how serious I felt about needing to get away from what we were doing to each other. You started to change my mind when you accused me of not appreciating you...you are totally right. That is something I need to address. But in order to do that, I need you to tell me what the hell made you turn against me so viciously before I got home from Yellowstone...because I felt a lot of mutual appreciation right up to that moment. *Please* let me in, Nadia. For our sake."

She took a very deep breath, like she had been submerged underwater for a few weeks.

"The Wednesday night before you came home...I had the worst low blood sugar reaction of my life."

"Worse than Quebec?"

"Worse. I woke up with it again. I didn't have glucose by the bed, and I knew I needed to reach the bathroom...only this time I couldn't take a step. I fell right to the floor and started dragging myself. I wasn't going to make it. I screamed and screamed and screamed, and all that came out was that horrible moan. I have no idea how Sister Mary heard me, but I wouldn't be here now if she didn't."

"Sister Mary" (full name: "Sister Mary Margaret McWeird") was our affectionate nickname for our neighbor on the other side of the bedroom wall. Her actual name is Grace, which I like better, but Nadia is convinced that she is a nun in some obscure sect that plants its neophytes among the heathens for aversion conditioning. She is around our age, very pretty and unfailingly cheerful when we see her, but she dresses like my grandmother and only seems to leave the house for twice-weekly church services. We are pretty sure no one ever visits her either, which does not seem to bother her. I shudder to think of the obscenities to which her virgin ears have been subjected while living next to us, but she never shows signs of being repulsed by us. A total mystery, in other words. But she always expressed concern for Nadia's health, so Nadia had trained her on first aid response for diabetics. This was the first time she was ever called upon--thank God, or whoever pricked her ears in the middle of the night, that she answered the call.

And thus it was confirmed: my choice to accept overnight jobs from Eldorado could be fatal to Nadia. The Destroyer entered our room that night, and I was not there to protect her. She was saved by an act of Grace.

I embraced Nadia snugly, choking back tears, and whispered

in her ear how sorry I was. She accepted it, still kind of flatly though. I could tell this was not *exactly* what she needed from me.

"OK," I said, pulling back but still holding her arms, as if I intended to shake her. "Now *why* didn't you *tell me that?!* Why did this have to play out for two whole weeks?"

"*Because* I know how you get when *anything* happens to me. You panic and you feel smothered by guilt, and you want to drop everything and never let me out of your sight. It isn't healthy for either of us. Better to make you suffer my slings and arrows to be honest."

"So you would rather that I act as though I *don't* care and go on like nothing is happening?"

"Don't play dumb with me. Those are not two exclusive choices and you know it. I *need* your *authentic self*, no matter *where* that leads us. I would rather die than live knowing that I kept you from doing what you love best."

She had expressed that sentiment before, albeit in less graphic terms, and I understand it. I appreciated the sense of freedom she was trying to impart, and I made sure my face said that. But I never felt the great rush of gratitude she seemed to expect from it, because that is never the whole story.

"But then I go away, and something goes wrong with you, and you get *enraged* that I wasn't there for you."

Nadia takes another deep breath. "Do I really have to explain that to you *again*?"

I looked away. No, she does not. Nadia is always point and counterpoint at once. Whichever is loudest at the moment is what I hear. There is nothing she can do about it.

"So a part of you will always be mad at me for wanting to go... and if I react to that and decide to stay, that drives you crazy, too. How am I supposed to live with that, Nadia?"

"Courageously. Authentically."

I looked back at her. The slightest of grins cracked the facade of her face, for the first time in my presence in almost a month.

"The only thing I've ever asked of you is to hold space for me while you are gone, and come home good. I want you to bring back something that shows me you weren't one of those auto-pilot drones just sleepwalking your way through the trip. If you have to go out into the world to make a living for us, I need you to *live* while you're doing it."

"And when you demand that I do something completely different at the same time?"

"Tell me to shut the fuck up. Seriously, it isn't that hard. I'm a very small person."

It was my turn to grin. I did tend to kowtow to her lioness nature, even when I knew that it was exactly what she did *not* want from me. She had told me many times that our fights often escalate because I *don't* challenge her, and by the time I do, I am in such a defensive stance that it gets belligerent and personal where it could have been something more like sparring. Then there are times when *she* takes something I say very personally, because she is already beating *herself* up and I am just piling on. It is not easy to tell the difference, she does not change colors when her shadow is in control or anything so discernible. But that is the risk one assumes when loving a bipolar--storm clouds are always on the horizon; sometimes you need to run for shelter, sometimes you should welcome the nourishing rain and be invigorated by the lightning and thunder.

"Well," I said, "I never promised you comfortable, and you never promised me easy."

This time our hug was mutual.

"But we did promise each other to stick it out to the end," I added. "And that I will do."

Nadia smiled. Another hard-earned peace was upon us. I may have been imagining it, but I thought I heard a few pelagic species of the class Aves distinctly squawk their approval.

That was Sunday, September 9. I fell asleep around 5:00, my body still reeling from the Grand Canyon run. Annie needed to put me to work right away, so she gave me an easy afternoon South SLO County wine run for Monday. (I was scheduled to do another one on the 11th, until a driver fell ill and she had to enlist me for the ABA Conference field trip). Nadia had free transportation to Atascadero for her eye surgeon and endocrinologist appointments, so I relaxed until the crack of noon and drove myself to work. We planned to have a special dinner at home that night to celebrate our newfound abundance. Things seemed like they were smoothing out just fine.

Until...damnit, I proved what an unregenerate bastard I can be. I never called her to let her know that I was going to be an hour late getting home. I got so wrapped up in defending myself from her rage that I forgot I was the immediate cause of it. Talk about failing to hold space for her.

GOD, YOU ARE THE WORST FUCKING EXCUSE FOR A HUSBAND!

I also guessed completely wrong when I challenged her reaction to the doctor's assessment. The signs were so clear that she had had a very difficult day and that was *not* the right tactic, and I did not read any of them.

YOU CAN HEAR A GODDAMN PIN DROP A MILE AWAY BUT YOU NEVER LISTEN TO A FUCKING WORD I SAY!

And here I am now, lost in the forest, unable to call her on what has to be one of the hardest days of a very hard life.

I WISH THAT KNIFE HAD STABBED YOU IN THE FUCKING HEART SO YOU WOULD KNOW HOW I FEEL EVERY GODDAMN FUCKING DAY OF MY LIFE BECAUSE OF YOU!

Sainthood, eh Thomas? So much for thinking that someone else's words could be my salvation. My idol is just as opaque as ever. All that theoretical knowledge and I still can't handle the most basic functions of a loving husband. I have been one who turns pages of the scriptures while rolling around in the mud, and wondering why I still feel filthy. Now I am even failing at dying. Is there a patron saint for *that?*

A few minutes later I come to a clearing. I do not see nor hear any birding activity, so I am not sure if this is a good sign yet. There were a handful of campgrounds in the immediate area, so no telling yet whether I have found Meseta Centrada or another one. A picnic table sits in the shade of an oak tree toward the edge. Yes, good. Rest would feel *tremendous* now. I sit, and I breathe. I don't move.

For a while. I think.

For the first time since those horrible words were whispered in my ear this morning, it feels good to be alone with my thoughts. I can see why people escape to the solitude of the woods when they need a temporary respite. There is nothing to fight out here. No reason to hate the wind, the rustle of leaves. Sunlight--back like an old friend, toasty warm after that trek through the forest canopy--it isn't invading my space. Birds are just birds, not names on a scorecard. I don't have to be angry anymore. I can just be sad.

Sad.

Many souls left the earth this morning. Fathers, mothers; sisters, brothers; sons, daughters. Millions of people have holes in their lives where living people were yesterday. This must be hell on earth for them. All this sadness and for what? *For what?*

Let it out...Let it go.

I cry. Like Noah's rainstorm I cry. Huge wailing sobs. And not just for a little bit. I use every tear in my body and then I make more. I cry for everyone I could not reach today. For Nadia. For everyone, all over this country, this aching world. For the millions. I cry for millions, every tear another drop of water in the oceans of grief felt across the world today.

I don't know when this ends. At one point I crumple over with my head nestled in the bend of my right arm on the table, and my body shifts seamlessly into sleep.

ACT VI

Time Unknown

Someone is holding my hand....
God, is that you? Hhave you come for me now?....

I am ready......I surrender this body and mind, the strain of life is too great...I will walk with you now, God

Please take good care of Nadia...and my family...ease their pain...let them understand why I had to go......

God...now that I am with you, can I ask you a question? Why do horrible things happen in the world? Why is there such suffering and misery? If we are all your children and you are always watching, why do you allow war and destruction and brothers killing brothers and so much pain and woe? Will it ever end?

What? No, I'm not laughing...

Nothing's funny, God...I just didn't expect you to look so much like Drew Carey, that's all.....

No, I didn't mean it like that....

Not at all, God, I dig the jester's suit. It is so you...Of course, very postmodern theological, trez chic....

Um, well, no, I never got around to accepting Him as my savior....He was serious about that?!?

Hey, why are you turning into a football player?a punter? Can't we go for it on fourth down?...wait, I can explain!......No, God, please, not into the end zone!

Nooo!...

Yikes! Where the hell am I? The picnic table, yes. Birds. *Birds!* *Ye gads!* how much time has passed? Don't know...doesn't matter. Oh, these goofy God dreams! Lord, why do you torment me with such humor?!

My head jerks up faster than my eyes can focus, but when they do, I see Betty Pickett sitting across from me. She is holding my left hand between hers and gazing at me. It is a penetrating gaze, unlike anything I have seen from her. Pale green eyes, artificially enlarged by her glasses, reach across the table as if they had arms.

These eyes have seen so much; even through the bifocals I can tell that. There is pain inside there, deep. I do not know what makes me think this, but somehow I am *certain* that she has outlived at least one of her children. Yet here she is, looking at me with so much empathy that I start to blush.

I pick myself up and mouth a silent thank you. There is that smile again, that everything-is-all-right smile I have quickly grown to cherish. So unforced, so real. Who can do that on a day like today?

I think back to our conversation on the bus, when it first seemed clear that Betty came from a different mindset than I. She did not agree with the Birds' decision to withhold the news from the passengers and keep the show going, but she did not appear to feel victimized by it either. She accepted the reality that she found herself in--she did not force her will into the equation. Something intuitively told me this was a spiritual practice, that Betty could accept the situation as God's will. She did not just passively accept the Birds' decision so as not to make waves--she was at peace with it.

But how does one do that in all situations? I can understand coming to terms with the drama unfolding with our leaders on the bus, but is it really possible to feel genuine peace when planes are crashing into buildings and our country is on the cusp of war? Trying to learn it from a book didn't work, but maybe Betty could impart some wisdom from experience.

Before I have a chance to ask, Betty begins to speak.

"You know, as long as I live I will never forget the day that

Pearl Harbor was attacked." Her tone is conversational. She could have been talking about the weather. "I was nine years old, sitting in my Sunday school class at the Methodist church in Lebanon, frankly kind of bored to tears like most kids. I remember it was almost over when the minister came in and called the teacher outside. She was gone a long time. When she came back she told us that someone had done something very bad to America, and we would soon be going to war. Oh was I terrified! My father was in the Army Reserves, and I'd been hearing all the adults in town whispering that if America got involved in the war in Europe, we would need every able-bodied man to join the fight. Now, here it was. I was so sure my father would be killed by the Germans.

"I ran home through the wheat fields crying. My mother was outside hanging the laundry. I know she was concerned too, but she didn't act scared, not with me anyway. She put her arms around me and hugged me real close until I stopped crying. Then she took me inside and got me some milk. We sat down at the table. It was just us; my father and brother were off hunting, and my sister was down for a nap. It was very quiet for a while, just a clock ticking in the other room. Then she said--and this is the part I remember best--she said I didn't have to worry about my father, because the angels would watch over him and bring him home. That's all she said, all she had to say really. I understood. The angels would bring him home.

"Sure enough, he soon left for the war, spent almost three years in Europe. We got a letter every week from England, France, Belgium. My mother was strong as steel. She reminded me of the angels often, told me to talk to them every night. And I did, and you know, I was fine because of that. I knew my father was safe.

The only thing that worried me, in fact, was whether the angels knew where we lived." She laughs heartily at the memory. "I even wrote a letter to the angels describing our house and the town where we lived, and I gave it to my mother to mail. She said she mailed it, but I think she saved it to show my father. It must have been the most darling thing for a parent.

"Then in November 1944, a couple weeks passed without a letter. I started to get scared. My mother told me to stay strong and keep having faith. She said faith is what keeps the angels working. I prayed to them many times a day. One evening we were having a quiet dinner--I was in a very solemn mood those weeks as you might imagine--and out of nowhere my *father* came *right through the front door!*" She claps her hands and laughs like it happened yesterday. "He was in Europe for God's sake! I didn't know if he was alive or dead, and there he was in the front door! Oh my feet never touched the ground all the way to his arms!"

I can see the jubilation in Betty's face even now. I bet it has hardly diminished at all in almost sixty years.

"Later that night, my mother took his last three letters from their hiding place and gave them to me. She had known all along he was coming home, but she wanted me to have the full impact of seeing him walk in the door. I also think she wanted to test my faith. I was twelve by then, and I guess she felt I was old enough for a trial. I suppose I was."

"Wow, that took some real nerve on her part. Some kids would have gone to pieces."

"You're right, but I think she knew I was the right age and temperament to receive that lesson. Alasdair was thirteen in 1941, and built from the warrior mold like our father; he was going to tough it out no matter what she told him. Ione was too young to understand what was happening, and maybe a little too delicate anyway. With me, I think she recognized a nature like her own: emotional, a little tightly wound, but willing to yield and trust. She used to tell me we're like strings on a fiddle, and we make beautiful music when we let ourselves be played."

That makes me smile a bit. I wonder if this will be the extent of her answer to my questions, this discipline of trusting the angels. Interesting, simple enough. And angels are known as "bearers of light" in many traditions. Not a bad context for a dynamic understanding of Inner Light. I am intrigued.

"So have you stayed in touch with the angels ever since?"

"Well, that experience prepared me for another trial I had seven years later. I was nineteen and had just been engaged to be married when my fiancé was called off to Korea. My mother was there for me again. She reminded me of everything I had learned before, and I spent a year and a half talking to the angels."

"And he came home safely?"

"Of course. He's over there birding right now."

"That's beautiful. Your mother was an amazing woman."

"Well there's nothing 'was' about her!"

"Really? She's still alive?"

"Ninety-two years young as they say. And she's never changed, not a bit. She still lives by herself on the family farm outside Lebanon. Virginia Moss is her name. Still raises the chickens and grows her own vegetables. In fact, if you ever pass through the 'Middle of Everywhere' again, you really should stop in and have a visit. You can ask anyone in town where to find her."

"I will certainly do that. She welcomes having random visitors stop by her house?"

"Oh, believe me, there is nothing she loves more. And don't think she needs someone to take care of her just because she's ninety-two. You would be an honored guest, and you'd get the same treatment you would at my bed-and-breakfast. Tell her I said to make sure you try her chicken soup, it's the best you'll ever taste."

"Well this chicken soup has been pretty great, too, Betty, and I am most grateful to you for sharing it with me. It's good to hear an uplifting tale today."

"Oh I'll never get tired of telling that story," she says wistfully. Then her voice changes, comes from a slightly different angle. "But the reason I wanted to tell you is, well, I sense that what happened today has made you afraid."

I nod. She smiles again. No one has ever spoken so much hope to me without saying a word.

"If I were to tell you the same thing that Virginia Moss told me--that the angels will be watching us, that they will guide us through this and bring us home--would you believe me?"

"I'd love to, and I do on some levels. But the deep-down faith you have is something elusive to me. I can't get my mind to shut up long enough to get in and fix the hard wiring that says we're all doomed."

"Well, if your mind won't stay quiet," she says, "then let it say the right things: there is nothing to fear; everything is alright; the angels are in control; there is nothing to fear...."

She trails off into silence, allowing me to absorb her simple message. It fascinates me that one moment of spontaneous wisdom created a faith that has sustained an entire

life, almost seventy years. Great religions must begin this

way. I want to be an apostle.

"I'm curious how your faith prevails through events like today. It seems easier to apply these beliefs to a situation close to home with people we know. But what about world events? Major earth-shakers pushed by forces far beyond our grasp? The Cuban Missile Crisis, for example. I mean, that was thirteen days of nuclear standoff with the Soviets, one push of a button from Armageddon, perhaps the most frightful times in world history. What was that like?"

"The angels worked overtime on that one," she says, with the closest I have seen to a sly grin yet. "I'm not saying they prevent things from being *interesting*. But I never doubted that the sun would rise the next morning. And the angels told me I'd be there to see it. I made a point of waking up before dawn every morning until it was over."

"My generation saw "The Day After" on TV and it was instant neurosis. I can only imagine how real live terrorist attacks will stoke our fears. World events seem to shake us harder than ever. We're saturated with instant images from the media and communicate at the touch of a button. I don't know how to keep equanimity in the middle of it all."

"World events don't matter, not like we think they do anyway. Remember, the angels are doing all the important stuff. We're just shadow puppets."

Silence. There's nothing I can say to that...in fact, *did she just read my mind?*

Betty checks her watch. "Think we'd better head back, they'll be wrapping up pretty soon. Don't worry, we aren't too far." She's right. We are actually at the opposite end of Meseta Centrada. Looks like I was led out of the wilderness after all.

As we start walking back toward the bus, I think a lot about what Betty told me. Why is faith so hard to keep? The people who have it, like Betty and Thomas Merton, make it seem so elementary. Sometimes I think that's what ticks the world off about religion--it's like a fish trying to teach people to breath underwater by saying, "Just use your gills!" I may be wrong--and God knows I probably am--but it seems like all spiritual paths come "some assembly required, battery not included," and until you follow the not-so-easy-to-read instructions, you do not have a bicycle; you have two wheels, two pedals, a frame, a chain, and a dozen loose screws that are going nowhere.

If that is true, Betty has some tricks up her sleeve. What are they? Why won't she tell me?

One other aspect of Betty's story starts to trouble me. Stops me in my tracks actually. Betty stops too and asks if everything is OK. I must have a paralyzed look on my face. Something is missing, something vital. I feel my shadow falling over the scene.

"The angels brought your father home from Europe, and your husband home from Korea, and they created the faith that you built your life upon. But many soldiers *were* killed in World War II--what if your father had been one of them? What if he *hadn't* come home? It's one thing to have faith when it works, but what about when it doesn't? What about the fathers and fiancés and husbands who never came back from the wars? What about the people who were supposed to land safely on four airplanes today? The ones expected home for dinner after a day's work at the World Trade Center and the Pentagon? The New York City firefighters who charged the south tower to put out a fire and never left? What did 'the angels' do for them? Are their sons and daughters just SOL when it comes to faith?"

Betty gazes at the ground, face slightly askew but with thoughtful composure. This really does not feel like the time nor the place, but I am afraid that all of my dissatisfaction with feel-good stories and "us versus them" religion is about to come out in one misguided stream of vitriol.

"I really don't want to be so dismissive with something that matters so much to you, and it obviously did wonders for your spiritual life. But please don't tell me that life comes down to a battle over who can manipulate celestial beings by having the most faith, or the *right* faith--we have all seen that nonsense play itself out ad nauseum. To me this just feels like another system that says some people are winners and some are losers, and that's why I'm not sinking my teeth into it. I can't put my faith in anything that says something so contrary to my heart."

Now Betty turns and looks straight at me, *into* me I think. It is all I can do to stay upright and not be knocked to the ground. Nothing in her face or the general atmosphere suggests anger, but there is blazing intensity. Her gaze could peel paint. Keep in mind this is a woman who, by mere physical appearance, looks like she would be toppled by a decent breeze, and here I am, about to be burned alive from within by her eyes.

Then she turns her head slightly, so that her gaze is now looking past me. Into what, I could not guess, but there is something that has her spellbound. Did I touch some raw nerve?

She speaks, calmly and directly, still looking into the Great Whatever.

"In my lifetime, I have found that a simple, child-like faith is all that most people want. All that they can handle really. Offer them more and you're in danger of being burned at the stake of their small, cynical minds. I sense that you are not one of these people."

"I'm sorry about that," I say. "My mind ate simple for breakfast, and it's half past suppertime now."

Betty looks at me and smiles again. The mood seems to lighten a bit, but that intensity is still there.

"Then it's time somebody fed you some Truth." Betty motions for me to follow her back toward the woods. "We should sit down for this."

We walk to a spot at the foot of a large bristlecone pine, the most ancient beings on earth. This one could have been 3,000 years old when Christ was born. We sit facing each other, a few feet apart. Betty closes her eyes and takes a slow steady breath. She seems to let the oxygen wash over her whole body before moving or speaking. There is a luminous quality about her now. I suspect that her shadow, if she has one at all, has become razor thin.

"There is more that you should know about my mother. Virginia married into the Moss family, but she herself is a Shipley, and comes from a long line of freethinkers and mystics. More than one of our ancestors were accused of witchcraft, going back to the Puritans and even to old England. But they were just people who never had a home in any established church.

"The Moss family, on the other hand, descends from a Scottish clan known for producing fierce warriors. The men are built like bulls, and they are also stubborn as bulls and see themselves as indestructible. One other thing they share genetically is a tendency to accumulate the invisible plaque--the kind that shows no outward signs of existence until it bores a hole in your artery and cuts you down within minutes. My grandfather died from it before I was born, and Alasdair met the same fate in his early fifties.

"And forty years ago, almost to the day in fact, my father was taken, too. He was fishing by himself up at the family camp in Nebraska for the weekend, but he did not come home Sunday night. They found his boat washed into the marsh at the edge of the lake Monday morning, his body slumped over inside. He had been gone for at least a day.

"My mother mourned for three solid days. She didn't speak a word, and I don't know if she cried privately but she never did in front of us. Personally, I was devastated. I was filled with the same disturbing thoughts that you expressed. How could the angels guide him through three years of war, and then let him go just like *that?*

"The funeral was that Friday, on a dismal gray day. I remember feeling like summer had ended and skipped right to winter. Even so, the whole town of Lebanon came out, and probably most of Smith Center and Red Cloud, too--Rowland Moss was a bit of a local legend for his hunting prowess. Our local congressman even flew in from Washington for it, they used to hunt pheasants together every year. There must have been a dozen eulogies given, each one very eloquent and sincere.

"Then it was my mother's turn to speak. I'm sure everyone expected her to pour out all the emotions she had been holding back all week. Instead, Virginia Shipley Moss told us this:

God cuts the gold thread,
The human being spreads his wings
And returns to his home.

That was all. She stepped down and didn't say another word. The crowd was absolutely stunned, no one knew what to do next. People kept coming up to her and asking if she was alright, and she would just smile and nod. I'm sure almost everyone thought she had blown a gasket. But a small handful of people understood, and they started coming out to the farm often to talk with her. I was one of them."

Several pieces of a puzzle in my mind--pieces that I was start-ing to think were remnants of something that shattered--snap together, just like that, and I smile. Huge.

"Wow. A haiku, even."

Betty smiles back, knowingly. She has seen this response be-fore, I can tell.

"That was 1961, I was 29 years old. Probably right about the age you are, I'm guessing."

"*Exactly* the age I am," I say, a little bit awestruck.

Betty taps the side of her head with her left index finger. "It's never too late to change that wiring, you know."

I pause and ponder that for a moment. My expression must become a bit more solemn, as Betty's does, surely meeting me where I need to go.

"Betty...can I tell you something that has been troubling me?"

"Please do."

I hesitate slightly...*say it! Get it out there!*

"Two weeks ago, I was hiking alone in Big Sur, and I reached the top of a trail that runs along the ridge. I looked out over the ocean and all around me. I'd thought that this was going to be a great joyful moment, because this was something I had dreamed of doing since...well, since I was a kid really, the first time I saw the California coast. I pictured it as the antidote to where I was and all that unhappiness we talked about before. I've even fantasized about *living* in a place like that many, many times...but when I looked around up there, I saw something that made me horrorstruck. I couldn't see another person anywhere... and suddenly, I felt as though everyone else were gone. *Everyone*. The whole world. And the part that still baffles me...is that I knew without a doubt that I was responsible. I killed everyone."

Betty closes her eyes and nods softly, but she does not seem ready to speak, so I continue.

"I've had a similar vision for years about my wife, and that always made sense to me because of her poor health. In fact it was recently shown to me that some choices I make that bring me fulfillment can contribute to her death...so I understand that. But what could make me responsible for killing the whole human race? And why would that vision be coming to me now? It is something I need to understand much better, because it happened again today. Up on top of Azucar."

"And you were alone this time too, right?"

"Yes, I walked back down the access road hoping to get a cell signal. This was just before our conversation on the bus."

"This vision is not as uncommon as you might think."

"Really? Other people have visions of killing the world while alone on a mountain?"

"The setting always varies, and they don't always happen while alone. Just last week, an eighty year old man came to see me at the B-&-B. He started sobbing as he recalled being at a University of Nebraska football game, and having a vision that he made everyone in the stadium disappear, including his wife who was next to him the whole time. They aren't always as intense as his or yours, but intensity is good in this case. It means you are closer to working out a solution.

"You were on the right track with the conclusion about your wife, but I think your perception of her frailty is clouding your vision a bit. You are not causing her death, nor are you killing the world--it is *you* who are killing *yourself*. It is not a suicide vision...more like a *soul*-icide, if you will. You are cutting yourself off from the source. You are isolating yourself from your wife in some manner, and this is fairly common. The mountain vision, however, comes from a universal experience--you are isolating yourself in the ego. Your individual mind has fabricated a prison for itself. Every human being does this in some manner. For you, this takes the form of a quest for solitude that is leading you into a trap, and it happens on a mountain because that is what you desire the most in this life.

"Getting exactly what we think we want most is a dead end. We become content. We stop seeking our way back home, and we wish that we could preserve everything just as it is. The universal Mind sends these visions to jar us from our complacency. I am glad you felt yours so vividly and let it drive you to distraction. Most people are not attuned to the universal Mind, and the vision is not strong or clear enough to break through. They only feel a vague guilt or remorse that they never fully understand. It is much better to feel the full force of the isolation and let it motivate you to be humbled and changed."

"Does this mean I shouldn't be seeking solitude?"

"No, not at all. Clearly you are a born contemplative. Solitude will be your greatest gift once you learn to let it nourish you. You just need to learn how to experience it differently. You need to share it better with others."

"That sounds contradictory. If I am sharing solitude with others, I'm not really very solitary. Am I?"

"There are two words used interchangeably that are actually quite different, and this causes your confusion. Isolation is an external experience that draws from the falsehood that we are separate beings with no connection to each other beyond social roles. It is the experience of being within only oneself, surrounded by a foreign world. But solitude is an internal experience, based in the truth that we are One. To be solitary is to know that Oneness is the sole reality, that there is no separation between oneself and others.

"The hallmark of solitude is attentiveness to the internal processes that bring the universal aspects of the self into sharper focus: intuition, conscience, the Mind, and the boundless, selfless Love known by so many names. People seek out quiet places to cultivate solitude because the senses can be distracting for a novice and must be stilled. But solitude can and eventually must be experienced anywhere. Once you find solitude, you can bring it to the busiest streets of any city and it will be untainted.

"The same is true of isolation--it can be experienced on a mountaintop, or in a crowded football stadium. I thought of this when you described what it was like to live in the city: people stacked on top of each other, yet living as if in their own private worlds. This is the epitome of isolation. If you seek solitude and instead find this invisible box of isolation, you should consider the state of mind you are bringing with you."

Merton's words come back to me, but not as verbal units composing rational sentences. Something more like synapses, connective tissue...edges of puzzle pieces coming together with electric sizzle.

"Yes...I'm bringing the city with me."

"Thomas Merton," she adds warmly. "One of my favorites, too."

"No kidding? I spent all of last week reading Merton. He really seemed to be helping with that bad wiring, but I think I got discouraged when my life didn't change overnight."

Betty laughs, with the levity a superlative doctor might show when her patient complains of a nagging tumor.

"Oh, I can't tell you how common that is. We all fall for the 'saved by the book' trick, as though we could study a map of the route we drove today and expect to see birds. At the same time, words are incredibly powerful at forming new ideas, and ideas shape the way our individual minds interact with the universal. So words, like maps, can guide us into new experiences. The written traditions will always inform the interior life, this is part of being human. But don't worship the words; honor them through the greater presence they evoke. Gather the ideas they generate and test them against your experience. Revelations will come as new, beneficial ideas that replace older habitual ones. This is how change happens, sometimes suddenly, sometimes gradually. For an American contemplative of this era, I can't think of a better role model than Thomas Merton."

I pause for a loug moment before responding. Betty just gave me at least a dozen new ideas, all phrased as questions, and all frantically raising their hands like eager school kids. I choose one.

"You've used a couple terms that are new to me, but seem like they might correlate to some of my new ideas. Can you tell me more about individual and universal mind? I wonder if that relates to the Quaker idea of Inner Light."

"Oh my, we have entire sessions to address just this topic. But yes, that's a very perceptive connection. The simplest way to explain is that the human mind has faculties that are tied to the organism--the five senses, conscious thought, brain stem activity and motor skills, everything that distinguishes the organism from its surroundings--and it has functions that are not tied to the organism. They are not bound to any location in space or time, and in fact they are not truly functions of the human organism--they are shared by literally all of creation, everything in the universe. This universal Mind is not something we can hold within the scope of our consciousness; it is consciousness itself, the awareness of all that is. It is the Light of the world that makes it possible for all things to know and be known."

"And we all have this universal Mind within *us*?"

"More accurate to say that the one universal Mind has us. We are its feelers and thinkers and doers. But from our perspective, it does appear to be within us, because the interior landscape is where we first find it. Our concept of the Mind is conveyed by many names and symbols throughout the world and across all cultural contexts. One of the more plain and simple of these is indeed the Inner Light.

"If you want more than that," Betty continues, "you'll have to have to accept that invitation to visit us in Kansas."

"Wow, Betty, I can't believe how right and wrong I was about you at the same time. I had a feeling you were a spiritual person, but I thought you were one of those harmless midwestern Methodists."

"Yes, we have most of the people back home foole,d too," she says with a wink. "They all think I run a simple bed-and-breakfast for birders."

Hearing the word "home" dislodges something in my heart, a longing that got stuck within me because it had no place to go. Now I feel like it might.

"Can you tell me more about the 'home' you mentioned? That has been the most elusive thing I've chased in this life. Even more so than faith."

Betty ponders for a moment. "I think you might be perceptive enough for this already."

She reaches with her fingers inside the V in the neckline of her rose-colored blouse. She tugs on a linked neck chain, then pulls out a large heart-shaped pendant, about the size of a ladies' makeup compact. It looks like well-kept, polished sterling silver, shiny but unadorned. Aside from its oddly elephantine proportions, it fits Betty to a T. A monastic reverence for detail directs her attention and motions. Something tells me this is a ritual that has been done many times before.

"I haven't told you about my boys," she says.

With great care she presses on a clasp with her thumb and the pendant pops open in clamshell fashion. Something inside it jumps to life like a liberated jack-in-the-box. Betty removes the object and, with the slightest hesitation, continues the unfolding process. It is a photograph, maybe a five-inch square print, folded with utmost precision into quarters to fit snugly inside the pendant. She holds it out for my inspection. It has the same grainy, textured color of my baby pictures, suggesting an early 1970s origin. I wonder to myself why Betty carries such an outdated photograph of her children.

Then I remember the premonition I had beneath the oak tree.

"This is the last picture taken of them all together," she says.

Oh dear...I didn't want to be right about that.

Beneath the deep creases of the photograph are five young men of various age and stature. Four of them stand shoulder-to-shoulder just behind the fifth, who is seated at a dining room table. He is the obvious focal point of their attention as well as the photographer's. A cake with just-blown-out candles sits in the foreground, while a florescent green and blue conical party hat sits cockeyed on the birthday boy's head. All of Betty's children are smiling profusely, but the biggest smile belongs to the smallest child. The four in the rear, all definitively older, lend congratulatory gestures to the shoulders and back of the young boy, who is clearly relishing the attention.

My first observation about the picture is the tremendous sense of fraternity. These people are *brothers*, in the deepest sense of the word. A profound presence fills the spaces between them in a way that only pictures of siblings reveal. The next observation is more troubling. Whereas the four older brothers may have, in some circles, earned the descriptive title "strapping young lads," the youngest child looks wispy and frail. Another telltale sign: there is no trace of hair around the sides of the young boy's hat. If my estimate of the picture's origin date is correct--and most of the hairdos suggest it is--I would bet the farm it was not a fashion statement.

Once again, Betty answers my question before I can ask.

"That's Elijah, our youngest. He had just turned eleven. At five he was diagnosed with leukemia. He wasn't expected to live another year. By the time this picture was taken, he had been through remission and relapse twice, and the third cancer was the strongest one yet. The chemotherapy wasn't working. Doctors told us to expect the worst. In our desperation we sent him to a clinic in Mexico that claimed to be beating cancer through a strict diet of nothing but organic juices and vegetables. We had never heard of such a thing, but something told me it was right, and it was his last chance.

"Two years later, just after Elijah's thirteenth birthday, the doctor said his cancer was gone. It never came back. Elijah just got stronger and stronger. By the time he finished high school at age nineteen, he was fully grown and solid as steel. He devoted his life to learning the science that saved him. Now he's a naturopathic doctor at that same clinic."

I look up at Betty, expecting to see that familiar glow in her eyes, but it is not there. They have shifted from Elijah to someone on the left side of the photograph. She points to a tall, broad figure with long, curly hair, a peach fuzz moustache and a carefree smile.

"Matthew is our second son. They were all honor students all through school, but Matthew was probably the brightest scholar in the bunch. He had just been accepted at Kansas State on a music scholarship, and was engaged to his high school sweetheart. Two weeks after this picture, while Elijah was still at his sickest, Matthew was driving home from the senior prom when a drunk driver crossed the yellow line and hit him head on. Matthew and his girlfriend both died instantly."

Oh dear...it has obviously never happened to me, but I have heard tell that the most painful experience a human being can endure is to bury a child. Betty and her mother, then, have shared the deepest depths of personal loss within their family. But I have never heard someone speak so inscrutably about the most personal events of a lifetime. She speaks passionately about her sons, but without judgment. She is warm, but clearly not sentimental. She describes the tragic, senseless death of her own child like it was just another phase in his life, like a straight-A report card or the pulling of his wisdom teeth. I just cannot figure it out.

And then I remember..."*God cuts the gold thread, the human being spreads his wings, and returns to his home....*"

"Elijah once told me it was Matthew's death that taught him how precious life is and gave him the courage to hang on," she continues. "But it has always been that way with these boys. They have always found inspiration in each other."

Assuming she is done, I start to formulate another question about the angels' role in these turns of fate, but she draws me back to the photograph. There is more.

Betty points to a taller, brawnier young man in the center, broad-shouldered and barrel-chested in an olive green T-shirt. He has little more hair than Elijah, and his garb and chiseled physique suggest this is for different but also involuntary reasons. His stature and position in the picture leave no doubt that he is the alpha dog of this pack.

"John is our oldest, a *Semper Fi* Marine if there ever were one. He's 21 here, a sergeant stationed at Camp Lejeune. He came home for Elijah's birthday. They are ten years apart, but John always treated Elijah like a son. There may never have been a person who loved and protected his brother the way John looked out for Elijah.

"John wanted to be a career Marine. In the spring of 1983 he became a lieutenant and was sent with his company to Beirut. It was always tense there but John thrived on it. He loved feeling like he was there to keep peace instead of preparing for war. But in August they were out on an exercise and a freak accident broke John's leg in several places. They brought him to the military hospital in Germany, but he caught a blood infection so they had to send him home for critical care. He pulled through eventually, but he had a half-dozen pieces of metal holding his leg together, so that was the end of John's career in the Marines."

Without further explanation, Betty points to a younger boy on the far right, not long past puberty by appearance. He seems to be mimicking John's demonstrative gestures toward Elijah and his bulging muscles.

"That's Paul. He was thirteen, and he adored John, wanted to do everything just like his big brother. Of course John wouldn't allow him to enlist in the Marines until he got at least a two-year degree, so Paul went to community college before he followed John's lead. He was just one year out of Parris Island when his unit got the call to replace John's in Beirut. And I'm sure you remember what happened later that year."

Yes, I do. She doesn't need to explain. I was eleven at the time but I still recall the stone hush that fell over our nation when militants bombed the US Marine and French barracks in Beirut. Three hundred people died in the attacks, including, I imagine, Pfc. Paul Pickett.

"They said Paul was sheltered from the initial blast, but part of the roof caved in while he tried to help. John was completely devastated. He blamed himself, like any overprotective big brother would, I guess. He believed it should have been him there to die for his brothers, and just could not let go of the guilt.

"Virginia Moss stole the show at the funeral again. The body Paul had inhabited was returned to the earth at Camp Lejeune, along with several others belonging to his unit mates. President

Reagan was in attendance, as were many of the senior brass at our largest Marine Corps base. In front of *that* kind of audience, Virginia had this to say about the passing of her grandson:

> *When a king is expected to visit a village, the officials turn out to welcome him with a great feast and joyous salutations. So it is with all creation when a person sheds the body. "Here He comes!" they say, "Here comes God Himself!" But the senses, while that man lies dying, gather around and mourn God's departure, as courtiers mourn when their king is about to leave.*
>
> *"When body and mind grow weak, God gathers in all the powers of life and descends with them into the heart. As life leaves the eye, it ceases to see. 'He is becoming One,' say the wise; 'he does not see.' As life leaves the ear, it ceases to hear. 'He is becoming One, he does not hear. He is becoming One; he no longer speaks, or tastes, or smells, or thinks, or knows.' By the light of the heart, God leaves the body by one of its gates; and when He leaves, life follows. He who is dying merges into his consciousness, and thus consciousness accompanies him when he departs. He is One, and he remains Awake. Nothing enters the ground but the mortal body, sloughed like the skin of a snake. Freed from the body, God merges into Himself, infinite life, eternal light.*

spent a whole month with his grandma after that, absorbing anything she could teach him. He never dwelled on Beirut again.

"John got into carpentry, does pretty well for himself. He has a wonderful wife and three teenage sons of his own now in Denver. He and his wife started a home church a couple months ago, and apparently it has grown so big that they need to find a new space for it. They just drove us to the airport yesterday morning in fact, and I have never seen him look better. There is a fire in his eyes like nothing I have ever seen before. I think that boy is going to move mountains before long."

I am fascinated by the story of John, but something in Virginia's teaching illuminated a large portion of darkness that has haunted me as long as I can remember, and I am anxious to share the understanding.

"So basically...the functions of the individual mind do not cease with death of the body. They just merge into the universal Mind?"

"Which they were a part of all along."

"And that means death is a passage to a place that we never really left.

Betty claps her hands together softly, joy spreading across her face.

"You're getting it."

"My God, Betty, I am so...this is just...there are no words for this...is your mother a *prophet*?"

"She's a farmer," says Betty, with another wink. "And a counselor. But she's an ordinary person--no superpowers, no special connections to the divine that we don't have. One thing I will say about Virginia is that she has extraordinary listening skills, and she has fine tuned them to incredible precision over the years. Whatever caused her inner voice to pierce her consciousness on December 7, 1941 and bring peace to us both, she caught on to what it was, and she has been listening intently ever since. But the first thing she will tell you is in no way does that make her special. Everyone carries that inner voice. We have a tendency to let it be drowned out by the noise of the world, until either we start to cave in or the voice finds its own way out. But it is there all along. All the answers you need are within you."

Two huge sections of puzzle connect the moment she says that.

"And faith is the ability to listen to that voice and act upon it. Because the voice is Logos...the Word of God. That must be what they mean when they say Christ is within us. It's another expression of universal Mind." I don't bother phrasing it as a question. Betty, quite amusingly, mimes as though she is holding an ink stamper and presses it into her other hand.

"BINGO! *And*," she adds emphatically, "faith also means to trust that the voice is still there when you *can't* hear it, and trust the wisdom it has already given you. This is what it means to *live* by faith and not merely have it."

Yes...Merton's darkness....

"That has been the tricky part for me. When I am immersed in the world, it drowns out almost everything I could hear within, literally. My ears are hypersensitive. It's a serious challenge for me."

Betty seems to trip over herself without moving. Her intense gaze comes back, and she tilts her head slightly, looking halfway up so she can use the lower part of her bifocals to look straight ahead.

"My goodness...you even *look* like him, in some ways...."

"Like whom?"

Betty points to the fifth child in the photograph, just to the left of John.

"That is our Pedro, in more ways than one."

He is the shortest and the most slender of the four standing behind Elijah, but carries an unmistakably athletic aura. I look closely at his face, and recognize my almond-shaped eyes and awkward full-lipped grin. Had I been a teenager in the early to mid 1970s, our hair would probably have been very similar as well, dark blonde and somewhere between wavy and curly.

"Peter is the middle child, and the only one who got Shipley physical traits rather than the Moss family like my brother and father. He was a very gifted athlete--that comes from the Pickett side. Peter was a natural at every sport he tried--basketball, baseball, tennis, ping-pong. You name it, and by the time he reached high school he could beat all his brothers at it, even John. His best sport was long-distance running. He held several Kansas high school records for many years. Peter was an ambitious student as well, and he went to Temple University in Philadelphia to study journalism. He was a track and field All-American his first two seasons and was excelling in his studies.

"Then right before his third year, he dropped out. Said there was nothing the university could teach him that he couldn't learn better himself--or as he put it, he was "withdrawing from the university so he could enroll in the universe." He also complained that he was having trouble concentrating and needed to get out of the city. Later on we found out that he had the exact same issue that you described. His hearing acuity was off the charts, one-in-a-million high, and he couldn't filter background noise very well.

"So he spent several years hitchhiking around the country, supporting himself with temporary jobs. We knew he wasn't completely lost, because he would find his way home a couple times a year and spend time with his Grandma Ginny. Melvin and I didn't quite know what to make of it, but Virginia convinced us we should let him be, that he was working out something beautiful in his mind. Those two always had a very special bond. When he was younger, I assumed it was because he seemed closer to the Shipley lineage than the other boys. Come to find out it was much deeper than that....

"All the while, Peter trained intensely and ran marathons, won quite a few. He said running was the best way he knew to get the quiet space he needed. As the prize money from marathon victories added up, he didn't need odd jobs to support his meager existence, and he trained more and more. Then someone suggested he compete in triathlons since he was such a versatile athlete. So in 1988, he tried the famous Ironman race in Hawaii. Oh, let me tell you, he absolutely loved it, and he loved Hawaii even more. There was a spot along the Ironman course on the Kohala coast that Peter found while cycling, near the edge of a cliff overlooking the ocean. He said it was the place he had envisioned all his life, long before he knew about triathlons and

and Hawaii. He called it his 'vision of paradise,' and he made it his goal to build there at that very spot.

"So he moved to Denver and went to work for John, building other people's houses. He married a Hawaiian woman he met while doing the Ironman, and she gave birth to gorgeous twin girls in 1991. They looked like a normal middle-class family rooted in Golden, Colorado. But Peter was bent on getting back to Hawaii, and he squirreled away every penny he could. Altogether it took seven years of hard work and good business sense to get the financial stability to move with his wife and kids to a remote section of Hawaii, but they finally did it, and in 1996 they built a geodesic dome house on a hill overlooking the ocean.

"What even *I* didn't know at the time was that all along, Peter and John had been immersing themselves in the study of world religions. They took every class they could find at local colleges, spent their spare time at libraries absorbing everything they found, even discussing together as they worked. Then they would take their knowledge and bring it back to Grandma Ginny and she would distill it into its most simple form.

"Then in the early part of 2000, we received a letter from Peter. He told us that he had finally mastered the ability to translate theological ideas into one universal context that could be understood by everyone, and he was going to lay it all out in a book.

"The key to Peter's idea was to see each religion as a unique language. Every word in a language has a symbolic meaning, describing a particular pattern of consciousness expressed by universal Mind and observable by the individual--what we call objects, images and thoughts, the world as it is. Peter grouped this together and called it 'substance,' as opposed to words, concepts, and ideas ABOUT substance, which are symbols--how we describe the world to each other. The relationship between symbol and substance is like that of menu and a meal, or a map and the territory it describes.

"Now diverse languages can coexist because we understand that symbols are not the substance they represent; we don't try to eat menus or drive on maps. As we behold the substance of a fragrant red flower with a thorny stem, we know it is true to call this a rose, and that it is also true to call it 'una rosa' if we are speaking Spanish. This is the same symbol that is used in Italian, and very similar to French and Portuguese, but translation gets more difficult with " a ardaigh" in Irish, or "Bir gül" in Turkish. But the substance itself is what we perceive, and it does not change as we give it different names. It is in the substance that we find its alluring fragrance, the beauty of its shape and color that inspires us, not in reading the word "rose" or "ardaigh" or "Bir gül."

"That makes a lot of sense," I say, nodding. "The name is not what it describes. I guess you could also say the birds we're seeing today are substance, and the names on the scorecard and pictures in field guides are symbols."

"Exactly," says Betty, beaming like a proud teacher whose student just won the spelling bee. "It is such a simple distinction to make once you see why, and then you have poked a hole in the veil that separates us from reality in our minds. The applications for this are endless."

"I had been contemplating why I felt such disenchantment with the whole birding scene, even before the news broke this morning. I think I would prefer to experience the substance of birds in the wild, and not fill my head with symbols about them. Is that why you're a 'non-birding' spouse?'"

"You could say that, yes. I do enjoy the company of birds, although my primary interest is a whole other class of winged creatures...but back to Peter's letter." I can almost hear the gears shifting as Betty returns to the topic, and I wonder if there is something about the angels I'm not ready to hear yet.

"So the revelation that he shared with us--fostered by years of private meditation, research and conversation with Virginia--was that each religion was an attempt to convey, through an often complex pattern of symbols, the inexpressible nature of the substance we call Eternity. Like the name "rose" for a thorny red flower observed by an English speaker, each religion is true within its own context, and they all point to one universal Truth which is Eternal. No name for God, not even 'God' itself, gets

286

past the point of being relatively true like a menu to the meal or a map to the territory. They are all correct because none of them are.

"From this, Peter deduced that the effectiveness of a religion is in its power to orient the individual mind to the universal, to bring awareness of Eternity to us while we live as finite beings. This is more effective when we don't confuse the symbols for substance, when we don't take our gospels as Gospel. 'When we keep God invisible,' he wrote, 'draped not with words nor ideas of Who or Where or Why, God appears to be everyone, everywhere, just because.'

"Peter believed that widespread awareness of this could herald a new era of interfaith relationships. He said language teachers have long understood that you cannot master a new language by translating everything from your native tongue, that you need to learn to *think* in the new language, to perceive reality directly and apprehend it in the new set of words in the same way that we learned our first language. Interfaith education has good intentions but makes the mistake of trying to teach English-speakers Spanish by way of English, so to speak. Peter said he had become fluent in a couple dozen theological languages, and in doing so, he said, he learned not to try to translate from one language to another, such as English to Spanish to French to German, but to go directly to the reality they represent and intuitively understand it in a new language.

"The miracle of this was that once you become fluent in more than one theological language, you cease to differentiate between them. Just as Juliet said, a rose by any other name will smell just as sweet, no matter how you translate that into words. If people could learn this about their faiths across cultural barriers, they would see that we are all worshipping the same timeless, spaceless, live-giving and life-sustaining force in our own language, and it truly does not matter if we personalize that force or not, call it God, Christ, Allah, Tao, Buddha-mind, Atman, Ein Sof, Inner Light, anything. They are nothing more than cultural differences in our attempts to label what is ineffable. The names and descriptions and stories we use only represent this experience, just as the word "rose" represents a rose but is not the rose itself.

"Once the symbol and substance of our experience of the Divine are distinguished, Peter said, people would no longer feel threatened by another theological language that seems to contradict theirs, any more than the reality known to English speakers is threatened by people who describe it in Spanish. The nature of interfaith relationships would move beyond mere tolerance of differences, into compatibility and collaboration of shared experiences. They would recognize that experience across cultural lines and cease to make enemies of people who speak other theological languages, and truly understand what the Universalists have been telling us when they say that we all come from and worship the same source. He foresaw a day when armies of the world would lay down their arms, soldiers recognize each other as brothers and sisters, and conflicts like the one that killed Paul would disappear from the human experience.

"His book was going to detail how he learned to become 'universally fluent,' in his words. But he knew one book would only go so far. So he planned to build a retreat center where people could come and learn from each other experientially. He pictured a Socratic scene with teachers and students mingling and learning from each other and taking their wisdom home to share. He hoped his center would become a model for others around the world.

"They were breaking ground on the retreat center when Melvin and I visited them later that year as a part of another birding trip. I can see how this place made him see paradise. Lush green hills sloping right into the ocean...I have never seen such contentment as I saw on the face of my son. He had just turned forty-two."

Betty smiles as she tells me this. Of course, we both know that Peter is no longer with us, leaving just one more year to live in paradise. She continues.

"Peter had competed in thirteen straight Ironmans, and he was training for his fourteenth. He was a very regimented trainer. He always finished his day with a light jog along the beach below his house at twilight. One day last December, he hadn't come home by sundown and his wife got worried. After an hour she went down to the beach with a flashlight to look for him. She found him lying in the sand. He wasn't breathing and he had no pulse. It was a heart attack. Just like the other Moss men. No warning, no signs. Peter had the invisible plaque in his arteries. All of his fitness training couldn't prevent it."

I do not offer any condolences. I can tell by Betty's expression that she does not need them, and I finally understand why.

"What did Grandma Ginny say this time?"

Betty smiles. "Not a word. She doesn't really have to anymore, people recognize the expression in her eyes. When those who don't know her as well did try to console her privately, she would simply say, 'What goes down, must come up.'"

That makes me shudder, perhaps visibly. Betty tilts her head and looks inquisitive. The familiar vision of my front door opening is back...except this time, Nadia stands in the doorway.

"Amazing. My wife said the exact same thing when I asked if she was afraid of dying young from diabetes. I thought she was being a wise ass."

Betty's gaze relaxes, the ebullient smile returns. "No. Just wise."

"Amen to that...What can you tell me about Peter's work toward universal fluency? I have had those same thoughts, but I'm sure they are not nearly as developed as his."

"Peter did all of his work in his mind, and he had not put much on paper. Most of his ideas left with him when his consciousness merged with universal Mind. I can tell you that if the ideas are 'out there,' and you are meant to continue his work, they are within you as well, in a place you will learn to access."

I think about that for a minute. It dawns on me that Peter...left his body...in the same month as Splash Rios. Perhaps it is a sign that I should go all the way back to the beginning.

"If I were to ask you: where is Peter? Where are Paul, and Matthew, and your brother, and your father? The people who died back east today...all of us eventually. What gives us life while we are here, and where does it go when we disappear...is that something you can answer?"

Betty closes her eyes and remains still for a moment, the corners of her lips very slightly turned up. The question seems to have brought her to a place of deep contentment, the kind only induced by a labor of love.

"Those are questions for which the answer will always be a mere symbol, a cultural interpretation of a Truth that cannot be expressed with words. The Truth remains in the realm of mystery, and not because we cannot experience it or know what it is, but because the knowing required is beyond the scope of the individual mind. We must access the universal Mind to experience reality in its infinite, eternal Truth."

"The beauty of this," she continues, "is that unlike finite knowledge, the answer makes no claim of absolute truth and bears no burden of proof. Its sole merit lies in the way it speaks to our lives and transforms the human mind and heart, not the power to enslave devotees to the gospels themselves. This is what Buddhists mean when they call their scriptures a finger pointing at the moon. The moon is the radiant light of the universal Mind, one beautiful Truth shining for all through the dark night of our shadow selves. Many fingers will point at this one Truth, and they will all be right from their own perspective. Follow their guidance if you need it, but if you seek the truth in the fingers themselves, you will miss the point.

"I can introduce you to one such relative truth, one language that developed through the collaboration of Peter and John with their Grandma Ginny, which we share with our guests. We've found it very effective for contemplatives with a mystic temperament such as yours and Peter's. I will try to lay a foundation for you before we must return to the bus, if you wish."

"I would love nothing more," I say. "And thanks for reminding me," I say. "I had forgotten we still exist on the temporal plane."

"A common perception," Betty says with a smile. "And true in most ways, but an occupational hazard for bus drivers."

Betty closes her eyes again and breathes deeply, steadily, before proceeding with utmost calm.

"All that is created returns to its source, which is eternal; it transcends any boundary the mind can draw around it, any shape or location or origin we create for it. Because we exist in the universe, we know this source permeates us, exists within us and connects us to all else. While we live, we call ourselves by the name we associate with the individual mind--we are an 'I.' But this name doesn't change what we really are: the source, the universal Mind made flesh, one Being existing as many.

"Because I am one 'I' communicating with another 'I,' when I speak of this Being, I will use the name 'I and I.' We are two persons, unique in our own minds, united as One by the presence of I and I within us and all around us.

"You observed earlier that death passes the individual mind to a place it never really left. Indeed, because it never stopped being I and I while it lived. All that disappears is what made us appear separate, the body itself, and yet even this is simply transformed into other forms of substance within I and I.

"Therefore, we know that they who have died have gone to where I and I always dwells, which in Truth is everywhere, space-less and time-less, as they truly were all along. It is we who are still here in our unique minds who lament, who suffer for their apparent departure. We do not see that it was I and I who dwelled within them, who is imminent before they were born and continues after they perish. Birth is not our beginning, nor is death our end.

Beings come and beings go, but that which inhabits our being, that which looks out from our eyes and listens with our ears and directs all of our thoughts and actions--this is the eternal, changeless I and I. It is not born into the body--the body rises from I and I like a phoenix from the flames of a previous life. It does not die with the body--the body stays behind while I and I merges into itself and finds a place to rise again. It disappears here, and it reappears there. It goes down like the sun in the west, and it comes up like the same sun in the east. All the while that we live, we live within I and I, and I and I within us. This is why nobody can truthfully say 'I am,' because only I and I is: infinite life, eternal light.

"I and I is the substance from which our ideas about eternity arise, the 'rose' that gives birth to countless names to describe it. 'I and I' is just one example of a primordial statement of our source and being, a name that is uttered to stand alone and need no further explanation. The ancient Hebrews knew this as YHWH, or 'I Am That Is.' To the Indus Valley civilization where both Hinduism and Buddhism were born, the source was 'Brahman,' a godhead with no describable attributes. To the Chinese, it was 'Tao,' the Uncarved Block. Much later, the earliest Christian scriptures written in Greek rendered it as 'Logos,' the Word of God.

"For a small minority of people, to meditate on a single name such as these, in full awareness of what it represents, is sufficient to develop awareness of the eternal source. But the individual mind of the human being is very active and imaginative at perceiving separation, and therefore most demand a symbolic depiction of the one Being and our relationship to it as apparent mortals--an explanation of how we lost contact with it, and how we may return. Our minds project separation rather than unity as the primordial state, leaving us with an existential puzzle which must be solved at great peril to our lost and lonely beings. Death of the body seems to close the door on everything we could ever be, rather than open it to what we really are. This is why I feared the loss of my father as a nine year old girl, and why my mother constructed a means to explain why I could never truly lose him. This grew into a mythological language of its own, the story of the angels who guide us home, a story we still tell today to those prepared to receive."

"I was curious about the nature of the angels, what roll they have in explaining I and I. It seems strange to hear you call them mythological now when I saw them as a pillar of your faith before."

"Ah, but this is the perfect example of finger worship. My faith is rooted in the home to which the angels point, not the angels themselves."

Something strikes me the moment I hear that. I look away from Betty, up toward the eastern sky. A waning crescent moon will rise there in a few hours, but what I see is luminous and large, rising above the pines of Meseta Centrada. I feel as it expands to encompass everything I see and think and am, leaving no doubt as to what I witness. This is my first time seeing Inner Light.

"On the other hand," she continues, "mythology does not imply a lack of grounding in reality. 'Mythos' is the broad term for a culture's collection of symbols, the 'bag of tricks' we call upon to explain the world as we know it. We already know that the truth of these explanations is relative within their cultural context, and they can never do more than represent an absolute truth. So it is with the mythology created by Virginia. It is a new cultural context to describe through metaphor our transition from an individual mind experiencing the illusion of isolation to the Truth of I and I."

"I see...which is why new contexts are needed. We forget they were *supposed* to be metaphor from the start."

"Or as Peter said, 'A prophet is without honor in his own home and without fault next door, crucified by one generation and canonized by its children.' Our need to deify the messenger and worship the finger is the greatest obstacle to Truth, so I cannot oversteer you clear of this. Likewise, do not give in to doubts about the reality of our symbols just because they are not what they represent. To me, the angels are as real as anything on earth, because I was taught to see them. To most people, they will hold greater value as metaphors. I am neither right nor wrong in my perception, nor is anyone else in theirs. I will tell you of my experience and let you perceive for yourself. This comes straight from the liturgy we present to our guests:

"We are all winged creatures. We must walk through this appearance in order to learn humility, which is what allows the singular mind to say, 'I relinquish attachment to this limited form,' and become One selfsame with all. This is the home to which all life secretly aspires.

"In the world before this, we perceived no separation, and we were also not aware of space and time, form and shape. Being born into this world, we are awakened and experience the four dimensions, but with that we also feel separation between ourselves and each other, and all things. This is an illusion caused by the human mind--a useful one that enables us to do everything we do, but still it is unreal. This is what is meant by saying we are shadow puppets--the limited concept of self projected unto a screen that veils the Truth from us.

"In the next world, the veil is lifted, and the emptiness of all things is revealed. We remain awake, so we can still perceive space and time, shape and form, but there is no separation. Space and time move in cycles and currents like water in the ocean rather than the linear progression of the stream. We will be able to look back at this world and see that this was always so, and we will feel love for those still living as though they are separate, and we will go back to this world in many appearances and try to save them.

"It is said, then, that the human being moves from being asleep as One, to Awake as many, to Awake as One.

"It is possible for the human to enter the next world while living here. But there are no land bridges to the next world. The human must experience the same humility that is ordinarily felt only in death. Most people will have their wings unbound upon the involuntary death of the physical body. It is the rare few who will choose to subject themselves to the voluntary "death" of the mythical shadow puppet. These are the ones who are said to earn their wings, and they are able to go back and forth between this world and the next, so that they may bring some of the peace of the next world to the chaos of this one. Others must be stripped of their body and five senses before having the will to help others, but even they are One in I and I, and there is no part of I and I that doesn't call all beings to come home.

"The Unveiled Ones are known by many names: angels, sages, seers, saints, buddhas, muktas, messiahs, saviors, helpers, friends. Some earned their wings and are visible; most were given use of their wings at death and are invisible. What they have in common is the humility and vitality to be empty and awake, and bring peace to those in this world who know beyond knowing that they are among us. Those who receive this knowledge are not content to keep it to themselves, for this is a form of arrogance. Instead they will begin their own path to humility so they can demonstrate the way for others."

"What is the way to earn one's wings?"

"Become more acquainted with I and I than you are with your-self. There is no one way to do this. This is what is meant by 'Truth is One, Paths are Many.' People are drawn to different paths by lineage or temperament or geography or who knows what. Three elements that most have in common are mentioned by Jesus of Nazareth in the Christian bible: prayer, fasting, and meditation. If practiced in the right spirit, with proper guidance by visible or invisible Revealed Ones, these will engender hu-mility and lead the shadow to disappear, the Light of the world to shine everywhere without obstruction.

"And the rest," Betty adds, "will have to wait until the next time we sit together, for I believe we will have some anxious birders waiting by the bus."

"I can only hope that will be very soon," I say while rising to my feet. "I don't know how I could possibly thank you enough."

"You can thank me by taking these ideas to heart and chan-neling the voice of Virginia Moss into your work. She will not always be with us, but her message needs to live on. I hope I gave you some new material for your book."

"I think you just rewrote my book for me." This idea makes us both smile, and we embrace like the old friends we suddenly are.

We walk just a few feet toward the bus before Betty stops.

"Do you happen to have a photograph of your wife?"

I fish out the one I carry in my wallet. It goes back five years to our earliest days together. We were vacationing in New Orleans, standing in front of a paddleboat that we were about to board for a cruise down the Mississippi. We were so new; carefree and burning with love.

I hand the picture to Betty. She looks and then immediately pulls it to her heart and holds it there, her head tilted and low-ered with a mournful expression. It looks as though she is try-ing to cradle us through the photograph. Then she takes out the pendant and pops it open again, removing a smaller item that I had not noticed before. It is also folded into quarters, and as she unfolds, it appears to be business card-sized. She inspects it for a moment, then briefly closes her eyes and turns toward the heavens before she speaks.

"When Matthew left his body, I had a brief loss of faith. The pain was overwhelming, and I forgot most of what I had learned in my inability to listen clearly. One of Virginia's students gave me this at the funeral, and it cut all the way through the shell of my suffering and brought me back to myself. I have kept it ever since, but I think it has served me well enough. I would like you to take it. You will need it in the not-too-distant future."

She hands me the card along with the picture. Tears well up and overflow as I read the words upon it--among the most beautiful ever penned in the English language. I was familiar with this passage of the mysterious John Donne already, but never in this context, never with such awareness of how near I am to "thee:"

> *No man is an island, entire of itself; every man is a piece of the continent, a part of the main; if a clod be washed away by the sea, Europe is the less, as well as if a prom-ontory were, as well as inf a manor of thy friend's or of thine own were; any man's death diminishes me, because I am involved in mankind, and therefore never send to know for whom the bell tolls; it tolls for thee.*

I feel a tingling sensation in the middle of my back. I can tell without looking that my wings have perked up. They are itching to be let loose and stretch to their fullest before taking flight, but the thread remains snug. Their time has not come, they are not ready.

I had turned away for a minute while absorbing the full force of Donne's words, but I look back at Betty intently. Her wings are spread wide and fully plumed. Her face is timeless, a blank slate devoid of age. I can see them all now: the terrified nine-year-old Sunday school girl; the jubilant teenager reunited with her father; the solemn, prayerful fiancé, waiting out another war; the exuberant wife and guiding influence on five souls; the mother who has said goodbye to three sons.

And, of course, the woman of almost seventy years, who stands before me on September 11, 2001 and knows no fear.

Betty could fly back to the bus, I imagine. Maybe back to the Middle of Everywhere...but she doesn't. She walks by my side.

2:30 pm (PDT) / 5:30 pm (EDT)

How strange.....I am not where I really am.

I must have fallen asleep (missed my second and third coffees, after all)...I'm not in a hospital room in Jersey City. I am lying in bed inside my boyhood home in Brighton Beach. Everything in this room is just as I remember from that crucial point in my life: posters of my favorite Giants all over the walls, Pink Floyd's "The Wall" playing constantly on the turntable. Right now, I am lying in bed staring at the ceiling. I'm experiencing the same confusion I felt as a young boy about how to properly address my Creator. This was before Mama died and I decided that it was pointless and absolved myself of responsibility to figure it out. Before that, I would worry myself sick, wondering if my nighttime prayers should be spoken to the Heavenly Father of my Catholic training, or to the Allah that Mama's family taught me about on the sly.

I hear myself ask out loud, "God, do you really answer our prayers anyway?"

Suddenly, the scene changes...I am sitting on a stage facing an audience. I can't move any part of my body, though my head seems to swivel around on its own power. Then I realize that I'm sitting on someone's lap, and that person has his arm reaching up inside my back. He is the one controlling my head. I look over and see the person is God. Well, a cartoon image of God; I recognize it from The New Yorker...and I realize that it was God who asked the question. It just seemed like I had spoken because

God's lips did not move.

Then God, in the voice of an old time Jewish vaudeville co-median, says, "Well dummy, who do you suppose is doing the praying?"

Just as the audience starts bursting into laughter, I hear a woman's voice shriek, "Stella!" I open my eyes to see Melody tiptoeing across the room, and easing into a slow motion pounce onto a waking Estelle.

With great care not to disturb her head and neck, Melody embraces her torso and lowers her mouth toward Estelle's, and they kiss.

And they keep kissing...deeply...soulfully.

I'm pretty sure this is another layer of my dream, and I shake my head vigorously. But they keep kissing...now I start to feel bashful. Should I be watching this?! Probably not...but I just can't turn away...*so this is what Melody meant by her "best girlfriend"*...

Finally, Melody pulls her head back, and the girlfriends whisper and giggle to each other, seemingly unaware that anyone else exists. The sound of footsteps coming to the doorway prompts a hasty retreat by Melody, and the nurse enters the room to find her only halfway on top of Estelle.

"Well hello there, sleepyhead," says the nurse, her expression suggesting she has quite literally seen it all. "You've had an adventurous day." She begins the standard tests of Estelle's vital signs, all of which seem to be looking good. "Do you have any recollection of events from earlier today, or why you are in a hospital?"

Estelle's brow curls as she concentrates on what seem like blurry thoughts trickling in through the fog.

"I was sitting in a car, watching a big smoky fire in a sky-scraper...then the skyscraper fell down, and everything went black."

"Ah, that's about what I would expect. Let's leave it at that for now. You'll piece it all together by tomorrow."

But Estelle has more. "And then I am pretty sure an angel carried me to safety."

Melody smiles and points to me. "Here's your angel, Stella. He's the one who saved your life."

I'm a little embarrassed by that. "I was just in the right place at the right time."

"You weren't 'just' anything to us," Melody retorts. "You're a true hero."

I lean over and take Estelle's hand. It feels soft and wispy in mine. I don't want to let it go. "It's a pleasure to meet you, Estelle."

Estelle squints to bring my face into focus, gears turning slowly. Then a weak but beaming smile.

"You're the man from the car. You stayed."

I smile back. "A promise is a promise," I say with a wink. What's your name, angel?"

"Joey," I say, then catch my slip and straighten myself up. "Um, ha, I mean Joseph. My wife calls me Joey. To everyone else, I'm Joseph."

"Your wife is a lucky woman, Joey."

Estelle trails off as her eyes close, and she falls back into sleep. Melody and the nurse look at each other apprehensively.

"She's had serious head trauma," the nurse says matter of factly, "Typical post-concussive symptom, called the lucid interval."

"And she just woke up," adds Melody. "Plus I'm sure you see that all the time with accident victims and the people who save them, right?"

"Oh yes, all the time," says the nurse, with a wink of her own at me as she leaves the room.

"Yeah, I'm sure," I add, my heart smiling for the first time all day...for many days.

ACT VII

3:00 pm (PDT) / 6:00 pm (EDT)

I am a new city, born again today in destruction and loss, but also in unity, and even small measures of triumph. In the place that some call Ground Zero, an American flag flies above the ruins of the World Trade Center, where it was raised by some of my Bravest. It will give proof through the night that we are still there.

Back across the river, I am once again Joseph Bijan D'Angelo. I scamper down the Columbus Drive off ramp for the last time, and hop into the passenger seat of Melody's car, waiting for me on the street around the corner.

'It's still there," I report. "The note I left on the windshield must have pacified anyone who wanted it gone."

"Great, well I guess you'd better get going," says Melody. "Do you need directions to the house?"

"Nope. We almost bought a condo on your street instead of the house. Wouldn't that have been something?"

"Amazing how the universe works," she says with a wide grin, "bringing the right people together at the right time."

"I am starting to see that." I consider asking the question on the tip of my tongue, but I hesitate. "So, um, are you heading back then?"

"Yeah, I want to be there whenever she wakes up until her short term memory improves."

I nod, a little absently. I cannot get that kiss out of my head....I have to ask.

"So, um...uh, you and Estelle...you're like...." I really hope she will finish the sentence for me.

"Oh!" she says after a short silence, and laughs heartily. "I'm sorry Joseph, I should have been up front with you so you'd be prepared. Estelle and I are lovers."

I nod again, softly but rapidly, and make that face where I am trying not to smirk.

"OK, OK, yep...and you're, um, but...you're...."

"Also married to men, yessir. Well, Estelle won't be for long, but yes I am blissfully wed. It's true that we've been best friends since second grade, I didn't make that up. But yeah, since our days together at UMKC, we've been a little more than that. I'm sure you can understand why we leave that out of most conversations."

I do, for sure, but I'm guessing my arched eyebrows ask one more unspoken question.

"But Ty knows everything, yeah, of course. No secrets there. He knew we were a package deal when he married me. He loves Estelle like a sister."

"Oh, OK, good. I just didn't want to get caught knowing a big secret between you as I'm getting to know you, that's all."

My face must have revealed more relief than I intended to show, because Melody casts a knowing sideways grin, then leans over and kisses me on the cheek.

"Thanks again, Joseph...now go get that adorable wife a'yours, y'hear?" She says in her best affected Mizzourah drawl. "We'll see you soon. *Both* of you."

"You bet. Dinner at our place this weekend. I'll make my killer *scampi fra diavola.*" I match her drawl with my cliché New York-Italian pasta jockey, punctuated with a *Bellissimo!* fingertip kiss. I hop out of the car, then watch and wave as she turns left on Montgomery and disappears behind the overpass.

Now comes the hard part.

Being alone used to feel like my refuge from the world before I lost Isabella. Since then, I've had a love-hate relationship with it. Right now, loneliness feels like my worst enemy. No one around to drown out the rising fear that I will have to raise my daughters without their mama.

I tread slowly up the off ramp and reach the shoulder of the expressway, the forever altered skyline of Manhattan back in view. The pillar of smoke and dust makes me think of a funeral pyre, mournfully lifting soul after soul to heaven. How strange: so many millions of people across the world were not directly affected by what happened today, and whether they think so or not their lives will go on more or less as normal tomorrow. Those of us going through the grinder today will either have gaping holes in our lives after the dust settles, or we will have triumphed over our deepest fears, like Melody, and our lives will forever change in *that* way. When I felt connected to Melody's triumph, I could handle not knowing on which side I will fall with Vera. Back in the world alone, my heart clamors for relief from unknowing. Faith is still there, I can tell, but my attention to it erodes with every moment alone.

In the foreground, one of the many churches of Jersey City rings in the 6 o'clock hour. I stop and listen intently to these chimes. I hear the same kind of bells from one of the churches in Union all the time, but I never really *listen* to them. They are a vestige of an era before electric digital clocks in everyone's home when church bells synchronized the lives of an entire village. I wonder if any of the urbanites of today even hear these chimes as they wear their headphones or watch TV in private family rooms. Yet the bells persist, feeding some need we don't know we have.

There's something about this train of thought, and the view across the river, and especially the church bells...it is harkening back to one passage that always stuck with me from that religious-themed literature course I took to satisfy my Humanities requirement at St. Francis: "No man is an island, entire of itself." Clearly, John Donne did not foresee 21st century America, the most insular society in world history. Yet even among our isolation from each other, I feel his simple answer ring true: be involved in mankind. I've tried to be uninvolved for so long, but life keeps bringing me back.

I never quite understood the line "therefore never send to know for whom the bell tolls, it tolls for thee," and I'm not sure I do now, either. But there must be something that connects us, and makes it possible to feel joy in Melody's joy, and pain in the pain of those who lost loved ones today. To the extent that we can feel both, perhaps, we are never fully alone, neither in life nor in death.

This thought bolsters my faith, and just in time, too, for as I reach for my car's door handle, I hear another chime, odd yet very familiar.

A call, the first one all day, is coming in to my cell phone. I fish it from my pocket, and see an unfamiliar 212 number on the screen.

My thumb hovers over the green button. This is the moment of truth for the rest of my life: it could be Vera, or it could be someone calling to tell me her body has been identified.

I swallow hard, heart pounding like it wants to break through my rib cage, and press the button.

"Hello?"

"Hi, Joey."

These two words eviscerate about ten tons of bricks from my shoulders (and how many more there would have been, had God not dissolved so many all day, brick by brick). I know that the delectably feminine voice that spoke them belongs to a woman of unimaginable beauty--long, wavy, almost fire-red hair, lips like plump strawberries, milky white skin and eyes a soft, lush green like the hills in the land of her forebears, all burning with a flaming vitality that I could imagine once belonging to a legendary Druid priestess. As a rather odd complement to this image, she stands a little under five feet tall, slender but powerful like the retired gymnast she is (she still works out with the Columbia University team for which she once starred, or at least she had been until about five months ago when her energy level dropped without warning or explanation). Though hailing from a family of tall and burly Scots, she owes her small physical stature to a birth so premature that she fought staggering odds just to survive beyond the incubator. After that, her limbs were supposed to stay so weak and underdeveloped that she would never walk without assistance. After *that*, her ovaries were supposed to be so small that bearing children would be out of the question. She is a perfect 3-for-3 so far at defying the doctors' most dire predictions, and at the moment, she is standing confidently at the plate, calling her shot, preparing to hit for the cycle. Having just survived the deadliest terrorist attack in American history--in which a jet plane crashed into an office tower no more than 150 feet above her head--there seems to be no reason to doubt her.

"Vera...oh Vera...I was starting to wonder if you had left me." I am well acquainted with Vera's disapproval at being the object of fuss or any undue attention--and almost all attention is undue from her perspective--so as usual I do my best to contain what she chides as my "unbridled Mediterranean passions" in simple verbal content. There is, however, no containing the tears streaming profusely from my eyes.

"Nope. God did not cut the thread today."

"Amen to that. Are you OK? Are you in a hospital or... what, where, tell me! My mind's been going crazy."

"I'm a little ashen and dusty, but otherwise all is well."

"So you were in the tower, and you made it out alright?"

"Yeah, I got out just fine. It was the going back in a few times that was tricky, and the--"

"*You went back in?!?*"

"Of course. The fire department needed help finding people on the damaged floors. It was useful to be small and know my way around the stairwells. And you said I was nuts for never taking the elevator."

"Oh my God, Vera, you are nuts for a million reasons and I love every one of them. I don't know why I'm surprised, I'm just...in your condition, sweetheart, I think--"

"Baby, you make it sound like I'm pregnant or something. I know my limits. We saw Tower 2 come down, so we had some warning that 1 was in trouble. I stayed with a group of Japanese bankers that we pried out of an elevator, and we got to a pizza shop about two blocks away before it collapsed. The fire fighters gave me a respirator after the tower came down--honey, I actually got with a group of Japanese bankers that we pried out of an elevator, and we got to a pizza shop about two blocks away before it collapsed. The fire fighters gave me a respirator after the tower came down--honey, I actually got to hold the hand of a woman who was trapped while they were digging her out. She's from your neighborhood in Brooklyn. I could feel the life force through her palm, it was so strong and kept getting stronger as they got closer to her. It was so exhilarating! I was supposed to be there today. So I stayed as long as I could hold out and I started walking north. I always knew I would make it home to you and the girls, darling."

"Yes, I am sure you did. Forgive me for even questioning. Where are you now and how do I get to you?"

"I'm in Times Square, and I--"

"Times Square? What are you doing up there?"

"Just sort of gravitated this way. Seemed like the place to be."

Actually this makes a lot of sense. Times Square was Vera's first image of New York City when she emerged from the Greyhound station as an 18 year old heading to her freshman year at Columbia. She was dazzled beyond belief, and it was the "first kiss" in a new lifelong romance with urban life, having previously only dreamed about it while growing up on a farm in the middle of nowhere (or as she prefers to call it, "the Middle of Everywhere"). If Vera needed any grounding today in her chosen home, it made perfect sense that she would seek it in Times Square.

"Well, I haven't been able to receive a call all day until now. I hope you weren't panicking about not reaching me." I say this mostly to make myself feel better, knowing well that "panic" is not in her vocabulary.

"You know the silly thing about these new cell phones? You program someone's number into it, and you don't bother to memorize it because you figure it's there forever on some indestructible microchip or something, but then you leave the phone on your desk while you step outside for a while, and next thing you know the whole building collapses. So then you're just *screwed* and you can't reach the love of your life all day."

I smile nice and wide. Vera is obviously better than fine. Her sense of humor is the only possession she really values, and it is perfectly intact.

"You obviously haven't given your number to anyone in the Jello family*", she continues, "which I *totally* understand and support, but it made tracking you down all the more difficult. Finally it dawned on me to call Cingular, because surely there must be some anonymous woman in Mumbai who knows your phone number. Lo and behold, I found her! By then of course I was completely out of quarters and had no access to any money--my purse went down with the ship, too--but the very nice gentleman who owns this porn shop let me use his phone to call you. People have been so kind and courteous all day; it almost feels

*When Vera and I were dating, she had a habit of using the common mispronunciation of my last name, saying the "D" like the "O" in O'Reilly instead of treating it simply as one word that sounds like "tangelo" with the emphasis on the middle syllable. I was already catching guff from my family for dating a non-Catholic, and I was afraid this would alienate her further from them, so I corrected her at every instance, sometimes not very patiently. Eventually she decided she needed a memory aid, so she started calling me "Danny Jello." My family, of course, then became the Jello family--or, when she really wanted to get my goat, the Jello mafia.

like I'm back home. It's been magical."

"Well, Toto, I don't think we're in New York anymore."

"Ha! Exactly! So yeah, this is the first time I tried. I figured I'd try the home phone next and then Small Wonders, but you saved me the trouble. So are *you* in New York? I was guessing you hadn't made it, you silly car-driving man. Are you home with the girls?"

"No, I'm neither. I was stuck on the Turnpike in Jersey City, and I'm still there...oh boy, what a long story...the girls are fine, they were picked up by...wow, what a *really* long story. They are fine. They are at Melody Weaver's house, with her husband."

"Oh wonderful, what a perfect plan! Tyrell is such a sweetheart with the kids."

"It all kind of came together. I met her friend today, Estelle."

"Right, her old Kansas City friend with all the health issues. She had just gotten to town last I saw Melody. How did you meet her?"

"She was right behind me in traffic. We were standing together on the shoulder of the Turnpike and she fainted, cut her head open pretty bad. I ended up taking her to the hospital.... Anyway, long story but I wound up contacting Melody and made the connection. Such a small world sometimes."

"Indeed, it's amazingly small and enormous and wonderful.... So you took her to the hospital this morning, and you're just getting back to the car on the Turnpike *now*?"

"I stayed with her, at the hospital. I don't know, it's kind of strange but...I felt like I *knew* her, even before I found out about Melody. I couldn't just *drop her off* like I was her cab driver or something...I needed to make sure she was gonna be OK."

"No, honey, I understand completely. It's not like you at all. I'm proud of you, baby....is she cute?"

"What?!? What do you--well, um, I don't...I wasn't *checking her out*, Vera! I mean, yeah I guess she *was* actually, but....

"Aw honey, are you still fretting the personal ad? How many times do I have to tell you that it's OOOOO-KAAAAY? I *want* you to be out there! And what better place than *that* site?!"

"I know, love, I'm not--OK, maybe a *little* fretting. But c'mon, I don't think that was really on my mind today."

(Oh, this woman's X-ray vision will be the death of me! Or the life, I'm not sure which.)

"OK, OK, just checking, baby. You never know, could be any number of reasons why a person comes and goes through the current of our lives. And we already have one connection to her. I just think you should try to be aware, that's a--"

"I will, sweetheart, I will, I'm just--I don't know if today is the right time to get into that, you know?"

"Alright, honey, if that's what you are feeling, that's fine... Well, I don't think I have to go to work tomorrow. Want to go hiking in the Skylands? It's been way too long."

I pause, not quite sure I heard her right. I've become so accustomed to hearing the most outrageous statements come out of Vera's mouth that I rarely if ever get surprised, yet there are times when even her most basic irreverence seems so incongruent with the world around us that I just have to check myself from a purely auditory standpoint. When I realize that I did hear her correctly, I burst into the most unexpected barrage of laughter. Here it is, the complete joy of realizing the love of my life is not gone, that we will wake up together tomorrow and our shared life will go on...and as I feel that, the pain of those who will not also hits me full force, for first the first time all day. My laughter becomes interspersed with choking sobs. How strangely real it feels to laugh and cry so hard at once.

"What's wrong, baby?"

It takes me a minute to calm my grief enough to even try speaking, I stammer as the words come out in jagged pieces. "The plane...I saw...the...the second plane...." I breathe deeply...*Let it out*. My theme of the day. "I saw the second plane hit the south tower. Right in front of me. While I was stuck on the Turnpike. I can't get the image out of my head...I wish God had taken my eyes before that moment."

"Oh, Joey. I can imagine the horror you are feeling. I am so sorry that you had to experience that. Now I want you to remember though, every one of the persons who died today has gone home. That is all that has happened. You can be sad, but be sad for the families who do not know where their loved ones are. They are the ones in pain today."

There was a time when I, drawing on my own perpetual heartache, would counter with a "what about the children" argument. But I've learned that this does not get very far with a person whose mother died giving birth to her, and whose father suffered a gruesome heart attack while driving her to school one Wednesday morning. Vera is living proof that nothing is too much to bear when the heart is open.

"I know...I believe you, love. I've been reminding myself all day, but I just...how can you be so *sure*?"

"I see their wings, Joey. I literally see them unfold and take to the sky. Oh baby, if you would only learn how beautiful this blossoming is, the city was so alive with it today! It takes training to see beyond what your two eyes are reporting to you at first, but I am so convinced that everyone can do it. But you won't see anyone else's wings until you can feel your own. That is the key.... You know you're welcome to come with me on Monday nights. Purusha could really help you develop your third eye vision. I know he intimidates you, but the best--"

"He doesn't in*timid*ate me," I interrupt, more meekly than I wanted to sound. I really cannot stand how right she is all the time. "He just seems like kind of a flaky hippie to me, that's all."

"Joey, he intimidates you. You decided he was a flaky

hippie before you met him, and you are holding on to that image because it belittles him in your eyes. I *promise*, you couldn't be more wrong about him, Joey. It's *OK* to admit it, baby, it's perfectly natural. He is a vessel of some very powerful wisdom. But I *swear* to you, honey, he is not that kind of teacher, he won't lord over you. The *wisdom owns him*. All he lives to do is share it, and the best way for you to get over your fear of him is to *accept* this gift and *empower* yourself."

I sigh. She is right. This is exactly what my heart has been saying for a long time, and I have been ignoring it out of fear. The call is getting too loud to ignore now. But oh, if Nonna Lioni, God rest her soul, could see me practicing Kundalini yoga, she would be calling for the neighborhood exorcist.

"I really would love for you to come sometime with an open mind," Vera continued, her voice a notch or two softer. "I can see you sharing this wisdom with others yourself someday. You have the heart of a teacher, sweetie. It is so obvious watching you with the girls...I don't think it would kill you to miss a few football games either."

Ah, another truth I have been diligent to avoid. "No, I think it would prolong my life based on reduced beer consumption alone. You're so right about everything, love. I just...I've had a real block with Purusha. Just the timing of everything, when you started his class, and when, you know...things like last night, and--"

"Oh baby, is *that* what this is all about?!" Vera lets out a snorting laugh and a sigh full of mock exasperation, neither of which would have seemed appropriate to an observer who was unfamiliar with our dynamic. But it was the quintessential Vera response to my frequent foolishness. How fortunate for both of us that Vera was blessed with infinite patience for the folly of men.

"Oh Joey Joey Joey. You are so good at getting yourself all worried about absolutely nothing! Now I know you like to pretend this isn't happening, and I can understand why, but baby, you are going to *drive yourself crazy* if you don't accept that my prana is not inexhaustible anymore. You were sitting next to me when the doctor told us that a depressed libido is one of the possible side effects of MS. I remember looking at you at that moment, and you had this glazed-over look on your face, like you might as well have been pressing your hands over your ears and saying, 'I'm not listening! I'm not listening!" Now I know we both thought there would be more time before some of the symptoms worsened, but that is not what we have been given--I am leaking prana and I am not sure why yet. I do know that if I try to spend sexual energy that I don't have, it would leave me that much more depleted. That is the *only* reason I would *ever* turn away from you, baby."

I shake my head in self-disgust. "God, I *knew* that! There was one stupid nagging voice that wouldn't let go of that ridiculous idea. Oh sweetheart, I am so sorry. The last thing you need to be dealing with now is one of my paranoias."

"Aw darling, I understand. You are so conditioned to think that every woman you love is going to leave you, one way or another. Now I know my body is beautiful and a lot of fun to have and to hold and all that great stuff, but if you could practice at being less attached to it, I promise you would know that I am always with you. We aren't two drops of water falling through the sky, baby. We're the whole ocean, you and I."

"You know, love, you've told me that so many times, and it's always bounced right off my thick skull...I think it's starting to sink in."

"There is hope for you yet, Joey! It's so typical for us as humans to look at the solution and see it as the problem. Kundalini is the art of cultivating and maintaining prana. We can learn to conserve it when it is low and shift it to where it is needed. Essentially, Purusha is teaching me to tap into my life force reserves and channel that energy more efficiently to you, not to give it to someone else, silly boy. Purusha and I talked about everything last night after class, that's why I got home so late. He has worked with MS patients before. He is very confident that I can keep my function level high with yoga while healing the auto-immune disorder through meditation and dietary changes."

"That's fantastic, love! I should have known that you'd be tackling this one just as hard as everything else."

"I promise you, MS will not get the best of me in the long run. But it will get a good chunk of me for a little while. And that's why I started thinking that, you know, maybe this is the right time for you to, well, *spread your wings* a little bit, so to speak, and--"

"Vera, *please*, I'm not--I can't...I don't need it that badly that I have to go find someone else!"

"Oh Joey darling, please give me a little credit for my vastly superior brain. I think I know my red hot Persian-Italian lover-man better than that. I didn't just marry you for your money, you know."

"Fine, but sweetheart, I am a one-woman man. I am *completely* devoted to you."

"I *know* you are, baby! I know you have been devoted when you've had opportunities to cheat, and I *love you oh so much* for that. I trust your devotion so much that I feel completely free to welcome a second woman into our lives. It makes perfect sense when you think about it."

"But sweetheart, I--"

"Honey, honey, please. This is one of those times that we talked about where it would be good for *you* to admit that you have needs, and then you can let *me* feel the joy of helping to meet a need of yours that I couldn't otherwise. Can we do it like we practiced, please? It's not as fun for me if I have to *beg* you to get excited about it."

"But I told you before, I couldn't be with another woman just for sex!" Even with no one possibly sitting still within earshot on the shoulder of the New Jersey Turnpike, I found myself lowering my volume as I spoke the last word. I can sense Nonna Lioni rolling over in her grave.

"First of all, get real. Yes you could. You fantasize about it all the time, you just think I don't want to know that. Second of all, that's the beauty of polyamory! Some people are looking to keep it casual, but there are many others who know that love is boundless and their hearts were meant to hold more than one true love. You could hold out for a another soulmate, or you could meet a sweet friend-with-benefits. It is totally up to you, baby. There are no rules. Just be honest with me and yourself and the other women and we'll all get along just fine."

"And that wouldn't make you jealous at all?"

"What in the world would I be *jealous* about, baby? I would be getting the space I need to heal so I can stick around and love you longer. I might even get a new sister. What a perfect trade!"

By now I am pretty sure that Nonna Lioni and all my other dead relatives are doing full somersaults...*to hell with 'em. I can't keep letting my whole life be controlled by a bunch of Sicilians who live in Greenwood Cemetery.*

"And you seriously would let me be with *anyone* I choose?"

"Whoever makes you most happy, darling. I trust you to choose wisely...well, if I could have one request, I would like someone with domestic skills. I'm going to need some help keeping up the house soon."

"Wow, sweetheart I'm...my God, you are *way* too good for me, love. I don't know why you've put up with me all these years. I don't deserve you."

"Bay-beeee, you're my Joey Angel. You deserve so much *more* than me. You have *no idea* what a gift you are to my life, and to our daughters. We will be needing even more from you for a while, and I wouldn't *dream* of asking more of you while giving less. We will get through this together, darling...with a little help from our friends."

"Oh Vera, how did I get so fortunate as to win the heart of a woman as wise as thee?"

"You know none of this comes from me, baby. I owe

everything to Grandma Ginny."

"Well, I could really use some time with your grandma. Let's spend Thanksgiving in Kansas this year."

"Why *Joey Bijan*, I never thought I would live to hear you say that! This isn't one of your sadistic *teases*, is it?"

"Not at all, love. I can say No to the Jello mafia every now and then."

"Oh *baby*, I can't tell you how happy I would be to go home for the holiday! You just made my year, darling. I will call Betty as soon as she gets back from California and make sure they are staying. They sometimes go to visit John or Elijah for Thanksgiving."

"Wherever you want to go is fine. I should finally meet these miracle cousins of yours too."

"For sure. If you love *me*, you'll go crazy for the cousins. They got to *grow up* with Betty. I only got those couple years after Pop left his body. Maybe we can get everyone to converge at the farm this year--oh what a yummy thought! So hey, I think I should give the porn shop man his phone back now, so I'm gonna head over to the Midtown ferry terminal and see if I can escape from New York by boat. Meet you over at Paulus Hook? And I don't think I got an answer about Skylands tomorrow."

I hem and haw, then hem a few seconds more. "Man, I have so much catching up to do after today. I was already at least a day behind...aw fuck it. Let's go hiking. I'll put in for bereavement pay, see if they buy that."

"*Whoohoo!* That's the spirit, baby! Let the paper remain on the desk unwritten, the road is before us!"

"Oh, and um, count me in for Purusha's class next week. Time to find out what I've been missing all my life."

"Whoa...I think my prana just peaked. Better come get it while it's hot! I love you, Joey Angel."

"I love you, too, Vera Moss Jello. I'll be right there."

I tap the red button, then dab my forehead with the back of my hand. I love that almost every long conversation with my wife makes me sweat, and often for the right reasons.

I reach again for the door handle--and again something makes me stop. This time it is an inward signal. My eyes train themselves upon that plume of dust across the river, still shrouding the buildings of Tribeca and the Financial District. It will linger for days while the city mourns, covering the vigils, the Missing Person posters, the fruitless searches where small hopes are smothered and fears realized. The world offers few antidotes for despair in desperate times. It clings to despair as an inevitable reality, while ignoring the reality just behind its eyes that swallows despair whole.

But I cannot ignore it--not now. That which was unstirred earlier is alive and awakened, and it emanates peace. Here and now, I feel it as a prayer.

I'm amazed that I remember this so clearly, word for word. My mother taught me this prayer when I was a young boy. It was handed down through her family from the obscure sect to which they belonged in Tabriz. Supposedly the author was a disciple of Rumi himself. The only time I have spoken it in public was at my mother's funeral. It was clunky and mechanical then. I was angry and wanted to bury everything my mother taught me along with her body.

If this prayer died, I am watching its resurrection unfold within me now. I close my eyes and sing it forth, from that place I forgot I had, in perfect Persian:

O Khuda,
Source and Destination of all, the door from Your world to ours is always open, and Your radiant Light ever hines upon us. It is we who build four walls and hide within them, for fear that this world will become too much like Heaven.

Merciful Lord,
these walls have turned to dust, and the vessels that carried my brothers and sisters are empty; They fly to You, rising like smoke from the fire of what was.

*May Your forgiving Glance heal their hearts and lift them from
the denseness of the earth.Surround them, O Lord, with the Light
of Your own Being. Welcome them through the door of Heaven,
which is our true Dwelling.*

*May their lives upon the earth become as a dream to their wak-
ing souls.*

-Khuda Hafiz

* * * *

Zoom across the continent, one last time. Now I am…well, my
Eldorado Stages nametag still says "Pedro," so I'll stick with
that for now.

Bus 477 rolls out of the forest and back into the great wide-
open. We turn left on Azucar Mountain Road, and soon we are
rolling along the edge of the plateau again, the great valley now
to our right, baking under the midday sun. We coast across the
steady undulations of the ridge like a ship on the waves. The
bus has a keen sense of the road, a natural way of pulling itself
forward, easing through curves at the perfect speed, like no other
large vehicle I have driven. When I let it, the bus almost drives
itself. I disappear--these are Mysterious Hands on the wheel, in
the name of whatever you prefer to call Him or Her, not me--and
everything is all right.

Betty's last words at the campground are doing loop-de-loops
through my mind. Every mile we drive now is taking us closer
to Cayucos...or so I think. I know that there is no place I would
rather be tonight than home with Nadia, and the rare simplicity of that desire has me feeling a channeled energy that should
manifest as a safe trip home. But I must be ready for wherever
the angels need to take me.

I suppose that is what the golden thread represents: the fact
that I have not yet earned the ability to call my own shots. I
am still bound to a chain of cause and effect, the karmic trail
through space and time that is both created from and sustained by the sum of all aspects of my personality: my actions

of the past, my feelings about the present, my thoughts about the future. Just as I would be powerless to untie the knot of a thread behind my own back, I cannot undo my own karma. I guess the solution varies depending on what spiritual language we speak, but one thread that seems to run through them all is letting go of the need to control everything like a god-in-a-box. No wonder the spiritualists of all traditions and faiths have always turned the world's finite wisdom on its head and insisted that self-determination is bondage, while true freedom comes through some form of self-negation: disappearance, blending into the universe, or simple involvement in mankind.

A lot to digest on one Tuesday afternoon? Yes indeed, so I will keep it simple and steer this bus toward Santa Maria or points anywhere, and leave that in the hands of my Pilot.

At one point, I realize that the radio is still on. It speaks in a hushed tone, reaching my ears with the volume of a conversation halfway back on the bus, but now that it has my attention I can hear each word clearly. It's a tremendously good sign for me that I have not been distracted by it since we left the campground. When my mind is still, I find the background noise becomes far less of an issue. So it is not impossible to overcome. I have just developed a fatalistic belief in my inability to keep it still...another great example of the bondage of my own thoughts.

Apparently, the media in New York are having a hell of a time trying to report an accurate death toll. Some are saying the number could be in the tens of thousands, based on estimates of the number of people who were typically in the towers by that point in the morning. Others are taking the conservative route and only reporting confirmed casualties, which will be a gross *under*estimate as long as an untold number of bodies are buried in debris.

This is an oddity of the human mind that has baffled me since I was a cub journalist and noticed the lengths to which we go to determine precise numbers for all the details of life and death, as if somehow, for instance, a tornado is more tragic because it kills six people in a neighboring state instead of five. If we are busy occupying the brain with a body count, I suppose, we are less likely to feel the impact of the diminishment within ourselves that comes from our involvement in the deceased. And paradoxically, it seems to me, if we deny this involvement, we cut ourselves off from the chance to know eternal Life, because we sever the connection that makes Life cyclical. We opt out of the Birth-Death-Rebirth cycle and keep our lives small and impermanent by our preference to think of ourselves as an island, as a drop of water detached from the Ocean all around it.

I feel a tidal wave of words. This is not going to wait until we get to Santa Maria. I have a pocket-sized notebook in my rucksack for this kind of occasion, and I carefully fish it out without taking my eyes off the road. I prop the notebook on my right thigh and scribble hieroglyphs that I will hopefully later recognize as words.

This is horrible decorum for a motor coach driver, but sometimes inspiration is so persistent it will not be shunted nor contained for the sake of etiquette. This is one of those times. Besides, I am very aware right now that angels have the wheel.

I fill two sides of the miniature paper, then survey the results:

Not Donne Yet

Never seek to know the toll when death visits your life; it is always One, for when anyone among us departs, we all die together; and it is always Zero, for while Life persists there can be no final death. It is in welcoming both Zero and One that we become empty and awake, both involved in humankind and beyond its earthbound limitations, and temporal death is overcome by Eternal Life. Therefore mourn neither for the living nor the dead, for a clod of soil falling into the ocean may diminish the continent, but the ocean gains--the wise one knows we are both. And fear not the darkness that follows the sunset, for what goes down must come up.

I quickly scan to see if any birders are watching, then tuck the notebook into my shirt pocket. That will definitely find its way into "The Valley and the Mountain." Not the conclusion, but it might do well wrapping up a chapter. I may have to create a new character for it–it would not be right to suggest that *I* said that.

As I return my full attention to the scene before me and the dashboard, I happen to glance at the bus phone when, lo! two bars on signal strength indicator. A sight for sore eyes! The wind must be blowing just right. That should be enough signal to make a call. I pull the wireless out of my pocket...only seven missed calls: one from the dispatch office and six from Nadia. I push the auto-dial button for our home landline...oh man, it is ringing. I feel a rush of phone anxiety, as if I'm calling a stranger with no sense of what to say.

Nadia picks up, then a few seconds elapse. I am probably waking her from a nap.

"Hello?" Definitely a rolling out of bed voice.

"Hi Boo." Not the typical high, rolling "ooooo" I often use that almost makes it a three syllable word. This time it is subdued and soft, like a prayer. I hear her breathe deeply, as though she had been holding it since mid-morning. It sounds equal parts relieved and exasperated.

"Hi." Then silence. It is clear that neither of us are interested in asking "how are you?"

"I've been in the mountains since early morning, had no signal all day...I'm sorry."

More pregnant pause, and another sharp exhale. "Not your fault. Just, you know...not a good day to be alone."

"No, I know. It wasn't." Not sure where to go next. None of our typical phone conversation topics feel like they will have any legs today, but we are not in a hurry to let each other go either. "Did you, uh, do any work on the self-portrait today?"

"No."

Oops. I forgot about the "cheap crumbly crap" I bought for her at the box store. I make a mental note to stop at the art supply store in SLO if it is still open. Another few seconds pass as I scan my exhausted mind for something that won't dig a deeper hole.

"So, um...I don't uh...I don't suppose you'd be up for some sushi tonight?"

There is rustling of papers in the background as she ponders that. I think she has moved to her drafting table.

"...I don't know. I don't think I can eat anything tonight."

"I understand. We'll do that sometime soon."

"Thanks for thinking of it, though. That would be wonderful."

Some sign of levity in her voice now. Seems like that might have helped. It is too soon to tell, and I definitely cannot relax into the conversation yet. There are two people on the other end of the line, and it is always hard to say who is going to get the upper hand. The invitation to dinner was also a reminder that she has no appetite, and that could just as well become a weapon to use against me. One thing you learn from living with a bipolar is to choose the gifts you give very carefully--one minute they can be gratefully received, and the next minute you can be defending yourself against them.

Another very pregnant pause follows, and as it seems to lapse beyond term I start to think I should quit while the quitting's good and let her go. I have the crazy roller coaster road coming up as the perfect excuse. Just as I open my mouth to say so, Nadia beats me to it.

"You know, when I couldn't get a hold of you today, it forced me to do a lot of thinking...and I had this one image that kept coming back, no matter how much I tried to shake it. I was lying on a couch in a room I don't recognize. It felt like it was ours but it was no place that we've ever been together. It was a totally swank room with a French door and a chestnut armoire and all that posh stuff that you hate. So I was lying on this luxurious designer couch with satin throw pillows....but I couldn't feel a thing. I was seeing through my eyes and my body was there, but I couldn't tell I was in it, like I was paralyzed. And I kept staring at the door, because I knew that at any minute you were going to be coming home, and I wanted to make sure I didn't miss it. The whole time I kept thinking I was about to see the door swing open and you'd be there with that big goofy smile you have after a great trip, and I'd think about how much it brightens my day to see it...but you never came home. The door just stayed closed. Minutes would turn into hours, hours into days, days into years...I never knew for sure if you had died, or if you'd just decided you'd had enough...but I was pretty sure you were still alive. That's why I kept waiting."

Goodness gracious. Someone is making a serious concerted effort on our part. I am giving Vishnu all the credit for this one.

"I really wouldn't blame you if you never came back though," Nadia continued. "I would have left me a thousand times already if I could"

"Wow Boo, that's intense. How did that make you feel?" I am pretty sure I know, but I have to hear it from her. There have been several times that I have threatened to leave and she has told me it would be the best day of her life.

"It sucked. I *hated* it. Like I would've given up everything just to have your stupid smile again"

She gets it.

"Well, you don't have to worry about that. I'm sticking around."

"Really?" She sounds genuinely surprised.

"Really. I gotta see how this ends."

More rustling of papers. "Good," she says. "I'll try to stick around, too." No other words--she does not need any others. Genuine gratitude reverberates from her words and ripples through her silence. No one shows gratitude quite like Nadia when she is feeling it, even over the phone. It has taken me years of lessons from her and I still don't quite shine like she does.

"Soooo..." she continues."Whacha haulin' today?"

This actually makes me laugh. I didn't expect that line at all. It is sort of a running gag that goes back to when I was long-haul driving. Nadia was always amused by the various items I carried, even something as mundane as a trailer full of plumbing fixtures for a Home Depot in Sandusky, Ohio. When I started driving motor coaches, she kept asking the same question, and I would answer the same way: "buncha Boy Scouts for a camping trip in Tahoe" or "old folks for the money mill at Chumash." I guess it has been one of our little ways of connecting her to my journeys, of reminding each other that no matter where her body is, Nadia travels with me always.

"Ha. You're gonna like this one. I have a bus-ful of birders."

"...*Birders?*"

"Yes. I'll explain later. Winnie the Pooh was wrong. My name is based on a half-truth."

She contemplates that for a moment, then laughs heartily. *The House at Pooh Corner* is one of her favorites. "OK! How about tomorrow? What's on the Eldorado docket."

"Well, I'm guessing she's gonna want to keep me with this group and have me swap trips with Floyd, take these guys to the Channel Islands. Hey, you wanna come along? *They're gonna ride on a boat for two or three hours* (I do a pretty tight impersonation of Floyd's gravelly voice), *go look at birds for an hour, tops, and two or three hours coming back. Ain't datta bitch!"*

An even more robust laugh. It is so beautiful to hear her laugh like this when it is least expected.

"Thanks babe, I'll pass."

"You know what? I'll pass, too. I'm taking tomorrow off. I'll call Annie right now."

"What? I think the signal went bad for a second. It sounded like you said you're turning down work."

"Ha, you heard me right, goiny. I'm off tomorrow. Let one of those California hot shots handle the Channel Islands. We have a lot of people back home to check on, ya know?"

"But what if Annie boots you off the golden altar?" She responds in a breathy mock desperation. "You may never see Yellowstone again! *No moh Chinese gullfliend foh you!"*

Pidgin English even. She is really on her game now. "True, true...well, I guess we'll always have each other, right?"

"We sure will." She then makes a sound that is so uniquely Nadia it is very hard to describe. Picture a cat, lying in a patch of sunlight coming through a window in a cozy house. Maybe it is winter outside, just to make that patch even warmer and cozier. The cat is nuzzling up with its best friend, perhaps a person, or another cat that is licking its fur, and it is purring. Now, give the cat human vocal chords, but do not burden it with linguistic aptitude or the ability to express itself symbolically as anything other than just what it is. That is close to what I mean. It is the essence of what she conveys in every one of her drawings: despite appearances to the contrary, everything really is alright in our world. The sound itself is peace to me. Even on a cell phone, when it sounds scratchy like from an old Victrola record player, there is nothing more divine.

"OK, so no sushi. How's this for Plan B: let's take a half-dozen blankets down to the beach, listen to the waves and fall asleep in each other's arms."

"Sounds wonderful."

"Great. It's a date…but, um, do me a favor please and like, eat a jar of peanut butter or something if you can. I don't want you turning to mush on me while we're trying to dig the stars together."

"Aye aye, captain. So when should I expect you home for this double date with ocean and stars?"

"Hmmm…this group's been running a pretty tight schedule, I think we'll actually make Santa Maria by 5:00…drive to the mothership, clean and fuel…let's say, 7:00?"

"Alrighty then, 8 o'clock it is."

"You know me way too well. OK babe, this road's gonna get gnarly in a few minutes so I'd better let you go…but hey, first I just, uh, I wanted to tell you.....thanks."

"For what?"

"Everything…all of it."

Purring cat sound. "You're welcome. For everything."

"I love you, Boo. See you soon."

"I love you too, Boo. Come home good."

Great. A day off. I am not going *anywhere* tomorrow. I can feel the rest seeping into my frazzled cells already. Annie will manage. Any monkey with a passenger endorsement can drive a bus to Santa Barbara and back. The owner is the fallback option when there are not enough warm bodies. He would be perfect for this run. I was looking forward to another day with Betty, but that's OK. I think I will be making a pilgrimage to Kansas soon.

My thoughts turn to my parents. They ought to be the first ones I call in the morning. Their homes make an axis that straddles the New Hampshire-Massachusetts state line, far enough from New York City to be out of harm's way, close enough to be singed by the flames a little more than the average American. Sidney Pierce works for the Department of Defense at a Lockheed Martin office in Nashua. I am sure the mood was tense there. He may have even been sent home as a precaution. Mildred "Millie" Pierce has been giving mother-infant care at the same hospital for 25 years, and will undoubtedly serve another ten more before she retires. A couple dozen babies may have entered the world in Lowell today, a reminder that even amidst tragedy; the Life within us is constantly born again somewhere.

I know my parents' lives became too busy for each other, and they both made choices they regret and would do over again if they could. But they are *good* parents, and good people, both of them. I do not tell them that nearly often enough. Not letting another day pass before I do.

I wonder if it bothers them that I never use my given name. Maybe I should start. I may not like all the associations I have with it, but it *is* pretty unique, and I bet it would make them happy. Life must have been so different for Sid and Millie in 1972--two carefree refugees of the hippie era, no inclination to think that their marriage was mortal or even that life itself was a vapor that appeaseth and fadeth away. It is quite a trip now to look back and think of the sense of whimsy they had when they decided that their first born should be known as Cottleston Pierce.

Suddenly a violent, shrill commotion erupts on the right side of the bus, the side facing the valley. Egads! did someone find a ticking package in an overhead compartment?

I grab the wheel at 10-and-2. The commotion is growing, but I quickly realize it is not fearful at all. Bird #1 is ecstatic. *"OH! PULL OVER! PULL OVER! PLEASE!"* As if by magic, a gravel turnout appears along the shoulder-less roadway, and I veer into it with much pebble-popping ado. All forty-four birders are now pressed against the windows like suction cup Garfields on the right side. If this were a cartoon, we would have tipped over.

"Ladies and gentleman," Bird #1 intones into the microphone. Clearly, at this moment, she understands why the Big Guy put her on this earth. "We have a *golden eagle* in the sky at three o'clock."

I sense absolute awe behind me. Even I can feel the transcendence of this moment. There is nothing more coveted by any American bird lover than an eagle in flight. It is in our blood. Nothing else comes close (I suppose a bald one would have been a little much).

Cameras click madly. Bird #1 had warned them to look out for raptors, so photographic units were on high alert. I lean over to see better, but the view is blocked, so I open the door and hop outside. Our golden eagle glides above the low scrub trees, and what seems like miles above the great valley expanse. It dips down toward the bus, then loops back, up and over, pure sailing grace. It does this a few times, like it is playing with us. I have heard of dolphins swimming playfully alongside boats, but I've never known eagles to sail with buses.

We stay and watch for several minutes. No one is thinking of leaving now, not even me. I can't believe I am birding an eagle. It soars, turns, floats on the wind--spectacular and yet the simplest act of nature. Nothing forced, everything flows. Flows, sails, soars above, looking down at us...like an angel.

Let me try something new. Let's stay in the present with this scene, but I will also speak of the future as it will later unfold. It will sound like the past because, well, as I am writing this, it is. (Maybe this is what time is like in the next world.)

After meeting Betty and getting this introduction to her sons' work toward universal fluency, I knew that the only spiritual context that would make sense to me was a universal one. So I read all the heretical writings of modern syncretists like Alan Watts, Aldous Huxley, and Joseph Campbell, and I immersed myself in the scriptures that inspired their work. From this jambalaya of influences, there developed a robust, sustaining faith in faith itself that also satisfied my sense of reason as I saw great diverse minds all over the world lend their voices to the same glorious story. And when the time came to say Goodbye, I was at least intellectually prepared to understand and accept what was happening. No small feat, considering where I was before Splash.

If this worked for me, I figured, there must be some of this happening on the macro level as well, for humanity as a whole.

From this, I developed a theory that religions have persisted well beyond the point in history where they conflicted with the superior reasoning of science because they carry extremely potent symbols and characters that go beyond the limitations of words to truly explain, on a super-rational level, the unexplainable.

This persistence becomes all the more important now that science has given humanity the means to deliver its own death blow, rather than quake in fear waiting for an imaginary vengeful *theos* to do it for them. At the same time, scientists like Einstein, Erwin Shroedinger, and Neils Bohr started leading us around the corner into a physical world much more pliable than the one ruled by Newtonian physics, while also conveying the joy of scientific inquiry in terms not unlike the spiritual. Now that the cutting edge of science is unveiling a world that looks a lot like what the authors of the Upanishads laid out over 3,000 years ago, perhaps it is time to reconsider the value of these old tales.

But, let us be wise enough to acknowledge that they *are* mythologies, not to be taken as historical facts, but vehicles for a presence much greater and a Truth much more inscrutable than any one tradition can claim on its own. For here lies their true power: they snap us out of the rational trap that says we are doomed, and deliver a death blow of their own to the idea that there is anything here to fear. Defending one against another brings them both down to the political sphere, where they are easy prey to both skeptics and political opportunists (usually disguised as clergy). But if they are understood to be unique manifestations of a universal story of deliverance *from* the dog-eat-dog world of politics, they can no longer be hijacked and fed to desperate souls to create fearless islands of hate or homicidal zombies. No *jihad*, no holy war, no Buddhist lynch mobs in Myanmar--we will all worship together, each in his and her own language, the Self who we truly are, with unattached love and respect for all of its countless manifestations.

We will need this in the not-too-distant future. The doomsday crowd has been so thoroughly wrong for so long now that someday they are bound to be right by self-fulfilling prophecy or maybe just dumb luck, and something will happen that may resemble the end times they have choreographed for us. Maybe there will be a point when all our sand finally reaches the bottom of the hourglass, though I am less convinced than ever that this will be the end of anything substantial within the Life as we are coming to know it.

But let us play devil's advocate (pun intended) and assume for a moment that the end of days is nigh. If my theory holds true, the actual revelatory events will not happen the same way for everyone--we will all perceive what our cultural filters make us inclined to see, and we will all be right. Most of us raised in this secular, technocratic culture will likely see some scientific cataclysm like a nuclear explosion, a giant cloud of anthrax or plutonium, maybe even a meteor blazing through the atmosphere. But who really wants front row seats to any of that? Christians, on the other hand, if I am correct, will watch the same scene and witness the long-awaited second coming of Christ and the kick-off of Revelations. Muslims will hear the horn of Israfil, heralding the Day of Resurrection and Judgment. Hindus will see the dance of Śiva. Betty and Virginia and all of their students may see legions of angels swooping through the sky, coming for to carry us home. Each has some element of the destruction of the sand castles we have built, but also a cleansing and redemption for the faithful that adherents will not want to do without. It will be a lot more fun for *all* of us, then, if these people are not pitted against each other to fight over which version is the right one, if we are *all* faithful to understand that each story has *metaphorical* value to teach us how to greet death fearlessly with pure heart and conscience.

My point--and there is a point here I think--is that this idea is by no means limited to images of the apocalypse. Most of the people here on Bus 477 probably see an *Aquila chrysaetos*--commonly known as "golden eagle"--a large, dark raptor with a pale golden nape, found mainly in mountain forests and open grasslands of western North America. And they are correct. I, not knowing most of those facts, see one of the purest forms of beauty I have ever witnessed. Some folks might agree with me. And *we* are correct.

I wonder what Betty sees. She is watching back there, as fervently as the rest of us. What is that in her sky? Is this one of her angels? Could it be her father, or one of her sons, bringing her good tidings and comfort? *Our Father*, giving us a spontaneous flying lesson? ("Just use your wings!")

I know I have not reached the place where this path will take me. There is much to learn ahead, and little I can claim to know. Gautama Buddha told us that all truth must be measured against our own experience or it is useless, and this is a process I have barely begun.

But of one thing I am certain: the sun will rise tomorrow morning, and we will *all* be here to see it. The road tells me so.

The eagle turns and heads east toward the mountaintop. I climb aboard and fire up the engine. We are going home.

Dedicated to the living Presence
who walked through this world as

Aubray Myett Tomkinson

From 1971 to 2005,
Then flew away

About the Author

J. Pierre Reville is a writer and philosopher focused on cutting edge spiritual theory for the next era. His blog, Heretic Asylum! (www.hereticasylum.org) explores many aspects of pantheism, "the first and final phase of all world religions." Reville has also been driving commercial motor vehicles for a living since 1995. He has probably logged well over one million miles in that time, but no one is counting. He lives in Ithaca, New York.

CPSIA information can be obtained at www.ICGtesting.com
Printed in the USA
BVOW07s1111201214

380219BV00003B/170/P